Kobor Tigan't
When Giants Walked the Earth - 1

Kobor Tigan't

When Giants Walked the Earth - 1

by
Christia Sylf

Translated from the French by
Michael Shreve

A Black Coat Press Book

Acknowledgements: A very warm thanks to Bernard Liessi for his support and understanding.

ISBN 978-1-64932-225-8. First Printing: July 2023. Published by Black Coat Press, an imprint of Hollywood Comics.com, LLC, P.O. Box 17270, Encino, CA 91416.
 Printed in the United States of America.

Introduction

Kobor Tigan't – *Chronique des Géants*, here translated as *Kobor Tigan't* – *When Giants Walked the Earth* – was initially published by Robert Laffont in 1969. It was followed two years later by its sequel and conclusion, *Le Règne de Ta* [The Reign of Ta] (1971), to be also published in this collection.

Christia Sylf was the pseudonym of Christiane Léonie Adélaïde Richard-Delecluse, born 28 September 1924 in Paris, who passed away on 28 November 1980 in Entrevaux in the Alpes-de-Haute-Provence. She was a major French fantasy writer who remains, even today, mostly underappreciated in France, where fantasy thrives in the shadow of homegrown imitators of J.R.R. Tolkien, Robert E. Howard and J.K. Rowling.

Sylf's published works included:
• *Kobor Tigan't* (1969)
• *The Reign of Ta* (1971)
• *Markosamo le Sage* [Markosamo The Wise] (1973) (which takes place in Atlantis)
• *La Reine au Coeur Puissant* [The Strong-Hearted Queen] (1979) (which takes place in Ancient China); and
• *The Cat's Paw* (1974) (a collection of short stories)

Sylf had announced the publication of five more volumes in her series: *La Geste d'Amoinen* [The Saga of Amoinen], taking place in Nordic Finland; *Amiona la Courtisane* [Amiona the Courtesan], taking place in Renaissance Venice; *Ertulie de Fons l'Abîme* [Ertulia of Fons-The-Abyss], taking place during the reign of the French Sun King Louis XIV; and the two-volume *L'Apocalypse de Kébélé* [Kebele's Apocalypse], featuring her immortal narrator and taking place in the far future. Unfortunately, these works were never published because Sylf died soon after the publication of *The Strong-Hearted Queen*. Reportedly, she was working on an additional novel, *L'Initié de Luxor* [The Initiate from Luxor], taking place in Ancient Egypt during the reign of Queen Pharaoh Hatshepsut, which was left uncompleted, but whose drafts were found by the association *Les Amis de Christia Sylf* in April 2007.

Born in 1924, Christiane had a life trajectory somewhat like that of the famous American medium Edgar Cayce, in the sense that, from a young age, she seemed to be endowed with the rare abilities of clairvoyance, to see auras and peer into the invisible worlds that in Hindu metaphysics are called the "Akashic records." Like Cayce, she was a modern sibyl, animated by a spiritual fire of great power and subtle energy. Very early on, she turned to the arts, wrote poetry, and was interested in alchemy and its symbolism. A self-taught artist since the 1940s, she gave life to a series of characters resembling those about which she would later write.

Reportedly, she said that she received visions and inspiration from ancient times and other incarnations. In any event, her work was truly unique in the sense that she was able to transform her experiences into novels and, with considerable work, produce fascinating and captivating stories bearing a message of freedom and open-mindedness.

Her many-layered, lyrical style allows us to experience, in a unique and precious way, such universal themes as friendship, the love of an ideal, the initiatory stages required to build a true human being, and also a warning against materialistic excesses. *Kobor Tigan't* tells the fantastic story of an antediluvian civilization that may nor may not have existed, an entirely original vision, filled with well delineated poetic archetypes...

Publisher Robert Laffont was quickly convinced of her visionary talent, to the point of creating an entirely new imprint just for her, *Les Portes de l'étrange* [The Gate of the Strange], which also published novels of other like-minded authors.

Sylf wrote four successive novels, recounting the journey of several characters reincarnating from one era to another, filled with marvelous and detailed descriptions, from the Age of the Giants to mythical Atlantis and Ancient China, sadly leaving her saga unfinished. She lived in a small village in the Ardeche region of France with her painter husband Kerlam, who occasionally illustrated her works.

Suffering from an unexplained illness, a generalized edema whose origin could not be determined, and which suddenly disappeared without leaving a trace, but which was followed a few days later by a right-side hemiplegia, prohibiting her from writing despite her desperate efforts for three weeks, she never made the slightest complaint, perfectly aware of her condition and anticipating her death within a few hours.

Christia Sylf left this world in the greatest serenity and in absolute peace on November 28, 1980 at 2:15 a.m., saying to her night nurse: "Goodbye, Madame, I'm leaving… they're waiting for me."

This was the autobiographical essay she wrote in March 1979:

My family was from the North. I was born Christiane Adélaïde Richard on September 28, 1924, in Paris, where I lived with my parents. My father was Gaston Richard, an industrialist, but also a poet in his spare time. My mother was a mezzo soprano singer at the Opéra Comique under the name of Amelia Delecluse.

My parents had a great spirit of tolerance, immediately understanding, as they said, "the world of their daughter." There was a great deal of love amongst the three of us, which remained constant during our life.

We told each other everything. There were no barriers between us. Lots of joy. We laughed together.

Of course, I was an only child! Music filled the house.

I was a fragile child (one of those who pick up every disease, solitary, a little wild, kind, serious and joyful at the same time, listening, constantly plaguing the adults with a flood of questions that I did my best to never leave unanswered.

The very first feeling I remember? That of the disappointment caused by the world of men, their ways, their duplicity, their lies, their false knowledge, their sufficiency. I always "guessed" what was behind it and saw that it was not beautiful, not sincere. And I felt that strongly.

Within my being, there was, very vividly, irrefutably (and, alas, inexpressibly because of my young age, which also made me suffer) the certainty of other values, other truths, other appearances than those presented to us by this world. I felt like a stranger in this world. (However, I still love it) But besides that, I knew that I was an exile...

So, cautiously, with circumspection, I applied myself "to do well like everyone else", with the bizarre concern (but not too much! As life will teach me later) "not to stand out"!

So, my first truth was: "I am from Elsewhere" (!)

I overcame all my childhood's illnesses, each time making progress with my being; they were, in fact, springboards. For example, no one ever knew how I learned to read. After coming out of a very serious bout of scarlet fever, I discovered I now read fluently... and I haven't stopped since.

During my childhood, every book passed through me. But, above all, there was the dictionary. It was like my teddy bear, I slept with it every night. At age ten, Anatole France, Balzac, George Sand, Flaubert, Zola, Gauthier, Hugo, etc. had all passed through me. Now, I return to them because I'm rereading them!

My inner life as a child was intense.

Everything was meditation; everything was subject to observation, reflection.

I "guessed" always better. I wanted to understand. I needed answers. And I quickly realized that these would not be those that a "classic and compulsory education" would provide me.

I played a great deal with dolls... baby toys? No! I made my "beings" myself — little characters, like miniatures, made of hat pins wrapped in embroidery cotton, dressed and painted. Basically, I played at being a demiurge, launching my characters into fantastic adventures, and all sorts of quests.

Thirty years later, I found one of them: a little magician with carrot hair, once condemned "to the clock" for life. It was still hidden in my grandmother's clock. I freed him from his "life sentence"!

From the beginning of my school years, I hated school, its methods, its mediocrity, its distorted teaching of banalities as it did not conform to my desire to learn. I didn't like high school any better. But for the sake of politeness, I became a good student.

However, I was studying, oh! how many other things, far less orthodox, where I felt that my Doors existed, and I haven't stopped since.

Little by little, I learned astrology, theosophy, symbolism, religions, folklore, traditions, the Great Past and the Vast Elsewhere, the Tarot and its Living Arcana, the One Tradition, the Rose+Croix, Alchemy...They truly nourished me and still nourish me, when my Being was (and still is) essentially hungry.

And I, who the visible world did not satisfy, quickly understood how passionately I loved, with all the fibers of my being, this Creature, this Woman of this Earth, this Being who did not dare to face this immense wonder, this heartrending and torn prisoner who confined herself in the rigid narrowness of conventions.

Internal certainties became truths. The meaning of my life dawned on me. And I wanted to say what I felt, what I knew, what I had patiently found, gathered, this same light expressed through a thousand facets. I wanted to give back to Humanity, through my writing, the truth of his veiled power, bring her back to Herself, to her natural transcendence, to her celestial origins, to all her divine possibilities.

I wrote from childhood, then in adolescence, poems. I always wrote about this world. It is perhaps the keys to my work as a novelist, as an ancestor storyteller.

Because I always felt so old! I wrote esoteric, initiatory poems. Gifts of Love, since Love is Knowledge. What the Initiates call the "Brain of the Heart", not the intellect, not the Mind. And I deny being an intellectual myself!

The dream world instructed me, very early on. Through my dreams, I learned, I was guided. So, the sources of my memory opened up, since I did not refuse, in the name of conformity, what was thus offered to me. Coming from nocturnal life, they then appeared in daytime life.

I gradually found my Past Lives in this way.

1950. A first marriage... which liquidated an old karmic debt.

I had been waiting since adolescence for "the one who must return, the one that I have always known". I shall know in advance his voice, his physical marks.

I continue watching. It takes a long time...

I always write. I study more...

The lightning inspiration of the great cycle of the Reincarnational Chronicles fell on me one day; the whole working mechanism to be accomplished was revealed in all its details. But the disease still engulfed me. My whole life was always extreme physical suffering. I learned a great patience that way.

The end of my first marriage saw me exhausted, no longer wanting to live. I divorced.

Death was approaching me. I wanted it...

Suddenly, I'm out! We're in 1961.

It took me several years before I found Kerlam, an esoteric painter, now my husband. I found and recognized him, because he, who was also waiting for me, found me and recognized me at the same time.

But then it was impossible for us to live together. It was still necessary to wait many long years during which we believed without hope.

In November 1964, together, we left Paris to live in a village in the Ardèche, in Saint-Montan where my elderly parents joined us.

Together, we deepened our esoteric studies because, of course, we shared the same approach to the world, the same concerns, the need to "understand". We constantly exchanged the fruits of our meditations, of our revelations. Everything was shared: we felt like a single, bi-polar being, who had switched their secret poles.

Kerlam painted fantastic, dreamlike, initiatory paintings. Me, I wrote the beginning of my Cycle.

Finally, I sent the first novel Kobor Tigan't, Chronicle of the Giants *to our friend Guy Tarade, who then recommended it to Robert Charroux; his wife Yvette read it first, and was very enthusiastic. Robert read it in his turn and quickly introduced me to his publisher, Robert Laffont, on the very day the first astronauts set foot on the Moon! It was in September 1969. Mr. Laffont liked the book, decided to publish it, and trusted me for the continuation of the series.*

His imprint Les Portes de l'Etrange, *with its gold cover, was created for and inaugurated by* Kobor Tigan't, *and welcomed my subsequent novels in the Cycle.*

To provide some historical and literary context to the above essay, we must begin with the meeting between writer Louis Pauwels (1920-1997) and scientist Jacques Bergier (1912-1978). Pauwels was then literary editor at the Editions des Deux Rives and Bergier very active in science fiction and fantasy circles. The two men teamed up to translate Charles Fort's notorious *Book of Damned* (1919), eventually published by the Deux Rives in 1955. This was followed by a collection of short stories by H.P. Lovecraft, entitled *Démons et Merveilles*,[1] also published at Deux Rives that same year, translated by Bernard Noel and introduced by Bergier.

This led the two men to collaborate on the classic *Le Matin des Magiciens* [The Morning of the Magicians], a book covering topics like

---

[1] Includes *The Statement of Randolph Carter, The Silver Key, Through the Gates of the Silver Key,* and *The Dream Quest of Unknow Kadath.*

cryptohistory, UFOlogy, occultism, alchemy, spiritual philosophy. The book was published in October 1960 by Gallimard, a very respectable and mainstream literary publisher. To everyone's surprise, it met with considerable success: 100,000 copies were sold in the first year and foreign translations soon followed.

Despite a hostile reception by skeptic reviewers, *The Morning of the Magicians* became a cult classic within the youth culture in France and abroad in the 1960s and the 1970s. Pauwels and Bergier went on to pursue their interest in the paranormal by launching the magazine *Planète*, dedicated to what they termed *fantastic realism*. Both the book and the magazine had considerable influence on the esotericism of the 1960s-70s counterculture, heralding the popularization of New Age ideas.

Its success caught the interest of commercial publisher Robert Laffont (1916-2010) who, in 1963, launched a new imprint grandiosely entitled *Les Grandes Enigmes de l'Univers* [Great Enigmas of the Universe] with Robert Charroux's classic *Histoire Inconnue des Hommes Depuis 100,000 Ans* [One Hundred Thousand Years of Man's Unknown History]. Charroux was the penname of Robert Joseph Grugeau (1909-1978), who had worked in pulp literature in the 1940s, writing scripts for a comic strip about an atomic-powered superhero, *Atomas*, as well as science fiction adventure serials such as *Professor Barthelemy's Flying Island*, etc. After the war, he turned to journalism. In 1948, he founded the International Club of Treasure Seekers, which he chaired for ten years. On the strength of this initiative, in 1962, he published his first bestseller, *Trésors du monde* [World Treasures], which lists more than two hundred and fifty treasures. In 1961, to promote the discoveries of his region, the Poitou, Charroux, passionate about prehistory, created a "Prehistoric Circuit" between Grand-Pressigny and Les Eyzies.

His *Histoire Inconnue des Hommes...* was followed by seven more books with similar themes, all published by Laffont between 1963 and 1977. It built the popular theory of "ancient aliens." The influence that it had on Erich Von Däniken, whose first book appeared in 1966, is now widely recognized. Concerned about plagiarism, Laffont contacted Von Däniken's publisher in March 1968, with the result that later printings of *Chariots of the Gods* and *Return to the Stars* mentioned Charroux in the bibliography.

Another author discovered by Laffont, who ended up becoming the editor of the imprint, was Francis Mazière (1924-1994), a French ethnologist and archaeologist, whose *Fantastique Île de Pâques* [Fantastic

Easter Island] became a worldwide bestseller, also translated into several languages.

Finally, Guy Tarade (1930-), a renowned French novelist and lecturer specializing in UFOs, the paranormal, and esotericism, joined the imprint in 1971 with his *Les Dossiers de l'Etrange*. Tarade was the founder of the Center for Studies and Research of Unknown Elements of Civilization. Many of his books are also about "ancient aliens."

This was the context in 1969 when Laffont published *Kobor Tigan't*, which led to a second imprint, *Les Portes de l'étrange*, which after such a remarkable debut, sadly published mostly esoteric non-fiction books, largely duplicating the *Les Grandes Enigmes de l'Univers*, with the sole exceptions of Sylf's four novels, a three-novel series by Jean Tur entitled *Memoirs of the Arkonn Tecla* about a fictional extinct Polynesian-like civilization, and a reprint of Maurice Magre's historical fantasy, *The Blood of Toulouse*.[2]

Sylf's novels were a breath of pure fresh air, but she was not alone in creating a new type of French literary fantasy that owed nothing to the great British and American masters.

Charles Duits (1925-1991)' *Ptah Hotep* (1971) and *Nefer* (1978) both take place on a parallel Earth with two moons—Athenade and Thana—during the time of Ancient Egypt. *Ptah Hotep* is the story of the ascension of a young prince to the throne of Caesar. *Nefer*, which takes place several years later, tells of the adventures of a young Egyptian priest who falls in love with a sacred prostitute. Supernatural elements are featured discreetly in these novels, but are an integral part of the author's spiritual "otherworld" rather than an artificial literary device. Duits, a friend of the Surrealists, was a gifted poet and a man who experimented with peyote. His novels were influenced by *The Thousand And One Nights* and the Indian *Ramayana*.

Jean Tur, a former art teacher at the Mohammed V high school in Casablanca, Morocco, created a Polynesian-like world of island empires in a world that never was. In his trilogy, *Memoirs of the Arkonn Tecla*, comprised of *L'Archipel des Guerrières* [The Warrior-Women's Archipelago] (1973), *La Harpe des Forces* [The Harp of the Powers] (1974) and *Sterne Dorée* [Golden Sterne] (1976), he narrated in painstaking detail the story of a peace expedition led by the Arkonn Tecla, a warrior prince of the Mavae Empire, sent to the neighboring Aginn Archipelago

---

[2] Black Coat Press, ISBN 978-1-61227-677-9.

to cement an alliance. The Aginn are fierce Amazon-like women, and by the end of the third volume, Tecla had only begun entreaties with them. The sea-faring world created by the author—perhaps the lost Empire of Mû?—owes nothing to the modern world as we know it. The first-person narration device is both poetic and epic, with many erotic scenes devoted to Tecla's tumultuous love life. As with Duits, the role of magic is sparse, but supernatural powers do manifest themselves during a religious ceremony in the form of a celestial harp.

Yves Rémy (1936-2022) and wife Ada (1939-) wrote a baroque and colorful type of fantasy. In their collection, *Les Soldats de la Mer* [The Soldiers from the Sea] (1968), and their novel, *Le Grand Midi* [The Great South] (1971), they chronicled the tales of a mysterious neverland dubbed the Federation, through its myths, legends and military history.

Finally, Christian Charrière (1940-2005) wrote novels that fit between the high fantasy of William Morris and the Symbolist literature of the previous century. *L'Enclave* [The Enclave] (1971), *Mayapura* (1973) and *Le Sîmorgh* (1977) are all about quests taking place in imaginary lands. *Mayapura* itself is an imaginary city that could just as well be located on Jack Vance's *Dying Earth*. The Simorgh is a colorful bird gifted with the curse of prophecy; whoever follows him can, after a perilous journey, find a land of paradise. Both novels created their own supernatural mythology, filled with religious icons, talking skeletons, animated stones giving birth to monsters, and monuments carved with secret symbols.

Jean-Marc & Randy Lofficier

SYLF

KOBOR TIGAN'T
chronique des géants

ROMAN

ROBERT LAFFONT

Prologue

*I keep vigil during the night in the high mountain plains
and my countless sheep shine white in the dark
along with stars.*

I am called Old Kébélé, the Wise Friend. I am a verdant old man and, to tell the truth, ageless. By nature, I am part tree. Like the oak with its knotty bark, burdened with years, outside. And the clear sap of present springtime within. Such am I, without ever varying.

People used to see me often on the mountain. I watch over the obscure valley tenderly. People used to see me often on the road—my journey crosses yours. While on the move, since I am always on the move, I straighten the plant bent by the wind, I crack open the shell occasionally too hard for the bird who is trying to hatch, I nudge the seed toward the soil when it has fallen randomly on rock, I nudge the pebble of pain that has rolled too long and burned in the sun, towards the river's relief.

Near the crossroads, where even the swirling dust falters, I smile, pointing out a side-road for the children, for the gypsies, those Sons of the wind, for the bees, for all those who do not resist

It is given to me to rectify.

The gatherers of medicinal plants, the followers of the sun, the lunar nomads, the thirsty, the frozen, the passionate and the very dark are my children who question me without knowing it and whom I answer without them suspecting it.

I am a traveler to meet.

Unconsciously, my kin search for me. And I find them.

…Here and there, between two journeys, I stay in my hidden sanctuary. My hermitage, my safe refuge for meditation and labor, it is the very heart of Time. I sit in the middle of my vast dream, before my loom and with the very threads of life I weave shining archetypes, I design the harmonic models of what is to come.

It is weaving. It is music. Whoever knows how to listen can, indeed, hear it. This creative gesture is also a prayer inscribed in the Laws of the Perfect, paying homage to it through a dialogue of reflections.

I, Kébélé, work in the Heights. I am the Mediator. My models will then be offered Below. Constantly moving, I gather gold and silver threads. The fabric is born out of this continuous marriage. At the same time, I embroider, and I inscribe. By the secret art I blend green and red silks whose forces repel each other. I set pure whites against deep blacks, like a carved-out shrine is supported by columns. In my hands that unite, oppositions agree to blend peacefully, correspondences develop together. It is the great sacrificial game of Light taking on Color. I embroider—the Laws bend, delighting in the struggle.

In the colorful game, the warp remains in harmony with the weft while my busy shuttle runs across the work. The details of the design appear, grow larger, following one upon the other... Nothing here is neutral nor gratuitous. Everything matters. Nothing is separated from the whole. Everything contributes.

What that inexplicable little ornament, seen on the site of this work, senseless like an eye opening on its own in a corner, in sooth reveals its nature in reverse, casts out threads, radiates around itself, and secretly makes contact with all the other designs.

The Great Tapestry shows only one aspect of its outer face.

I alone know its shifting underside, replete with all the solutions. Above all else, my hands have quickened what appears to your senses.

I know from which knots, every now and then, following a rhythm, certain threads, always the same, come together. Thus, periodically, they repeat a particular design, useful to the whole, a flower of lightning, a dragon of beauty or the cantata of prismatic lights.

I know why this thread runs, solitary and shining, into the land of others, like a rushing stream full of desires and wishes goes headlong toward the sea. Then everyone leans over its cool shores, but it only brushes by them, without knowing them, and joins with nothing. Another, which goes unnoticed, which might be passed by, runs earnestly from one to the other, never stopping its work of binding. It is hardly recognized; it looks neutral; and yet everyone knows one another through it...

And still another, precious, reluctant, uses an antenna to probe the spiritual that shows through its subtler senses. It seeks where to change, it seeks a real place, a center to enhance. Has it found it at last? Straightaway, the whole work blossoms and radiates!

... A thread flashes in broken lines, lawless, anarchic! It goes, always straight through, like a trailblazer. Does it bring order? Does it simplify? Does it create anew? No one knows. It simply goes, with all its might, until a patient obstacle meets it, holds it back, absorbs it into its mass… It advances, underneath, hidden for ages, only to reappear one day, apparently out of nowhere but, in reality, foreseen in the overall plan.

Thus, it is with the development of spirits on the transcendent loom where the lustrous fabric of futures is woven.

I, Kébélé, have woven certain pieces with six threads. I cherished six threads for a long time. So much so that I could call them my off-spring, my own six threads.

I will tell you of them, so as to reveal to you, from the underside of the tapestry, the mysterious ties that bind and unbind, from one life to another, certain groups of humans. Under the wise gaze of heaven, they form karmic families learning the best love.

The way to the light is long and dark. What flickers in one existence can be blinding for the next. The error committed here is engraved over there. What could not be completed in one go continues on and on. Those who have been separated find each other. Those who are together are separated. The darkness gradually lets the day shine through. The impatient grow calm. The blasé go a little faster with every step. Successive lives form the stages of the journey and the sleep of death renews the strength of the soul for the next stage.

Yes, there were six in my hands, six threads of different quality, different tension, six predestined threads that are going to work on themselves while working on others.

As a point of reference that will not change, I will give you the translation of their secret name. So, in the archetype, at the beginning, there was: He-who-always-loves, He-who-is-always-opaque, He-who-is-always-an-angel, He-who-always-destroys and the Two-who-always-form-one.

I wove them and they lived, bitterly, painfully, with failures and triumphs, with crimes and miracles, without faith and with it, against the light and then for it. They lived. They live…

He-who-always-loves seeks God more directly than the others. That is his sole preoccupation. He never stops having found him. He finds God to lose him, like losing memory. He remembers finding God and his torment of love leaves him no respite. He pursues his divine prey. He hunts it, like a lover his beloved. Finally, he gets hold of it, possesses it… and embraces nothing but emptiness. In all things, he looks for "his divine". He seeks it in all beings and in every possible way.

He sees everything as divinely penetrated. Out of the depths of the night of beings and things, a flame beckons him. He rushes to it, forgetful of past experiences. And just when he seizes the being or the object bearing this flame, it goes out.

He finds himself, once again, disillusioned by an empty envelope, a meaningless lamp.

But the light shines elsewhere and is already calling to him! He runs to it, never able to tell the difference between the content and the container. He desires the perfume, but he only knows how to grab the flask and cannot smell the myrrh. He has no respite. His ardent desire for reintegration, for communion with the flame, drives him on searching wildly for the most beautiful image, the highest vibration, the most intense ecstasy.

Hence, untold errors, untold failures, illusory paradises, illusory hells, untold gestures, passionate and ravenous, that chain him down, encumber his debts.

He has the sense of God within him. He is madly in love.

And thus, he will remain alone through all his incarnations, alone in the world of manifestation, despite appearances to the contrary that make him build countless relationships and never be alone. Everything in him, for better or worse, all things being of relative value, will be more pronounced than in other members of his karmic family.

He will always suffer from his secret solitude. The multitude of his loves will never populate the desert of his yearning. Sometimes possessed by his carnal passions, sometimes possessing them, he will never feel truly connected. A lucid wall of crystal will always isolate him from the contamination of human Eros. Whatever he does, he will never be able to break this invisible barrier, which will preserve in him, in the core of his being, an inviolable purity, a requisite purity.

For a long time, he will remain a rebel heart, until he understands that this mysterious Beloved is part of his malady of solitude, wherein lies the secret quintessence, and that this emptiness, this hollowness he feels, this Absence, was, in truth, the Presence Itself, silent, infinite, unformulated, alongside which every actual human presence becomes what it really is: an absence.

At last, he understands that, in the Presence Itself, he was losing his love, from the beginning, but he was unaware.

All his work on himself, therefore, will be to master this awareness, awakening from his false ecstasies. And it is only when he finds himself exhausted, after the struggle has stopped, when he finally accepts this solitude that he will see the true meaning of it.

He-who-always-loves will frequently cross threads with He-who-is-always-an-angel.

They will be polarized because the first is searching for God while the second possesses, unknowingly, the power to reveal God. In fact, it can be said that he "designates God", that he makes him visible, and, quite often, just by being there, God is closer, without the angelic being noticing because it is for him a state of being, without intellectuality. Like the rose gives off its scent, He-who-is-always-an-angel exhales the divine scent through his being.

Unlike my other five threads, all quite human, this one is emanated from a wave of parallel life. He is from the Plane of Angels. The multiple unity of his ardent, inspired, original nature was prone to a lively interest, a compassion for things of the earth. At his request, the Law judged it good to mingle him with the other threads so that as a free spirit of light he can make matter evolve by penetrating it.

Going through the human is, for an angel, both a pathetic sacrifice and a glorious adventure.

He abandons part of his grace. His intelligence, permanent contemplation, needing to yield to time, will be subject to eclipses. Instead of *being* in the plenitude, he must *become*, experience toilsome growth, the slow, fragmentary acquisitions.

But thereafter, he will be more actively useful to general evolution because he can then gain access to this chosen sphere reserved solely for Man.

He-who-is-always-an-angel knew the Law. He had chosen freely, in complete clarity, in total desire. But by donning a density heavier than that of his first nature, a veil dropped over him, he forgot a part of his transcendent knowledge. The honor that was his felt like exile. His subtle composition suffered from being integrated into a heavy envelope. And he did not like the components of his human body, even though he had come down only for that.

All his work, therefore, from life to life, will be to evolve this matter, to refine it, to make it glimpse a possible release, a transmutation, a permanence.

During long incarnations, he will feel only bitterness and outrage against the thick nature of his various bodies, and disgust for the other bodies that will appear heavier, denser, rougher and deprived of any power.

But in this being, (filled with grace and gifts nonetheless!), inspired, a seer, he will be able to interpret the rhythms of nature, the musical harmonies of the universe. He will have knowledge of plants; the animals will approach him, particularly birds, called by the lingering effect of his former aerial state. He will be loved without even trying. He will be a beguiling, elusive, unforgettable being, concerned only with nostalgia for a happiness men cannot understand.

He-who-is-always-opaque appears like his complement, his inevitable constraint, because he very accurately represents this earthly matter to be worked on, at its lowest point.

Both, therefore, will be constantly challenged, united or opposed by destiny.

He-who-is-always-opaque is a being without transparency who cannot imagine letting himself be penetrated by the light that disturbs him.

Solid, compact, attached to the things of the earth, he loves the short lifespan of the body, the pleasures driven by the flesh. The graspable now is his. Tangible things belong to him, are pleasing to his ear, glitter in his eyes, feel soft to his fingers, tasty to his greedy tongue, intoxicating to his nose.

Fortified, opulent homes are his domain. He covers himself with colorful, rustling, embroidered fabrics. His jewels are heavy, his weapons massive and destructive. A hunter to provide for his kitchens, he does not, however, willingly kill his enemies in war because he respects human life.

Unable to see beyond appearances, death is a hopeless end for him and, since he is not evil-hearted, he rarely inflicts it.

He does not ask questions.

In him, there is no openness to mystery, no spiritual quest. It is as if he lacks the necessary organ. His thirst and hunger never rise to the plane of the soul. When he is thirsty, he drinks; when he is hungry, he eats.

A lover, he makes love, appeases the flesh. He is only familiar with easily satisfied appetites. He reproduces his children euphorically, pleased to make many of them in his image and of his scent. He knows all about governing his household or his people.

The different aspects of He-who-is-always-an-angel never cease to fascinate him, befitting the attraction of opposites.

He will always go toward him, search for him, try to catch him, to smell him, to taste him, to touch him, to make him sleep at his side, to see him eat his fill like him. He will naively endeavor to resemble him and also make him resemble himself. He will want to procreate with him. He will love him truly and will get drunk on his presence.

Unfortunately, He-who-is-always-an-angel feels his lifeblood being sucked dry by He-who-is-always-opaque!

Nevertheless, he will always assume his responsibilities because, in essence, he is the Master and the other is the student. The other can only develop through him. It is necessary that the one agree to teach and the other agree to learn. The student who, wildly, comes up and desires with his flesh what the other can only grant though his soul, is wrong of course but deep down is merely obeying, in his awkward way, an urge that is inscribed in accordance with the Law. He lets himself be swept along without discussion toward his master. And this is good, even if he takes time to understand, even if he is unruly, a lazy thinker, slow-witted and pigheaded; this is good, nonetheless, because he does not go astray.

The master, however, does wrong by trying to avoid the task originally accepted. And the karmic debt, increased from one life to another, will weigh more heavily on the master than on the student...

The-Two-who-always-form-one are like two parts of a bright star, exploded and extinguished on its fall to earth.

They are more than brothers, more than twins, more than predestined, but closely identical, of the same nature, two poles of a single body that knows real existence only through the action of a vitalizing current of love, sprung from this union of two poles.

This earth is both night and solitude for them. They grope their way along, like a special kind of blind person who can see nothing down below here but their own reflection. The light that designates the world can only shine for them after the restoration of their original mystic lamp. Until they have found each other, they float at the whim of the currents of a destiny that, it seems to them, is no concern of theirs. Deprived of their union, they are nothing.

Each taken separately, they always seem a little absurd compared to what surrounds them and in which they refuse to take root.

Strangers full of strangeness, they only cease to be an enigma, an unsettling fragment, when they are together. They justify themselves by completing themselves.

Until they meet, they constantly yearn for each other, they imagine each other without knowing each other.

They are really two parts of a wound that can only close with their nuptials. Nothing on earth can replace one for the other. Nothing, in truth, can bind them to anyone but themselves.

Moreover, during their rebirths, separated by Time which sometimes causes them to be born many years apart, separated by differences in region and rank, separated by barriers of the same sex or of incest, disconnected, rent asunder, they will slowly learn, on the open planes of matter, to make flourish, to give form to the Spiritual Androgyne of which they were the double seed, both of them so aptly called: soulmates.

Now that leaves He-who-always-destroys...

He is everyone's trial and tribulation, bearing in his substance the gift of creating the necessary reaction. He must lash out at each and every one. The Law uses him as a very severe instrument to weigh, measure and compare.

He represents cold darkness, the perilous night, the swamp of dark temptations, everything that allows one to treasure the miracle of the return of the sun, terrestrial or spiritual.

In truth, he accentuates the dawn. But the exact meaning of his role is not recognized immediately because the pattern of his evolution is traced mostly on the underside of the tapestry... He-who-always destroys brings the consummating challenge to his karmic family.

Everything that he touches, he will ruin. He is like the Absinthe Star: in the mystical honey he will instill the bitterness of doubt. Just by travelling them, he will make straight roads twisted...

He will be a permanent danger to others, the hidden enemy, making it impossible for them to rest on their laurels. All in all, he is an element of severity that whips and goads.

All his incarnations will distill temptation, fanaticism, obscurity. This distinctive quality is extremely strong in him. He likes to determine things. His unfailing will allows him to carry out his plans. Unaware of the disorder and drama he incites, in keeping with his Idea, always in keeping with his Plan, he calculates, evaluates, formulates. He works incessantly.

He loves power, the most active kind, the power that remains ignored. He never shows himself directly. To attack, to strike, he sneaks around and coils up. He acts from a distance, from below, but constantly, employing a kind of magical force in the action, so great is his will.

All means are good to him. His words dictate it. Devious and treacherous, they pave the way.

His supreme illusion is to believe himself constructive whereas all he does is defile.

He arrogantly ignores the suffering of others as he himself feels no pain.

He will have to become aware, lose his power, grow gentle.

He will need time, and yet more time, more than any other but, heavily burdened and the very last to free himself, he will, in truth, have mysteriously assisted all the others.

"This then is one existence of my six protégés. It will not be the only one.

They will have other lives after this one.

… But first they lived in KOBOR TIGAN'T…

CHAPTER I

It was one of those mornings of the ages when renewals renew after the general oblivion and extinction of everything.

The spiral of life is reconnected up above by passing back through its point of apparent death. Out of the end, the beginning comes again... And, after an immeasurable nighttime, came an immeasurable morning...

A huge, muddy, volcanic continent was floating on the fuming sea.

Along the shores, the liquid element was still thick, the earth still almost fluid. They became differentiated from each other slowly, painfully and arduously, decanting their mixture along with the initial androgyne that gradually withdraws one of its joined parts from the other, to split in two and fall, to the left and to the right, into the place of the separation.

The unity of the Cosmic Wedding gave way to the wounded opening, the fissure, the differentiation, the solitude.

Cries, rage, fear and fury had manipulated the elements, then the immeasurable upheavals had grown relatively calm, moving on from widespread disasters to localized earthquakes. On this continent, vast regions were becoming safely habitable. The animals here, to a certain extent, were losing that constant distress that had kept them migrating.

Starting already in age-old generations, the Giant Men had settled their nomadism far inland, on peaceful lands where they built enormous cities.

They barely remembered their ancestors who, before the Time of Fear, had lived along the sea, only to flee afterwards, for generations on end, hounded by the horrors of the sky and of the earth, endlessly hounded and decimated...

Although the interior lands had grown peaceful, there were still large zones, especially coastal areas, where volcanoes continued to vent their fury. There were still storms on high and in the depths, still rumblings underground, and at least during the calmest periods, there persisted an incessant purr. The borders of these perilous zones were recognized by the fact that no one could walk there without feeling a shudder in their heads, emitted from below. There it was "like Before."

Tormented by ancestral fear, the Giant Men had banned these places. They never visited them. They never talked about them. And the west was both cursed and sacred.

There, faults continued to open, swallowing up trees laden with birds. And it happened so quickly, sucked into the chasm in one big gasp, that they could not even spread their wings! There, the mountainous ramparts split in two, releasing mighty rivers that had been held back up to that time, while other mountains, opposite, rose up as dams. The liquid masses poured in, destroying virgin forests, drowning all animals—a rolling deluge! The subsequent earthquake closed the access to these gaping mountains. The rivers resumed a modified course beyond, once again sloping down to the sea, leaving behind the region completely transformed into a stagnant lake.

This lasted an excessively long time, deserted and silent, sleeping under the white sun or storming with the winds. From the floating foam, aquatic plants were created, then veritable woodlands with deeply sunken roots. Forms lived in the water, fighting one another. Packs of eggs clustered together. Slimy animalism emerged, painful, random births, imprisoned by steep walls... Then, in one convulsive night, new chasms sucked in all the water and closed up.

So, a swamp, filled with putrid silt, carcasses and rotting wood, evaporated in the flat light. The ground oozed. Watercourses snaked around. This lasted as well. A time and times.

Little by little, the animals repopulated. The air streams carried seeds, dust, pollen and insects. Then came the ravenous birds with their fertile droppings. When the savannah became tall and luxuriant, large reptiles appeared, attracted by the abundant growth. Would they get out of the mud? Were they stuck in their protective burrows by lethargy? The predators came later to this rich hunting ground.

This lasted. A semblance of symbiosis created a balance in this part of the world... But then the land dried up and there was no trace of water. The animals left. All the aquatic creatures had already perished. The rest died of thirst, strewn hither and thither, because the way to a fluke spring was long...

And, during time, during a time of nameless duration, it seemed that it would never rain again. Everything turned into dust, the ground turned from black to gray, then even paler, almost white, changing into rancid powder tossed about by burning winds. Strangely, fire would sometimes flare up and scorch through like a passing snake, devouring this powder.

Big bones and barren trees tangled their ruins. They crumbled with a ghastly noise... then, suddenly, the center of this desolation gaped open a purple seam of lava!

For a long time, for ages, the volcano was active. Its smoke covered everything. Its pasty lava flow spread out, boiling with large bubbles. Slag and ashes built up along the edges. The crater rose up... It never rained... Then, it rained. Another deluge! This lasted. Still another age. The fire and water warred with dreadful hissing, the explosions of opposing planets.

Then the volcano, drowned up to its yawning mouth, turned back into a little lake, set very high in a mineral ring, looking down over a liquid region where it rained gently, gently, for ages...

And this went on until it was named, in the memory of the Old Giants, "The Land of Eternal Rain"... Like it had been named before, deep down in their memory, "The Land of the Fire that Never Ends"... Or, according to the secret of the ancestors, "The Land of the Dead Dust"... And far, far back there was another name that could no longer be pronounced.

Fog covered almost all the land. The layers of clouds, very dense, very low, did not lift, barely moved. Over almost all the valleys loomed a dreary twilight, a funereal aura. Leaf-eating monsters led a downtrodden life there, lumbering on when they exhausted their pastures. And the intense humidity, good for vegetation, hastened regrowth. So much so that these monsters just had to walk in circles, and they thrived effortlessly.

Moreover, they were inoffensive, silent and lacking in intelligence. They didn't see much with their big, white, bulging eyes that could move independently on each side of their muzzle with its drooping jowls. The milk produced by their females was drinkable and so abundant that it flowed freely. Other creatures followed the white trails of this excess—insects, reptiles and all the parasitic animals lapped it up.

The Giant Men who inhabited this world hated the fog in both the chasms and on the peaks. But they loved the milk! So, they went into the valleys only on short expeditions to hunt or to milk. They never stayed, convinced they would fall sick, despite their vital power. They said that certain plant intelligences and certain hidden stones fed on human lives there by a kind of absorption of desire.

Apart from these tasks, which were honored because they were dangerous, the Giant Men preferred to live on the High Plains, in their tranquil lands, far from the volcanoes. These plains got sun and the fog never rolled in except during the bad season.

In this populated region, there were still some those odd mountains, black and shiny as jade, on which nothing grew and to which they attributed a celestial origin; The Sun Sleepers, or in the language of the Giants, the R'Lil.

They also said they were the condensed seed of the sun, drops fallen from the summit of the origin, sleeping creatures whose sanctity lay in their sleep. They adored these harsh jewels of nature, despite looking like gloomy mausoleums. Traditionally, they considered the region a very propitious area. They knew that their oldest migrations would not have stopped and built for posterity except in the vicinity of such landmarks.

Were these the very same Sun Sleepers to which the successive waves of ancestral exoduses had once come? They did not know and did not look for the difference, satisfied with being there, with having built.

The R'Lil, the guardians, the guarantors of longevity.

All day, these black mountains sparkled, reflecting countless fires onto the polished ramparts of the colossal city of metal and stone on the High Plains: Kobor Tigan't.

I, Kébélé, was living there too, in my way, already old, always old. The lives of the Giant Men were longer than those of the oldest trees. But still they marched by me without a wrinkle on my body changing. I was so insignificant that no one noticed me. In my immutability, I always incarnate the negligible amount.

Moreover, sometimes I would go away for long periods of time. Therefore, people had plenty of time to forget a figure that was so easy to forget for anyone not interested. In such cases, my face never is just a dull, gray, shapeless mist in the poorest memories. And when necessary, every trace of me is completely erased. I am not an historical individual.

For whom I am responsible, I am more like a state of being, a meeting place, a balancing point, a nurturing environment, a rest for perfection or, in some cases, a mysterious door opened for a mysterious two-way trip for knowledge. I am inseparable from the effect I produce. And this effect, in the memory of those who have benefitted from it, remains so striking that it completely obscures the memory of my presence, however potent it may be…

Over against the Sun Sleepers, there was another mountain, the tallest of all, one of a kind, covered with flowers and fruit trees, rife with

28

easy game, veined by beautiful rivers, honored by birds, a paradise of sorts.

It was bursting with colors and so fragrant that, from a distance, you could recognize its scent among a thousand others. Built up from the base between the natural ramparts that rose only a third of its height, it stood out for its gigantic mass. It dominated everything with its size, shape and spirit. In the distance, it seemed to stand in isolation, welcoming the first ray of the morning sun at the tip of its cone—an extraordinary white flash, almost tragic, that sprang violently over the horizon like a weapon being unsheathed...

Under the moon, which was very low and very fat and really blue, the mountain turned into sapphire, adorned with a flight of phosphorescent nocturnal butterflies.

It watched over a certain point of the land beyond which the Giant Men had never ventured or, at least if they had, they had never come back.

It formed a border that was known on only one side. Nothing was known of the other. Some people claimed that the mountain was completely different on the other side, dark and barren, ragged, dangerous. These were sad people who were the butt of jokes since most people believed the contrary, saying with obvious pleasure that the mountain was even more beautiful on the other side, inhabited by a population of large white birds with golden heads who played with lightning.

The name of this mountain was Kah'B'La.

I often preferred to stay in the city. And I saw both sides since I was no more involved in the taboos of that time than the cloud floating overhead, watching...

My travels also took me occasionally to the western coast, along the edge of the vast sea. Volcanoes crowded around there. No one except for me ever went there. This could have been a result of the persistent earthquakes, which made it dangerous enough. But the real reason had deeper roots because the ancestral dread was connected to the west.

The Giant Men called the region: The Great Over There or, if you prefer, in their language, the Great Va-Hôh.

Without knowing anything specific about it, without wanting to know anything, they passed down the horror through tradition, like a racial imprint.

For them, the west was the region that they could only give the name Va-Hôh, in itself a source of discomfort, unseemly, almost an insult to morality, above all synonymous with one of those unspeakable and permanent threats that might be warded off by alluding to it as little as possible. There are things like this that grow stronger in the thoughts of men.

Every time the storms of the bad season returned, they caused panic in Kobor Tigan't because the winds carried with them sounds and odors that supposedly came from the Great Over There. To remedy this, they burned scented herbs on the terraces and wore strong perfume while horns and drums drowned out the noise of the west wind.

In the Great Va-Hôh, I used to sit on a rocky bluff in the middle of a half-circle of mountains facing the sea. From there, one could see far in the distance.

The breeze, which often changed direction, ferried thick fragrances, sulfur or iodine in turn, followed by an inseparable trio of scents: rotted soil, ashes and, strongest of all, the bitterness of the volcanic fire, visible in almost all of the fissures.

The light, sometimes blinding, sometimes so faint that it was nothing but a bit of filtered daylight, would carve out or wipe away the faces of gods or demons on the rocky outcrops. The color of the rocks, red mottled with green, as shiny as if they had been polished, and spontaneously organized into indecipherable architectures, added deeply to the feeling of solitude and hostility, of Elsewhere.

This was the secret theatre of that devouring femininity to which we owe the beginning of every race and which demands the timely return of extinctions. This was where the dreadful genitals converged, whence the first-born came and whither the last dead inevitably returned to be swallowed up.

She who reigned there said, "I spawned you. I reabsorb you. But I am different from you."

Yes, this was the fief of the Different Woman... The true identity of that power was veiled from my clairvoyance by a kind of gleaming magnetization. But I knew her well and I knew what I was dealing with. The obvious sign was to be found at a certain distance...

Around my bluff, noises and movements all over the place kept it in a permanent state of catastrophe. The underground commotion spread to all things. The turmoil below ground shook the peaks. Down below, the soil, black or yellow depending on the location, rippled occasionally. The chasms gaping everywhere bellowed. Water, steam, sulfuric mud and lava, poured out. On the smooth surfaces, holes suddenly opened up. Almost everywhere, ashes fell and stones bounced around. Heavy falls, one after the other, distorting the savage tones.

Although there was no trace of man, there was also no trace of animal or plant life. Sterile, virgin, without generation, nothing but the land, unstable rock, the heights doomed to collapse, a sky full of conflicting clouds and the colorless sea, which a blinding white light turned even whiter. A great, ponderous sadness loomed.

The terrestrial putty had not reached its definitive state. It was preparing other things than what was already there. It would not rest for many cycles of stars. It needed a long time to be kneaded, dried and remoistened, a long time for its architectures to crumble, to sink its ruins in the sea, the mud, the ash and dust so that higher, more ephemeral peaks might once again grow out of the grueling gulfs. Rise, fall, turn back, open, close, for a long time, passively, as if hopelessly in search of a supremely distant perfection. Ruins upon ruins, constantly decomposing, building the mysterious future.

Along the shore whose contours changed continually, the sea, thickened by the volcanic ashes, steamed, barely disturbed by heavy folds. Its apathy contrasted with the terrestrial activity. It did not flow freely, only coming to life in open waters. Far off, it foamed in infinite motion, with bright, flashing clusters. The diamond line of the horizon sparkled.

On the shore, no sand, nothing but a beach of yellow mud, riddled with bubbles and boiling in places near the lava flows. The light burned hard. The stones turned white, flaked. Their edges standing out against the sky shined like metal. The water evaporated; the mud cracked into vast geometric plates. The odor of the subterranean fires rose up. Around the volcanic craters the fires buzzed like a billion swarms. Sparks and flames flew out of all the cracks. Sizzling, answered by sudden flashes shooting up in all directions. A panic, a clash of undisciplined forces.

The place became a glowing forge. The heat grew stronger along with the intensity of the light. All of a sudden, something snapped, turned back in this shimmering universe, some clouds, which no one had time to ever see coming, burst and with a tremendous stench of ozone, let loose a terrible rain, reddish water that flowed down into great gullies, and loosened entire blocks.

In the double thunder of the sky and the earth struck by the falling rubble, everything crumbled, was shattered by the liquid lashing. Swathes of earth peeled right off the peak of the mountain, exploding loudly as they fell onto the muddy shore. Torrents of pebbles went rushing into the sea while waves, so powerful that they leapt over the thick coastal waters, raced in from the horizon, strong and seething, crashed into craters. Under this water, the lava flow let loose shrill hissings as it turned into jets of steam.

The downpour stopped... Had it really happened? Without transition, a kind of dream replaced the violence. It was another world, shapeless, featureless, unlocated. Everything everywhere was smoking, evaporating. Veils of ash, grey powders, the sulfuric layers and all the fumes blended into a fog. A twilight, an opaque time during which nothing could be seen, neither sea nor horizon, nothing solid, nothing but an aural landscape of muted sounds: lumbering flow of lava, purring of underground fires, lapping of muddy bubbles.

A bitter wind blew. The clouds were routed, swept away, shredded. The mists dissipated, strips of fog rolling back in all directions, melting away. The sea rose up all at once, visible as far as the horizon, colorless. The sky was bare, without awareness, the sun stationary, haggard... The wind turned into a breeze carrying scents that wove, strand by strand, a strange composite harmony...

Oh, how far were the High Plains of Kobor Tigan't! Far away from the most sheltered heart of the continent but, especially, far into the past.

For, although this coast of the Great Va-Hôh endured in some way in its genesis, the race of Giant Men came to an end.

It had come from the west in bygone days but it had forgotten, no longer wanting, no longer daring to remember. It wore itself out in that place, incapable of renewal. Of course, the flood that would later carry off its last vestiges, would also come from this anarchic west, from the inexhaustible west.

Thus, the junction of two times, which had become too different, would be accomplished. The new beginning would rejoin the end for a tranquil submersion and the reign of a unified age. Until, gradually, the same differences, the same distances develop, with subtle variations in rhythm. Evolutions that diverge until they are vastly far apart: one stubbornly persisting in a youthful disorder while the other, stemming from it, already weakened, drags along its enfeeblement and does nothing new. It is the offspring that wilts before the old tree. The lineage to which the progenitor does not pass down all the mana, keeping it for itself, and with it, for itself, wild youthfulness. "You came from me. But I am different. I prevail. Because I am the Different Woman!"

This mother earth holds herself back. She lets her sons leave, those innocents who believe that by leaving her they are going far away from her! Without moving from her chaotic bed, she measures how fast they go. She knows it well, this mother, since she circulates in their blood. They constantly move faster, farther. She persists in her magic, not aging as they pass on, reaching the end of themselves after their denial of her. For, they no longer want to know her. Their race dies advanced and lost. They can go no further.

Then, the beautiful cruel mother sets out. The Different Woman reaches her old sons. The intelligent head of this serpent rejoins her absurd tail, sees herself in her own distance. She clamps down and bites and is renewed, heir to her own fruit.

Flood, earth and sky mixed up! Two ends of a single formation that seemed always separated from each other are brought back to the same point...

The middle lands where the Giant Men live are protected behind a defense of mountainous barriers. It was not impossible to make one's way from Kobor Tigan't to the Great Va-Hôh because there were natural passages. But, of course, it would have been necessary to leave the hospitable heights and be ready for a journey full of physical hardships, mental constraints and dangers of the three worlds.

Any determined or independent man would certainly have succeeded. But only if he forgot the tales of the old Huge Mothers, those druids of a sort, those bards: the B'Tah-Gou, who hold sway over public opinion.

That was the hardest part of the undertaking because these old women wielded an almost magical influence on the brains of the males.

They told of such things, so persuasively, that they froze the blood of the proudest of men, removing any vague desire for adventure. Moreover, by a kind of deeply imbedded mental depravation they grew indulgent. They asked for more because it was finer to have one's personal B'Tah-Gou. It was an indication of caste, a sign of intellectualism, a refinement.

They chose B'Tah-Gou in youth, either by joining a group or finding one on one's own. They went to hear her in the evening and get advice from her—they started thinking through her. The Huge Mother became the Brain. They brought bosom brothers to drink in her words, in a drunken binge of oddities. Groups occasionally visited each other. The most successful meetings turned into collective delirium because the Storytellers had highly developed gifts of invocation. They were the store-rooms of racial myths and a real armory of secret words, of verbal formulas.

A B'Tah-Gou did not move around, did not touch anything, she simply spoke. But with such art! It could be said that she possessed the Word. The tone of her voice was altogether special, very deep, very low, very hoarse. A B'Tah-Gou was appreciated because she made the air vibrate when speaking. And those listening felt the physical effect deep in their chests.

A whole ritual of respect surrounded the Storytellers. For example, you could never touch them. The slightest touch was improper. You stayed three steps away. You greeted them, spoke and looked at them freely.

They did not hold conference in the morning, only in the evening. Each in the back of her dwelling, they started speaking at nightfall, often without even waiting for their listeners to arrive. They could be heard chanting from outside. The men entered, in silence, one by one, and sat in a semi-circle. The incantation of the legend grew and led unerringly along the winding thread of an imagination that never was at a loss. The listeners rocked in place, contributing throaty hums at times, marking the rhythm, participating with short responses. The night passed. They would forget their bodies. The B'Tah-Gou bore away their minds.

The Storytellers lived to be very old, their art increasing with age. The more decrepit their bodies grew, turning gray and grainy like stones, the more alert their minds became.

Those fortunate ones who possessed the oldest B'Tah-Gou wore belts that set them apart from others. They ranked higher than the other men and walked ahead of the other groups.

Spouses and mothers hated the Storytellers for the hold they had over husbands and sons and also because they were sterile women, a dreadful blemish in their eyes.

Nevertheless, this single activity of the mind was not enough for the men. There were brave ones among them, in particular the collectors of Dongdwo eggs who went down from the High Plains into the Calamitous Valley for this harvest.

Many superstitions surround this Valley. The B'Tah-Gou take pleasure in adding to them, but they are careful not to cast the slightest prohibition since they love those eggs and know that there is nothing more pressing for the men than to offer them some on their return.

But, apart from that, truly, this Valley is in a bad place. So deeply hollowed out between such steep walls that the fog never lifts. Everything there is damp. Everything is hazy. Everything is as if swollen with a secret mental existence, a diffused intelligence, floating everywhere.

People have to travel through it with no bearings, walking on a spongy soil that never holds any traces of previous expeditions. Every time someone goes there, it is like the first time. The last victory is of no use. Travelers have to start all over again, undergo a new trial against which they cannot prepare a defense.

Although men only go there out of necessity, animals and insects, on the contrary, never go there at all. The entire place, therefore, is strangely silent. The father you go, the more the silence you drink in through your pores builds up in you, runs through your chest, stays there, swells, weighs you down bit by bit, as it to moor you there forever, enchanting you with a melancholic fatigue and an almost delectable disgust. The effort required to walk becomes harder and harder. The fog is full of fumes that make you drowsy.

All that is found there are wild plants, a vegetal madness with thick, translucent stems and limp leaves, wide as wings. Touching them is like touching dead, cold flesh, a little sweaty. They are not plants but presences that grow there, anchored with stubborn roots. They have a bitter attitude and accuse you, the guilty one! Soon, you believe it is true. Farther on, you question yourself under your breath…

The darkness at the heart of it seems to have sowed chaotic seeds here. Like a tangible sadness, a bad memory, a restless sorrow that stretches arms out of the ground. Arms and more arms! Vehemence and testimony!

These plants, being weak and strong at the same time, are called the Widows of the Moon or the Vindictives or even the Desolates. Their real name, which no one likes to utter is the Aâz.

Men fear them and rightly so. They grope and feel you everywhere, like the blind. They recognize you! They tell one another! You feel as if the news spreads everywhere! And then you too, suddenly, you recognize them! In front of you, you see the part of yourself that had always been hidden: the unsettling stranger, the psychic vegetation that you weed in vain! It is there, overgrown, it knows, it accuses, it holds you!

To vanquish these plants, you must trample on them, move them out of the way, break them off. They only break off after they have been stretched out, then they turn into a runny sap with an intoxicating odor.

But more often, instead of breaking off when pulled, they are torn out of the soil whole, in a shower of white roots. And still, they do not let go! You have to keep walking, dragging them behind you.

Young men have gotten lost in this valley. They went mad, going round in circles without ever finding their way out. They believed they were dragging a corpse behind them…

It is a sad lot, all the more absurd since the race of Giant Men normally have an infallible sense of direction. But the Vindictives, the Widows of the Moon, cloud this sense if you are not careful. Can the traveler allow himself a short rest, a slackening of his energy, even a simple doubt? Then it is over: the two interior directions on which he relied, the starting point and the goal, disappear from his consciousness. He loses any notion of them. He will never find them again… They know that only pure young men with strong minds can withstand such confusion.

Fortunately, by walking in the right direction, to the end of the Calamitous Valley, you finally reach other regions where the ranks of the Widows of the Moon thin out. Small, stunted, malnourished by a terrain that is no longer suitable for them, the last ones to appear are covered with spots and wrinkles.

Travelers are pleased to see this. Soon, over large, bare spaces, they are treading on thick moss. The air is hotter, fouler. They start to see more clearly and farther away the natural configurations. At first, they are merely vague shapes, appearing as thicker banks of fog. Then, you can see, on either side, the walls of the gorge that narrow into a sharp turn. The passage grows wider after turning. On one side, an expanse of black water shimmers. On the other a light halo indicates the exit that opens onto another plain. The fog has lifted from the ground. Thinner, but not yet dissipated, since it is still impossible to see the tiniest patch of the sky, it is like a ceiling diffusing hazy light. Above that, the sweltering heat of a hatchery.

The ear picks up hoarse sounds, heavy breathing, neighing, gurgling, belching. The stench, once inhaled, is suddenly replaced by the musky odor of giant reptiles. The ground sinks more and more. Every step makes it ooze water. It is the area around the vast swamp where the last dragons live: the old Dongdwo, whose eggs they eat.

For ages, they had stopped trying to capture the ancient saurian. Vestiges of a mythic time, they were almost sacred. Very old, very weak, they stopped breeding. Still, they were taking a long time to die out, since their lifespan was as long as that of cities. Kobor Tigan't was barely being built when they had already declined to that state, the Last of an Age. Some storytellers claimed that the city would die along with them. This was not certain. They could very well live on for an indefinite time. Other B'Tah-Gou had a more original opinion: "The Dongdwo don't die. For them to disappear, the earth has to swallow them up like it swallowed up their elders who were even bigger!"

The Dongdwo were truly gigantic. From a distance, they could easily be mistaken for hills.

They lived in the middle of the swamp on an island made of solid land where the forest provided them with shelter. They liked the shade and fled from the rays of the sun, fearing they would be burned. The protection of the fog was barely sufficient. They also needed the tightly knit domes of the trees and the vegetal night of thick undergrowth.

Weakened by age, and no doubt deteriorated, they were losing their scales. People harvested them to decorate their hunting shields. Their flanks, stripped bald in places, presented pink flesh. The thorny armor down their spines was falling off as well. What remained of this dorsal crest had atrophied or been paralyzed and could no longer stand up straight.

Some Dongdwos were blind, their visual organs having been reabsorbed. Most could barely see anything anymore. They shook their heavy, lumpy heads in which their yellow eyes with their vertical pupils, once as bright as topaz, now dull, looked like overripe fruits.

Still, all of these old, pitiful dragons had one last power: they could mottle their hides with different hues, depending on their mood. This particularity got stronger the more emotional they got. They whimpered in fear over nothing: a shadow, a noise, an unusual scent. They could not bear being looked at by men without suffering. Even the blind ones felt the contact on their hypersensitive bulk. Incapable of fleeing, they whined and trembled, each wave of shivers triggering a wave of colors over their skin. A pale gray at the first shock of fright, then they turned bilious green, then to yellow, followed by a congestive red mottling their dewlaps while their snout became purple. That was when they would collapse to the ground, unable to bear the tension any longer.

The Giant Men, aware of these characteristics, took pains not to alarm them. It was a matter of not exhausting them since the precious Dongdwos tired quickly, moving about with great difficulty, their knock-kneed legs barely able to support their mass. They could not flee and even less, as they had once done, gallop through whole regions, devastating them like an earthquake. No, those days were over, they never left their island. Had they been tempted to do so, the only practicable way was a narrow rocky peak, jutting out of the swamp on the other side of the island that would have collapsed under their weight, dragging them down into the sludge. On this side, they faced the smooth wall of the High Plains, a vertical cliff, dotted with caves, the bottom lying at the very edge of the swamp.

There, I knew, the place was becoming a cemetery. It was there, from the very top of the cliff, that the big, wrinkled bodies of the nobles or dignitaries among the Giant Men were piously thrown down with their finery and jewels.

During such ceremonies, the usually quite noisy dragons would fall silent. They waited. Then, when the heavy body, at the end of its fall, sank into the swamp, they all howled together, lamentably, and started growling in unison without eating for long hours ahead. It resembled a litany. Inexplicably, the duration of this homage was always proportional to the virtues of the deceased.

Up on high, the Giant Men stood still without moving from the place. They would not leave until the Dongdwos finished their song. They believed that their brave ancestors were speaking through the voices of these guardians of the dead.

The Dongdwos ate grass and the steaming rot of the swamp. The females laid their bunches of sterile eggs in the silt, where the Giant Men came looking for them. It was the favorite delicacy reserved for the noble caste who believed this food contained magical and aphrodisiac powers. The most famous of the B'Tah-Gou were always kept well-stocked by their devotees. Ordinary people did not eat these eggs and would never have dared to do so, convinced that it was a sacrilege, that only the nobles could reconnect with the ancestors in this way.

The job of egg hunter was highly honored and, because of the difficulties and the expertise require, it was always held by the best. And they were proud of it. The way in was hard and dangerous but the rest, finding and gathering the eggs in the nest was even more so. Very real perils were awaiting the adventurer. Not that the old dragons were the least bit dangerous, but the swamp itself was toxic, as a result of it being a mass grave. Foul fermentations spoiled the already stifling air. The damp fog steeped their clothes in the stench.

And above all, a sadness, a curse seemed to loom over the region. The breezes whispered quietly; misty shapes crawled about pretty much everywhere. Everything was half deceased, half sunk, grasping for purchase, a solid shore to hold onto. They said that anyone spending too much time there carried inside them forever the melancholy of finite things, the disdain for the destiny of man. This is why they took on this task only during the years preceding maturity, because it required the vital fire of youth to successfully fight against invisible influences.

To get to the swamp the steep cliff of the High Plains was impractical. It was impossible to climb down from them. The only possible access required a long detour through the Calamitous Valley. Then, once the adventurer had reached the swamp, he had to climb up natural slopes through a series of plains to a third way up the cliff where an opening yawned. The men went in, plodded through and climbed back down through a maze of caves and tunnels. From time to time, they caught a glimpse of the void through crevasses. They wound their way over dark terraces, slippery slopes while gusts of wind blasted around them. Finally, they came to a vast cavern that opened out onto the rocky ridge that led to the island through the swamp.

When a man reached this cavern, before taking the rocky bridge, he would blow a horn to warn the Dongdwos who, familiar with the signal, would immediately stop whatever they were doing. Worried, shaking and shivering, they fell silent and, stuffed with uneaten leaves hanging from the jaws, they backed away, very clumsily, to hide deep in their lairs. They did not move again until the expedition was over.

And, while his acolytes waited, a single hunter walked along the ridge and, once on the island, made a methodical tour around it without ever being bothered. If by chance, he spotted the muzzle of a straggler in a bush who was weaker than the others, the hunter avoided laying eyes on the creature so as not to frighten it.

So, he walked along the shore, searching the hollows and under the mounds, to find the hiding places made by the females. From the mud, he extracted clusters of eggs that looked like huge bunches of white grapes and wrapped them in leaves before putting them in a leather sack he carried on his back. Sometimes, he searched a long time before finding anything and occasionally there was nothing to be found.

The eggs were becoming rarer and rarer. Laying was less frequent and less abundant. Degenerate females ate their own eggs. It was always more and more difficult. And, as a result, they were more and more valuable. Furthermore, it was said that the eggs strengthened their quintessence from their rarity. They were more pungent, more fortifying, more intoxicating.

In Kobor Tigan't, the radiance of the royal caste, the beauty of the queen, the vigor of her spouse, the inspiration of the renowned B'Tah-Gou came from the regular consumption of this delicacy.

When the egg hunter had completed his harvest, he went back the same way along the ridge to be greeted joyfully by his companions. Before heading home, they sounded the horn again, releasing the Dong-dwos. It was only time they shed their apathy. They recognized the signal so quickly and so clearly that they would all start snorting, sneezing and gurgling in high-pitched unison. Often, as well, while relaxing, a few females would lay eggs right there. When hearing the specific cry that marked the event, the hunters smiled. Next time, they were sure not to return empty-handed!

Apart from the Dongdwo, the egg donors, and the Mouh-Tou, the milk donors, there was another type of domesticated reptile at Kobor Tigan't in a pit under the palace: the Ananou, which people preferred to call the T'Lo when they were renting them individually for personal use. Ananou was their name as a group, T'Lo their name as individuals.

They belonged to the crown, which meant that they were well cared for. No one ever heard them screaming. They were quiet and happy to lead a vegetative life, spending most of their time sleeping. A musky odor, strong but very pleasant, was the only indication of their presence. They were given food that enhanced this scent.

The Ananou were the vestiges of an unsettling mystery. When the ancestors of the Giant Men reached the High Plains, where they would later build Kobor, they discovered these strange creatures who seemed to be waiting for them. They made no effort to escape, stayed nearby until people took an interest in their mysterious appearance.

The B'Tah-Gou, who were already teaching, revealed the secret by calling them Creatures of the Error. These beings were the result of the insane matings of the previous race, the race of the "Larger-than-Us", so the Storytellers said.

This race had been overindulgent (quickly turned into a sacrilegious cult) to the tame saurians. Thus, they spawned the Ananou, creatures which, without being truly human, were no longer really animals either. They terrorized all other beasts. As for humans, upon seeing them men were torn between horror of their origin and a curious sense of the sacred, no doubt due to the ancientness and the strangeness of the act. The result of this feeling was their preservation.

The Ananou hated animals but showed adoration for mankind and total submission. The people loathed them. This was not the case, however, for the debauched nobles who paid the crown very high rates to use some of the creatures. They coupled with them in their orgies, proudly pretending to imitate their mighty ancestors and be the equals of the "Larger-than-us". One good reason for this was that the queen did so, too.

These hybrid monsters, smaller than the Giants, had delicate, pink skin covered in places by pearly scales that shimmered in the light.

Most often, they stood upright. Their slim bodies never grew fat, stretching their slender limbs, their movements marked with reptilian grace. Their long, thin necks often tilted to one side or the other under the weight of their round heads, which were totally hairless but the tightly woven scales formed a kind of helmet. The typical flatness of their faces, their cleft mouths, the slight projection of their noses with wide holes, their eyes as golden as the sun, made them look like big frogs. Thin webs connected their fingers. They had no fingernails.

The Ananou were hermaphrodites. They all had double sexuality.

Male or female, anyone who paid to use a T'Lo took such a fancy to it that they could not bear to be separated from it because of a kind of enchantment the creatures possessed. Use quickly turned into passion, then into an irrepressible need. Eventually, except for moments of erotic relations when pleasure was long-lasting and all-consuming, these abuses put them in a permanent state of twilight pleasure. In truth, it was as intoxicating as a drug.

Once out of the pit, the T'Lo attached itself unreservedly to its mistress or its master. It was very gentle, very tender, docile beyond words, tireless, always available. Its sole concern was to satisfy its owner. As a result, it developed an odd intelligence that really only worked on one track, manifesting itself in perverse research and utterly extraordinary amorous inventions. This intuition for the refinement of sensation was their genius.

They were living instruments of love, entirely dedicated to the ecstasy of their human partner. Most of the passionate dramas that troubled Kobor were caused by the T'Lo. Frightful tales of licentiousness or touching examples. The T'Lo had been seen escaping to join their masters in death and commit suicide by throwing themselves into the Dong-dwo swamp.

But, since they brought a fortune into the royal treasury, such matters were brought under control. Palace officials were assigned to recover the T'Lo as soon as its owner passed away. It would be captured if necessary. Most often, the family of the deceased individual would bring it back on their own. The creature would be given a special brew that would remove its memory and it would be put back in with the other Ananou. It would quickly find another master because initial training of these creatures took a long time and people preferred to avoid this work by choosing one that had already been prepared.

One could inherit a T'Lo, the mother or the father passing it on to the eldest of their children who thus assumed the noble prerogative. In the best families, tradition required the main T'Lo to wear the ancient jewelry and what was used as a coat of arms. There was no limit to the number of T'Lo a family could have, a mark of how wealthy the masters were since they cost a fortune and were only ever leased out. The crown received its dues on a regular basis.

In the case of an inheritance, the law mandated the T'Lo to still go back down into the pit before being reclaimed. To better preserve everything it had learned, the drink of oblivion would be replaced by a sleeping concoction.

Among themselves, the Ananou never reproduced. They did not even try. There had never been an example of it. Human desire alone aroused them to the sexual life. Their male organ did not fertilize women. On the other hand, rare as it was but often enough to keep their numbers up, the seed from a man could fertilize their feminine side.

But their offspring were always other Ananou. They got no human characteristics other than those they already possessed.

They did not advance, did not improve, nor did they degenerate. Their species remained forever between the human and the animal, a non-integrated link, a bewildering hybrid.

The offspring born in human homes were returned to the royal reserve right after they were weaned.

CHAPTER II

Kobor Tigan't, a mightily built system, not a city with districts but, in the huge Body of the holy city of Kobor, set on the quintuple terracing of a mountain, four cities topped by a royal estate, four ascending, progressive cities, fitted together, articulated, proceeding in order from one to the other, four complementary and hierarchical cities plus one, like Man with four Limbs and a Head.

Kobor Tigan't was called Kobor Tigan't like an individual living species, like a living entity. It was called Kobor Tigan't like Man is called Man!

Kobor was beautiful, and tragic as well, like all great holy things.

Kobor was terrible because its construction reflected an order of forces, a succession of planes of forces where the inhabitants lived on their level according to their secret rank. Neither too high nor too low, each placed where he had to be on the scale of values.

For, everyone of that time, like those of other times, did not have the same density of being nor the same vibratory combination. Always among men there are the heavy and the light. And in Kobor, the heavy and the light did not live mixed up together but were partitioned from top to bottom according to their true weight, each living on his proper plane.

Thus, Kobor had a religious force, although no religion was practiced there. There were no temples nor priests. But the forces of the cosmos were there in order, reflected there and producing their works. And Kobor, visited in this manner, illuminated and resonating, Kobor was a mighty instrument connecting the Above and the Below.

The sacred Whole, therefore, was called Kobor Tigan't.

Below, the Black city represented the terrestrial base. It was called Kob'Lâm.

In the rampart, the large central gate, surmounted by a golden disk, opened outside onto the gentle slopes of the High Plains whose successive levels dropped into the deep valleys, the swamps, the shadow-filled gorges where buried rivers shimmered. Just under the gate, a stone bridge stretched over a bottomless chasm, the round mouth of a black pit that seemingly plunged through the entire depth of the earth. People threw waste and small corpses into it. It exhaled a very cold breeze. The hunters hated the feeling. When crossing the bridge, they always sped up.

Large scavenger birds with furry wings dove boldly into the chasm to feed. People liked them so little they never bothered to name them. What an insult! They were simply referred to as "those birds" in the most scornful of tones. No one killed them. Their blood would have tainted the reputation of the weapons.

Kob'Lâm housed silos, depots, storerooms of all kinds and the cellars for Dongdwo eggs. These cellars were so deep that they always remained at almost freezing temperature whatever the season. The massive houses crowded against one another. Their overlapping rooftops cast shadows over the facades. They were made of flat, black, shiny stones, a kind of marble, which called to mind the R'iil, grouted with red clay not for sturdiness, since their weight sufficed for that, but for decoration.

The common people lived there along with the old people from the three higher cities who voluntarily came down to end their days in the lower city. They all lived together amiably. Sterile women, who no longer wanted men, took care of them. In the evenings they would sit on their doorsteps and chat from house to house. The ordinary people loved listening to them and never tired of asking them for stories.

Every morning, Kobor Tigan't woke up from top to bottom, but the feet first. For it was Kob'Lâm that stirred first. The royal officials responsible for food supplies, waking up before everyone else, took food out of the silos and storerooms to prepare the shares. This was particularly important for the grains and products made from Mouh-Tou milk since, for the rest—picking fruits and certain plants, small game—the supply was free and easy to get.

There were many of these distribution officials. They set out in successive processions, heading back up to the higher city. The people waited in clearly designated places to receive their food.

The first served were always the B'Tah-Gou, the Huge Mothers, the storytellers, the glory of their race. Each of them lived alone and never went out. Each of them was served by a young girl who had asked to do so. There were always young girls who longed for this. Their parents never refused. It was considered a mysterious calling. One out of three of these young girls became a sterile woman. They were disgusted by men, took care of the elderly and then, in turn, became B'Tah-Gous, carrying the torch of inspiration.

Some other sterile women formed a special caste of prostitutes. Very beautiful and intelligent. Men sought them out in secret because, in the gynecocracy, the free and conscious desire of males was considered a vice, almost an act against nature. In any case, the men saw magic in these women and went to see them in the hopes of acquiring a special quality of influence that would channel other women's desires towards them, particularly a woman from a very high caste.

In the world of the Giants of Kobor, the Woman took the Man.

Again it was in Kob'Lâm that the fabric makers lived. There was no actual weaving, but by soaking a kind of gigantic leaf, they obtained a supple, vegetal cloth. The soaking process was used on a corrosive vine. It destroyed the fleshy part of the leaves, which looked a little like parchment when dried but without the stiffness or brittleness of parchment. It goes without saying that animal skins were treated in a similar manner.

Once the food distributors had served all of Kob'Lâm, they moved on to the next city above and so on through all the others until they reached the top.

A central gate, also surmounted by a golden disk, connected the Black City with the Green City: Kob'Vâm.

There again, you had to cross over a stone bridge spanning a large, round pond in which water or rather a perfectly green, mysterious liquid, deep and glistening, stagnated. They were very careful not to throw anything into it. It was a sacred pond and, to stress the fact, a golden coping had been built around it.

Just below it, at the base of the rampart, on the Kob'Lâm side, stood the houses of the B'Tah-Gou.

Kob'Vâm was a burgeoning of rustic tiers, filled with flowers, leaves, springs, waterfalls and small rippling rivers, gardens, orchards. The houses were spread out in a pleasing matter. Most of the women were very beautiful, curvaceous and cheerful, renowned for their beautiful arms and luscious hair.

A rampart with two side doors, also marked by two gold disks, separated the Green City from Kob'Râm, the Red City, the city of fire, forges, cast iron and metal work.

Handsome men were almost always born in Kob'Râm. In the center of this city, always lit up at night, there was one very remarkable detail that was particularly important in the Spring festivals during the Queen's Battle. This ceremony took place on the site which was, on semicircular terrace like an overhanging balcony, another sort of pond—a huge crucible containing perpetually molten metal. This crucible was also decorated with a golden rim. People were in the habit of throwing the weapons of the dead into it to melt them down and mix them into the mass that was like the wild heart, the volcanic heart of Kobor Tigan't.

At the back of this terrace, the forges glowed red. The bellows panted day and night because they kept them constantly working. The blacksmiths labored patiently, taking great pleasure in their work, alternating with each other. They did not only make large items, but also jewelry in the smaller, more detailed workshops.

Kob'Râm was always very busy, a little feverish, even at night. A lot of people came and went. At the end of this tier were two side doors with golden disks joining it to Kob'Iâm, the Blue City, the aristocratic city.

Columns, arcades, porticoes, walkways, dizzying terraces and grand staircases that crossed every which way. Everywhere, jets of water, natural geysers sprayed the air. An immense waterfall, an iridescent arc, fell from high above. Vast residences perched here and there, in unfettered chaos. Light flooded into the inner courtyards. They were home to the best families.

Due to the altitude, the air people breathed was lighter, almost intoxicating because it was fragrant with flowering bushes, brought there long ago from Kah'B'La, the beloved mountain. Each house had its own bush and took special care of it. A withering bush brought shame and despair like the admission of a hidden flaw in a family. And it was not uncommon for a family, stealthily in the night, to plant others carried down from the mountain in order to repair their honor in the critical eyes of their neighbors.

Then, above this, at the very top, above this Blue City, stood the holy city, the Queen, the Golden One, the one called Kob'Ooh'R, named after the sun, Ooh'R.

There lived the queen, the Ooh'Rou, the Fully Golden One, the One who resembled the sun. And in the epoch that concerns us, this queen was Ooh'Rou Opak.

The double doors, decorated with a gigantic gold sphere, led into a tunnel through the triple rampart and, once inside, you had to cross three thresholds guarded by sentinels.

In Kob'Ooh'R all of the splendid outbuildings of the immense palace, a city in itself, were covered with gold plates, blinding in the sun. In the peak of summer, it was a maze of fierce refractions. Walls and doors made of a soft, white, smooth stone, much like ivory, and amber yellow tiles, shiny, precious, grouted with gold.

At the top of the highest tier an ultimate golden sphere shined, surpassing all of the others in size and splendor. The base was decorated with streamers whose different colors represented the noble families. Directly under this sphere was the terrace where, every year, for the good of the people, the festival of the Fertilization of the Queen was held.

Yes, anyone who has been to Kobor Tigan't remembers it forever, stored in the imperishable marrow of his being!

And anyone who has been to Kobor Tigan't forever misses the Potent Life and forever fears the Potent Death that broods below, within...

The Palace was in the exact center of Kob'Ooh'R and in the middle of the Palace, in the Center Chamber sat (and never left) Abim, the queen mother, revered in silence by all.

They did not talk much about her. But all thoughts were secretly preoccupied with her. When, however, it occasionally became necessary to allude to her (which only high-ranking people were permitted to do), they called her: the Very Huge.

She was the supreme shakti, the occult "sarah", the most formidable one. Few people knew it. Those who suspected rejected any train of thought in that direction, forbidding themselves to go further. They were afraid.

Just below Abim's chamber, there was the Ananou Pit. Thus, on this upper level the same position in terms of hierarchy and force was reproduced as on the lower levels of Kob'Vâm where the houses of the B'Tah-Gou were huddled together below the green pool. This showed a hidden analogy.

If anyone, through clairvoyance, could have made a kind of vertical cross-section in the system of Kobor Tigan't, they would have noticed, ever so frightfully, that Abim was enthroned at the top of a hollow column of black fluid.

Abim was like a fermenting bubble in a layer cake but, unlike leavening in bread that makes the dough rise as if through a rapturous ascent of the Wheat Being, her power was exerted in the opposite direction, from Above to Below, in a tragic descent. To stay like that, sitting motionless, alone, over the course of ages, the Very Huge had plunged the vertical shaft of her influences down to the very core of the Black City. You could say that she made the bread of life rise backwards, transforming it into the bread of death, the bread of stone. She was a reverse leavening. A thing that people cannot imagine without trembling. This was Her Force. This was Abim's Key.

Crouched down, *never showing her feet,* she had used her lowest vibrations to bore a secret route that ensured her eternal dwelling through all of the cities. She now felt extended into the darkest of the land like a huge taproot. She possessed four paths of emanation that she took in her descents. First was the ambiguity of the Ananou, then the smelting energy of the crucible in Kob'Râm, the green spirit of the pool of Kob'Vâm, which was connected to the astrality of the B'Tah-Gou and, finally the dark whirlpool of the gaping chasm under the last gate of Kob'Lâm.

Sitting. Motionless. Alone for ages. Never growing old, for ages!

Under such circumstances, this non-action benefitted from the concentration of the telluric emanations. Abim diverted them for her own use, whereas these emanations, at the top of their ascent, should have freely gushed forth through the coronal sphere of Kob'Ooh'R to flourish and spread their vital blessings over the entire race. But Abim blocked them.

And that was a most terrible crime. For, it made Kobor Tigan't like a piece of wormy fruit. A dead man who could not admit it diverting life for his own benefit.

The seed-bearing spirits of the Sky, aroused by the prodigious system of the quintuple cities, when they descended onto the coronal sphere, could not join forces with the terrestrial spirits. Abim turned the sky into a widower! She forged a lesbian union with the sacred Femininity of the earth core.

Abim infused herself with the telluric Kundalini! Kobor Tigan't was drained of its marrow. Abim held the lever of the world, for herself, for herself alone.

Sitting. Motionless. Alone. Constantly intoxicated, Abim let the force penetrate her, gathering more and more of it. She had an almost limitless capacity for absorption. Nevertheless, when she reached saturation point, she knew how to reverse the force in order to be transported by it, as she pleased, and descend and plunge and head out west... Her consciousness did not know the full extent of using the force, but she reveled in it. That was all.

The Giants were massive but their height was not so remarkable in a landscape that was itself gigantic in the size of its mountains, trees, plants, flowers and animals. Also, to the naked eye, the size ratio between man and the mountaintops was no different than what we are used to.

Their lifespan was very long. They had the time to see trees grow, age and fall before even starting to feel their own strength decline.

But the Giant Men grew tired of living. Their thickened race got its looks from the land itself, its fluvial power, its volcanic vitality. The strength of the blood in their veins could be compared to the circulation of metals liquefied by fire in the veins of the earth.

However, it was really the end of the race with all the secret lethargy it entailed. The ancestral burden was heavy. The layering of all the pasts was crushing their souls. The problems accumulated by history were crying out in the marrow of the living for solutions that grew more urgent every day. Fathers asked their sons for answers to anguished questions. An unspoken torment pestered all their minds.

Weary, yes weary, the race had seen too many tedious dawns, too many rumbling nights and too many terrifying flights that clouded its mythical past. And so much deceptive peace had foundered without providing a real balm so that they all grew sick of dying so late in daily boredom. Their strong life slipped away so very slowly! They were never really sick. They saw the cycles pass over them, around them, without really understanding anything, with a vast melancholy from which, little by little, they acquired a disturbing intelligence, bizarre delicacies mixed with their roughness.

The changes they noticed disturbed them. And there were more and more of them. Among the animal species, the beasts they had known, loved or hated, were disappearing. They discovered others, unknown ones, in the woods or on the mountain. They alone did not change, did not dare to, were not able to. The plants, flowers or trees they had gathered, eaten or admired stopped growing, replaced by others that they took a long time to get used to, even if they were better or more beautiful. They regretted the fact that everything changed while they themselves did not. This annoyed them. They had been stuck there for too long. But was it not already too late? Such numbness was spreading through them!

Of course, that was not exactly the way they thought about it. Everything was more obscure in their minds. They felt these things more in their hearts, so that broad feelings, tides of nostalgia washed over them.

The race was corroded internally by disgust, by wear and tear. It was being mineralized since it had never gotten new blood through alliances with foreigners or even those simulating currents from contact with other civilizations. No, the Giant Men lived in isolation, with the impression that it had always been so. Come from nomads, once they had settled down, Kobor Tigan't, after it was built, had fixed them in place for all time.

They detested adventure. Fiercely conservative, they never set foot outside the walls of the city. Their trips were deliberately short trips, gone and back in no time. They did not like to camp outdoors. The magnetic aura of Kobor held then within its walls like an abusive mother, denying freedom to her children. Being born meant not going outside but sinking deeper into the mother's bosom. And staying there.

The mountains, given their almost perfectly circular arrangement, made it even worse—by protecting them, they imprisoned them. It was normal for them to think that neither the land nor anything else imaginable existed beyond those heights, over by the great Va-Hôh where the frightful sea shimmered.

Obviously, as always, the symptoms of this malaise were more evident among the nobles than among the common people. While the latter whined and wept in the night to tales of bygone days, the nobles leaned toward excess. Their need for distractions grew constantly more frantic: feasting, hunting, exhibition fighting and, above all, luxury.

But nothing came of it. The morose lake trembled for a moment, then the gray water closed in again, restored itself, tranquil, sad. Disappointing efforts! The people started to imitate them too late, spoiling things. There arose grand poetic outpourings, boundless despair, silent mediations that merely made them stop speaking, fleeing from one another only to come back together in their sterile excesses. In short, a dazzling life with the search for oneself. The old tribal spirit slowly faded, replaced by individualization.

Decadence sensitized them. The degenerative poison fermented slowly in their depths. They would have had to go beyond themselves, to breach the invisible limitations. Pipe dreams, alas! Protractions of the heart, contortions of the soul! Nothing soothed them. In their urges they found nothing but false exits, always the same, relentlessly banal: hunting, feasting, jewelry, intrigues, luxury. The influence of the B'Tah-Gou. The influence of the T'Lo. The influence of the self-enclosed rituals.

The Giant Men were passionately sad: shocking scoffers, loved a good laugh, not cruel nor evil, but sad, very sincere in everything, very serious and solemn even in the worst excesses.

Breathless, stiff, always the same, utterly mystified, the race was waiting for something it could accept, some fitting rescue, some delivery, waiting and had no real idea what for.

Only one person understood the scope of this quagmire: Abim, the queen mother. Yes, she alone, paradoxically, understood. She alone was aware of these dramas, in general and in detail. She alone knew because she was not really like the others, because she "escaped" thanks to her personal resources. But, above all she knew because she loved her race, her kingdom, like one loves a long-cherished idea. Secretly she mutilated Kobor Tigan't but in spite of this (or perhaps because of it, who knows?) she loved Kobor Tigan't.

Abim was a holy and horrific mountain of fat, a gigantic toad that just sat in the center of the kingdom, in the spot in the palace that her weight had hollowed out!

Her rooms were there, off limits to anyone not belonging the royal family. Without much talk about it, Abim was considered the indispensable pivot of Kobor, the center of gravity. You would have thought that she had magically emanated the city, that it represented a projection of her inner nature and that, perhaps, the circle of constraints that was crushing the race was nothing but a manifestation of her despotism. People preferred not to think about it.

Sitting, hunkered down, Abim was still taller than the tallest of men standing up. A vestige of the extinct race of the "Those-Bigger-Than-Us"? No one knew. No one said anything. People were afraid to say it. No one looked like her or acted like her, not even Opak, her eldest daughter, the reigning queen. As for Ta, the youngest, she looked even less like her.

For Abim, sitting represented the state of plenitude, the splendor of permanence! The many cushions of the folds in her buttocks wedged her comfortably in her hollow. Contrary to the inclination of her kind, she wore no jewelry, no weapons, no clothing. She was only happy when totally nude. Her dangling breasts, her huge belly, her colossally rounded hips drooped around her as she squatted.

She was very dark-skinned, almost perfectly black, which gave the contours of her body a reddish, shadowy reflection in the light, a deep purple mouth, eyes with very wide, black irises, the whites of her eyes rather orange and a full head of brittle, white hair.

She was extremely old, weathered and worn by time, as old as a continent on which waterfalls, avalanches and earthquakes have turned the soil many times over, dragged the depths up to the surface over and over, repeatedly buried what once burned in the open air until eventually becoming extinct for good, the volcanoes latent, the ocean stormless, the earth finally motionless.

Abim summed up her planet. She, the Witness. She, the Memory. She, the conquering vestige. She alone had gone through everything without weakening. She alone held the thread from the beginning. Having reached this state of immutable fulfillment, she no longer ventured out. The fire of her vitality smoldered inside.

She did nothing but think, all day and night, saying nothing about it, with fervent perseverance, with the special patience that endlessly mulls over the details of a complex problem without solution. Over the years that no longer affected her, she had, with her self-mastery, come to scorn the expression of feelings. She spoke only in a low voice. She rarely responded. She knew that people would come close so as not to miss anything and, even with no one around her, she knew that her thoughts went where they were supposed to go.

She almost never moved. People in the city talked about it for months if Abim lifted a finger! Her gaze was enough to support her decision. A short flutter of her eyelid was more important than a shout or authoritarian gestures.

She had stopped reigning such a long time ago that no one knew how she had once fared. Good and bad, everything she might have done was gone, obliterated, forgotten, as if her real, actual actions had never been truly important. What was important was that she was there like this, mythic and inexplicable in her origins and passive longevity alike.

The people were convinced that she had always been sitting in the heart of the kingdom, not like an old queen (people never dreamed of picturing her as young and, besides, she never talked about her past) but like a living being, inherently eluding age, like a living stone of eternity, the symbol of the reign, a being above human, a sort of transcendent animal, great her attention, her secret vigilance, living, always living, as a matter of principle living...

People only ever saw her very rarely, by accident, when the stone doors to her rooms swung open, and always from a distance, through curtains, a dark mass. Out of propriety, a fear of sacrilege, no one ever described the vision.

Her presence alone bore the weight of her longevity over everything. Abim governed. Because she did nothing visible any longer, it seemed like she acted through the invisible, with a muted strength, underneath events, like the rudder under a boat. She was present at the heart of things. Abim was sitting in all the centers! There was no need for her to go anywhere—she was there! Her breathing blanketed the kingdom. She kept all her secret desires in unutterable cohesion. Her roots spread through all beings.

Thanks to her ability to concentrate, she had long ago perceived the race's troubles, its danger. Behind the thriving façade, she identified the signs of ruin and behind the noise of life, she heard silent death working away.

She did not connect this to her hidden action. No, for her, it was different, two separate domains. Such that Abim also waited for the liberating or transformative event. But she waited consciously, actively. It had to happen! She wanted it without knowing it, but with constant vigor, certain that she could thus incite it, possibly hasten it. Above all, she wanted the event to be her own creation.

Was she not capable of making fruit ripen on the tree before the season? Did she not secretly control the fertilization of the women? Did the Ananou not owe it to her for keeping their numbers stable? Did the B'Tah-Gou not receive their clearest inspiration from her? Abim did not formulate all these things in her mind. She was satisfied with merely knowing them, with all her substance, because she "thought", in fact, with all of her fleshy bulk. She was full of her thoughts. Every fold of her body was permeated.

However, for a little while, she had discovered other skills. She caught herself dreaming as if outside herself and beyond anything she knew. She no longer guided her meditation, she lost control. Immediately, a prophetic current carried her elsewhere, stealing her away into another country, among other beings.

During this state of traveling, she spied countless details. But she saw without understanding. The visions had no name. Therefore, she could not control them, only suffer them, be enraptured by them. Thrown straight into the future, she could not swim where she wanted and had to settle for floating in the luminous regions. This unknown universe intoxicated her. She let herself be carried along for a moment, then as soon as she wanted to see so she could remember, to understand so she could bring it back, everything disappeared.

Suddenly there was nothing but Abim in her palace, Abim dissatisfied, shipwrecked on the shores of her dream, remembering only a vague feeling of bright light, white flights, the sound of thunder, a certain kind of laughing… No one laughed like that in Kobor! She experienced a desperate longing, a bitter desire to possess these things.

"This is needed for the kingdom," she grumbled.

This was the solution. Possessing this! But THIS? What was it? She had no idea what it was! She labored silently in her troubled mind. In vain. Nothing would become clear. What was more, the little she had retained suddenly escaped for good. Vexed, all she kept from it was her crushing desire, her rage. She would have stolen those things! She would have stood up to get hold of those things! Yes, yes, she would have killed and stolen and moved, even if it meant revealing the mystery of her feet, just to be able to bring those things back and give them to her race!

…That day, like the others, once again thwarted in her personal quest, failed in act, she took out her bitterness on Amo.

Amo, he was the rottenness, the limpness. For the thousandth time she deplored the fact that Opak the Queen had chosen him as her male. Under her breath, she hardened in her opinion—Abim would never love Amo! She swore to it with furious determination.

Her eyes closed halfway since, being prudent, she told herself that she should never let anything show, at least not too much, just enough to keep from exploding. She would suffer her perpetual dissatisfaction because of him until she managed to make her move, under the invisible pressure of her hostility. She would do it! She had to! It was he, yes, he who was preventing the Event! Amo was preventing Abim from attracting the Event to herself… Oh, the Event with its laughing and its thunder and its whiteness and the levity of its incomprehensible happiness…

The old woman pouted, sticking out her lower lip…

CHAPTER III

It was evening. Since sunset, the ceremony of the Fertilization of the Queen had ended. All of Kobor Tigan't, in jubilation, was making up for the ritual chastity. But Princess Ta, instead of joining her male like all the other women, had to serve the Very Huge.

With a jangle of bracelets rising and falling, following the steady tempo that she tried to maintain, Ta was combing Abim's hair. She respected her silence and was waiting to be asked, as she usually was, about the events of the day. But the question did not come quickly. Worried, Abim remained formidably lost in her thoughts. Ta performed her duty well. Still, she was visibly bored and was twitching nervously. Roused with desire, she thought about To, whom she loved. She wanted to join him. Immediately! To run to him, to cry out in joy, after throwing down the comb with a dramatic flourish! But she did not dare. The respect she owed her mother Abim held her back.

Ta did not have dark skin like the old queen but, a warm, coppery hue, the same, incidentally, as that of the man she loved. For the time being, her face looked a little sour, which was not lacking a certain charm on her. Whenever she was away from To, she almost always looked like this. A way of protesting—she could not stand being without him, even for only a short time. However, behind her pouting lips, you could glimpse the malice that was always at the ready. And although her head tilting to the side looked plaintive, her eyes, on the contrary, sparkled with a lively fire.

Ta had an original character, deep-rooted. Without saying a word, as was her custom, Abim was studying her with interest, not without concern. This younger daughter was nothing like the older, Queen Opak with her strong qualities albeit softened somewhat by her frantic sensuality. Ta always seemed submissive. She performed her duties well enough, with flashes of malice and mischief and independence here and there, which were not unwelcome to her mother although when it came to this matter as well, she showed no sign of approval or disapproval, merely recording everything in her inexhaustible memory.

Ta, who was capable of good humor as well as biting sarcasm, only loosened up in To's presence.

Until she met him, people thought she was superficial, fickle, unable to commit herself, to retain any lasting interest in anything. Everything was a momentary fancy to this girl who shamelessly changed her jewelry as often as her men. She detested everything that faded. Her love affairs were nothing more than irritating games that never tied her down. She bit into a piece of fruit only to throw it away with a laugh. And even as she bit into it her eyes were already searching for another!

Independent, she fled to the countryside as soon as Abim let her loose. From a distance, people would see her running off as if chasing something. Or else she settled for just wandering around. She would go to the foot of Kah'B'La, pretending to be seriously interested, picking up leaves, turning over rocks, walking into caves. No doubt, this did nothing to satisfy her.

She returned to the palace in roundabout ways so that she could slip away from some disappointed lover. And there, in the palace, anxious again, she wandered as usual through the maze of stone corridors, then climbed her way up to the highest terraces. She never got lost. Her eyes scrutinized the nooks and crannies without finding, apparently, what she was looking for. She dared look west. Abim was not unaware of this...

In the same way as she strolled around, questioning all of nature, she occasionally meandered among the courtiers, the common people or the artisans. She glanced inside the houses of the B'Tah-Gou, even though a woman had no right to do so. Thus, she attentively studied all of the faces but quickly turned sad again.

In an effort to calm her, Abim suggested one day that she rent a T'Lo. People were raving about one that had just entered the Pit. If Ta wanted, he could be reserved specially for her.

On hearing this proposal, the young woman had burst into laughter so loud that the old woman left her alone but still kept a close eye on her. She put up with more, namely Ta's sterility, since her youngest daughter was in no hurry to procreate.

And yet, all through Kobor, it was a subject no one tired of discussing. People even wondered if Ta would turn into a B'Tah-Gou in her old age. Was not her name a presage of that?

The young woman answered this gossip with arrogant contempt. Since Abim's indulgence protected her, things never got worse until she found To, all of a sudden, at the Festival of the Choice of Men.

From that time on, it was a complete change: she never left his side, immediately dismissing all of the men attracted to her, a scandalous gesture for a woman from the upper caste whose reputation depended on the number of males attached to her person.

People said that on learning of the news Queen Opak had gone half a day without touching her favorite foods. But since no sign came from immovable Abim, the opinion of the Queen and everyone else remained cautiously in suspense.

Encouraged by this mood, Ta's innate independence grew stronger, joining with To's, which was equal to hers in this.

He was just like her: fickle and unstable.

But once joined together, these two instabilities transformed into an unshakeable stability. People quickly noticed this. And they were all the more surprised. It was actually said that Ta would forever be talked about in Kobor!

The spirit of freedom of these two lovers was enjoyed at the expense of others. Everything that was not them, them alone, annoyed them.

Here again, with half a smile, Abim let it go. She knew how to savor the progress of destinies as she should, slowly like a gourmet. Moreover, the focus of her youngest daughter's love affairs did not hinder any of her projects: the crown was secure since Queen Opak, hale and hearty, was procreating at the desired pace... Yet, with that thought, the Very Huge always winced as she stumbled over the same detail: the detestable influence of Amo, the Queen's chosen male. The pair had many children, all very beautiful, but no Great Child... Fortunately! It would be better if he did not appear right away. Until that time, she would find a way to get rid of Amo. And the Great Child would not be fathered by him...

To and Ta, unconcerned by these gnawing political intrigues, paid no heed. They lived only for their love.

When, by chance, they were not together, people saw them waiting for each other, wild and ornery, not getting distracted by anything, keeping even friends at a distance. Or else they went looking for each other with fidgety fingers. And if they saw each other? If only from afar, they ran to each other, grasping the other's hands, squeezing tightly, then running off, wasting no time, at the same nimble pace, while their laughter spurned the world of others.

They wanted to live together, apart from others. Such a desire was not normal in that time of tribal communities where people felt like moving parts inside a vast, motionless, social body. At the mere thought of separating from the whole, the people of Kobor felt their souls freeze! Everything always took place in common and people always used their personal goods for the good of others.

Nevertheless, the respective duties of the two young lovers did not permit them total liberty. They deplored it but continued to perform their duties because they were bound to their rank. Rebels in their emotional life, they never forgot that they came from noble stock and remained very sensitive to honor. No one found grounds to criticize them. They even admired them for it.

To was the most skilled in the entire kingdom at finding Dongdwo eggs. He supplied the queen. And Abim, who ate nothing else and refused to accept them from anyone but him. That might explain why he was in good favor. Since his romantic idyll, the young man had made it a habit to discreetly save the most beautiful eggs he harvested for the Very Huge, unbeknownst to the Queen who, however, had priority because she traditionally had to produce as many royal children as possible and the eggs were known to enhance fertility.

In Kobor, the Queen had to be prolific first and foremost.

Abim, who was fully aware of the situation, smiled slyly, never flinched, accepted the attention. And To knew, through the reports that Ta never failed to give him, that a tacit agreement had been established.

"If Opak's fertility slows down for a while, from consuming eggs that are less rich and less of an aphrodisiac," Abim told herself, "we could perhaps blame it on Amo?" So, she would wait for the first signs, growing stronger herself... She could have lifted the palace simply by puffing out her silence a little bit!

As the youngest daughter, not destined for the throne, except in the event of an accident, Ta owed her mother homage and provided care that her mother accepted only from her hands. Luckily for Ta's independence, not very often since the Very Huge cared more for her solitude than her person.

Her nudity simplified many things and by an oddity of nature, by extreme concentration, she never seemed to get dirty. Never damp, never glistening, even in the hottest season. Without odor. Skin cold and taut over the compact fat. A stone! In fact, the care that she demanded from her daughter was a way of having her play another role unwittingly: that of political informant.

When asked, Ta told her what was going on in the city or in the palace, without realizing the significance of what she was saying. Anyway, she didn't really care!

The only events she cared about were strictly between To and herself. Concerning this she said nothing at all. But gossiping, recounting everything that caught her lively eye worked well for her—time passed more quickly. She went on and on, from one story to the next, never drawing the slightest conclusion. Out of her mouth, then out of mind. This was just fine for Abim who remembered everything and rejected any opinions her youngest daughter might harbor provided that she, the Very Huge, held the secret links of real power in her hands…

One evening, then, the young woman finished tying up her mother's long hair. The silence from the start persisted. It had to be broken at any cost! Ta hid a smile and, as serious as possible, started piling up her hair using shiny hairpins.

Abim suddenly stirred from her lethargy, like coming out of a bath, still dripping with dreams. She motioned with a finger: enough vanity!

Without arguing, satisfied, Ta waited for what would follow. Wrapping up her thoughts, Abim was still nodding her head a little, brooding. She finally stopped, her face lit up and she cast an inviting glance at her daughter.

Ta started talking immediately, with obvious pleasure, quickly drunk on her twittering like a bird. She toyed with her bracelets, wiggled her fingers, laughed, forgetting all about her attentive listener.

Abim soaked up the gossip, eyelids half closed, hands dropped randomly on her bulk. She looked like she was resting. Nothing made her even twitch. Calm. Like a trap ready to snap shut soundlessly…

Ta was raising her voice now because she was recounting the most important ceremony of the year, the Fertilization of the Queen, which had taken place just after the Festival of the Choice of Men.

Instead of going into detail, the narrator gave free rein to her passion. The highly colorful festivities pleased her enormously. An erotic egregor evolved in the liberating explosion that, at the end of its condensation, all Kobor was in communion with…

But what she did not say was that she had planned to escape from the collective restraints, to flee with To and mate with him in the solitude beyond the walls of Kobor!

Unfortunately, before fulfilling her wonderful project, she had had to come to Abim... Her disappointment made her furious. She controlled herself, however, being careful to hide her emotions.

"Oh! What a truly great day!" she said. "A perfect day, from start to finish! Certainly, the result will be remarkable. All the participants said that this time the Queen will give birth to the Great Child!"

Abim raised an eyebrow but said nothing.

"Yes, O Very Huge, Opak officiated majestically. From dawn until sunset! Without fail. But how could it be otherwise with Amo the Inexhaustible, right? He is certainly worthy of Opak in every way. The best males of the first circle who were, as always, watching out for the slightest lapse on his part, found nothing to complain about. Oh, I saw their faces droop, mother, while their women across from them were getting hot, feeling their breasts swell... And then, as the ceremony proceeded, they forgot their bitterness since they were overcome by that devastating love and they knew they were getting it directly from Amo who was transfusing them with some of his force..."

The old queen listened to this panegyric without saying a word, even though she did not like it much. She knew it was an echo of the general sentiment.

So, the task would be tougher than she imagined. Detestable Amo! Two pale grooves formed on either side of her mouth. Infuriated, she exhaled.

Ta, who had noticed nothing, turned to a more personal topic, despite herself.

"But it was long, a whole day like that for us women, without our males! We burn with desire and have to wait... I saw To, across from me, among the men who were all sweating, red and eager. To was paler, as his love drifted grievously toward me... Unable to mate for an entire day!"

She suddenly stopped talking, angry that she had said too much. But Abim, exceedingly patient, simply remarked that "any mating would have profaned the royal act which had to be performed alone, had to be the only one so that the sun, Ooh'R, could mingle his seed without risk of error."

Deep down, she was furious that the revolutionary Ta had not defied tradition. The royal union would no doubt have been tainted and it would have been possible to show, using trickery, by influencing minds from a distance, that Amo was just a trap since a tiny breach could strip him of all his prestige... She tried to surmise if Ta were concealing some evil deed like that. But she was unable to break through the barrier the young woman had built around her private thoughts.

She was terribly annoyed. And, to wreak her vengeance, she ordered her youngest daughter to calm down and give her the details of the entire day.

Ta was livid but had to obey. Abim thoroughly enjoyed it. That silly fool, whose heart she heard whining!

CHAPTER IV

Ta had met To a year earlier, during the Choice of the Men.

That day, she had gotten up before dawn, dissatisfied with her usual companions who were still sleeping. She had spent the night snubbing them, frustrating them to such a point that two of them had fought. Brawling men in Ta's house, now that was intolerable! They were immediately chased away.

As a sign of her anger, she left the men's chamber and claimed that she wanted to sleep alone. In all honesty, she barely slept, hoping against her will that one of her males, someone able to comfort her, would show up. But they were so foolish, so demoralized, and so respectful of royal authority that the thought never even crossed their minds! Moreover, she had played with them so cruelly, exhausting them so thoroughly that they quickly fell asleep. Ta was utterly vexed. She did not calm down. When she could take no more and decided to go out, as soon as she had pushed open the door, she found the two men she had sent away standing there, shamefaced.

Her expression kept them at bay. They stayed where they were, terribly saddened, watching her walk away. She swaggered so seductively, slowly and steadily swaying her hips until she heard their cry of dismay, which she had been hoping for. Then she burst out laughing and turned to face them, baring her teeth with a vengeful snap of her jaws. And they ran away.

An uproar of laments exploded from her dwelling. Waking up too late, the men were all consoling each other. Alas, they had displeased her! It was over for them. There was no hope for them to be chosen this year to remain for the next.

They were not mistaken. While strolling through the morning twilight, Ta swore that she would completely overhaul her Men's Chamber. She would keep only one. They were all too stupid. "May all of their B'Tah-Gous be struck mute!'

She knew that they would all run to their Storytellers for consolation. They were brainless! And she would so much have liked to see them with brains. Were not willpower, thought, desire and drive always the prerogatives, the superior faculty of Woman?

Kobor's gynecocracy gave women all the rights over the consenting herd of males honored in this way. The woman was responsible for all sexual initiatives: choice and selection. Her desire alone was law. It was remarkable to see that the women almost never stole males from each other. If a case of rivalry over a male developed, they all got together as a group to decide what should be done. The most sexualized of the two rivals always won, based on the assessment of her companions. Their judgment was nearly infallible.

The strongest sexualization was always personified in keeping with the hierarchy and the queen was always at the top. The noble status of a man was ascribed only through his union with a high-ranking woman. The rejected male lost this noble standing. He could then only be chosen by a woman of a lower status. With the exception of the queen, her sisters and her daughters who took their men from all levels of society, which enabled honorable redemption. The levels of the system itself in Kobor reflected this: the intense eroticism of the palace, of the Blue and the Red City, decreased from top down, all the way to the Black City where the people with the dullest senses had simple, slow and placid tastes, ending with the strange institution of the B'Tah-Gous, who were cold and sterile.

The Festival of the Choice of the Men permitted the renewal of couples according to the needs that feminine instinct understood without fail. They were free, of course, in the case of a perfect union, to re-select their favorite partner or partners.

The Festival started early in the morning throughout the whole verdant territory of the gardens, fields, woods and crops of the Green City, among streams, fountains and waterfalls. In a symbolic race, the women had to hunt down the men until they had them captured and, no less symbolically, tied up with their belts.

It was a grand spectacle, overflowing with joy. Herds of males spread out, laughing with pleasure. Heavier in the race, all of the men gladly let themselves to be caught. They flaunted their hostage belts, ritualistically surrendering to the feminine power of entrapment.

Ta had just arrived at the lowest terrace of the Red City that looked out over the whole expanse of the Green. She saw nothing yet but inhaled the drowsy scent of the plants mingled with the slightly sour coolness of the ponds.

She heard fish jumping and nocturnal reptiles slithering back to their lairs. She was still furious, despite all of the calming odors. "I will take the fattest, the tallest, the stupidest males, a royal heap of males and establish my domination over them." But what was the point, she suddenly wondered.

At that moment, her mother's treacherous insinuation unwound its coils around her heart: "A T'Lo? Maybe a T'Lo?" The young woman stopped abruptly, unable to move on, sad, almost frozen, with a feeling of impending danger. She felt as if she were standing on the edge of a chasm... "Why not a T'Lo? A T'Lo has a double nature, obliging like a woman and understanding women, more passionate than a man could ever be and exhibiting it tirelessly and obediently..."

The sinuous image was forming. Ta thought she felt a vague caress, like an invitation, heralding unknown delights... So was it true what the love addicts gossiped about, that only the use of T'Lo opened secret doors, that other dizzying powers were discovered putting all others to shame? Abim had spoken so softly when she said that...

Then, suddenly, at the summit of Kah'B'La, the white sun flashed! Ta cried out in joy, stretched out her arms, felt exorcised, bathing in the light and cooing like a child. And then she no longer understood, was all alone, stuck in her solitude, facing the broad landscape at her feet. Her arms fell. She stood there in the light, ashamed.

Shortly thereafter, before the others, when the advancing males spread through the terraces, she ran off to bury herself in the densest thicket of the Green City. She always knew where to find impenetrable hiding places. She sat down in one of these hideouts, listened to the festival for a moment as it grew livelier... She must have fallen asleep...

When she awoke, To was sitting close to her, so perfectly identical to her that she thought he had come out of her own body. She jumped up.

"I am Princess Ta!" she screeched.

He replied calmly, "I am To."

And it was like an echo. He smiled... and ran off. The young woman stood petrified. A whirlwind of sensations roiled inside her. Everything was topsy turvy. "He was fleeing! She would lose him! She would not be able to catch him! He did not exist!"

All this was spinning around in her mind. So she rushed off... and ran straight into To, on her way out of the thicket! She was speechless. She touched him with her hand. No, no this was like nothing she was used to. The laughter of the others was fading in the distance. The Festival was coming to an end.

"Put your belt around me!" he ordered in a gentle voice.

She obeyed. No, this was like nothing she had done before! Once the belt was fastened – and she noticed that he tied it himself, which went against tradition – he laughed mischievously and said, "Now, catch me! Catch me for real, Ta!"

And he ran off. And he ran across the entire territory of the Choice without letting her catch him. And refusing to let her catch him, he crossed the Low City from one side to the other, creating a stir among the old people. Ta saw nothing, heard nothing, she ran, she desired, he dragged her in his wake... No, no this was like nothing known before. Everything was upside-down. She realized that she had gone outside the borders of Kobor Tigan't, suddenly feeling the aura of the city fade away... And To kept running farther and farther.

He let her catch him near Kah'B'La. Ta recovered enough of her dignity to murmur, "You're not reasonable, To. I chose you!"

She touched him again, tenderly. He narrowed his eyes, the spark of mischief re-appeared. "How many men did you choose today, Princess Ta?"

By the treachery of the Aaz! Ta shivered. So, she had completely lost her senses. And what about her rank? A single man brought back by Princess Ta! What would the women in the palace say? What about Opak? Though the queen had her favorite, he was not the only one and the Royal Chamber of Men was so massive!

"You have just me, isn't that right, Princess Ta? Since you forgot to put your mark on all of the men who were waiting for you. And since everyone knew they were yours, no woman chose them! They will, therefore, all be alone for a year! They will have to go crying to the B'Tah-Gous or else seduce some poorly guarded T'Lo."

He burst into laughter. Appalled, Ta watched him, mouth agape, her hand still on him. And she was filled with the pleasure of just looking at him! Outrage and pleasure made such a strange brew for her that all she could say was, "I have only you."

"But I'm enough for you," he replied calmly.

He was going beyond all possible boundaries. But she understood that he was speaking the truth. Still, she repeated her words again, without realizing it, "But, you're being unreasonable. Don't you want to be reasonable?"

"No," said To. "I will not be reasonable. I am never reasonable. I know you well, Princess Ta. I've watched you living for a long time and getting upset with all your men. The Woman I was with knew about my wild tastes and kept me deep in the back of her Men's Chamber. And I can tell you that I was her favorite, that she tolerated all of my whims and that she was a high-ranking woman. I only left her home to gather Dongdwo eggs. Yes, Ta, I supply the palace and you never saw me! I was waiting for you to ripen. Every day, in the Men's Chamber, I pictured you in my mind and when the woman made use of me, I still pictured you. Last night, I was so bad, so unruly, so annoying to her rank that she threw me out! Exactly as you did your two males. I saw them. I was in the shadows and I called you soundlessly. I saw you go out. I followed you. And I sat down by you."

Ta was fascinated. Without realizing it, she kept caressing his shoulder.

"You're not being reasonable," she sighed again.

"No," he said. "And you'll see. I'm going to chase after you!"

She recoiled. Had she heard correctly? But he was coming at her like a hunter. Then, everything started spinning around in her head. And she, Princess Ta, found herself running away from him!

… She fell on the ground, in the litter from the ritual, which he completely crushed by lying down on top of her! And, because she had such an intense desire to mate with him, she wanted, as was customary, to straddle him so he could enter her, but he held her down on the ground and overcame her, had his way with her.

The roles were reversed.

… Night was falling as they slowly headed back to Kobor Tigan't.

Their return was as weird as their Race. They held hands. No, the man was not walking behind the woman, as tradition would have it. To and Ta walked side by side, savoring the deep satisfaction of being carried along in a common rhythm.

They had dared to make a revolution of their difference, against the tribal system. They had truly "left" the city. They had discovered and sanctified their freedom. They were other, together. Together they freed themselves.

They could not stop smiling at each other. They knew they were complicit in audacity. They knew that from now on they would experience this audacity together. Slowly, they went back. Late. And they walked slowly through Kob'Lâm and Kob'Vâm, through the empty streets, past the uninhabited houses, before finally arriving, both of them, together, at Kob'Râm, the Red City where everyone had gathered.

That same year, at the same time, the Queen's Race had taken place.

Nothing surprising had happened. For years, Opak had selected Amo first. The other males chosen for her Men's Chamber barely counted as she so eagerly flaunted the difference between them, mere accessories, and her favorite, the real Queen's Man.

This fidelity that used to seem laughable to frivolous Ta, was seen in a different light this evening. She knew that henceforth it would be the same for her, that she too would no longer change. She stopped mocking her older sister and what was more, she honored her with a certain consideration she had never shown before. "Opak is truly a Queen," she told herself. "A Queen able to experience powerful things!"

She felt a little humiliated at not having understood sooner that her sister had in a way beaten her to this revelation. "That's what the others cannot understand. I'm from the royal caste! I will keep To like she keeps Amo. I will keep him even better—I will keep him alone."

Ta told herself that she was surpassing the Queen...

Of course, in Kob'Râm everyone was immensely surprised to see the two of them together like that. But Ta's face displayed such sparkling audacity, such triumph that they bowed before it. After all, she made the law, right after the Queen.

Opak said nothing. She did not concern herself much with the fantasies of her younger sister since they did not bother her. For the Queen that was what mattered most: not being bothered. The rest was unimportant. Ta wanted just one male? Great! And the Queen smiled. She thought it was kind of a special vice...

Abim did not criticize her either. No one said a word. People sang all night long in Kob'Lâm about the strangeness of the princess.

CHAPTER V

Yes, Ta obeyed, Ta told the Very Huge all about the Festivities, sparing no details.

She made a great effort to satisfy Abim, but the tension tired her excessively. It was like she felt sick. Her anxiety escalated. Her voice was slipping away, away, distorted by the acoustics of the vast room. To's absence grew more and more intolerable. As time flowed it expanded the distance like a wound opening slowly. Life was retreating and there was no stopping it. The intimate images grew sharper, more colorful... Her voice now escaped her, withdrawn into the back the room, prey there to a slow whirlwind of echoes...

But Abim was there, dark, sitting in the middle. And Ta had to continue, it was too late to break her focused attention... With her head spinning, she continued, therefore, speaking faster. There was still so much to say before she would be free!

Every year, after the morning selection of the Men, the rest of the Day of Choosing was dedicated to the Spring Battles, which took place in the square in Kob'Râm the Red City, in front of the smelting crucible.

Everyone gathered around the Queen and her chosen one, who had to signal the start of the Games, beginning the first battle. People waited impatiently yet respectfully.

Everyone was coming back from Kob'Vâm. They were still excited from the Race and their faces were flushed. Their eager eyes glistened with pleasure. They breathed noisily and the sound mixed with that of the forge bellows that were puffing away in full swing.

The blacksmiths were working with their wives, who were helping them on the occasion. For, the weapons forged during the Royal Battle were noble and indestructible. The wealthy always ordered their blades on this day.

Murmurs and laughter ran through the crowd. The reflections of the fires danced. It was scorching hot. Men and women standing in a semicircle rubbed each other's hips and shoulders, unwittingly testing the forces that set them apart and brought them together. The vibration of desire was nagging all those bodies. But they knew that the union of male and female was forbidden until the next evening after the Fertilization of the Queen. Except for the devotees of the T'Lo who, that very evening, would withdraw from the communal festivities to surrender to their individual eroticism in private, behind closed doors.

The Kob'Râm festival was simple: the couples faced off, man against the woman, in games of strength, cunning and fun, a kind of love parade, a dance of muscles, a skirmish of grasping and sweating that fanned the flames of desire, accentuating the merits of their bodies and their beauties, while also glorifying the scent of the hair all over their bodies. People said that the fire forged the male's virility.

The Ooh'R'Ou Opak, the Red Queen and her male, Amo, no less flamboyant, facing each other on all fours, on furs laid on the ground, shoving hard, shoving back, with all their weight, determinedly, banging shoulders.

They acted with a kind of sacral slowness and restrained power that was theirs alone and in which was marked, right away, as the weight of nobility.

Little by little, Opak became more and more impassioned, moaning with joy. Her lips curled while laughing with joy. The satisfied crowd expressed its pleasure with a similar low moan. The Queen intensified her assaults. Amo's eyes sparkled with love and pride every time she got the edge on him. Secretly, he helped her, restraining his own muscles. He was noble. He loved her.

The men in the crowd, who had not missed this detail, expressed their approval.

Amo loved seeing Opak triumph more than anything. She did not know this. She lacked finesse. She was a royal beast, the royal female animal.

Shortly after the battle began, she started sweating. Her smile broadened. She put both her hands against Amo's chest, trying to push him over. He moved back, very little, for the ritual, but did not waver! He stayed there evenly matched, calm, peaceful. The precision of the action was immediately admired and talked about. Surprised, Opak furrowed her brow, got angry but still in good spirits, and put all her effort into vanquishing him. Her clothes fell open. People could see her breasts, her heaving belly.

The people whispered appreciatively for a long while since the nudity of the Queen being exposed during the Battle was a very good omen.

People liked to watch the Queen living. They liked the sound of her voice, her heavy gestures, the fertile display of her flesh. Her odor pleased everyone. They enjoyed nothing better than the majestic spectacles of the Queen eating, playing or mating. Her open intimacies were endowed with a supernatural spark. She was the one who always did more. Harder. Higher. Longer. In everything. Nothing of hers was irrelevant. Her whole being acquired importance beyond all importance.

Seeing her live with Amo was seeing the kingdom and the race live. Everything she did had profound significance, always beneficial. She incarnated the life of the race. A fluid flowed from all her activities that invigorated the land and the people. The strength of her people was linked to her strength. They lived at her rhythm, through her rhythm. The bigger, sturdier, more muscular, more tireless the Queen was, the more her capacities surpassed the norm and the more her prestige expanded. Her fertility stimulated that of the other women, the animals and the land. Peace and prosperity were magically bound to the number of her children.

Her exaggerations, her excesses were just signs of racial vitality. Her defects, even her vices were glorious and sublime. They imitated her in everything.

In the Kob'Râm square all the forges were firing up as the Queen's game went on. Gradually, as if by inspiration, the other couples started fighting, more and more of them, until everyone was involved. Joy, laughter, effort. It lasted for hours in ever-growing jubilation. Night fell. Everything blazed with red light.

In the middle of the crowd, the heart of the crucible looked like a steady flower of fire.

From time to time, the weary couples rested, quenched their thirst, became spectators again, went to see the forges. After a while they joined the others again.

They did this all night long. At the approach of day, they followed the Queen to the very top of Kob'Ooh'R. Everyone, nobles and lesser nobles, the common people of Kob'Lâm who were entitled to enter this sacred place once a year, everyone went. Everyone except for the B'Tah-Gou, who never got involved with anything, never disturbed their solitude. During these two days of festivities, they closed their doors, which they never did at any other time of the year.

Their faithful flock did not visit them.

There are many taboos concerning the Day of the Fertilization of the Queen, the most important one about the T'Lo whom no one has the right to be with.

Everyone has to imprison their erotic servant from dawn to dusk in a room reserved for this purpose and then lock up the house when they go to participate in the collective mating outside that brings the Ritual of the Queen to an end at sunset.

The T'Lo, though lacking intelligence, have a remarkable intuition for everything that concerns their master emotionally, near or far. On this day, they feel what is going on, apparently even understanding the meaning. A few hours earlier, they were more tender, more attentive, more dedicated, as if secret antennas were warning them about their imminent neglect. Thus, by increasing their affection, they seem to want to hold onto their masters, to prevent them from abandoning them.

It is common knowledge that the most unforgettable love inventions of a T'Lo are spawned on the night preceding the Day of the Queen because the nobles who sacrifice themselves to the custom of the love slave have the right, not really authorized but tacitly tolerated, to mate with their domestic T'Lo after the Spring Battles. Hence the popular saying: "Inspired like a T'Lo on the eve of The Day!", which is often used for someone who undertakes something too big without imagining that the next day will mock him. It is like a "shot in the dark". A useless exercise.

As soon as every T'Lo is locked up and left alone, they let loose their despair. Unable to cry out because they are incurably mute, they start beating on everything within reach. They hit each other with their metal jewelry. They clap more and more loudly. There is no use tying them up, they always manage to get free thanks to their consummate flexibility.

From house to house the banging echoes back and forth. They do not stop at all during the day and their clamor will continue to grow even at the climax of the community ceremonies. So much so that, in their Pit, their unevolved brothers, the Ananou, are aroused and awaken from their torpor to start slapping their hands against the prison floors in unison.

Their masters are greatly concerned about this ordeal they have to put their T'Lo through. But they are quickly exhausted by their grief since, without making a sound, they weep great big tears that choke them. Occasionally, their hearts break. It has happened that people have found their T'Lo dead. They deeply dread this calamity, for various reasons, the least of which is not the threat of total ruin.

When a T'Lo dies in a house, it is very expensive for the family because the palace collects a fortune in fines. Then, that scathing syllable is added to their name: Ol'T, the reverse of T'Lo, indicating to all the world that a love servant, the wealth of the crown, has been lost through negligence.

Worst of all is the general feeling that develops around these marked families. They are forbidden to enter the palace. Friends stop visiting. The people, already hostile to the owners of T'Lo, regard them as ogres. Cruelty is frowned upon in Kobor.

One of the worst insults for people of the high caste is: "I hope you lose your T'Lo!"

Another variation on that insult is: "I hope you lose your B'Tah-Gou!"

Anger alone is the only excuse for either.

If, after such a snub, the family in question is not completely ruined, there is only one way for them to recover their prestige. By making an oral appeal to the Queen to get permission for a new T'Lo, promising this time, however, to successfully fertilize it so that the royal treasury can recuperate its losses.

Usually, after a more or less long period of punishment, permission is granted. The Queen herself chooses the Ananou from the Pit that will become their new T'Lo. She has it turned over in her presence to the head of the repentant family on whom she pours out a strongly worded tirade. The new lease costs double the first and is granted for only one year, at the end of which, if the birth of a compensatory Ananou has not occurred, the T'Lo is returned to the Pit while the family is forbidden another lease until the guilty master has died. At that time, the slanderous suffix, Ol'T, is removed. Then everyone takes part in a grand gala to celebrate the family's reintegration in the noble caste.

And the head of the family, by the transmission of power, whether it be the wife of the deceased, the eldest daughter or the son, hastens to get another T'Lo! Nevertheless, most of the time, through that mysterious balance that ensures the continuity of the Ananou, the hoped-for birth takes place and immediately eliminates all traces of the previous misfortune. This, too, is celebrated lavishly. Everyone is relieved. Those affiliated with the worship of the T'Lo shower the hero of the day and his slave with gifts and the love slave will be considered a living talisman from then on.

The fact is that the families thus redeemed are among the happiest and enjoy a kind of immunity to the hazards of life.

However, in the very recent past, many T'Lo died one after another at the end of the Queen's Day. What had only been an exception seemed to become the rule. The next year, more died. The best families wailed and wept. A wave of panic spread.

This coincided with the Choice of the Queen for Amo whom she would no longer leave because of her great appetite for him. This connection was not made immediately because all of Kobor had been aroused to passion by the contagious virtue of the newly chosen one. Everyone agreed that the ceremonies were unforgettable and that the erotic egregore was denser than ever. Then, given the repeated deaths, people realized that the fatal despair of the T'Lo came from the fact that they deeply felt the control of this love egregore over their beloved masters. The pleasure they took in communing with the royal union caused such a diversion of strength that the T'Lo died, as if the energizing cord joining them to their masters had been snipped.

Given the scope of such a catastrophe, the affected families joined forces, held secret meetings. About their decisions they remained discreet and never discussed it. But people noticed their obvious relief. The following year, the slaughter did not occur. People had wondered about it the previous day. Little by little, rumors spread, which could have been plausible since there was a certain logic to them: The aesthetes most attached to their T'Lo apparently came up with the idea of a compensation ceremony in which they rendered homage to the love slaves—a secret ceremony, it goes without saying! But so firmly established in the custom that it was regularly practiced ever since.

Gossips even claim that the Parallel Festival takes place several times a year. The members gather at night on a hidden terrace along with their T'Lo. They get so frenzied for so long that eight days later, people can still point out the participants by their dolorous expressions.

Although aware of the gossip, the palace took no position on the matter, which, all things considered, suited its interests. The gossip died down on its own and became a matter of occult folklore.

For her part, Abim had not missed a thing. She delighted in it since the turn of events got her a little revenge on Amo. But oh, how angry she had been in the early days of the favorite's influence when the T'Lo died one after another! During the whole period, Ta could never manage to untangle her mother's hair and there was no question of chatting. The Very Huge never stopped her meditation.

Finally, inspiration came one day. She was the one who came up with the idea of the Parallel Festival. She concentrated even harder, closed her door to all, until through the agency of certain B'Tah-Gou, who passively intercepted her thoughts and spread them unknowingly, a few nobles received a revelation about the course to take. A marvelous tour de force of which Abim felt exceedingly proud, which in turn put her, for a long while, in an exquisitely good mood.

It was then, however, that she started to stealthily make gains against Amo. Triumphing over the beautiful man became her main objective.

It should be noted that she was especially lenient with the Ananou and the T'Lo. Vestiges of ancient times, for the most part incomprehensible, they were part of legend. For, although the nobles knew of the visible aspect and how to handle their favorites physically, Abim knew their invisible aspect and how to use them according to very particular fluid mechanics that will be discussed later.

CHAPTER VI

In the very center of Kob'Ooh'R, Ta was still with Abim, recounting the Fertilization of the Queen. The end was in sight, however, and she plucked up a little courage at the idea of being with To again. But her mother seemed determined to be unforgiving. Thus, at her request, Ta had to give detailed assurance that all the ritual taboos had been observed.

In fact, for the Fertilizations of the Queen to retain its magical value, being the Sole Deed on the Great Day, they made sure that no male approached any female. They even separated the pairs of domestic animals.

All the families sorted their children, girls on one side, boys on the other.

Other symbolic acts were performed. They unsheathed their swords. They did not make necklaces. They tied no knots in strips of leather, made no braids, stopped weaving. They drilled no holes in stones or wood.

Ta was telling how, in the middle of the night, well before dawn, all of Kobor Tigan't had surged back up to the royal city to fill up all of Kob'Ooh'R, the people being grouped together from top to bottom, around and under the platform on the summit. Total silence ensued. The first gray signs of day were floating hazily.

All the nobles encircled the platform, the men on one side, the women on the other, facing one another. Where the two semi-circles met two fragrant braziers burned. The reflections from the fire danced like apparitions on the golden sphere that stood over the scene. Votive streamers waved in the wind, snapping briefly once in a while.

On a large, square carpet made of white skin, covered with all the flowers from the bushes of Kob'Lâm, unclothed for the occasion, were Opak and Amo.

They were both completely nude.

The Queen's Man, lying on his back, his red-brown mass sprawled peacefully, coppery hair glistening, he waited, his phallus erect. His body looked like a heavy altar stone prepared for the sacrifice. Opak stood over him, legs spread, not moving either.

Their immobility gradually affected everyone. The silence seemed to deepen. The wind died down… All that was left in the braziers were the pink coals. The pale smoke was hovering like a canopy.

Then the night lit up. All the faces turned anxiously toward the summit of Kah'B'La, the holy mountain that was now unobstructed in the distance. They were waiting for the sun to strike its peak.

In the gullies all around the High Plains, a mist lingered, the last trace of the bad season. Tomorrow it would be gone. They were waiting for the light of spring!

Slowly, Opak, open, kneeled down without taking her eyes off the mountain… And suddenly Kah'B'La turned pink! The queen took the phallus and mated with it.

The sun sprang up as the golden sphere reflected it. Opak let loose the full-throated cry of the royal defloration. For the tradition, the queens were always virgins at this time of the year, meaning rejuvenated, young, recovering their source of youth.

The ritual cry was, moreover, the first lesson they learned. The defloration released the torrents, increased the heat, set in motion the era of the sun, decided, decreed!

And it seemed to be true that the all-powerful magic of this rite suddenly swayed nature. Yes, all at once the world had turned, like a sleeper twitching, then waking up with a happy face.

Onto the sacred, stationary mating of the Queen and her Man, the spring morning poured its splendors. The air had changed; soothing were the breezes.

Birds shooting up into the air, drifted on high, the animals called out to each other in the valleys, the clouds retreated, the sun rose, the land became fragrant, red flowers bloomed in the foliage and the grand waterfall could be heard cascading while the open floodgates poured the joyful water into all the canals, from the top to the bottom of Kobor Tigan't.

The Sleepers of the Sun, the R'Lil, refracted dazzling shafts of silver, astonishing to see on their smooth, black mass.

The Ooh'Rou had to stay joined to her male until sunset. All around them, the circle of nobles, men and women apart, were swaying, moving, speaking to the couple slowly, warm and tender words to help and support their self-control. Everyone transfused them with their psychic forces, all joined together by the intervention of this unique and restrained Act.

76

… Come to this point of her account, having almost said all she had to say, Ta felt To's absence more cruelly than ever. She remembered his pallor and how he gazed at her from the other side of the circle during the royal mating.

Instead of participating in the ritual, warmly and faithfully, adding his voice to the constant stream of sonorous praises, he kept quiet, stubbornly, did not even look at them, kept walled into a sacrilegious coldness. He spurned the Act. His eyes were glued on the woman whom he loved, isolating her from the others by the intensity of his stare. Had not she said they would run away together? He wanted to do it immediately.

Unable to make up her mind despite this silent call to join him, despite this command, Ta did not move a muscle… Then, he shut himself off in a haughty gloom, his eyelids closed. Was she betraying him? Nevertheless, he still, now and then, cast an ardent eye on her, thus telling her to escape with him, to mate with him, freely, beyond the City, beyond the grip of Kobor. Thus and more piercing with every new glance. The pain of desire between them got stronger all the time. Ta wanted to run away! But the more she wanted it, the firmer her feet clung to the ground…

Why did this image of the Very Huge impose itself so strongly in her mind? The Very Huge who did not move and whose feet were never seen, buried under her like roots? No, it was forbidden to think of Abim's feet. The worst taboos concerned this mystery.

Ta, therefore, got a grip on herself after being absent, in a way, for who knew how long. Across from her, To had disappeared! The low-lying sun proclaimed the end of the royal mating. And without having time to search for her beloved, she had to go to the Very Huge. And talk, talk, talk to her!

Ta realized that she had, indeed, stopped talking for a while already. Close by, Abim said nothing. It was night. Only a faint glow illuminated the room. The greenish reliefs on the polished pillars glistened. The curtains fluttered slightly, like creatures of the night, blind birds, silent birds, half asleep.

Under her, a distant rumbling crept up, coming from the Ananou Pit: they were clapping their hands to an unusual rhythm.

Looking up at Abim, she believed she caught the shadow of a sympathetic, knowing smile. What bond was there between the Very Ancient and the Creatures of the Mistake?

The sound ceased. The smile vanished. In the black face above her Ta saw the slit of the half-closed eyes glow. She suddenly had a strong feeling that the old queen was a dreadful danger, that behind this sleepy appearance there simmered an implacable hostility.

The silence became unbearable. Abim was a stranger. A strange Thing...

Impulsively, Ta started talking again, a little randomly. "Very Huge, the Ananou have moved and clapped their hands in uncustomary ways. They feel the love that has infused all of Kobor. For, it is late, very late. Everyone is loving each other at the moment... Are you listening, Very Huge? All the women are mating now. And me? I'm alone here with nothing to do. You don't say anything. You're sleeping. To is waiting for me. I could have left without you knowing!"

"No, you could not have. No, I am not sleeping. No, you haven't finished. Your account is incomplete." Abim took her time to deliver the blows with a kind of boundless negligence. "Therefore, my daughter, I ask, at sunset, what did they say about the queen?"

Exasperated, Ta almost shouted back, "What they say every year!"

Abim opened her eyes completely, which was enough to make the princess turn pale. "And what do they say every year at sunset, what do they say about the queen?"

Hushed now, Ta murmured gloomily the ritual response: "They said that the Queen was hopefully fertilized by Ooh'R."

"And maybe also by shining Amo?" the old one added with a snicker.

The princess thought the moment had come to get her revenge. "Certainly," her voice rang out, "fertilized by Amo! By Amo who is like the sun! By Amo whom the sun fills up! By Amo who made everyone say that this time the Great Child cannot help but be born, the bearer of the Just Sign! And everyone also said that The Very Huge will finally proclaim that it's the One, it truly is the Great Child of the Reign!"

She had to be quiet. Abim was groaning.

"No, younger daughter! No, paltry female with only one man! Little scandalous woman whose Chamber of Men is destitute like a low-born wench, you're wrong! There will be no Great Child! Just like every year! It will be a little child like the others, without the sign, without the mark, without the glory. A little child of the womb, that's all, who falls to the ground when born. No Great Child from Ooh'R! Oh no, nothing but a little child from a male and female to stick with the others. I won't name it. Nameless! Nothing for the reign, nothing from Amo!"

She had spit out the truth of her hatred. Just as quickly, it was over. There was no transition.

She followed it in a low whisper, "Go…"

Believing she was free, Ta leaped up without further ado.

But Abim held her back, "Go tell To that I want to eat some power. I feel weak."

Stunned beyond measure, the princess could not believe her ears.

"My daughter, I need freshly gathered Dongdwo eggs."

Ta's rage exploded, sweeping away all fear, "My Very Huge Mother, they don't hunt on the day of love, you know that. Your supplies are fresh and whole right there within reach. You haven't touched them."

Abim did not budge. She muttered, "I touched them…" And she crushed the white bunches with the palm of her hand. "They will hunt on the day of love for the Very Huge! Like that the nourishment will have the special virtue I demand. Go tell To!"

Nothing could change her mind once made up. The princess knew it. Furious, powerless, standing there like a frightened bird pecking her beak and scratching her feet, she snipped, "And in the meantime, so that you can wait patiently, I'll brush you?"

"Of course, if you want to, even though it's already been done. Your hands are good and give me pleasure."

Ta snapped back, "I'll undo all your braids to redo them to make them look like the votive streamers of Kob'Ooh'R! And I'll oil them and since we'll have so much free time on our hands, I just might, oh Mother, unless they're too firmly rooted," (she slowed her voice her) "I just might be able to see and admire and understand…"

Abim looked at her, but Ta finished nonetheless.

"… the mystery of your feet?"

Something happened that she did not understand afterward. Her entire body felt devastatingly nauseated. It was like she was a sack turned inside out while from the depths of the earth arose an irrepressible force and the same nausea… Was Abim suddenly standing up to crush her? No, nothing of the kind. She was just staring at her with her true, fiery eyes.

Ta thought, "I'm going to melt away!"

Dark red blotches had spread and, in a way, transfigured the enormous body. It emitted a pungent, burning odor. All around her was an invisible whirlwind sucking things in. A kind of quivering ran through the young woman in her life source. She was drained, crumpled over, bent double, shapeless, disfigured, she thought she was dying...

But no! A swift gesture threw her to the ground, reviving her at the same time.

"Get out!"

The nausea faded. The quivering had stopped. The mysterious burning force died down in the Very Huge. She was dark and motionless again. Cold. Ta ran away.

She lost one of her bracelets that went rolling against Abim, who stared at it.

CHAPTER VII

Abim is rocking back and forth, moaning, at the mercy of the inner jolts that are ravaging her.

Fury, nothing but fury! Her hands feeling all over her body. Moving, strangers to the stability of this eternally sitting mass on which they are not dependent, they go about their business. The fingers grab the fatty folds, pinch and move on. Abim feels nothing! Somewhere else, try again, her hands knead the dough of fury. Abim shakes her head, groans and breathes, bubbles pop between her lips. She looks hard at the bracelet, but she does not see it, she did not see it. Her anger clouds everything. She does not even know that she has just heard something. Or what it is. It sped down into the depths. And everything had been fury, nothing but fury!

Faster the movement. They are not really thoughts that are whirling around in her. It is not just battering inside her head. It is filling her whole body, circulating through it, deep in her limbs, just under her shivering skin. Noises, words, faces, names that snap, sharp fragments that hurt, that scrape their way in, that pile up anarchically, that fall apart, that slip away, that she pursues with her vigilante hatred. To grab them, sort them out, line them up, understand them. To be done with them.

Everyone, everyone, arrogant, uncooperative, hard-headed: Amo, the Queen with Amo, heavy Opak who knows nothing, who understands nothing! The Great Child! They are expecting it! It will not be born of Amo! Most detestable Amo! And Ta? What did she say, what did she dare to say, the younger sister, the nerve of the girl...

And here, for Abim, everything speeds off at a furious pace again. Her vital torrent bears along crippling little stones that shatter as they crash into one another, ricocheting farther along, deeper down, in shadowy places where they get stuck, disappear except for the dull pain that grows and grows until it all gives way and crumbles under the surge of the circulatory movement.

Abim rocks back and forth. Her hands slap her skin, lay flat on it, clutch and pinch it, fly off, and come back down.

Very faintly below, the sound of the Ananou on alert can be heard again. They too are slapping their hands and there is also something about the sound like a veiled breath that rises from the earth, extracted from an abyssal reservoir, to comingle by rising up to the Very Huge.

She pays no attention to it even though the red blotches are starting to reappear on her skin and the quivering is rippling over the ground. She jerks: something else, it was something else that caused all this flurry of activity! Ta? Of course! The younger daughter, what did she say? A little whirlwind like a hiccup that hauled up the offense that was sparkling in the foam of other bile: "Your feet!"

The Very Huge identified the thing with alarm: "Your feet, the mystery of your Feet!" Ta had said it. Her nervy but scared voice pronounced it clearly.

That was what had started it all. That was what had caused the tidal wave. Now she remembers the crux of the matter: "The mystery of your Feet!"

Who ever before today, before Ta, who ever dared? Abim reflects. Nobody! As far back as her memory goes, she finds no example. All the people, all of Kobor has always been silent on this matter. Certainly, their thoughts linger and spin around it, but their tongues stay quiet. The Feet of Abim? Nobody has ever seen them. Does she even have feet? It certainly seems like there is something else there. Who knows what. The night of the night, the deep of the deep. Yes, a root, if you want... But how to explain it, how to think of it safely? One "cannot" know because this thing called "The Feet of Abim" is too far from the men of today. The Feet of Abim are unknowable.

Of course, the Very Huge does not know it but the B'Tah-Gou sing stories in which they indirectly refer to this secret. They are about great, mythical women who are almost plants and who grow in a single spot or they are almost stones and endure in a place without ever changing or growing old or falling. The B'Tah-Gou say that it was a terrifying marvel and these women could use the force from the earth's core. Plants. Stones. Who are stuck in the ground and yet can travel without anyone knowing how, without anyone ever seeing them do it. The storytellers leave it at that. There are limits that cannot be passed...

All of a sudden, the anger is gone, completely.

The hands of the Very Huge drop down. The wings clipped, all at once, they freeze in the mineral assemblage of this vast body that does not move, seems not to breath, once again becomes a monument. The chin digs into the chest. The neck is stiff. No more anger. But extraordinary concentration.

The Ananou stop moving down below. The unidentified wind has died down. However, it continues softly along with the subdued quivering. Invisible coils turn very slowly somewhere under the palace halfway between the Ananou and Abim's slumping. A lull, basically. Everything that had spread out, that had come as if answering a call, stayed there in mid-course, on hold, available. A lull… The inner panorama had lit up. The old queen realizes that, all things considered, she is not really so upset with her younger daughter. The wispy female has her brave side, after all, which flatters the royal blood.

How interesting it is to witness such behavior! Later, who knows, it might prove useful? She must remember this.

Abim has worries about this, she knows that she never forgets anything, even if the memories are a little slow in coming sometimes. For the moment, she is not concerned with the projected plans or even the obnoxious insult that will go no further. Ta was just trying to get out of her chores. She succeeded. Very well, grant her that. The courage it took to do it that way deserves the reward! Childish bravado. Children have more courage than adults. Abim smiles. Had not Ta paid her an enraged tribute? Who can truly oppose the Very Huge. Besides, the insult comes at a good time to remind her that she sometimes has to awaken her powers.

So what if Ta is running around fancy-free in her harmless fantasies, that little female tying herself down to one man… For a moment Abim stops to consider the strangeness of this kind of love. She feels something there that is beyond her, that annoys her or touches her tenderly, she cannot tell the difference between her emotions very well. The rest is just comically bizarre.

"Your Feet!" she had shouted, that one-man female. Oh, it is too funny! Just one man! And shamelessly to boot! That Ta, more proof of her odd bravery.

In the darkness the laughter shakes the sitting giant. But it ends abruptly.

Now, she has to consider more serious things. Ta is still nothing. What Ta said is still nothing. So, she can put aside this worry. And the primary outrage comes back. But this time coldly.

Amo. How to topple him? Where to hit him? For, there will come a time when it will no longer be possible to refuse to acknowledge one of his children as the Great Child, the Female marked with the sign of

Ooh'R, the one who will, later, when everything has utterly passed on, succeed Opak.

It is incumbent on the Very Huge to give the Name that, more than the birth, will grant the chosen child an official existence. So far, all the queen's children are considered as non-existent. They have no name, nothing but words that refer to them according to their particularities. They are royal children but not creatures for the throne. It is the sun Ooh'R that designates. It is the Very Huge who identifies and names... She will not name! She is adamant. Ta will reign instead, if necessary!

But it is not a question of Ta... but Amo. She must dismantle him.

Come now, she has daydreamed too much recently. She needs to get power and recharge herself. She will regain possession of her Agir... The clicking syllable starts murmuring around her again. The Ananou stir...

Tonight the Very Huge will officiate with her terrifying magic.

Leaving her physical bulk in place, she will travel in her vast subtle body dragging along in her tide of force all the passive ghosts of the sleepers that will become her servants for her ceremony at Grand Va-Hôh!

During this time, To and Ta were running together all over Kob'Lâm.

Their breached duties were making them drunk on freedom. They were overflowing with eagerness and joy. Holding each other's hand, they tumbled down to the Low City by the shortest route with no fear of the dizzyingly steep slopes or the terraced drop-offs that they jumped down without hesitation, without slowing down, since their forces were so harmoniously balanced.

Nobody paid heed of their passing. On this night of love, everyone had retired to their Chambers of Men. The inhabitants were buzzing with the same hum of pleasure.

In their Pit, the Ananou are panting softly. Lethargy is slowly over-taking them. But they are still clapping their hands to the rhythm of the waves that pass through their sensitive organisms.

They cannot help raising their heads toward the dark ceiling of their prison. Above them, Abim's force of attraction... They are beginning to suffer...

To and Ta had left Kob'Râm. They were crossing Kob'Vâm whose gardens and pastures gave them a foretaste of open nature. Beyond, beyond, quickly! They were running.

In the Low City, the B'Tah-Gou Méè-Nê is startled awake, astounded.

Her big eyes open in the night, she sits up in bed. Her ears are also wide open. With her hands flat on her knees, she spreads her fingers to better capture the invisible. it seems to her that it is expanding... She feels around and queries toward the Ananou but cannot make sense of what is happening over there.

All of a sudden, she loses contact. She is left with her astonishment and insomnia. It is, however, the night of the biggest sleep, the only night of the year when the storytellers regain all their strength during the repose of death that they do not come out of until the morning, rejuvenated.

She catches something again from the Ananou. What is it? She does not know...

It is light in Abim's room.

It is the body of the Very Huge that is red like a ruby. The pungent odor it emits would be unbearable to anyone. The mysterious quivering that was just rippling the ground has reached the very center of Abim's flesh and seems to be transforming it. The way is open now. From the earth's core, the summoned force leaps up like an underground spring whose stone lid has been removed. Abim fills herself with this power in one interminable orgasm. The clicking syllable beats, throbs in her and replaces the usual toil of the heart. The power of the earth's core has taken its place and she identifies herself with it. Now Abim can use a foreign, invisible organ that beats inside her, that has replaced her heart and that circulates the vital, telluric current that possess her.

She hurts. But she cannot complain. She is a prisoner in a body of stone. She is going to leave it soon.

She looks for an exit, guided by the clicking syllable that she has to get close to, that she has to get drunk on.

Her consciousness is carried over. In the momentary blindness, a red day appears. Abim opens different eyes on this light.

The throbbing is huge. Everything is shaking. Everything giving way. The stiff body of the Very Old is run through with a brief shock.

Her whole mass cracks, wavers, stops still, lifeless, but rises up irresistibly. Abim is rising up!

The body of stone straightens up, so tall that it grazes the vaulted ceiling. The statue remains standing, straight, cold. Abim has left it, like being wrested out of armor. She is gone, using a different body of subtle density.

Klimm!" she says. "Klimm, Klimm!"

In their Pit, the Ananou are writhing on the ground. Then, one after another, they lie still. Something has passed over them, taken them out of themselves. Their fluidic life has left them... "Klimm!" said whatever it was that carried them off... Abim is enlarged by a docile material.

A great danger, something ferocious brushing past disturbs the borders of Amo's sleep. Will the enclosed edifice of repose resist much longer? Who is trying to consume everything around there? The tension of the siege grows stronger, unformed, but everywhere at the same time.

The sleeper jumped up.

Opak, with her mouth against his ear, was surprised, "Why do you scream? And why are you sleeping? You dropped off into sleep like into a hole."

He opened his disoriented eyes that were resurfacing behind his eyelids as if sleep had sucked them in. He looked deathly tired, like a part of him was missing.

The queen made a sign. There was a swish in answer: T'Lo Dê obeyed and lay next to her, against her back. She knew that this would excite her male's passion by angering him even if he would never rebel against her will.

She was not mistaken. Amo grumbled in annoyance, shook off his numbness and, furrowing his brow, hastened to take back his queen with renewed force. Inexhaustible Amo!

To and Ta had passed through the rampart of Kob'Vâm. They were rushing into Kob'Lâm, the last step before freedom beyond...

Eqin-Go, Amo's best friend, was also sleeping, drunk on what the T'Lo had given him, which he was passionate about.

But Oda-Néè, the woman who had chosen him for the fifth year in a row was indulgent because she had the same tastes. She smiled and because she naturally slept little, she called back her T'Lo to commune with the same drug.

Another male of her Chamber of Men joined her at her behest.

She paused her erotic games several times because Eqin-Go was moaning in his sleep. She ended up becoming worried since he seemed to be suffering. Where was his spirit travelling? Shouldn't she wake him up? She held him close and caressed him.

He woke up right away. His face looked tragic and his mind appeared to be wandering. The woman called his name softly as she rubbed his forehead. Sympathetically, the other male blew on his temples to help revive him.

Finally, he recognized them. He hugged Oda-Néè tightly and buried his face between her breasts, not wishing to talk.

She felt guilty for not waking him up earlier. But despite her battery of questions, he did not want to say anything about his dream. He trembled for so long that the other males of the Chamber came to comfort him. Finally, he calmed down under their caresses.

Méè-Nê gets up. "Someone passed by!"

She cracks open her door. All is deserted. Everyone asleep. The elderly of Kob'Lâm retired early. All the houses of the other B'Tah-Gous are shut tight. There is no light anywhere. They are not supposed to leave. But she leans out. What does Méè-Nê see? Over there on the bridge, that fleeting whiteness: two brief silhouettes no sooner seen than gone... The princess Ta, the hunter To? Méè-Nê tells herself it is a dream, without a doubt. Why leave Kobor Tigan-t on the night of love? Oh, a sudden premonition overwhelms her heart. She feels like she is falling, down, down, swallowed up. Her body is no longer her body. She is drifting away like steam towards the Revelation that summons her. The ground sinks. And in this state of dissolution, thus becoming more lucid, she sees the five-fold terracing of the Cities tremble like a mist. The architecture mutates. The sky sways. A sickening throb shakes the earth. A clicking order repeats itself. From the west comes an immense, pale puddle, an echo of the order...

But that is all. It stops there. Méè-Nê has not really understood. She recovers herself, standing up straight again, bathed in sweat. She is hanging on with both hands to her door. Quickly, she closes it. She cries in her closed fists because now everything is despair. She should have slept. She has been duly punished. All the B'Tah-Gous are supposed to sleep this night. To know nothing. She disobeyed. She saw... Oh, what she saw!

She stumbles back to bed in the chaos of her stifled screams. She must not awaken her servant. Quickly, to the back of the house in the darkest shadows! Quickly, to that refuge where the interrupted sleep will evaporate! Quickly, it is waiting there, sweet oblivion, the remedy! She plunges in. Tomorrow, tomorrow morning, she will know nothing. She swears to it. She wants to abolish herself. No, tomorrow she will know nothing...

Without stopping, To and Ta had crossed the bridge over the gulf by the gate of Kob'Lâm. For a short instant the cold vapors blowing on their legs felt repugnant to them. Then, right after, on the slope they were bounding down, there was only the warmth of nature, the night with its plants and stars and fat Nood whose blue sphere cast its light on the peaceful face of the mountain Kah'B'La.

Immersed in joy, they stopped, turned to face each other, unable to talk. Seeing each other like this, each in their young glory, each gleaming with love for the other, they were sure they had escaped common fate, had been saved from whatever was threatening Kobor Tigan't. The willful upsurge of their love had just triumphed over some influence. And they would always have this.

They almost immediately forgot the premonition. But the benefit from their act was not lost because it will remain within them.

Ta's smiling face clouded over, "Do you hear?"

To pricked up his hunter's ear, "Yes. It sounds to me like a rumbling coming from the top of Kob Ooh'R. The Ananou were clapping their hands just now while we were running. I don't know what this is now. It's coming down from up there like the wind."

Ta dragged him forward, "Come on, let's go, let's not stay here, let's get to Kah'B'La."

The anguish was gnawing away at her. She thought that in the breeze descending on all the cities she could recognize the clicking syllable... "Klimm! Klimm, klimm!" the far-off Thing was saying and it was getting closer. She thought back to the hidden aggression that Abim had directed at her in the hope of controlling her.

"No!" she screamed very loudly.

She pushed To, who was surprised. They ran for a long time. The distance increased quickly. Finally, they were in the hollow of the valley.

The grass rustled around them. They slowed down, calmed down. Here there was no trace of Abim!

They soon climbed a path leading up the beautiful mountain. The night suddenly became darker.

"Nood is hiding," To said.

Ta raised her arms, "Come back, Na-Nood," she prayed using the tender diminutive. "Come back, O Na-Nood, all blue! Show yourself on Kah'B'La so that we can be happy tonight!"

The clouds slipped away and once again the nocturnal star was watching over them…

Shut up in her home, Méè-Nê sleeps. Most assuredly, she is sleeping. But she is not at rest.

Deep in her consciousness she feels like she is suffering great torments. A foreign willpower has seized her, trying to steal a precious treasure from her. "Klimm! Klimm, klimm!" the will is clicking around her. Then it strikes and opens a little passage, a narrow tunnel toward her treasure.

Méè-Nê groans loudly. She would really like to wake up now. The trap, it was sleep itself! She should not have gone back to sleep. She should not have. Suddenly she knows it! It flashes on her… but it is too late. She is sleeping now… and she leaves…

She tamely follows where the clicking leads her. She is sleeping. Oh, she is skirting great dangers. She feels terrible dread. And it is long. Oh, what are they doing to Méè-Nê? What are they doing with all those who are with her in the same Gehenna… Oh, what sadness! Oh, what shame! Oh, what torture! Oh, there is no end!

In the royal Chamber, the vigilance of T'Lo Dê never slackened. T'Lo Dê never slept. He was the perfect guardian, always at the ready. Calmly, he lay there, eyes open. Giving and receiving caresses and love made him not the least bit tired. He never got enough of it either. Just boundless gratitude, awe and his usual, inextinguishable desire to commingle in human embraces.

His big, golden pupils gazed on Opak and Amo deep in sleep. The T'Lo stayed attentive so that he might catch the faintest call for his services. He tried to imagine it in advance. A vague gentleness brightened his face.

Among the other T'Lo on their furs, the other queen's men were sleeping, too. But T'Lo Dê was not concerned with them. His devotion was solely to Opak and Amo. Both of them. He loved them both. With a tremendous, formless and sad sentiment. He struggled to deserve something. Opak and Amo would give him something precious one day. He was waiting for it. He almost knew. In their loving embraces and amorous remarks he almost identified something. He was already able to recognize it and greet it in the light. Deep in the flesh of Opak and deep in the flesh of Amo, that light!

T'Lo Dê was reaching desperately out to humanity. But like all the T'Lo he was a psychological cripple. He lacked a level of his being; a hinge had been removed: a bridge had collapsed… In this entity lingered the injury from a flood, the defect from an irrevocable ruin. T'Lo Dê was no longer an animal. T'Lo Dê would never be a human. T'Lo Dê was stranded on an island of banishment in the middle of a vital ocean. He could see the near shore, the human shore. He never went there. They came to him on the island.

Lonely, very lonely, T'Lo Dê…

His eyes on Opak and Amo, he was ready for anything. Whatever the two of them wanted from him, he would do.

T'Lo Dê was the slave of love. When were they finally going to call him over to them? Why were they not moving? T'Lo Dê desired them so badly. He desired their comforting, promising communion…

Across the distances, through the mazes and walls of the palace, T'Lo Dê saw Abim rise up.

He had always seen through the densities. He knows how good it is for protecting those he loves. It is good to be warned like this because T'Lo Dê also knows that humans do not see much. So, for him, it is a supplement to all his strength, in silence of course.

He did not care that the Very Huge got up! It meant nothing to him. That fat, unnamable root who was pulling herself out of the ground left him cold. Not surprised, just attentive—a spectator uninterested in the show. T'Lo Dê was thus the only one who knew. As usual!

T'Lo Dê also "heard", better than humans, farther than ears. And again, it was a good thing he never neglected… And so, he was listening. He heard a syllable, a pronouncement of force that was moving like a being. It was signaled at first. Then it came. And now, ah now, it is here in the nocturnal substance, in Kob Ooh'R and already it is getting ready to invade everything! From top to bottom it is going to go all the way down to Kob'Lâm, then to flow westward where it will settle into an incomprehensible assembly.

There it is. T'Lo Dê hears "Klimm, klimm!" outside in a ball of vital emanation that is passing over the five cities. "Klimm, klimm!" every which way, going and coming, repeating, multiplying, becoming legion and yet only the one "Klimm", One only, but multiplied by the play of furious activity, expanded into all of its possibilities.

All around, everything must mirror it. And so now it is moving with the same grating, clicking, sliding sound. The klimms intermingle with the klimms and are built up, like interlocking sonorous strips, into a kind of enormous monster with shiny, gibbering scales, a grand composite vehicle that fastens on whatever interests it and that moves on carrying away its prey... All this is Abim!

Red-black, black-red, the Very Huge guides everything. She is already down below, ready to spring westward. The disordered Klimm rush down to her almost lovingly. She is its center, its source, its medium. T'Lo Dê, however, sees that Abim is still standing in the center room, inert as a dead stone. This mystery does not interest him. He has no opinion, he just looks. He is not affected. Attentive.

All the B'Tah-Gou have been pulled out of themselves. They are floating over there in gloomy vapors. The departure is sucking them in, drawing them grievously into the confusion...

All of a sudden, T'Lo Dê starts. His vigilance is focused again on the royal chamber. It seems that Amo just gasped. What happened? T'Lo Dê touches his master. Yes, he is breathing, sleeping. But what a weird sleep, all hollow, all empty!

There is no more noise outside. Westward is completely shut in by the black that cannot be seen through. Where has Amo gone?

In frustration T'Lo Dê watches over the body that lies there breathing gently. He can do nothing else. He understands, he knows that Amo is no longer truly there and that this body that the T'Lo is so in love with, this human body is free. A part of Amo has been taken away by the Klimm.

Oh, the temptation is terrible. He would like to enter it, him, T'Lo Dê, to enter Amo, to be one with Amo, to live as Amo! He touches his hands, mingles their breath together. But he does not know how to go about it. For, from him, as close as he is, for T'Lo Dê there is an insurmountable distance. This so close abode so very far away.

T'Lo Dê weeps. From his dilated, golden eyes tears flow ceaseless-ly. He hears the warm heart of his master beating. And the reptilian cool-ness of his own skin horrifies him.

As usual, Ata-Réè slept near her B'Tah-Gou this night. She went to bed sad and anxious, but without having time to clear up her foresight because the interruption of her sleep was so abrupt. She slept. And then she woke up. In the middle of the night. As suddenly as she had fallen asleep. With a painful jolt, a rupture.

She woke up in a way she had never done before. Her sadness and her anxiety grown beyond measure; she was standing up without know-ing how she had gotten up. She knew who she was. She knew that she was still Ata-Réè. And yet, she was standing in front of her own body that was still sleeping on the small bed in the alcove. And she saw it clearly through the darkness, just like she saw the bigger body of Méè-Nê who was also sleeping in her usual place.

Méè-Nê was standing up just like the girl, next to her own body. she looked like a statue of steam.

Ata-Réè also knew that she had become a pale ghost.

Her B'Tah-Gou looked at her with both despair and tenderness, her eyes shining dully. They could not speak or move. A mortal weakness was making their images tremble. They communicated their desperation to each other in silence. Ready to faint. In great danger...

Around them, outside the house that was now just a fragile defense soon to be breached. There was this throbbing motion that was emitting powerful waves... and was now coming in, was everywhere, filling eve-rything up and about to penetrate them, suck them in...

Oh, how hard Méè-Nê and Ata-Réè resisted! They held on with the last of their strength. They fought against the morbid control, gazing at each other with a tenderness that was slowly fading away...

And something snapped in their consciousness. A blank void. And then Méè-Nê and Ata-Réè were next to each other outside with all the other phantom B'Tah-Gous, entangled in the viscous fluid of the Ananou, blended into a mysterious, magical clicking, a multiple body of action in the center of which reigned the single Will of the Very Huge who circulated, tremendously, through all the docile components she had captured.

A descent. An irresistible plunge, drawn out, long, tragic. The night deepens and darkens. Submergence. Nothing and no one can resist. Abim hurtles onward in her reptilian deployment! And after all the shocks and struggling the restless consciousnesses of the abducted are snuffed out and reawakened.

There it is. After a long oblivion, the group of ghost prisoners are revived…

What is it? What is that? It hesitates. It is taking shape. And deforming. And then suddenly it is done! All of them are part of it.

It is a circle, greenish, glistening. It is hostile and repugnant. It contains everything despite its imperfection. And it lets nothing escape.

"I am Méè-Nê, however!"

"And it's me, Ata-Réè!"

"Oh, B'Tah-Gous, my sisters!"

"What are you doing here, what are you doing?"

"Oh, B'Tah-Gous, our shadows! And the Circle of High Black Stones! Everything is warped here. Green circle. Pale circle: US! Black circle: Them, the stones! AND THE TALLEST in the middle: THE DIFFERENT WOMAN! THE ANCESTRAL!"

…Nothing should come here. We didn't want to.

"Oh, B'Tah-Gou!"

And how many others who didn't want to come here either. And who is here. Unable to free themselves! The green circle glows and ripples all around.

"We have to wait."

It's cold.

"I want to leave. I want to leave!" It is a cry.

… No voice carries. Nothing has any strength…

"Who are we, all in torment?"

"I see you. You see me."

"Oh, am I in the same state as you?"

… And time passes. Of the unconscious. A kind of death. On awakening, it is the same. Unchanged.

"Did you answer something just now?"

No answer.

"For how long?"

No answer. Ignorance on all sides. Passivity. The green circle ripples and glows.

"Why do we have to wait here like this?"

"Listen! I'm telling you there's a cry, a long cry that doesn't end."

"Yes, a cry, somewhere else, a cry, calling out to us—COME BACK! COME BACK! That's what the cry is saying."

"Listen!"

"COME BACK!"

"We can't, we can't go back, alas!"

"Outside the green circle: heat, life and our memories! All this is outside now, alas… And we are here, inside, in the circle, alas!"

"Oh, B'Tah-Gou, we can never return home!"

"What are you talking about?"

"I don't remember leaving. And yet here I am."

"Are you saying it's The-Very-End?"

"We're going no further."

"Oh, turn away. YOU HAVE NO MORE FACE!"

"What's that? What are you saying? I have no more face?!"

"But it's ME, Ata-Réè!"

"And it's me, Méè-Nê!"

"Oh, B'Tah-Gou, my sisters…"

The green circle ripples and bends. The cry has not stopped. Vibrant. ALIVE.

"COME BACK? COME BACK!"

"Oh, yes, there is someone, free, ON THE OTHER SIDE, who's running, all over, all round, outside, look! He is bringing his face near, into the circle, look, he dares!"

"COME BACK! COME BACK!" he cries. He wants to know. What to tell him, alas?"

"Oh, don't come in! Oh, not like us!"

Red as fire, he has kept his colors!

Inside the Gehenna, ground of sand, sky of ash, gray night, dry night. Domaine of Stones. Everything is mineral. The heart dies of thirst. I have lost life. Everyone here, all of us are not living. But our life still exists without being open to us. Oh, what are they doing with us? The green circle lights up: Klimm!... The red circle lights up: Klimm, Klimm!... I'd like to sleep to get out of here. I'd like to wake up… Our shadows are lighting up, white: Klimm, Klimm, Klimm! Setting us alight, one after another. And we are all here bound together in a big, phosphorescent ring at the foot of the Stones. THEY HAVE EYES, they are looking at us, content. They have arms, mouths, genitals, wills. How tall they are, towering over us!

"Let me leave!"

… The biggest Stone is in the center. SITTING… Like WHO, sitting? ?... THE DIFFERENT WOMAN, THE ANCESTRAL.

She is growing towards us, on all sides, her coarse pores, fully opened, fully greedy. And… OH, NO! She is pulling us, she is sucking us in, KLIMM, KLIMM, KLIMM, the clicking beats in our bellies in this frightful pleasure that is foreign, so foreign to our nature! WE ARE INVADED BY SOME OTHER THING! And… oh, here it is—we are dripping away like pierced wineskins, like overripe fruits, rotting and leaking, in this foul pleasure of dripping away. And… Yes, all of us here dissolved, scattered in nebula whose substance the Great Stone is absorbing. All of us, liquified, we are flowing back to Her!

And the Great Stone starts to live, slimy and malleable in the circle of its peers. And… Yes, IT IS STANDING UP, THE GREAT STONE! From below there she goes, pulling up HER TERROR, HER ROOTS. Dark red, pointy, immense.

Everything passes away, except HER, red-black, straightened up towards the summit of the night… THE DIFFERENT WOMAN, THE ANCESTRAL… And there, in what has never been the sky, and yet ABOVE, opening like a mouth, this: A BLACK STAR, unknown, and HOLLOW, drowns this phallus, descends, an inverted abyss, to engulf everything…

But the green circle bursts! The red circle bursts!

Outside, the one who was calling, the beautiful, tawny male who was crying out, "COME BACK, COME BACK!", launches himself, ALIVE, strikes the statue, strikes the root, battles, fights, and tries to throw THE ANCESTRAL to the ground… It is…

"Amo!"

Ata-Réè wakes up. Lying in the alcove of the home of her B'Tah-Gou, who is still sleeping nearby.

The day has risen, fresh, joyous. She gets up. Her head is buzzing. "Amo, it was Amo!"

Like she does every morning, she goes to open the door. She staggers. She is still trembling. But she does not want to show it. She breathes in, with all her might, the heat and the golden weather like a remedy. She must erase the awful memories. The memory must fall silent and nothing show through to the outside. The trembling eventually stops. The images of the night recede, buried in her consciousness…

Ata-Réè gets busy picking up the provisions piled on the doorstep. Thus, she connects to life, the light, pours herself into the menial household chores in which her will works freely in blissful naivety. Like this she tries to recapture some happiness!

There is a choice of victuals because Méè-Nê is a respected B'Tah-Gou.

The exquisite fruits, the plants, the succulent meats: pleasures, comforting pleasures!

The girl is fully back to her habits, one after another, that weaves her morning together. There cannot be the tiniest rift in the order of the day. So, she makes the usual jokes to those who have left the food. She laughs at their replies, also usual, always the same.

Unvarying smiles: pleasures!

Her eager eyes soak in the images of Kob'Lâm as it comes alive. There are the grand, decrepit elders already arriving, sitting down gingerly, their joints cracking. The gather together to enjoy the rest of their life.

"Another day and another tomorrow and after and many others to come!"

Ata-Réè greets them thus without pausing her chores.

They answer her cheerfully, "Come on, girl, we'll still be alive to see you as the Great Brain when you take over for Méè-Nê. We'll be your first followers, ha, ha! You'll tell the stories in the evening and we'll listen. Ha, ha! Aren't we better than those young men of Kob'Râm who have no memories yet and who just regurgitate the deluge of knowledge that their B'Tah-Gous give them, like babies after suckling when the milk drools out of their lips."

They laugh, the old ones, it is so funny, it feels so good and the girl looks so carefree.

But Ata-Réè knows that she is still trembling. Inside of her, deep down inside, the panic is there. Restrained but ready to spring forth. Too many, too many things learned last night! Méè-Nê must not find out. Or anybody! Never.

Ata-Réè sprinkles water all around the house. Even when she becomes a Grand B'Tah-Gou, by spiritual heritage of the one she is serving at present, nobody must know, no, no. She makes a promise, clenching her fists, biting her lips, stomping on the ground with her heel.

Then she brings the food inside.

… It is still dark in the back of the house where the B'Tah-Gou is sitting, full of a secret woe.

The girl's eyes adjust to the obscurity to notice her preoccupation. With a nervous hand she offers the food to Méè-Nê whose gaze falls on the hand and traces the arm all the way to the child's face.

Both of them look at each other, long since harmonized in mind and spirit. A great sadness binds them as if they were moaning together. But neither one breathes a word of it.

When the knot in her throat loosens a little, the girl speaks words of hope and courage. "O, Huge Mother, tonight you are going to talk again. The men will come cling to you with their empty minds. You will give them all your nourishing ideas. You will enter them like men do women. Your seed is good. Without you they would be sterile."

Méè-Nê titled her head, "Amo will come first."

She wrapped it up with that. They smiled. They stared at each other. They understood each other perfectly.

CHAPTER VIII

Amo, the male with the great, tawny mane, Amo the passionate who loved the beauty of the sun ecstatically, Amo who had big, warm hands and a gentle chest for a woman's repose, Amo loved Queen Opak. The weighty majesty of her, the mountainous contours of her body and her face, above all, big and round and blazing with an orange tint, all infused him with wonder. Her contact enraptured him and when mating with her he called up a scared fury from the dark cave of his sex.

For him, there was nothing above Opak, nothing to equal her. He fulfilled his queen, him, the first male of Kobor Tigan't! he was truly the only one capable of communing with such perfection. For him, she was superhuman.

She alone could support the most exuberant passions! Proud of her and often surprised, too, because the least of her impulses seemed fantastic to him, Amo lived by her side, always in a state of desire, against her, in her and yet even then never sated, always exhilarated, revived in his exhilaration by everything she said or did, by her limitless capacity for food and love, by her craving for existence, by her disregard of fatigue, by her mercy when she hunted. For, Opak hated cruelty.

Amo was in love with the royal apparel, ensnared by the royal jewelry and truly wedded by the queen.

Always, under every circumstance, he kept his eyes on her, scrutinizing the movement of her mouth when she ate and how her lips snatched the meat, how she licked the grease off her chin, he laughed at that! And how she swallowed, with that slurping noise, gulping down the too big pieces that stretched her throat, that turned her purple to the whites of her eyes!

Was she laughing? Amo blossomed. Was she solemn? Amo turned to stone. Did a shadow pass over her? Amo tensed and looked around for danger. Was she speaking? Amo, without being aware of it, imitated with his lips, silently, every word. Incomparable Opak! She was the All Beautiful, the Infallible Woman, the Queen of her race and her Sanctuary! He was the devotee of love.

Their frantic and tempestuous conjunctions went on non-stop. Day and night, Amo coupled with her. Her sensuality ravished him and knowing, rightfully, that he was the favorite, he went so far, out of sheer devotion, as to admire and desire the other males she often brought to bed with him. Everything selected by Opak was tinged with female royalty, became worthy of being loved. Amo, therefore, accepted the whims of the Chamber of Men as the goodly instruments of the erotic worship being fulfilled on this world by means of the Queen.

And yet, he was not truly happy.

Sometimes, more and more often, he felt oddly, painfully full, like the nausea caused by hunger and exactly like the nausea from eating too much. He was glutted with love. And he was dying of hunger!

At the end of the night, in the Chamber of Men, while all of Kobor was still asleep, he was startled awake. He smelled the odor of his own fear. Dawn was near. He was coming out of such a deep sleep that he wondered where he was coming from so alert. At the end of an uncommonly long separation, did he not make a leap to get himself out of a terrifying hole, to escape from some engulfing darkness?

He noticed that his brain was repeating, "She was already digesting, she was already digesting and yet I struck her in the circle…"

He got scared. It was meaningless! But where did it come from, then? What happened? He squinted in the early morning. The familiar scenery looked unknown to him, hard to understand, left behind a long time ago and now he was back from a boundless voyage.

With great difficulty he picked out the everyday details, one by one, to put them in order in his head after identifying them. He looked at the queen lying next him. She was sleeping on her back, spread open, one leg stretched across him. He looked at her with no reaction, like a stranger, drawing a blank… After a moment he jumped and said, "Ah, it's Opak!"

Opak! He felt better, recovered a little. He looked again, more carefully. He was refurnishing his empty interior.

There on the furs and fabrics, the usual T'Lo were half-awake, very gentle, well-behaved. When his gaze fell on T'Lo Dê, the latter shuddered with comfort and a wave, almost a smile, crossed his golden eyes. Instead of responding in kind Amo frowned. No, he did not like the T'Lo!

The other men of the queen were also lying there in a jumble. Opak had worn them all out as she was supposed to do to display her queenliness. Looking at these tired bodies, Amo felt angry and sad. Then he smiled darkly, thinking of his own body with its strength intact, already rejuvenated. "Amo the inexhaustible, the first male!" They kept saying this all the time! And recalling it fed his bewildering anger. An ungrounded anger that found no object...

What was wrong with him? Had his sleep dragged him into some evil place?

Suddenly, he was frightened, in a panic for having gone west like the childless dead who cannot fall back into the sleep of the ancestors and who are caught in a frenzy of moving around. They go west and come back bearing curses. They leave behind these noxious fumes and go back to Grand Va-Hôh. They come and go. They never stop. Nothing relieves them.

Amo shook off this thought. He gauged his strength. He felt heavy, dense, alive. He laughed: he, at least, could awaken the queen! But just as he was leaning over, he became totally disgusted with this woman! He froze, petrified with fright. But the nausea was already gone, in a flash, just like it had come.

What is all this?! Was he still asleep without knowing it? He jumped to his feet. Opak, thrown off, rolled over without waking up. In the eyes of the T'Lo, a brief flame flickered. With no hostility he stared at them, all of them lacking any sentiment except being ready to serve him, to serve her, male or female in turn or both together.

Did he desire to see them play with the queen? A T-Lo had slipped in next to Opak while keeping his eyes on Amo. The others were also fidgeting. Their musky perfume got stronger. Amo realized at once that they were observing all his thoughts. Their pug-nosed faces were reaching out to him, their slender hands beckoning... Slaves, slaves full of danger! He recoiled, burning with anger. In obeisance, all their gestures froze, but their eyes did not blink. They were waiting for his signal.

Opak was sleeping, sleeping. Her sleep spread throughout the room. She was sleeping, sated with love, saturated with semen. A devouring land, fattened on everything she had captured. She was sleeping in such an immense plenitude that she incarnated, in the absolute, one of the most terrible aspects of the Sacred: the insatiable female, the "Always-Again" abyss.

But she was beautiful! On the mountain of her body, her hair, her mouth, the double areola of her breasts, the slit of her sex made five fiery centers. Beautiful! Buttocks, breasts, belly, arms and legs inviting embrace even while at rest, all of it firm, full and abundant. Flowery shadows, satiny curves, all oiled with aphrodisiac balms. And the two cups of her upturned hands, dark pink fountains... T'Lo Dê was peering now at Amo, not disturbing anything, just waiting.

This creature emanated an ambiguous ambiance. Amo felt the insidious emanation that wafted around him. This spell of the T'Lo was quickly intoxicating like a volatile drug.

Amo remembered the last time T'Lo Dê had mingled in the caresses he was giving Opak... And how, when he had penetrated his queen, at the climax the T'Lo had slipped in next to him and... T'Lo Dê who was holding Amo in his gaze made a movement more precise, slow, detailed... Should he? With his whole being, he was asking. The other T'Lo were asking in the same way. They were moving around gently. Amo looked at them as if he knew nothing about any of this, as if it was all new to him and he did not understand. The pug-nosed faces were tender towards him, the big, golden eyes had a precious gleam, the strange, bisexual bodies offered themselves, deft, docile, loving.

Touched in her sleep by latent eroticism, Opak smiled, without awakening, opened up, formidable, desirous again, always, always desirous! Why did Amo love this woman? Was she really the object of his love? In a panic he wondered why he loved her, whether this was love and whether it was necessary to love. Was he not wasting precious time, blood, noble strength and light? But beyond her, the Supreme, the Divine, to whom or what could he raise himself, to what could he offer his inner fire?

He ran outside as if he were called.

And he found himself almost at the top of Kob Ooh'R, in the morning light, staring at the sun in despair.

He realized that he was alone, facing the sun alone. Around him in the air his love strayed off unanswered. Around the sun, likewise, love strayed... Amo did not love and was not loved! So, what was it to love? And was it necessary?

The hoarse voice of Opak reached him. She always woke up when he was not there.

He ran, surprised to be running, surprised that he had run away.

He took comfort in her heat, inhaled her odor, penetrated her femininity, deeply, forcefully. And he was searching there, in her limits, an answer to the luminous enigma glimpsed in the sun, an answer to his own enigma.

Without seeing anything, he took the lead, imposed his rhythm, forgetting the law that demanded that the Queen dominate. He kept up with her, matching force to force, like fighting blindly in the night against a heavy beast, a harmless beast, formidable only in its dark mass.

Surprised but not offended, Opak melted beneath him, revealing secret tricks, more dangerous for having been hidden until now. She evaded and intensified, more exquisite to conquer him the better!

Under her tempest he felt himself hypocritically indulging the feminine danger. He was discovering what it was like to be a man, brought to life by a will different from his own. And knowing her as a woman, far from savoring the union, he felt (much more than the difference) the despair... Suddenly Opak yielded. And at the same time, in his own terrifying pleasure, he was completely lost with the squirt of his semen, he was lost, swallowed up by the pitiless mystery of the royal womb... Alone. He was alone. He did not love. He was not loved. Was it necessary to love? The queen loved his fury. In a passiveness that was totally new to her, she had just discovered a new form of power, another face of triumph. She did not at all understand where it all came from. And it did not matter much to her! This angry possession filled her bulk with life. She needed violent sensations. But until now, ritually, she only got them from her own violence.

Opak could not do without other men or T'Lo. The exclusivity of rank accorded to her favorite for a long time was due solely to the plenitude of pleasure that Amo alone knew how to give her. Nobody had yet equaled him. She kept him, therefore, in his place out of great respect without regrets or sorrows, almost without thinking of it, simply because he was always the one who gave her the longest pleasure.

But what if another man suddenly came to surpass him and Amo was left relegated to the rank of accessory. And without drama, without remorse, as a logical thing with respect to merits. And it would be improper to see it any other way.

However, this was not the case. Opak told herself that she really did have the best male of the realm!

She therefore had to work at keeping him in this new and delightful state of aggression. By any means possible. Starting with T'Lo Dê whom she swore to use constantly. Pushed to the extreme, Amo would always end up rushing over with this grunting and amplified power. And she would be waiting, on the lookout, in her tenderest flesh, pretending to disappear, to no longer be there, she would be waiting in triumph for the staggering union of all this tempest!

It was really from this day on that Amo felt true despair.

CHAPTER IX

At the end of the magical night, everything had to stop. Abim was carried back to herself by the day. Or by the irruption of a daring and dazzling force that she associated with the sun.

Under the onslaught, all the charms thinned out at the same time. Sounds, colors, forms: all gone! Suddenly weary she stopped maintaining the cohesion of what she had built. She returned in a vastly weakened state. Like a plant whose roots have been cut, she collapsed.

But she was coming from so high up in the strangeness and so far away in the bizarre that the return was a bitter, dizzying fall. The gleaming day, or what she believed was such was painfully stifling.

The various fluidic borrowings of her circulation had been destroyed when her will weakened. Nothing belonged to her. None of this was with her except for a short time. For a moment, just a moment in the night, she had been able to command in the shadows, to snatch away like a thief, to fuse through abduction and darkness, to organize her bastard construction. For a moment she had been able to separate the dynamic energies from their legitimate supports. For her own good. But only for a moment. At night. By the darkness of Nood.

But now it was over, everything has gone back to its source. Everything had to be given back. Stifled by the brightly gleaming day, she went hurtling backwards, in full flight, with a single outcry. More than naked, flayed, beaten, red blood, all the hordes of the light on her heels! The light that sometimes resembled a redheaded man…

She finally ended up in the depths of herself. The red glow of her inner furnace was extinguished. The suffering too. It was nighttime again, a shroud. But grueling and hostile. She barely felt herself in the dense, uncomfortable, cold body. Almost dead and reluctant to revive to inhabit it, but starting to settle into her personal repose… Still, she had managed to come back. She lay there, still hearing a faint echo that was the last to retreat: "Klimm, klimm…" She had been divorced by her magic. That, too, was only borrowed…

Oh, she had brought nothing back, nothing that really mattered. What staggering certainty! Abim's consciousness cried out in despair.

She was in the blackness of her body, all her strength used up.

A little air whistled into her chest. The span of her existence resumed its work where she had left it. Resumed grudgingly. It was still not possible to move this body, even a smidgeon. Not even lift an eyelid. But deep down inside, this gentle whiteness? What was it? What was waiting there, like a habit, deep in her lair? It was sleep... Abim surrendered to the usual influence that owed nothing to magic.

There she did not command. Did not will. Did not know. But she was there. Piteously taken back by the very thing that escaped her when she wanted to see it and that only showed itself when she gave up.

...The glimmers come forth. The laugh, the marvelous laugh rises up and makes them shimmer. They quiver in the lightness, in the liberty, in delight. And the laugh goes from one to another. Then, satisfied, "the white form" appears. It was going in the colored circles. Then Ooh'R arrived like a friend coming to meet someone with the same laugh. And Ooh'R bursts with joy, surrounded by spheres like it. And the White Creature transforms them into birds. Unbearable whiteness of all those wings, this unbearable joy reflecting in all directions, growing unto the ends of the earth! And then at the end of it all, the crack of lightning applauds the supreme good of Ooh'R...

But Abim got nothing. She only knew that it as This that she was searching for. This that her race needed. She had always known. Everything halted for her. There was a total break.

Then, slowly, with a mocking click, the bitterness of the Klimm left her through her feet, yanking out something like long entrails. From the top of her head down through the middle all the way to the bottom it left, bearing its tribute, leaving its mark, its empty channel, to come back later, to be summoned again later. Oh, she must have been bleeding, bleeding. Everything was red...

Well, it had been a long time since she had dropped into the encased pit of her old body. In the old days, there, in herself, she was Abim. As always. Alone. Huge. Disappointed. Full of mighty power. No one was like Abim anymore. Disappointed, disappointed, disappointed! No, she had brought back nothing of what she was chasing in vain. But what was it, then. Where did it come from?

Well, she would destroy Amo first! Apparently, she had to start there. The people were going to be visiting the nursery where all the little royal babies grew up. She knew very well how the good people gawked at the little females hoping to find one of them with the mark of Ooh'R that the Very Huge might not have seen because of the gloomy dimness in her room.

Abim suddenly opened her eyes. It was daytime.

But where was Ta?

CHAPTER X

They were following a road sloping up, very steeply. In a jumble of branches and reeds the tall, thick vegetation made a dome over them.

Kobor Tigan't had no more hold over them.

Here it was Kah'B'La. Verily, a different place in the world, fragrant, almost perfectly silent because no animal on this mountain raised its voice louder than a peep or a whisper.

The murmuring of the insects harmonized with the vibration of the sunlight filtering through the transparency of the foliage. The magic life of the plants, which grew without ever saying anything, penetrated To and Ta. On their way, they were resting as if balms were seeping into the nooks and crannies of their nature, healing old wounds.

A feeling of happiness, thrilling but peaceful, carried them forward. Never had they felt such blessing, which their mutual consent made stronger, more beautiful. They kept looking at each other with rapture in their eyes, ecstatically sharing their common gratitude. Their thoughts were going side by side like their bodies, harmony and perfect echo.

Over time Ta realized that this exceptional joy was linked to the very specific feeling of finally experiencing something long-desired. She knew, at the same time, that To also shared this certainty. For both of them it had no name, no face. It was an ancient desire of reaching a place in time, a positive excitement, an intense eagerness. It was: "Soon!"

All of a sudden, their path split into different directions. Not knowing which way to choose, they stopped, becoming aware of a certain weariness and above all a fear of going astray. Where should they go now?

They tried a few, but they felt like they were going away from their joy or, more precisely, that their inner light was fading. So, they let themselves be guided by it and it was only in feeling it without any shadows that they were certain of being once again on the right path.

However, nothing around gave them this impression. It was just rocks, rubble, barrenness.

After a sharp turn where they had to clamber up a steep terrace, they had made the transition. Before them resumed the tunnel of green, the golden green of plant light. The slope was even steeper, but they climbed, reinvigorated, their faces raised towards the end of the tunnel that, high above them, opened onto clear skies in the bright sunlight. The heat became sweltering, the golden shimmer intense. They went on, thrilled, a little disoriented by a kind of weak delirium and they no longer felt their bodies. Nothing but the delightful blending of their double subtilities.

They did not know how long or how far they had traveled since the turn, but up there in the round clarity on which their dazzled eyes were fixed, a tall figure was silhouetted against the backlight.

They had no reaction on seeing it, no surprise, no inner movement. They kept climbing. They were now almost deprived of senses. More and more subtle. More and more together. Above all, oh, happy, totally happy! They were in the good of the world. They were living the best of times. The fervent spirit of plants and animals bore them along. The fragrant delights of Kah'B'La honored them. The light nourished them. They mingled in the grace of the event.

Without a sound, without effort, the silhouette came down to them. Were they still going up? Who was walking? Who was going? Who made the movement? It or them? Even though getting closer, it remained vague, a gray shadow, haloed by the rapture of the sun. It came forward... An image. Almost without features... Who was hastening closer? It or them? Who did the euphoria belong to?

All of a sudden, the image got denser. They saw it better. And yet, their minds remained still, producing no personal thoughts. But: only receiving. A clear mirror that warped nothing, that did not interpret. They saw, therefore, the truth in an indisputable way. They saw like in the repose of their entire being.

It was an old man with a very long beard, with a mane of white hair both soft and intense. In the hair, in the wavy beard, there were strange little birds, very colorful, clinging on, nesting and chirping, also fluttering around his shoulders, which they adorned with a simple splendor of feathers.

He passed by To and Ta without touching them in the least even though the path was very narrow.

"Beautiful children who resemble each other perfectly, remember not to ever separate, not to ever let them separate you! Remember!"

A voice? A thought? Better still, a higher caress, the best that they had ever felt. Through it their mutual mystery was confirmed: the twinning of To with Ta. For a brief moment a new bond was established between their two bodies. Maybe it had only been hidden and they were

107

seeing it appear? A bond of almost tangible light in which they had the revelation of a possibility of fusing their two natures, much more effective than a physical union because it was this that remained, veiled, after their young lovers' orgasms.

In the love that binds and unbinds, there was this other love that has no need to be renewed because it never stops. For, it is Sustenance.

They learned that for them, always, hostility and death would be called "separation". They knew that on going back, to defend themselves, they would always have to maintain their cohesion, not let anything alien to them ever get between them or join their alliance, nothing, no matter how sweet or enchanting.

Always, for them, the life triumphant, the wisdom that reintegrates would be called "reunion". Everything around them could be scattered unto the ends of existence to be brought back together and then re-scattered, again and again. And this might always seem almost hopeless. Except for those who, like them, have discovered and mastered the secret force of "sustenance".

They came out of the dizziness trembling. The whirling of a spiral dropped them back in place in the green tunnel of the path. Very quickly they turned around to watch the old man going away, but he was already gone. The path wound down as far as the eye could see. There were little feathers on the ground.

To and Ta realized that they had not seen the stranger's face. The extraordinary hair and beard, yes, the noble shoulders and the inexpressible mix of force and floating that moved the body, and that youthful old age and the whiteness... Yes, all that they remembered. But the face, no. Nothing remained, nothing had been seen. And yet, they knew how the warm eyes had gazed on them. On them who had seen, in the beard and hair, that the round, black, merry eyes of all the little birds!

"I always thought that Kah'B'La was a good mountain, the best place and that great benefits awaited whoever visited it," To said.

Ta smiled at him. And without any apparent connection to what he had just said, she blurted out in a whisper, "I'm glad he's of our race."

"How do you know he's of our race?"

"I just know it."

"Yes, you're right. And I know it too. Without having seen any more than you did."

She hesitated a little before, "To, listen, I really think I met him before."

"Yes," he said, "I don't doubt it. It's the same thing for me."

She pondered. "When I say I'd already met him, I mean he was there near me… When I was a child. Yes, right there, I really think so… In the dark, the night. I wasn't sleeping, I saw Nood watching me… And him, he was there, but I don't know where. It was in the warmth of the heart, imageless, and I was there with him… A kind of continuity of my childhood."

To leaned closer to her, "Remember what I told you, the story that you're always asking for. I never knew who woke me up in the cave by the swamp of the Dongdwo when death had cast me to earth from on top of the stairs. Life just suddenly lifted me up! And I didn't suffer from the fall. Someone was leaning over me, calling me with a tender ferocity, with a tremendous will. Impossible to resist. I had, however, already surrendered to my fate, bogged down in death. And yet, I felt like a fish floating up to the surface, captured in a net of domineering light… I thought I was being brushed by feathers or curly hair, filaments that framed an invisible face that was leaning over me. I had no more strength, I was already at the bottom of the swamp of death, I was already transformed by death. But still, I came back up! Because someone was telling me, "Come back, Son! Make an effort! You have to do it! To has to live because Ta is alive!" After that was said, I found myself alone and alive on the ground like a newborn babe. I'd just been born, for you, Ta! Oh, at the time you didn't care about me. And me, I couldn't picture you, well not too well…"

He was going to add something when a long, rumbling sound echoed from the other side of Kah'B'La.

Ta threw herself against his chest. He bent his back and covered her with his arms to protect her. It was neither a storm nor some volcano but a shifting of an unknown force. A quaking, an oppression, the temporary dimming of sight… They wobble, hanging onto each other. The mountain also wobbles. The arch of the path is sagging. It is like the details are vanishing. The leaves are dull. Their cheery little green spots are melting into a gray patch that is stretching out in every direction like a veil. A sharp pain drills the ears of the two young people. Then, nearby, a tree snaps off, cracks and topples over. All along the path the ground is slipping away in streamlets. Elsewhere, rocks are tumbling down. A burning gust blows by, then disappears. But it is over! Everything is already back in place.

Myriads of insects scatter the ground. They are not dead because some are moving, fluttering, flitting off. The silence that is looming again is broken: all the birds are singing as loudly as they can in a bizarre frenzy of joy!

"Something happened on the Other Side..."

The Other Side of Kah'B'La, the country nobody goes to see.

To and Ta boldly peer at each other. Of course, they have the same idea. The summit, close by now, is attracting them. From there they will see the Other Side. They will dare to see it. New forces are circulating in them. Drunk with courage. Craving revelation. They spring forward!

The instant they reach the summit, they jump back in surprise. Clacking their feathers, huge white birds with golden heads glide by over their heads. And soar up, up, ever higher and higher!

Birds on the Other Side? To and Ta rush forth and lie on the topmost stone, their heads hanging over the void, watching, the first ones!

On the Other Side of Kah'B'La there is nothing.

Everything is empty and deserted. As far as the eye can see, a vast expanse, flat and glistening, dull gray sprinkled with red patches where unmoving bubbles thickened.

Nothing living. Nothing moving. No place. And it has been an infinitely long time since it has been like this. Grass, plants, trees? None. Nowhere. It seems that here it is unthinkable. That this corner of the world knows nothing, that is even ignorant of the possibility of the most meager germination. Stone. Just Stone. Stone dead since time immemorial after a sudden drama, in a vitrification of all its elements. Yes, unto the horizon, a desolate terrace of stone, almost perfectly smooth. Dead. And having forgotten it. Dead. And having forgotten everything. Dead and still here, set apart and no longer able to become again, any more than to become once. Seized and frozen like this. Without emotion. Without torment. Without expression. Without memory. No regrets. No desires. No nothing. Nothing, nothing! Tranquil, indifferent and bare. Magically isolated by virtue of that state of oblivion. Empty!

"Nothing. There's nothing!"

To and Ta repeat this ad nauseum. This platitude stupefies them much more than any other revelation. Because in their most daring imagination they could never really have pictured such total barrenness. Nothing. Really nothing wherever their gaze fell. Nothing that broke the monotony.

And yet, properly considered, what unbelievable enigma remains suspended in this scarcity? In the vacancy of the stones without visitors, what awestruck questions go unanswered? And from the other point of view, what crowds does this infinite retreat invoke? This termination, what beginnings does it invoke? This suspended immobility, what former, teeming activities does it invoke?

Is it, then, for all these unspoken reasons that To and Ta gradually come to feel a completely different sentiment than at first?

Once the initial shock of amazement is worn off, they suddenly think that maybe the only real Place, the only Place in all the memory of their world that is truly situated is this Place here, which one day stopped "becoming" so as to forever "be".

This closed surface strangely invokes openings and opens onto the above…

So, the young couple search above in the sky. And way high up they see again the white birds with golden heads, which they had forgotten.

Straight up from the summit these birds are gliding without any other movement but a slow circling. Then, To and Ta look down along the sides of the mountain below them. They notice that from top to bottom it was formed into successive corbels, jutting crags that make an extraordinary stairway. But a bird stairway! For neither To nor Ta, despite their stature and agility, can use such steps, too big even to jump down without a pair of wings.

Halfway down, on one of these balconies whose center is hollowed out into a cradle, a being reposes. Arched over, head under its arms, it is covered in an extremely fine, white robe.

On seeing it, the two onlookers jump in surprise. So then, the one detail of the landscape, the mark, the gem, is this unrevealed creature!

They cannot tell if it is feminine or masculine. Under its veil it is all mystery. It hints at an indefinable beauty as well as power. The right balance, a secret harmony, its bending over is perfectly fitted into the hollow of stone.

Petrified remains? Certainly not! Because there is no permanent rigidity in the body. It is there, that is what matters. It is a valuable witness preserved by a grace for some future message. Living? Dead? An embodied ray? The melodious expression of a star molded in matter? Who can know?

Aghast, almost distraught, To and Ta raise their heads. Very high up, the birds circle languidly over this being. With their continual, patient movement, what does this mysterious guard have to do with it? Under the aerials watching over it, the Beautiful Being seems to be sleeping or more precisely to lack life. Which is not the same thing but is not the same as death either.

The young pair understood that it was not dead but in some totally other state. It was only deprived momentarily of life, in suspended animation, without losing its essence.

Maybe its life drifting on high in the gyration of the birds?

Ooh'R, who had been brooding behind the clouds for a while, made a sudden appearance. Unusual rays, almost crystalline, bounced off the birds' feathers. They were transformed into dewdrops of very bright light that fell upon the inanimate beauty.

The air seemed to flare up around To and Ta. Myriads of invisible insects pricked their skin. Gnats of light dazzled them. And in the throes of terror, they could not move, only watch the encirclement of white flames around the sleeper. Its body almost vanished in a sudden transparency. Then, the dewdrops of light withdrew or were absorbed, perhaps... The stone had turned white. It was once again perfectly visible. And in the peaceful air, it started to move.

Very high above, the birds stopped turning round to fly in formation, each in its place.

Ooh'R held a steady brightness.

To and Ta clasped each other, paralyzed with emotion.

The Beautiful Being awoke. All alone like on a fine morning at the beginning of the world... All of Kah'B'La participated. All of Kah'B'La knew. To and Ta were at the start of a miracle of re-creation. They were caught in the bubble of this marvel.

Under its robe, the sleeper shivered. Its head rose out from its arms. Its hair unfurled, golden like the crests of the birds. It stretched its neck, revealing more of the head. Blurred by the distance, its face was nothing but a gentle, astonished void. Beyond childhood, it seemed. Its big, oval eyes glistened like an evenly lit liquid so that one could not tell what direction was targeted by that vast vision, which seemed to take in everything together rather than fix on a single detail.

Several times in a row, it shook in an angry way as if to throw off some defilement or some unpleasant contact. Kneeling down, with its chest straightened up, it examined its surroundings avidly, impetuously, turning every which way, more and more amazed the more it gazed upon the arid landscape.

Then, it had a dizzy spell. It sucked in big gulps of air. Shuddering, it fell again, its face into its hands, stopped moving, bent double into its initial position.

To and Ta felt the suffering. They hugged each other harder. By sympathy they, too, had held their breath. And now they, too, were standing still. Stinging tears welled up in their eyes. A deep sorrow. What was happening? What was the meaning of all this? Was the Beautiful Being ever going to come to life? They truly felt that a wondrous event was dependent on them.

Suddenly, the Beautiful Being jumped to its feet, stood up straight and it was tall, it stretched, making a kind of unbelievable effort to pull itself off the ground.

"It's a bird!" the young woman exclaimed in a whisper.

It did not fly off! It was not a bird. Maybe it believed it was? It remained standing, head down, on the edge of the void. It was searching for a reason. So thin, so long, so slender and appearing to weigh less than barely, no, it was certainly not a bird!

Evidently, it was trying to find around it the memory that was escaping, the meaning of itself. Who was it? Where was it? What did its presence in this place mean? The clouds, the sky, the sun, the horizon, the flat stone of the ground, the mountain. It named all these things, pronouncing words that were lost in the distance. But the young couple saw its lips move. All kinds of desperate identifications that obviously led it nowhere because it shook its head or stamped a foot, by turns frustrated or furious.

It calmed down and seemed to sum up the futility of all its efforts with a strange gesture made by holding out its hands in front of it with the palms cupped. The youths noticed that the hands were different from theirs: the fifth finger was much longer than the others. To and Ta exchanged glances. Yes, who was this?

To said, "It doesn't know! It's amazed. The clothes, body, hands, everything amazes it. As much as all it sees. It knows nothing. It knows less than we do. Until now it was a sleeper in this place on the mountain. The Sleeper who knows nothing."

Yes, indeed, it knew nothing. But it was learning. It grasped its own details. It put its hands into the light. It touched its face, breathed on its hands, felt its hair, its chest, its whole body under the light robe covering it. Then it felt for something invisible around it as if it were defining the borders of its being. It shook its head again in discouragement, but less than before. And every time it resumed its search until it found the desired clarification.

Now, To and Ta had the impression of watching a mysterious exercise, quick and intense, whose successive actions were highly satisfying to the stranger.

The birds were still gliding overhead, which it paid no attention to.

It sat down, deeply absorbed, spreading and stretching its fingers, one by one, slowly, in a sequence that the two spectators did not understand. After this, it fell into a reverie while absent-mindedly fingering the hem of its garment.

Without it seeing them, the birds came lower now, very, very slowly. It was like every piece of memory was bringing these birds closer to it.

In a sudden movement it flipped some fold of its robe or else opened a secret pocket and shiny gems of all colors came flowing out and bounced on the ground.

To and Ta marveled at this. The Giants knew only one kind of gem: the rubies that were found on the outskirts of Kobor and that were reserved only for the Ooh'Rou and for their commemoration these rubies were mostly embedded in the side of the biggest of the Sleepers of the Sun.

With this discovery, the Beautiful Being had jumped to its feet and let out a cry of joy. It burst out laughing, then stopped as suddenly in order to inspect with a sharp, piercing eye, the rocks and shadows.

It saw (and To and Ta at the same time noticed) that the mountain was strewn with these same gems all over the place, clotted together, nestled in the cracks, clustered along the rocks.

Right away, in a rediscovered connection, it became aware of the birds. It called out to them, lively and joyously. And the birds obeyed, came down in a thrill of reuniting, squawking and beating their wings, while it laughed and laughed like it was hearing some fantastic joke.

They did not laugh like this in Kobor Tigan't! This laugh, did it not transform everything around it? Leaves turned greener, the light higher and hearts lighter as they began to feel something hopeful! That was what To and Ta were feeling, carried away despite themselves by the joyful balm.

"It's the Son of Kah'B'La!" To said in a sudden revelation.

"The last Son of Kah'B'La," Ta clarified in an odd, subdued voice as if she had hit upon a secret source of information. "The Last! There were many others, undoubtedly, like this one, in other times. And we knew nothing about them. They appeared here and disappeared. Like thoughts that come down to us and then leave. Oh, yes, I feel it, he's the very last! Look, he doesn't have the strength of the mighty Others! And even though he has rediscovered his joy, he knows almost nothing about himself. Maybe nothing at all about the Others like him. Alone, he was sleeping in a preservation of time. He would never have woken up if our eyes had not fallen upon it. The golden-headed birds were also sleeping in the same preservation. And we woke them up and set them in motion without knowing it. Our living eyes stirred the suspended life in them... We came here just for this. Only the Old Man who knows everything..."

Her radiant face faded. With a sad smile and sounding apologetic, she said:

"I do not know or understand anything beyond that. And I am not sure now of being able to repeat these things. They arose in me like a little herb quickly withered! But you, you've heard, haven't you? Even if you forget very soon, you have heard?"

"I've heard and I've understood. The whole time you were speaking. I didn't dare breath so as not to disturb you. My heart is still! When you'd finished, then my blood stirred heavily to carry everything far away from me to a place where, whatever I do, my riches stay hidden and protected."

"Oh, To, we have known! And it's been wiped out. Completely. We no longer know. Oh, To, it's gone, it's lost!"

She was almost crying, hanging onto him and he thought that this made a weird contrast with the joy that continued down there with birds. He made an effort to remember.

"We were looking at this... in a place, I think..."

She looked skeptically hopeful, "What place?"

He lost the thread he thought he was following, "No, it was, I believe, in a direction..."

"What direction?"

"No, I'm mistaken, it wasn't that. I don't know any more what it is. I don't know anything anymore either, Ta. Nothing more..."

She was crying while looking at him, vehement, "But we really did know, didn't we?"

"Yes, Ta, we really did know."

"Maybe it'll come back someday?"

The quivering laugh, so light, penetrated them with its harmonics. Oh, not really, they did not laugh like this in Kobor! No, this was a completely different kind of joy. They saw clearly: this joy "persuaded" everything around it. It colored everything its own, nothing escaped it, it allied with everything and worked, transformed what it penetrated...

And the young couple, their sorrow lifted, started to laugh also, before even realizing that they were laughing! Their amazement at this was boundless. But what followed was bound to carry them beyond even this amazement.

The golden-crested white birds had calmed down and were gathered together at the feet of the stranger. As before, silently, pensively, he held out his cupped hands. Then, he wrapped his very long little finger in the four others of each hand. This was a state of concentration, a call or contact.

After a while, a very soft sound began exhaling from his chest, modulating gradually, getting louder, changing and developing and continuing, like the light varying its brightness on nature through the clouds when it hits the rugged landscapes.

He was singing. He was all music.

But To and Ta did not know what it was, had never heard it anywhere, could never have even imagined it.

For, they did not sing in Kobor Tigan't. The genius of the race suffered a cruel lack of elevation and music could not come forth. They did not know it. They were unable to know it as if a delicate internal organ had failed to grow. Or else it had once broken away, affected by the bleakness of its support... Words, laughs or cries, huffing and puffing too, yes, they knew these in Kobor to express themselves or pass things on. But not this possibility of pulling out of one's being this language of infinite resources, this forceful expression that was in tune with nature, that was immediately "received" wherever it reached. Higher magic! Prayer to the primordial state! Action column of Below that praises on High! And that carries with it every creature in the course of its elevation...

A liturgy as well, no doubt? And this unknown Being had the rank of priest. But this, too, could not be understood by the race in Kobor. To and Ta were simply swept away. They felt like they were hearing the thoughts of the stranger, understanding them, communing with them, becoming these thoughts, always having been one with them in secret.

And the thoughts ravished them and they told them or reminded them of countless extraordinary things, unexpected and yet known by them. Things that could not be said otherwise because neither the laugh nor the cry nor words were fitting.

And there was no obstacle between their mind and that of the beautiful stranger and these things and the rest, sky and earth! No, no obstacle. Both of them, To and Ta, were with the Beautiful Being, together, happy, happy, not separated in any way, all of them united in peace, in an infallible existence that nothing was threatening, that, on the contrary, everything was joining, at the right time, in the right place, and not cheating, not pretending to be something other than its truth. All united. The birds, Kah'B'La, Ooh'R, down to the tiniest blade of grass there before them who were participating in the benefit of all this supremely wise togetherness.

The Beautiful Being was singing its original music. And this developed like an act of love. Nothing could resist it. Everything rushed along with it, echoes of it, ascending, escalating its vibrant, exalted sounds full an unshakeable knowledge that opened radiant thresholds above.

Everything that was carried along joined together more fervently, more closely, to continually blend better in this euphoria of resemblance, by gradually diminishing themselves, by successive identifications, in one single power, right and glorious, aspiring to its completion. To the inevitable, complementary meeting. Beyond the Beyond. In the blessed abyss of the highest Height... And the Perfect Wedding was achieved! "There is no more injury. Nothing is missing!"

This cry? The lightning bolt had crashed at the feet of the Beautiful Being in a benediction of fire, ratifying the pact, the promise made on this earth.

The Beautiful Being sat down, gently. The birds shook themselves and seemed to doze off.

Nothing moved anywhere.

To and Ta stood facing each other. Looking at each other. Loving each other. The vestiges of a distant age of glory. Sadly, they had become differentiated from all the rest.

And all the rest was lying around them in the same state. Full of the glorious memory. And everything fragmented...

They slept deeply right there where they were.

CHAPTER XI

At that very moment, Amo was hurtling through the successive cities like To and Ta the night before.

But he was far from feeling their lightheartedness. On the contrary, anguish was tormenting him. The day had been abominable, as oppressive as the previous night whose dire turmoil lingered in his heart. He could not remember what he had dreamed. It was like evil spells had been cast on him. He felt exactly like an egg hunter when the Aâz are trying to make him lost. His inner bearings, the direction of his being, no, they were gone! Maybe he would never find them again?

He had to see Méè-Nê at once, confide in her, ask her great sun brain for light and comfort. She always had an answer for everything. About the torments of her devotees, she was always forewarned and always, even before they confessed their suffering, she had already prepared the perfect cure.

She was a little like the treasure-trove-brain for them. Everything was kept in her, nothing ever lost. On the other hand, everything developed in the warm and gentle haven towards a slow but constant progression of its quality. Everything grew and was fed by her. When they came in search of something, she offered them the ripe fruit, brought to maturity, ready to be digested. The nursemaid of brains!

Amo ran in a hurry for help. In his haste for consolation his problem was already easing a little, growing a little numb. But Amo was mulling it over, more somberly lucid.

He was upset with Opak for having hurt and confused him all day long. What was her problem? All day long she had withdrawn into herself. Not being there, ever. Fleeing.

He had taken her again and again without really finding her. He had dived into an absence, crashed into the depths of her devouring evasion without finding her. Her! While in her sudden abduction she-the-female cooed, invisible, carried farther than him, beyond, him, by her powerful night. Thus, at no moment could he join with Her. When he collapsed at the limit of his male light, she—the dark moon—surged up into her personal realm, established, unlocatable!

In the extreme blackness where he had no access, there where he was dying, she came to life to steal and carry off everything he had given her without leaving anything in exchange and without giving him anything. Her pleasure occurred next to his, not along with his. There was no way to blend them together.

When he had come down, she was still drawing it out endlessly in stealthy waves extending around her, the limits were always retreating. Oh, why, why so much difference? Why so much duplicity in what was constantly saying "come with me" but that was never there together!

How many times did Amo, gloomy and dull, brought back by her in the night, but alone, how many times did he rekindle his fires of dawn to climb back up in glory and take her again? Well, she made herself vast, gentle, slow, withdrawn into her inner valleys that she occupied one after another. At every step along way she was no longer there, always elsewhere, under a veil of stealthy distance, having already come and gone.

She forgot about him, basically. The more he took her, the more he lost her. The more he lost himself, especially! Where was she? And there she was skirting around him, come unexpectedly! She curled herself around him, pretended.

Captivated, he himself became Ooh'R! He bore her on his tip. She, the flame, spirit of the zenith, ocean of light—she the same as he! Again, the night fell suddenly. All light dwindled in a victory of shadow. She was not there. The Same as He had never been there!

And He, where was he then? Lost. Defeated. Scattered. Denied. Dead.

…Amo rushed into the home of Méè-Nê.

The reverent silence of the place washed over him like a cool bath. He sat down, the first.

The attentive eyes of his B'Tah-Gou fixed on him. Ata-Réè squatted off to the side in the shadows, never getting involved, modest. In a very soft whisper, Méè-Nê started reciting, as a sign of affection to her loyal listener, the most famous of her poems:

Kobor Tigan 't, I carried you,
I, the sterile storyteller!
I carried you in the mold of my heart Like a very big child.
Too big to be reborn after your death,
O Kobor who appears only once!
I carried you, me, the sterile storyteller Full of words and whispers
Like battalions of children!
With my poems around me Flying into my black and hollow house.
Hollow like my sterile, storyteller's womb!

I carried you, Kobor Tigan't,
Great and terrible child
Who is like the mystery of the sky
And all its levels!

Without a sound, men had come in, one of whom was Eqin-Go who sat next to Amo because he was his older bosom brother.

The B'Tah-Gou fell silent. There was a lull during which Amo sank again into the depths of his trouble. He could not keep himself from speaking out. "Oh, Méè-Nê, I don't know where my heart lies anymore! My head is reeling like water. And my sex just hangs!"

Surprised, the men were jolted.

Méè-Nê smiled, "It's not true. On the contrary, you are always ready. Some say like a T'Lo."

"Ah," Amo sighed, "should a man long to be like a T'Lo?" He looked up at his B'Tah-Gou who was in a shadow. "Méè-Nê, explain to me, share your mind with me, it's too great a torment... and yet..." He tried to make himself understood. "You see, I am all bright..."

"They call you the Golden One," Eqin-Go nodded his head.

But Amo went on without hearing him, "... all right on the outside. But inside, the light does not enter. I am all dark. And I hate this darkness!"

Méè-Nê sighed and laid her hands on her knees. Her voice had changed as it rose up like when inspiration seized her. "There are men who are sun sick. Darkness is favorable to you. It envelops you well, it receives you and you enter its womb like the slipping in of evening's flesh. For, the Queens are all day on the outside and night on the inside. But you have stared too long at the sun with your heart. You wanted the sun on the inside. So, you opened your eyes at the end of your climax of pleasure when all men, or almost, keep their eyes closed tightly... and you saw that at the end of your shadow standing erect before you, deep down in the woman, there was suddenly a sun come out of you and springing out of the dawn at its zenith! A sun that you lost at once..."

"Yes, Méè-Nê, yes! It was the spirit of the sun that came out of me in the steaminess of the sperm! And instead of creating the day, by taking it in, the woman dissolved it and made it dark. I have the sun, oh Méè-Nê!"

"Of course you have it, Amo."

"I have the sun and I lost it in her. I don't even see a spark. It's lost, lost, you understand! She remains dark, thick, lightless. And I wear myself out trying to brighten her. All the suns I put in her womb, all the suns from my pelvis! And they are extinguished like torches dropped in the Dongdwo swamp!"

He stopped talking. All eyes were on him, disturbed and distressed.

In the door frame another very close friend appeared. His name was T'La-Voh. "We hear you, Amo, outside. We hear words from you so strange that we believe we're hearing Méè-Nê speaking through you."

Other men looked in. They were all talking together.

"What's wrong with you?"

"Have the Aâz got into you?"

"Did you sleep facing west?"

"Be quiet," Méè-Nê grumbled. "Men, men, I share my mind with you so often that is it any wonder that sometimes I talk through your mouths?"

They all sat down and while Amo kept silent, they rocked back and forth paying homage to the Storyteller:

"Oh, Méè-Nê, it's true, your great brain shines and we, all of us attached to you, we float around like the votive banners around the sphere of Kob'Ooh'R!"

The force of the collective rocking affected the B'Tah-Gou. Her eyelids half closed, letting nothing show but a bright slit and, like in a dream, she started to recite another of her poems, one they asked of her at every meeting.

I would like to sleep like a stone.

"E-i! To sleep!" the chorus said.

Standing up, in the western sun that swallows the memory!

"Oh, I would like to sleep" the chorus said.

I would like to keep standing up, black, in the sun…

"O would that she stops!" the chorus wept.

With its ideas that are stirred by the impact of ancestors!

"E-i!"

I would like my head to be full of strengthened stillness.

Like the head of statues that are standing up

Forever on the western shore!

"AAAh!" the men say

All of a sudden, Méè-Nê opens her eyes wide. A terrible event has surely resurfaced in her memory? Everyone watches her without daring to move and sees her already pale skin turn livid. They also feel that her life is paused: a blanket of cold air spreads around her and penetrates them. What has sprung up in the Great Brain?

Ata-Réè, who knows, guesses, because she saw the thing come back in the words of the prophetic poem, covers her mouth with her hands to stifle a cry. The terrible moment has come! Since this morning, the B'Tah-Gou has refused to remember although her eyes were filled with it. Ata-Réè saw it clearly when bringing her morning meal. And now, the rest will come.

The girl knows this too. With her seeing eye she recognizes on this or that man the same mark, the same fright even though they do not yet know it. Amo and Eqin-Go bear the trace of the nocturnal touch more markedly than any other. And the former more than the latter because the bosom brother, who is basically like the younger when they are together, often only reflects weakly what happens to his would-be elder.

Ata-Réè understands that Eqin-Go will have few memories. As for Amo, she does not dare look at him.

Méè-Nê speaks! Her voice rumbles, resonating out of her depths. It is a surge. The words flow one after another. Nobody talks. Nobody moves. The great breath of revelations is pouring out its strangeness. Méè-Nê improvises, at least they think so. Méè-Nê improvises! Yes, that is it, they are listening. And it is almost the same for her. Otherwise, she will not finish.

But keeping up with the improvisation, the Storyteller finds the hidden sense. She speaks before herself. Her voice goes forth, expanding the words. And there before her, in the delay of her thought, which no longer belongs to her, she starts to understand when the words shine a little in the resonance of the room.

On this night... I was sleeping, this night, certainly!
The B'Tah-Gous always sleep on this night!
A clicking word struck me despite this night.
The other B'Tah-Gous were also struck despite this night.
It struck and struck again until I awoke out of my night.
Oh, alas, I woke up beyond my night! I woke up beside it, stripped of my body, stripped of my night.
And I was in the clicking word that replaced the night.
With all the B'Tah-Gous, white, naked and without night.
A bad death was bringing all of us down! O my night!
I was falling, you were disappearing far behind, up above, lost, my night!

Amo clung to Eqin-go's arm. Méè-Nê was speaking true things. He, too, like her, like the others, last night, he was made to go down below, sucked in by a clicking echo. When he realized that his body was sleeping behind him, it was too late, he could not go back. White, naked, defenseless, he could do nothing but run to the end of the perdition in the dark. Run or rather slide or fall, it was all the same! And with rage because of that clicking syllable, that treacherous syllable that was saying... What was it saying? He could not remember. He only knew that he wanted to get revenge on it, to exterminate it.

Eqin-Go shudders. What was that green glow that he saw the other night? He was sleeping in the green and could not get out...

T'La-Voh believes solemnly that something happened last night. But he does not understand anything more. Nevertheless, he is scared. After Amo was just talking in that tortured voice, he got scared...

Ata-Réè knows. She saw: last night the double of Méè-Nê was twisting like a vapor under an invisible, serpentine flogging that was saying with every lash, "Klimm! Klimm!" And thus, the poor double was taken away from its body's shelter. Vanquished, it was forced to go outside... Then, she, too, left but of her own free will because the formless attacker did not bother with her. Maybe because she was too little? Outside, the whole troop of B'Tah-Gous was floating in the darkness that was clicking all around.

And then came the infinite descent and the infinite voyage! Klimm, klimm! Lower! Clicking, undulating, the dreadful conveyer carried them outside of everything. In front, the huge, black form forced everything to follow it. Everything was following. The green followed. The red too.

Ata-Réè wants to vomit. She doubles over. The voice of Méè-Nê bemoans:

Kobor Tigan't
Your fruit is no longer healthy.
It is devoured, your kernel.
No more seed. You will not reproduce.
Your succession will not be seen.
In the fruit the place of the seed is empty.
Kobor Tigan't
You will not return.
Before you go,
You have already gone.
Oh, it is ended before the end.

You heart, it is a round chamber.
Yes, it is a dark bell there.
A black stone clicks inside.
The obstacle is sitting on you,
Kobor Tigan't
It has been sitting for a long time inside of you.
And the land's desire of love
Can no longer reach the threshold of the High.
The obstacle diverts the sap that rises
To strengthen the dominion of the obstacle with it.
How could the sky respond to the threshold of the High?
Kobor Tigan't
The sky is uncoupled from you!
Pointless, outside, disordered,
It loses its seed like a madman
Whom the Woman has not chosen!

Ata-Réè leans heavily against the wall to keep from sliding down because it is blatant even though the Storyteller has not exactly spoken the truth because the words used are another veil. The sitting Obstacle is a Stone... A sitting stone: Abim! There it is. Now, Ata-Réè knows All. She is trembling. It is too much to know All. Will it be possible to keep on living? Be quiet, stay quiet, that is what she must do. Make even her thoughts quiet. What has been given her must remain there, of course, but in silence.

Amo remembers. Big, disconnected pieces come back to him every time the voice of his B'Tah-Gou fades away, he thinks. By the humming of the words he guides himself through his own mazes. Yes, here is his dream coming back: in search of Ooh'R, he ran for a long time. Without thinking. Like a star. With free and pure joy. First a game. Then, it changed into a laborious obligation. He saw that shiny globe, that glory that was rolling in front of him. He saw that Ooh'R was an independent stranger who was not waiting to be joined... Afterward, an immeasurably long time after, he realized what was fleeing like that in the night, It was not Ooh'R but a red sphere, dark like lava, angry and thick, menacing, vindictive. He did not want to follow it, but it was dragging him in its wake even though it was fleeing from him, apparently, deeply hostile. Just then, he remembered having seen a passage ahead, the crucible of Kob'Râm, empty, cold, the mute forges, deserted, the walls crumbled, weapons and jewels on the ground, abandoned, long cracks crisscrossing the terrace, a leprous growth had invaded everything...

Oh, in what face of time had he looked upon these things? He feels like he has always known them because they do not surprise him and they correspond to the distress lying in the pit of his being. He cannot unravel the chaos. He tries. The desired images reveal themselves, then disappear. An afterimage quivers a little, but it makes no sense. The images dissolve. Were they even there? Amo starts to doubt it. Méè-Nê's voice comes back to the forefront:

Oh, we must run!
Oh, we must flee!
Leave everything and leave one another!
Always go further away and cast off more!
All, stripped bare, helpless,
We must go down and westward in a troop of white woe...
The green ring, the ball of fire,
Like us descending and rolling,
Brought by the great, black stone
Who inhabits the west, the west!

T'La-Voh is aghast. Fear and devastation wither his heart. Still, he remains ignorant of the reality of the facts. His mind is not abreast. Only his instinct speaks. It is serious, very serious, all this.

Eqin-Go remembers the red ball! So, wanting to find some clarity for his defective memory, he looks at his bosom brother. But Amo keeps his eyes closed and even though Méè-Nê continues her litany, it is obvious that he hears nothing any longer.

Here is a fragment: the red globe had jumped ahead of him! Impossible to catch up to it! Carried blindly on his thunderous descent, Amo trips over a metal rim. He recognizes the pool of Kob'Vâm. He falls headfirst into the green fluid.

The memory is so strong that he yells and opens his eyes.

Eqin-Go is leaning over him, brimming over with concern. But the voice of Méè-Nê prohibits them from talking to each other. She goes on. She has not stopped.

Stand up where you are in the hollow of the west, B'Tah-Gou,
Like all the other B'Tah-Gous around you are standing up!

Emerging for a moment, just to hear this, Amo sinks back into himself. And it is for the worst memory! Later, much later. Here it is... He was coming and going. Totally exhausted. An absurd act starting over and over again and always failing. He was walking. Going back and forth. Along a green wall, vaguely transparent, through which he struggled to see. The need to see was tormenting him! Tirelessly, then, he was changing places, trying here and there, searching for a better vantage point.

… Sometimes he was running around in circles. Interminably. Because the wall, the cylindrical obstacle was completely enclosed. He grieved there on the outside, consumed by care for those who were shut in against their will on the other side, inside. Oh, how he burned with desire to free them! He heard their hearts screaming in him while listening to his own heart.

… Finally, in certain places, the material of the wall seemed less dense to him, less governed by whatever was holding it up, more anarchic. Its thinner film allowed a glimpse of the pale, deformed shadows of the imprisoned beings…

It was thus that he identified, among the emanations of the B'Tah-Gous, the form of Méè-Nê.

… The desire to free her became so intense that Amo crossed the wall! This root of the black stone, this root, he had to cut it! It was not just Méè-Nê whom he had to save, but all the people, all of Kobor Tigan't!

The recollection is unbearable. Everything is exploding in his head like the night exploded when he struck the foul root. Into smithereens, into whirlwinds, everything exploded and everything is exploding. Oh, he screamed, screamed and Opak pulled him out of there:

"Why are you screaming?"

He is screaming, screaming.

But now it is Eqin-Go who is leaning over him and shaking him. Here before him Méé-Nê is no longer talking. And next to her, Ata-Réè with her eyes agog.

Amo stops screaming. But it is too much—he falls over stiff, unconscious.

It takes a long time for his bosom brothers to bring him around. They carried him outside at the behest of the Storyteller who did not want to say anything more this evening.

Amo comes to his senses.

The fresh air calms him.

They all go back, close together, holding hands, without breathing a word, looking overwhelmed and nervous.

They turn their heads at every noise from the shadows. Each of them carries within him more or less of the terrible revelation.

Life is ruined.

CHAPTER XII

To and Ta returned.

At the end of their voluntary departure, they suddenly missed Kobor Tigan't and despite the charm of Kah'B'La, they had to go back.

Right away, Ta visited Abim, bravely, without even a Dongdwo egg to excuse herself. To her great surprise, she was very receptive. So much so that she could not help talking. To justify herself perhaps or by the naïve pride of being a pioneer of wonders, she recounted everything that she and To had seen. Everything except the meeting with the Old Man on the way up. She did not mention it not out of distrust but because during the whole time she was there in front of her mother, *she did not think of it!*

Never had the Very Huge been so attentive to, so interested in a story. She did not close her eyes, she leaned forward with her lips parted. Thus, without saying a word, she drank in her daughter's tale. Not once did she interrupt the account. Ta was astonished to see her mother's eyes fill with admiration for her, respect for the narrated events, emotion, too, and almost happiness.

When she had finished, Abim said, "Younger daughter, you have blessed audacity. Disobedience is your best quality. You alone, when you go against the rules, do well. I've seen this almost always. Something what inspires you escapes me. If your older sister didn't exist, I'd say you were the Queen, Ta! Because like true queens, you will, in time, find the cure for your race."

The young woman received the compliment like an overweight jewel—she teetered under the weight because, oh no, she had no desire to reign! But what was said last amazed her, so she asked, "The cure? What cure, O Very Huge?"

Abim deigned to reply, all smiles, "Yes, Daughter, I say that without knowing it, you found the cure! But Abim knew how to recognize it!"

Her smile grew bigger while she was already beginning the gesture of benevolence that would let her go free.

"Go, my Daughter, as thou wilt from now on, following your instincts since your will chances upon what is favorable. Whenever you come here will be fine. As you want. You will serve me better like this, see. Go and tell To that for the Dongdwo eggs the Very Huge says: whenever he wants."

Favors, irony, wisecracks? Ta did not prolong her bewilderment. Flattered and free, she ran off to see To.

And there, all the rest, the adventure, the mysteries, the compliments, the whole cascade of the unexpected, well, it was just all the rest. What was most important to them was being together in the world and that it, in the end, did not distract them too much from each other.

"So then! So then!" Abim mutters, continuing to go over Ta's story in her mind. She is deeply moved. She recognized the white Being that her own visions had been unable so far to apprehend completely.

"Well then, It exists! Well then!" And the laugh also exists. This laugh that she had heard inside herself for so long... And the glory of joy that she desired so strongly...

She feels like she can still hear her daughter saying, "Above all, my Mother, the first thing that made us see it as a creature with a lighter essence than ours was that *it was laughing*. But it was laughing very differently than us. Effortlessly. It was not joy closed in on itself that made the stomach vibrate and that was abruptly stifled without anything around paying attention to it, without anything answering it. No, no, quite the contrary! When this Being laughed, everything laughed with it. It was an open joy. The entire landscape took an interest in it. You could participate in this joy freely. It told you, through its laugh that had just found you: Come, come, all, and share with me the best! How can you resist such a thing? I'm telling you, Very Huge, we don't know this, this power, because I assure you, the light became brighter every time it laughed like that! Ooh'R responded to it with its strength... That's why I believe that in the mountains around it, there were those colorful rocks, precious, pure and shining. Solidified drops of laughter from Ooh'R, all its blessings!"

Well then, well then! Abim is more shaken up by the memory than by hearing the story. The more she dwells on it, the stronger her emotion. She rewards herself like this for her infinite patience and for her faith as well.

Let's see, how did her daughter describe the Being? She must remember the exact words... Ah, yes: "It was very white. It eyes? Like water. The direction of its gaze? We couldn't even guess. It was like it was seeing the entire landscape all at once without, like us, glancing here and there. It seemed to reflect everything, all together with all the details. Yes, just like water. On each hand the last finger was longer than the others. Except for this, it was almost exactly like us. But thinner... We thought it was a male because it had no breasts. And yet, it attracted love to it like women. However, sometimes, it was almost scary how beautiful it was, how powerful its attraction was... No bracelets, no chains, no weapons. Nothing on it but a white fabric, very light but still enough to cover it up. So that the rest of its body couldn't be seen. Plus, the white, golden-headed birds were flapping their wings so much around it that they hid it a little from our view..."

Abim's breathing accelerates. She is getting to the most important point.

She trickles it out slowly, with a kind of strange delicacy so as not to tarnish it and in order to understand it well.

"So, ITS VOICE... It was no longer a laugh but it was not words. And yet, a language. First like water, yes, hushed, trickling, steady, iridescent. Then as if it were growing feathers and it was a bird that knows it can fly, looks up, makes a little leap... And the wings spread, stretch out, rise to join the most intense light... That was its voice! And free, free to play in space! And so, playing and reflecting its joy of being able to join Ooh'R... Well, nothing could resist. The spirits of Kah'B'La, the scents of the plants, the stature of the trees, the vitality of the animals, the busyness of the insects and the gentle and burning of our heart, all this rose with the voice, was carried away all together beyond Ooh'R. After? We don't know. The lightning struck. The tingling air around us awakened life. We wanted to stay there forever with everything, not separated. To stay together in that great good thanks to the being... We slept deeply that night. The next morning the birds had disappeared. And the beautiful Being was lying there, bent over, unmoving in the hollow of stone, like in the beginning. We waited all day and then another. It didn't move. We dared to shout at it and roll little rocks down, but in vain. It never budged. We couldn't go down there, it was too steep. It's still down there..."

"It's still down there." That is when the Very Huge makes her decision: the Beautiful Being will replace Amo! This will be. She wants it. At once she applies all her fierce willpower to the task. It is through the Being that Kah'B'La must create the Great Child in the womb of the Queen! And Abim will recognize it! Right away!

The scheme lights up her eye. It is just a matter of arousing her daughter Opak by retelling her, with plenty of embellishments, the story of Ta.

She summons the Queen.

When Opak arrived, she recalled that it had been a very long time since her mother had called for her.

Amo waw with her, sulking. Worry weighed down his steps. He lagged behind and the Queen had to turn around to wait for him. She was not angry. She knew how much her male always hated to be near Abim's rooms. She herself got no pleasure from it. It was more like a chore. How hard it would be to hide the very thing you wanted to keep secret. Abim was certainly going to grumble about Amo…

When about to leave her favorite waiting at the door, as was customary, Opak looked at him and immediately had a thought, like a jolt, "that it was about keeping him."

A thought that astonished her. Why think such things? Nothing is threatening the Queen whose will trumps all! She smiled: she had not had her fill of Amo. Not at all. She promised herself new pleasures. The image of the T'Lo Dê came once again to mind.

Opak lingered, her hand on the door. T'Lo Dê was very useful.

With a bigger smile she turned to Amo to encourage him. The Very Huge might very well say what she wanted to hear…

And she went into her mother's.

Amo waited alone. Nobody came. Total silence. Along the long, stone corridor, on the rounded openings, regularly spaced, the shades were raised. The air from outside wafted in with distant sounds from the Noble City.

Amo barely looked around. He felt far from everything. Vaguely worried, uncomfortable, he suffered from his immobility like a prisoner.

The door of the Very Huge looked dangerous and sinister to him. The stone, which was glistening, reflected Amo's image like in a blurry dream. It was this, no doubt, that kept him from moving.

The Very Huge did more than necessary during the meeting, which she had good reason to be satisfied with.

Her daughter had barely entered the room when Abim got right to point, no wasting time. "This year," she said, "the Queen bears no fruit! Kobor Tigan't will have a bad season and the fogs will come quickly."

Hit hard by this straight shot, Opak had to sit down. "The Queen will bear no fruit!"

Yes, the Very Huge had said this. She was repeating it now. Without even bothering to alter her tone. The words themselves were enough. Opak sat breathless, her head lowered. The Very Huge always knew everything. Once again this was proven. Nothing ever escaped her. Floored, the Queen suddenly confessed whatever was wanted. She revealed what she naïvely thought she could hide just a moment before.

She had not conceived. She was not expecting a child. She did not understand. Why had Ooh'R stayed away when no fault in the ritual had been committed?

Abim burst out laughing. "Ooh'R did not stay away from the Queen. Ooh'R is like the Very Huge: he doesn't respect Amo. Ooh'R is tired of seeing the same man every year at the Festival of Fertilization. So far, Ooh'R like the Very Ancient has been patient, settled for not putting the Sign on the children who were begotten. And the Very Ancient has named none of them since there was nothing to name, nothing but kids from the womb and never the Great Child of the Reign. Your mother is weary, Opak. And Ooh'R is weary of your behavior as well. So, this time, he didn't even put a deflection of his light in you. You are empty, that's it. The Queen is empty like a common woman. Empty like a B'Tah-Gou!"

Out of fearful respect for her mother, Opak felt ashamed, wretched, almost cursed. An unknown sentiment in her that left her unresponsive, at the mercy of the Very Huge who, making no mistake about it, took her time and left out no details.

It was beautiful speech and Abim is bound to remember it for a long time as one of her proudest.

"What, my Daughter, you the Ooh'Rou of Kobor Tigan't, you're slipping behind your younger sister! What will become of the reign, what of the grandeur! And you owe everything to this realm. Always the same Man! And one who pleases neither Ooh'R nor me! You shouldn't make him exclusive. Have you ever seen Ooh'R shine on only one spot? He spreads himself over everything, he touches everything, his rays reach out tirelessly. And you who are like the female sun, you, Queen, you should be searching in all your men for the one who is most pleasing to Ooh'R, who will reflect Ooh'R in the seed.

"But instead of this, what do you do? You keep one man, a worthless man. You believe you're a great Ooh'Rou and you make the people believe it, but I who am ancient, I who have seen real power where the Queen was truly above all, surpassed all, and thanks to that the people were full of vigor and joy, I tell you this: I barely recognize my lineage in you! Can you imagine my disastrous grief? Your people are asleep on their feet because you don't spread among them the animating Force, the Royal Force that should settle, like the sun, on one Chosen Male and then another Chosen Male.

"You always give the people the same show and without knowing it they're bored. If you don't refresh them, they will never be refreshed. Bad Queen, the people are the reflection of your foolishness. They are old and sick and you don't care. You're heading down the same path as Ta. What she does, fortunately, has repercussions only on herself. She is not supposed to reign, so maybe she'll end up a B'Tah-Gou. She's not far from such an oddity, the sterile princess… Oh, what kind of children do I have, poor me! Ta is a scandal and Opak is a sin!"

Abim took a deep breath, glanced briefly to check the effects of her speech. Opak sat with her head in her hands, rocking back and forth and moaning.

The Very Ancient went on:

"Oh, my daughter, look at yourself! You didn't use to be like this. Before Amo, before this stubbornness, you were prettier, fatter, brawnier, your hair was longer, you ate more, you ran longer. You were truly the Queen, the one who was more and better than all the others in every-thing. You always needed more. It was good. And the people, like you, wanted more, did more. You showed them the way. And they followed you without, of course, being able to ever catch you because a Queen goes faster, farther and better! Just by seeing you the nobles were enrap-tured… Remember, you had powers almost equal to the heavens. When you shouted, the clouds moved. Indeed, I assure you, I saw them. And I was happy, o my daughter, because I could say that in a short time she will be moving the sun!" Abim leaned over confidentially. "Listen well, Opak, I who know, I used to tell myself that the Queen will experience the great trance that will herald the Great Child!"

Opak looked up, her tears had dried. Abim held her in her gaze, turning red, and whispered.

"Oh, my daughter, you think you're happy because you're ignorant of the true happiness of the Ooh'Rou. But I who know, I tell you, your life is a complete failure. You are unhappy, Opak! You're heading for ruin. I tell you, I who know: your womb will remain empty forever if you don't do your duty as Queen. And what will become of your people? And who will we put in your place?"

Opak jumped to her feet, pallid. "My mother, what are you saying?!"

"I'm saying that we will be there very soon and I don't balk before anything, even if you are my daughter."

Opak wept silently, standing there. Everything was confused in her mind and in her feelings. She was surprised to be telling herself that Amo, however, gave her joy and most exquisitely recently since he had become more somber since she had mingled with the T'Lo in their sexual frolics to goad him. She thought she was happy. And now her mother told her she was not. Now she revealed the existence of higher pleasures, those reserved for Queens... pleasures, delights, powers that she had never known!

Abim was easily reading her mind. She let just enough time pass and then she started putting balm on the wounds she had made.

"Opak, you are my big, fat daughter. After me, in all the realm, it is you who are the tallest. There is no other possible Queen but you. I'm not telling you to reject Amo. Keep him with the others in the Chamber of Men. What does it matter? Not at all. Play with him... and the others as much as you like. You are the Queen. But heed my advice. I want to help you. I know where there is the one who is the favorite of Ooh'R."

Opak looked at her now.

"Yes, I know where he is! I've been tracking him for a long time because I knew there was a mystery around you to keep you attached to only one man as if you knew that it was not in Kobor that the great Queen Opak would find the Man chosen by Ooh'R."

The Queen stammered, "I knew nothing at all."

Abim ignored this pathetic interruption that proved once again the state of internal spinelessness of her daughter. She pushed on, nevertheless, harder, to prove her point.

"Yes, Opak, you knew. Just like me. In my visions there was always a light I was going toward, always white birds and a laugh, my daughter, a laugh that would regenerate all of Kobor Tigan't. I saw, I knew. But I located nothing. Well, your crazy younger sister ran off with To and encountered the Man of Ooh'R. She knows nothing about it. But she told me about the light, the whiteness, the birds, the brilliant laugh that infused everything with joy. And I recognized the Being of my eternal visions. Go see, Opak! Go see on Kah'B'La! Go see, alone, without saying anything, without bringing anyone. And come back and tell me. Then I will tell you what must be done."

Opak followed her advice. With courage and wiles she did not know she had, she managed to leave that night without being noticed. She went to Kah'B'La. She saw there, without being seen by them, To and Ta. And she watched what they watched…

Amo searched for her all day long. The men of the Queen's chamber lamented and they, too, scattered every which way until an order from Abim reached them, carried by one of those old, stone-colored men who guard the threshold of her rooms. "The Queen's men will hold their peace and not panic the people. The Very Ancient makes it known that the Ooh'Rou is not in danger. They will await her return."

So, they stopped running around and went back to wait, bewildered, with the T'Lo whose golden eyes were filled with questions at their return.

But Amo was already too far for the order to reach him. He asked nothing of anyone, just ran hither and thither searching for a clue. He, too, finally took the road to Kah'B'La, remembering that To and Ta were going there often.

Halfway there he met Opak coming back, tired, obviously having made a long journey. She was merry. She was laughing. She did not want to speak. Amo followed her without understanding anything, his head in a whirl, his heart full of anguish. What was happening? He felt threatened without knowing where the blow was coming from.

In Kob'Ooh'R, instead of following him into the Chamber of Men, Opak hastened off innocently to see the Very Huge, from where she had come out transfigured in the morning.

Back in her own rooms, Opak gulped down some food and summoned all her men, all her T'Lo, Amo along with them, for a kind of feast where she surpassed herself in a gluttony of all the senses.

Mysteriously, the news of the feast spread from the highest to the lowest of the five cities. The people came out and visited each other. A sparkling joy electrified the air. They were saying, "The Queen knows, the Queen has seen that this year the Great Child will come."

Up above all, in the center of all, alone, concentrated, Abim saw everything and smiled gravely while telling herself that the people were the people, easily governed, easy to exploit and that she, Abim, was still exercising power through her daughter Opak.

She knew very well that Amo could not put up with this semi-destruction for long. To overthrow him for good, it was shrewder to treat him as insignificant. This would avoid turning him into a hero in the eyes of others. For, had she openly overthrown him, rejected him, tossed him aside, he would have rebelled with that mighty force that she hated and that was truly royal—this she knew! But she would rather die, explode, vanish forever before admitting it!

She would wear Amo down, therefore, day after day, until the Beautiful Being was in Kob'Ooh'R, mated with the Queen.

Opak, however, after she got over the initial astonishment at what she had seen on the mountain, could not decide to act right away. Countless, contradictory feelings were stirring in her, which secretly put Abim into a rage, as she was impatient to see her projects come to fruition.

The fear of the unknown paralyzed Opak. What she was supposed to do, no Ooh'Rou had ever done before.

However, what she had seen of the Beautiful Being haunted her. She craved, violently, because it was her full power as Queen to possess this Being, to get from it the Gift of Ooh'R, to know the Great Trance, to have powers, and in the end to be the Ooh'Rou of Kobor Tigan't.

But Amo in all this? She was keeping him, plain and simple… And yet, when she got to this point in her thoughts, she felt it was not simple, that a danger lurked, a tragedy was hiding there. She rejected this eventuality.

Waffling back and forth like this, still without deciding what to do, she went through a period of torments that left their mark in different ways. She went from excitement to total dejection. She wanted all her men at the same time and rejected them all together, tolerating only Amo whose presence seemed always to calm her.

Then, abruptly, she sent him away, shut herself in with her T'Lo. They appeared to console her. Their contact gave her that kind of drugged numbness that they got from their weird magnetism. She slept heavily, therefore, and stayed like this for hours on end, in a daze, half asleep, eating non-stop, but half-heartedly.

She always ended up crying, unable to resolve her problems, which had a knack for throwing the T'Lo into despair. Her men were in a panic, anxious to save the Queen and the precious T'Lo. No one knew what to do. They ran all over the place in total chaos.

This ended in shouts of rage from Opak who was exasperated by all the commotion and sat up, woke up, terrifying, unapproachable.

Then, she called for her children, all her children. They brought them to her. She separated out the males to keep only the females. And she spent hours handling them, turning them in every direction to try to see if maybe the Sign was not on one of them.

But as her mother alone knew the nature of this Sign, poor Opak ended up, obviously, with nothing. Disappointed, furious, she abused her children. In time, Amo dragged them away from her, giving them back to the women in charge of their care.

Opak went back at night to Kah'B'La.

Amo did not dare follow her. Like the first time he went halfway and waited there, alone, for her to come back. He sat on a big rock at the foot of the Holy Mountain, helpless, not knowing what to think. His Queen's distress upset him. How could he relieve it?

Several times he saw To and Ta, magnificent and free, who apparently, since subject to no constraints, were sauntering back to Kobor only to go as they pleased on other pleasant outings. Amo hid from him.

He envied them. He wanted to be the only male of the Ooh'Rou! And yet, when he thought about it, he knew that Opak was not enough for his inner quest, he knew that he was thirsting for some other possession, for some other conquest than this dangerous female body.

What did he really have at the end of the ecstasy? That was what he wanted to get! He looked desperately at the sun, to burn his eyes out... There, beyond this pulse of fire, there was a poignant mystery, an echo of himself, an echo of Amo!

Then, Opak came back. He joined her now, still in his same spot. She was expecting him. It was almost a habit. They made their way back together. She wanted to confide in him everything that she had seen, but she could do nothing of the kind. And he felt this, found her more beautiful, more desirable. And even more inaccessible the secret desire glimpsed deep down inside...

During one of his solitary waits on the big rock, Amo happened to be yanked out of his gloomy reverie by the touch of a hand on his shoulder. Not very clear-headed, a little muddled, he raised his head and saw above him the face of an old man leaning over, backlit by the sun, whose features he could not distinguish, haloed by the white light of a mane of curly hair. Colorful birds were fluttering and chirping all around him. There was an iridescent fog in the air, a strange scent, an exquisite mildness.

"Be strong, Amo! Think of the sun, think of the light of Ooh'R... Love the sun, Amo!"

Before he could say anything, already distant from him by his supple silhouette, the old man disappeared down a path through the shadowy leaves. Amo ran after him, but too late. There was nothing there except the rustling of the grass that was not even trampled and no path. Who could have passed by here?

He did not know whether he had dreamed or not. Nevertheless, he guarded the sweet image in his heart. And since that day, he felt less troubled. Or rather, troubled in a different way. Something opened inside him. It was a wound, of course, but he had acquired a growth of consciousness that he gradually became aware of.

He told nobody about this incident.

Queen Opak started talking that night in her sleep. Amo listened, picked up snippets. He was able to question the dreamer in a whisper without waking her up. He got more muttering that he patiently pieced together.

Finally, he understood. Opak wanted another man, an inaccessible stranger, a man of another race, in white robes, who lived on the other side of Kah'B'La, who handled lightning, seemed to be a giant bird, laughed a laugh that brought Ooh'R out from the clouds…

Amo promised himself that he would save Opak and kill his rival.

When the Queen finally made the decision desired by Abim to capture the stranger, Amo was ready and was not surprised.

CHAPTER XIII

The expedition is underway to Kah'B'La.

It includes Opak, richly outfitted; Ta followed by To, both agitated by the turn of events that is going to endanger the Beautiful Being; there is Amo, very somber, with Eqin-Go, his bosom brother, worried too; there is also T'La-Voh, who does not know what to think; and then other of the better males.

The Queen is in no hurry, speaks little. She is hungry, so she eats often, sitting down and everyone does the same. Then they set off again.

They each walk casually, wandering off here and there but never going too far thanks to that group instinct that unites them all more strongly on this unusual voyage.

Each of them is lost in thought. The bizarre circumstances make them uneasy: an expedition to Kah'B'La with the Ooh'Rou Opak—this has never happened.

Oh, they were first very happy except for Amo, To and Ta, of course. But the others only saw the glorious presence of the Queen, her beauty, her jewels, all the dazzle gleaming on a brisk morning when the sun struggled to pierce the bad fog that had been covering Kobor Tigan't for a while.

In the whirlwind of action, the shouting and preparations, all the people had accompanied them until they left Kob'Lâm.

But now the little group is alone, the excitement of the departure has died off. The adventure is taking a melancholic turn. The confused men feel far from their kingdom. The isolation of nature weighs on them. Why is the Queen staying silent? Why is Amo's brow furrowed? He does not eat at the breaks, just waits, standing up, a little off to the side.

The travelers see before them the mass of Kah'B'La still a long way off. Behind them the fog has closed in around Kobor. In front of them low clouds stubbornly veil the mountain. They are not so favorable omens for this bizarre undertaking that entails leaving home to capture an Unknown Being…

The men sneak questioning glances at one another. When the Queen is not looking, they nudge each other. Isn't it a little foolhardy to attempt such things when already (not for long, true) the happy season after the Fertilization of the Queen is spoiled? Evil winds have blown through

Kobor. The Ananou were agitated, inexplicably. The B'Tah-Gous tell much more harrowing stories than usual. There were, that night, noises and odors as if coming from the Grand Va-Hôh. Isn't such a dark uprising of adverse forces a warning?

They do not know. They are afraid. They are pessimists. But they keep on, heads lowered. They had just passed by and paid tribute to the R'Lil, the black and shiny mountains they loved so much. They drew a little comfort from them because the sun Ooh'R fell upon them right at that moment. But alas, for only a short while. Just a little sign of encouragement. Then the clouds closed in again.

They climb the mountain through the heaps of fallen rocks, the natural pathways.

To and Ta tell themselves—and hope—that maybe the Beautiful Stranger will not be there, that maybe they will not be able to capture him, that maybe they themselves will manage to warn him, to make him understand that he has to flee...

The princess who happens to be by Amo cannot help noticing his worried face. She is suddenly struck by the extent of the trouble and grief that is gnawing away at the handsome redhead. And To, too, has noticed it. Both of them understand that Amo loves the Queen. Who knows if he dreams of being like them, alone with Opak, the only man? Alarmed, they trace his stare to Queen Opak, heavy, tall, leading the group, a little faster now, with the sun on her face because they have come out of the low clouds above which is only clear sky and the presence of Ooh'R directly overhead! Opak, beautiful Opak, with her chains clinking on her chest at every step. She keeps her hands on the weapons in her belt. Her hair is tied up so as not to get in the way during a possible battle. She breathes noisily, her nostrils flaring. Her lips are drawn back, baring her teeth, in a kind of smile and far from being tired, as the slope gets steeper and the paths more difficult, she goes faster, clearly impatient to reach her goal.

Amo reflects all this like an echo. He parts his lips, breathes harder, speeds his pace. He is thinking, however, very deeply: "Yes, I will surprise them all by killing the Beautiful Being whom they want to capture without hurting it in the least."

What expression passes over his face then? To and Ta are on either side of him, anxious but friendly, trying to understand and to help.

To touches his arm gently. Ta does the same, holding his hand. All three of them look at one another in turn, understanding, feeling close and brotherly. Amo stares into their clear eyes with astonishment. Who are these two, really? Full of freshness and grace? What marvelous mystery surrounds them? It is such a sudden and total revelation that Amo is enlightened. He feels, he knows that he, too, like them, aspires to freely form this double being of a Couple. He feels, he knows that To and Ta are one, single Double-Being. Yes, they possess a treasure whose power protects them.

Amo smiles at them enthusiastically and receives two confident smiles back, bursting with comforting love, so full of respect for life that in contrast his heart suddenly sinks: He, Amo, who loves and respects life, he wants to kill, he is going to kill! He must...

They have fallen back. Above them they see Eqin-Go climbing over a barricade and pointing the way for them to follow quickly. They acknowledge. Reassured, Eqin-Go disappears behind the rocks. They hear again, a little muffled by the distance, the clinking of the group.

To and Ta help each other to climb. Amo follows them. While he struggles to scramble over the loose rocks, one of them slips out under his foot, goes rolling and bouncing off the path to the right through the foliage. He watches it. It goes far. It is deep. He leans over... What sudden calm! How nice it is! What a sweet smell he breathes in! How good life is, so gentle deep down in his big body! But what is he seeing? At the bottom, a kind of narrow, rounded valley, a view of meadows. The sun casting pools of gold on it. And there, at the foot of a tree is sitting the old, white-haired man in his flowing robe. Colorful birds are fluttering around him, perching on his head, on his shoulders, clinging to his beard, nesting in his folds. The old man keeps his head down. Everything about him bespeaks solemnity, meditation.

Amo is startled. And now To is coming back. He leans over next to him. And whispers, "I know him."

Amo replies, "Me too.

It vibrates between them like a pact. Why? They do not know. But that is the way it is. There they are, bonded.

Ta had turned around and come hurrying back. She slips and falls. The two men run up to her. It's nothing. She laughs, already on her feet. They whisper to her. "The old man..." She understands, wants to see him, too. So, they all lean over together.

Down below the little valley is empty. The sun, which had been clouded over, sinks into the shadows.

They look at one another. Yes, the same mystery unites them. It must not be shown to the others. Something caressing floats over their group. A colorful bird swoops down and drops the small fruit it was holding in its beak. Ta picks it up.

Her eyes open wide and she murmurs, "What will the Old Man say if we bring back the Beautiful Being to Kobor Tigan't?"

Who could answer that? Amo least of all since he was thinking, while shuddering, "What will the Old Man say if I kill the Beautiful Being?"

Without a sound the troop has arrived on the shelf where they can see the Other Side of Kah'B'La. The men, who are breaking this taboo for the first time, shiver. The stories of the B'Tah-Gous surge up in their memories. Amo is not the last to be troubled. He feels like he can hear the deep voice of Méè-Nê in the middle of his chest. But curiosity wins him over.

The excitement of the event gets the better of all of them. They are thinking of nothing but fulfilling their mission. Amo is determined. He is tense, on his toes. He will seize the right moment to do what he promised…

Silently the trap is laid on the shelf. It is a big net with weights around the edges that they will throw over their prey from their higher vantage point. Everything is ready. They are waiting. Opak is trembling on her shanks now like an exhausted beast.

There is the Stranger down below who is getting up from his rocky cradle! The sight of him strikes everyone with astonishment, then with admiration. Can there exist a Being with so much grace, lightness and beauty? He is a cloud, a ray!

"The Son of Ooh'R!" Eqin-Go mutters in ecstasy.

Amo also looks. His sight is blurred by so much beauty. He forgets where he is. He feels dizzy. His heart sinks. But still, he clenches his fist on his weapon. Come now, he wants to stay focused! So, this is the one who caused such a stir in Opak? A Being so essentially different from her—thin, long, transparent it seems… But then, really, what is it? A man or a woman? "Ambiguous like the T'Lo," Amo grumbles. He stays quiet, upset with himself for this thought that he "knows" is unfair.

They get ready for action. They push the net to the edge, being careful not to cause a little rockslide of pebbles.

To and Ta, at this final moment, look at each other. "No, no, they don't want this!" Therefore, To, on impulse, breaks the order of silence. He shouts a cry of alarm for the Beautiful Being. The Stranger raises his head, sees them.

The group is thrown into confusion. No one dreams of retreating. They are on the edge, baffled by the incident and even more enthralled by the exquisite face turned towards them.

To shouts again, waving his arms, "Get out of here! Leave!"

Huge surprise for Opak who looks daggers at him. But the stranger does not move, not even concerned, but filled with curiosity about them. With amused interest he smiles, is going to laugh very soon... What about them is so funny to him?

It is obvious that he does not understand why To is shouting so vehemently. Maybe he thinks he is just calling out to him? Undecided, he sways, seems hesitant to join them. Nonetheless, he climbs up a little way towards the group that does nothing but stare gaping at him.

His eyes light upon Opak, scrutinize her. Then he stops, frowning with disapproval, almost with disgust. And straightaway he laughs, a high-pitched laugh like a child, throwing back his head. Between his outbursts of amusement, he points a finger at Opak as if he cannot believe his eyes. Offended, she turns red. All her men look stupidly at her without really understanding. But are they about to start laughing as well? This is too much! By an embittered, feminine reflex, almost without realizing it, she gives the sign to attack.

Those holding the net obey. The trap is sprung. It falls over the Beautiful Being who collapses in the middle of the mesh. Stunned by the weight, he does not move.

Opak turns pale, bites her lip. It all happened so fast... To and Ta are frozen to the spot. Amo, pale and cold now, waits for what comes next. He feels the "moment" approaching.

Meanwhile, as was decided beforehand, the nimble men shimmy down the ropes attached to the net. Down below, they tighten the net, keeping their prey from moving but without hurting him.

The Beautiful Being wakes up when the net starts rising. He struggles. He lets loose loud, shrill cries.

From deep in the clouds, the white birds rush out and others, too, all the birds of the sky from every direction. The rocky shelf is darkened by them. Furious, they attack with their beaks and claws. There is total confusion. The men defend themselves by swinging their weapons. The birds are hit. A rain of blood among whirlwinds of feathers.

Half standing under the weight of the net, the Stranger looks horrified. Outrage turns his eyes pale. His voice rises again, louder than the tumult. This is no simple cry. It is a dolorous order, strangely intoned, that soars off, spreads out, stirs up echoes. The birds surge back up in a kind of spiral. They are quiet. The sky suddenly blackens. The white cloud of birds disappears. The sun becomes pallid and dull—a metal disk that emits no rays. Everything turns gray. Lightning flashes. Torrential rain pours down.

To figures this is the right time to free the Beautiful Being. He slashes the net. The Stranger leaps toward the edge of the shelf. Is he going to jump and crash down below? Or is he going to fly away?

But Amo is ready, gets close to him, weapon raised. He can, he is going to slay him... But inexplicably, while the other dives pell-mell into the abyss, he holds him back with an iron grip. For a second, he holds the wondrous body at arm's length, feels the lightness and breathes in the aroma despite himself. The thin, white fabric of the robe, an unknown material, crumples in his fist and he sees up close, staring at him without fear but wild and beautiful, the face with the huge eyes that do not reproach but are astonished, just astonished, to no end, at such inexplicable violence.

Amo pulls the Beautiful Being back onto solid land, wondering why he was doing it. He loosens his grip. The Stranger stands before him, an irreal apparition, mute, motionless, luminous by purity. All of a sudden, thunder cracks and lightning strikes so close that Amo is blinded. The shelf is split. He staggers, hands on his head, and feels himself disappearing in the dark...

He comes around with a feeling of total strangeness. Feathers, clouds, veils or rather strands of long hair or a white beard have been floating around him. This finally fades away and he witnesses the battle between Opak and the Stranger.

He cannot intervene. His limbs refuse to obey. He just watches, lifting his neck. The clouds are cleared, the sun glares, the light makes everything sharp-edged. But still it is raining, sheets of rain, shiny water, sparkling like silver. The pitiful corpses of the birds litter the ground. There are injured men who huddle together in a confused group in an angle of rock.

The shelf is a quagmire in the middle of which the Queen is battling the unknown. They are not even shouting at each other. A bizarre silence. The rain steams when it touches their heated bodies. They both move (and this seems absurd) like two ghosts in white vapor. The large, wet sleeves of the Stranger flap noisily like wings. He really does look like a furious bird. He shoots a fiery glance at his adversary. His slender teeth look ready to bite.

They hear the heavy pounding of Opak. She is clasping him, forcing herself to beat him without hurting him. But he has more hidden strength than she could have imagined. With a sharp blow, completely unexpected from him, he breaks free and throws her to her knees, so swiftly and so roughly that she stays there, dazed, her head hanging down. He is about to flee. To and Ta are filled with a warm feeling.

But Amo can finally jump in, grab him around the waist to hold him back. Facing off, they stare at each other. They meet again. No, there is no hatred. The fight is absurd! What subtle sweetness do they share... The Stranger has lost all the fury he had shown against Opak. Amo sees this. He realizes also, very clearly, that the Stranger does not love, will never love the Queen. It is so suddenly obvious that he is almost content, he almost forgets the reason they are holding each other.

Oh, the vast, pale pupils, so full of astonishment and reproach, whose penetrating gaze drills deep into the heart. They bear witness to the immense foolishness of fighting like this. Why, why? It is a silent discussion. The Stranger does not budge. He does not try to break free. He accepts it with a kind of friendliness. His breath slows... And for Amo, it is exactly as if he were holding in his arms a woman of divine essence...

But the pale pupils quiver, his eyes drop. Amo sees the Stranger is wounded. His eyes close after a sort of smile surfaces from the depths, which is meant for the one holding him. He gasps, then passes out.

Once again Amo has every opportunity to kill him. He does not even think about it! He becomes slowly aware of his surroundings. There is a commotion of dismay. "Is the Beautiful Being dead?"

Opak, still on her knees, just starts snorting and shaking her head. "What's the meaning of all this?" Amo is fully aware now and remembers. A sudden surge turns him red as the other slips gently down to his feet. A black veil in his head, a rumbling, a startled reflex: Amo has brandished his weapon!

With a heart-rending cry, To pounces on him, knocks down his weapon. Ta is there, too. And as if this were not enough, she punches him with her young fists. She is weeping. To repeats, "No, Amo, leave him be, leave him be! Oh, let him go!"

All is as before. Amo is once again the Queen's handsome man. He has recovered his dignity, put away his weapon, helped Opak to her feet and gathered everyone together.

It is decided: he will bring the Beautiful Being back to Kobor.

They make a litter to carry him. It is very sad. The wounded lies there without moving. Opak helps them carry him. She is crying. She caresses him, laments, fears that he is dead.

The return was hard. Amo was quiet. To and Ta held each other and walked at a desolate pace without saying a word either. The men grumbled.

Opak insulted the bearers who stumbled, then ended up hitting them for every blunder that put the wounded at risk. A hundred times they thought they would break their necks on the craggy paths, in the torrents of rain and gusts of wind. It was so dark that they got lost several times. Uprooted trees barred their way.

The troop turned around, went back to find other passes, the ones they had taken to get there were turned into raging rivers or blocked by fallen rubble. They lost hope of ever getting back.

Nevertheless, they made it to Kobor. Like castaways, muddy, in rags, with a dying man, after a trip that no one talked about.

Were all the evil spells of the Grand Va-Hôh focused on the City? Never had they seen such desolation! What fate had Kobor Tigan't been stricken with?

This rain that followed the Queen on her return plagued the city ceaselessly. Ooh'R only showed himself in the far distance, only on Kah'B'La. He lit only the summit for a brief moment at dawn before disappearing behind the heavy clouds.

It is raining in Kobor Tigan't.

The springtime has withered on the stalk. The flowers have fallen. They rot pretty much everywhere in all the hollows of Kob'Vâm, once so pleasant. The grassy terraces turn to manure. They cover the green pool as well as the everlasting crucible of Kob'Râm, under threat of going cold and for the bellows that the maintenance teams take turns on.

The stale stench of swampland festers. Here and there bactrians hop about after rushing in by the legion. Water snakes slither by. It is, indeed, the breath of Grand Va-Hôh that blows through.

Alas, alas! They sigh and cry. For, they have seen the young leaves, barely out of bud, turn yellow and curl up like in an early autumn. For, the unopened blooms get bloated before drooping in full decay. The irrigation pools overflow. The upper waterfall is a cataract whose current sweeps along rubble, rocks and branches.

From the top to the bottom of the five cities, muddy water streams down from one terrace to another. All the stairs turn into spillways. At times the growing storm pushes this water in waves against the closed-up houses, spraying water everywhere. It is an assault come from Grand Va-Hôh! People shut themselves in at home. They sleep a lot. They stoke big fires on which they keep throwing perfumed powders. Oh, the detestable rumblings of Grand Va-Hôh that get confused with the howling winds. People speak in whispers. They pull over their heads the headdress for a long wait whose brims shadow their eyes. They stay squatting, huddled together…

For the first few days they had tried to be hopeful. They had figured that this dismay of nature was due to the Queen not leaving her rooms where they had carried the wounded stranger. And they had waited for an improvement that was a longer and longer time coming.

Great was their bafflement! The nobles, seeing nothing coming out, had stopped waiting in front of the palace. Opak did not show herself. Amo would run by, mute and rude. To and Ta had left for who knows where. No influence seemed to be emanating from Abim's secret center. They also knew nothing about the Very Huge. Neither what she was thinking nor what she was doing. She was there, that was all. She, too, was waiting.

All life, therefore, was on hold for the fate of the Stranger. About him they knew nothing more than they did on his dreadful arrival. No information filtered out. They were left to their guesses. The little they had seen of him, lying on the litter under his white robe stained with mud and blood, had raised awe and wonder and respect, and for Opak and her men disapproval because they did not understand why she had attacked the Beautiful Being when it surely would have been enough just to say, "Come to Kobor Tigan't!"

The simplistic and meek logic of the people was, therefore, shocked and everyone eagerly wanted the stranger to survive his injuries. Even just to satisfy their all-consuming curiosity.

Oh, yes, they were yearning to see him, to hear him, to understand him! They were burning up inside. This was all that mattered!

But the excitement faded quickly in the downpour. Other concerns, more serious, replaced it. Supplies became scarce. They had to call upon the winter reserves in the cellars and silos of Kob'Lâm when they were craving fresh food. The hunters brought back little game that rotted fast. Many of them got lost in the wet fog amasses deep in the valleys. They fell into water holes or were swept away by torrents. Many who made it back got sick and could not go back out again for a long time. The others were loath to leave.

Many days went by like this without any change in sight. Weariness struck everyone down.

Opak stayed in the wounded's room. Her men were almost always alone, bored, sleeping, dreaming, eating.

All the T'Lo were on pins and needles since they had brought in the stranger and they felt him there, in the room next door. At the exact moment of his arrival they were gathered together in a corner of the Chamber of Men. Afterward, they performed a kind of vigil, night and day, their golden eyes staring in the direction where he lay, watching him, no doubt, through the walls with their peculiar gift. They really looked overwhelmed by the events and straining with great effort to understand. The out-of-the-ordinary almost made them ill.

Sometimes, under the impotent pressure to understand, a kind of distress, almost panic, showed in their faces. They gave the impression of being ready to jump, to commit some crazy act. But, no, nothing happened. They kept staring straight ahead.

In the pit, their primitive brothers, the Ananou, had also reacted to the stranger's arrival, clapping their hands continually all through the first night.

One morning, To came out worried. Amo had called him. They conversed briefly. Then, the young man bolted off with the leather satchel of the egg hunters. Ta stayed behind. They saw her sitting in the window of the Chamber of Men, waiting. She did not leave her post until she ran out in the rain to meet To on his return.

The harvest of eggs was meant for the royal apartments. But, no, it was not for the Very Huge. The people noticed this and were greatly surprised. And then to see the young hunter go back out almost right away!

He shuttled back and forth regular much to Ta's displeasure since he took their life with him.

The people supposed that they were trying to nourish the wounded. Maybe he refused normal food and, in this case, to keep him from dying, they were forced to give him royal delicacies—the Dongdwo eggs?

The rain stopped, replaced by a thick, depressing, noxious fog. It enshrouded all of Kobor Tigan't.

They had lost the strength to even wonder how long the situation would last. They decided to sleep as much as possible.

But there was something else unexpected. Amo, To and Ta, first of all, noticed that all the birds had deserted Kobor. Nary a one remained. Even the surrounding countryside was empty. Even in the outside pit at the gate of Kob'Lâm, "those ones", the contemptible but useful scavengers had disappeared.

This inexplicable desertion of the winged species seemed to everyone to be a bad omen.

Moreover, the frogs and toads multiplied at an alarming rate. Soon they were teeming, filling the cellars where they ruined the reserves and boldly invading the houses. Every night the sleepers were startled awake on feeling the cold, wet bellies on their faces before they hopped away silently.

They had to exterminate them en masse. It was disgusting work. The sweet stench of the carnage seemed to saturate the fog permanently. So, they burned more scents on the big fires until the intoxication threw them into a kind of drunken binge.

CHAPTER XIV

Opak was living through a drama. Despite all her care, the Stranger was not getting better. His wound had closed up but he remained sunk in this sad lethargy, without complaining, panting softly like a baby bird. His arms lay motionless at his sides. His eyes opened sometimes but focused on nothing. He was silently delirious.

Unable to feed himself and refusing anything brought to his lips except for a little water, he was visibly wasting away, paler, almost luminously white in the half-light. His hair was also losing color—was it from lack of sunlight—its gold turning to silver, the curls losing their shine, sticking out like the feathers of a sick bird. He seemed to have many points in common with these creatures…

The Queen had surrounded him with the richest luxury. His white rags thrown out, he was dressed in a sumptuous velvet robe made of different colored stripes. He lay on a bed of furs under a multicolored canopy. Oily fragrances burned in the room lined with heavy skins.

On the first day, he had been fully conscious. Without saying a word, he watched everything with a scornful eye. Over and over again he had refused whatever they offered despite the regretful moans of Opak who knew not what to do and who, mindful that she had wounded him, dared not touch him anymore lest she hurt him more. Furthermore, he glared at her in anger. And she saw it! She ended up sitting in a dark corner, letting Amo come and go noiselessly, more capable than she since he managed to get the wounded to drink his first sip of water.

Then, as evening fell, the fever came and the Beautiful Being fell unconscious. All night long, he looked rattled by great, blind anger. His eyes were dilated, staring belligerently at the bright fabrics, trying to tear off his robe only to fall off the bed. He cursed everything around him, screaming in Opak's face in an unknown language, such maddened rants that she backed away, panting while big tears skipped down her cheeks reddened with shame.

She took no comfort for having put him in this state. And as time passed, her grief grew deeper. How could she do such a thing? Did the Very Huge really have to push her to edge? Yes, but what about the Favor of Ooh'R? The Trance of the Ooh'Rou?

Towards dawn the Stranger quieted down. He still rolled his head from side to side like someone stricken with despair, but then the drowsiness came and persisted.

Opak did not leave his bedside except for the vital calls of nature: to eat and to mate because the emotions escalated her needs and basically, she needed to feel better by appeasing her two physical appetites. But nothing else because she had almost renounced sleep.

With Amo, therefore, or other men, as sad as herself, she had her hasty pleasure just like she ate in a hurry without paying attention to anything, eager to return to the wounded.

There, she resumed her gloomy vigil. But she did not sit still; she paced around the room. She knocked objects to the floor and the patient groaned a little more. She stopped, then, terrified. Was he about to die? He calmed down. After a while she forgot about her clumsiness and went back to plodding more heavily, tormented by a single thought: "Was he, the Beautiful Being, oh, was it going to die?" Her city and her realm were nothing but fumes to her. Her mother? She forgot all about her. Her children? It was as if she did not have any. Amo? "A piece of furniture!"

Only one feeling kept her going: "The Beautiful Being, when oh when would he be able to love her?!"

Everything about him amazed her, ravished her, threw her into a world of confused notions that gave her a headache.

She gaped in admiration when she uncovered him to admire his body. But she wept right after on seeing how much weight he had lost. Oh, was he dead? She had to touch him to be sure he was still alive, still there. She saw him flinch at her touch, pull back from her, scoot over to the far side of the bed, while still unconscious. For her it turned into a form of torture.

He was like a door closed on its treasures and she did not know the secret to open it. Where was this secret? What did she have to do to open it? Puzzled, she touched the Beautiful Being's hands, those elongated fifth fingers, what did they mean, what were they for?

Most often, however, tired of being alone and fearing to make some irreparable mistake, she kept Amo by her side for her convenience.

Obedient, diligent, silent, he was the safe link with the outside. He did his work well. For example, the Dongdwo eggs were his idea. Plus, his presence had a calming effect on the wounded. But except for this, for her he was a soulless body, a reliable tool that she was using. Clearly, Opak had forgotten that he was her favorite for a good long while, the

Queen's Man! And he, in his personal downfall, did nothing to refresh her memory.

He obeyed scrupulously without the slightest deviation. By doing so, he found a bitter relief. His face was frozen. He looked like there was no sentiment or sensation in him, just the calm of inner emptiness, contrary to the obvious anguish of the Queen, tormented by her impotent love for the Beautiful Being.

And Opak kept pacing the confined space. She wanted to hold onto the stranger but he was slipping through her fingers like water. Do something! But what? Wouldn't the slightest action on her part push him further away? So, she stopped moving, just like that, abruptly, in the middle of the room. She dropped to the floor. But doing nothing, not knowing how to prevent it, wouldn't the stranger's life slip away even faster? Over and over again, Opak did not hear him breathing and lunged at him. He was just sleeping, a little more calmly. But her hapless action disturbed him and he started moaning again and burning up.

She really had no idea what to do, she did not know, she wept, then foamed at the mouth.

There were, however, moments of calm when she did not make too many blunders. She stood leaning over him, stock still, unable to take her eyes off so much beauty, unable to understand the sense of this beauty, unable to understand the relentless sleep and the failure to eat.

This last detail was what really tore her apart. Not eating! That threw her into an abyss of confusion. For her it was a monstrous refusal, aberrant, unnatural, a sin! Not eating! She was struck with pity, sorrow, then right away with rage at not knowing what to do to break through to him.

Not eating! Was there some kind of strange ploy in this, some dark vengeance? The Beautiful Being was thinking behind his closed eyelids. Yes, that was it: he was thinking! Right, you cannot stay sleeping like this all the time! He was not eating to make his escape by dying! This wonder was escaping!

Opak was sweating. No, she could not let him die and escape like this. She could not let him foil her plans like this! So, she got feverishly busy to make him eat at any cost.

But she proved to be as bumbling as always in her marvelous intentions. She did not realize in time that by holding him in her arms she was brutalizing the weakened body. She leaned his head against her chest, forcing meat into his mouth along with the Dongdwo eggs that she crushed with her fingers to make them easier to swallow.

He groaned, struggled, half-suffocated by her embrace. Sometimes, however, in spite of everything, a mouthful went down. He opened his eyes in horror, saw Opak and screamed. But he held him, even though he tried to break free. And she started again to part his lips, to present a cup full of blood that he managed to refuse by spilling it.

Seeing himself like this, covered in blood, dirty and stained, he was utterly sickened and sagged in her arms, white and senseless. She gaped in fright as this outcome. When he came to, she started again! Again and again, torturing him without realizing it.

When To and Ta visited the sick stranger, they protested in vain. They tried to get across that he was more urgently in need of peace, that it was imperative to not touch him and that, obviously, the Dongdwo eggs were not to his liking.

Opak turned red with fury, "The stranger is mine!"

Ta replied as curtly, "The stranger is free and only freedom will bring him back to life. By acting like this the Queen is killing him and no doubt will finish him off very soon."

They parted very angry and the young couple had to space out their visits because every one of their appearances unleashed this screeching bitterness from the Queen. To and Ta were convinced that the Beautiful Being would not survive. To this grief was added their remorse at having participated in his capture. If he were less weak, maybe they could have helped him to escape?

Amo was also witness to these fruitless attempts. He grew more and more irritated at Opak's relentlessness, which snapped him out of his mental torpor. Surely, he, too, was ignorant of the reason for this weird refusal of nourishment since he himself had verified the quality of the food. In the end he figured that the Queen was banging her head against the wall instead of trying to go around it.

There had been high hopes of nourishing the Beautiful Being with the Dongdwo eggs. But To and Ta were right: they were no more to his liking than anything else. What did the stranger eat?

Amo went out into the countryside. He walked in the vain hope of pulling himself out of this slump. Too many questions scampered around his skull. Impervious to the fog, he paid no attention to where he was going.

Another unknown that remained unanswered pestered him: why did the birds all leave Kobor Tigan't?

On his stroll, he clearly felt, like all his race, the moment he passed the magnetic borders of the "aura" of the city. By the usual inner reflex, he noted this but gave it no mind.

It was a little later that he heard the sound of wings, a bird flying by, tweeting overhead, but invisible in the fog. Shaken up, he stopped to listen. In a short while there were others that were all headed in the same direction, away from Kobor.

Amo set off again guided by the sound of the birds. He noticed that it was leading him to the foot of Kah'B'La, to a place where the fog was thinning.

Now he heard the birds singing, a huge flock, it seemed, of beating wings, fluttering feathers, a whole merry hullabaloo, intense activity concentrated there, at that point of convergence where the birds gathered!

Suddenly, at this same place, the fog was rent asunder, a curtain ripped open. The birds whirled over Amo who had come to the entrance of a narrow gully, a kind of rocky gorge that he entered in stride without a second thought. The birds dove in as well, with innumerable cries of impatience, their wings and beaks and feet grazing him. He was stunned, beyond himself because it was like an outpouring of joy!

Very narrow at first, almost dark between the steep walls, a kind of crack opened in the substance of the mountain, the path abruptly widened, lit up. And like at the end of a long journey, Amo came out in a place that was truly Elsewhere: a lake enclosed in a vast crater where all the birds who had left the city were taking refuge. They perched on the shelves, in the crevices, settled in the sand on the shore, hunted, fished, hopped around, flew back and forth in all directions, in joyful action that was all their own.

Amo was in their home, in the birds' home!

He saw that the fog languished again, not far away, in dense masses that gradually lifted.

He sat at the edge of the water and saw how pure it was. He absent-mindedly contemplated his own reflection and dipped his hand in, from time to time, to stir it up and watch it resettle. He was a little dazed and felt powerless. But it was a pleasant feeling, this painless frailty. The squawking of the winged creatures blurred his thoughts, wiped them clean… He just listened, breathed, observed.

He dreamt for a good long while. Yes, he had finally got some rest! His soul was calm. The ripples on the lake, their reflections at his feet were soothing caresses that wiped clean, wiped clean... Kobor seemed so very far away! The suffering he had endured was becoming vague. Had he suffered so much? He doubted it.

He was even surprised to think one could suffer. His recovery was complete. Then, in the liquid mirror, he saw, right above his head, the fog retreating like a scroll rolling back. The clouds scattered and in the curved sky over the lake Ooh'R sprang out, flooding him with his radiance.

Amo, lifted by joy, jumped to his feet, raised his arms and puffed out his chest. He was alive, he was happy, Ooh'R saw him! Both of them looked at each other, recognized each other!

Once again, everything seemed to have undergone a transformation. This region, recently gentle, irreal, dream-like and where even the flurry of countless wings was softened by tenderness, suddenly turned into sharp edges in the solar intensity.

At present, echoes extended the cries of the birds. The constant flights projected a complex matrix of light shadows, woven and rewoven again. The final wisps of fog eddied around the lake, some invisible force pushing them toward the exits of the place, the cracks like the one Amo had slipped through. The fog condensed at these openings. Thus, the domain of birds, now dazzling with light, was defended from any foreign intrusion.

Amo noticed on his right, some ways off, a strip of land almost forming a peninsula. Trees were growing there along with thick foliage, bushes scattered around in small clumps and high grass. Birds of all colors were frolicked all around it.

Then, with a shock to his heart, Amo saw in the middle of them, under a tree, the figure of the tall old man he had meet before. Without moving, captivated, he admired the scene. On closer inspection, all the birds looked different from one another, in color and hue and in the speed and energy of their flying. They were certainly the winged servants of this Old Man, the companions of his thoughts, whose rise and return they were, perhaps, following. Were they talking together? An interplay of harmonic sympathies, a whole ritual of sensitive discourse.

And then the Old Man saw Amo. An inviting wav, "Come, come close to me!"

Amo was already running over there.

From that moment on, he completely forgot about all his troubles. It was as if all his burdens had been lifted during his journey. He was alive again or rather he found himself in the very heart of an overabundance of life, of new and free joy, which needed no excuse at all to be joy but was its pure principle freed of all contingencies.

The day, therefore, was going to unfold like a dream without him being aware even once that it was actually unfolding, meaning that it was going inevitably towards its conclusion.

Grace upheld him. Indulgence protected him against any attack. When he got to the Old Man, he felt like he had never left him. He felt closer to him, more intimate with him than any other being he had ever known. He was not shy or embarrassed. A vast, inner contentment, total satisfaction. Everything was good, logical, ordered. Hadn't everything suddenly been put back in place in the universe?

The Old Man talked to him like a friend. It looked like they had their habits, their little ways of doing and saying things, particularities in a pre-established understanding that was theirs alone.

A conversation ensued that seemed to be a continuation of a previous talk.

"So," the Old Man said, "you couldn't stop it, just like To and Ta. And the Queen captured the Angel?"

Amo was surprised and repeated, "Angel? We named him the Beautiful Being."

"You named him well. But Angel is his name. He is not of your race. In a way he is a being from the other side of Kah'B'La where things happen."

"But that land is dead, empty, I've seen it."

"And yet things happen there... where stars dip down on dark nights sometimes dropping off beings different from you. This one, when he arrived, was sleeping and could have slept for a very long time. So, Angel was awakened from his stone cradle?"

Amo nodded, "Yes, awakened. But the first time To and Ta saw him—they told me—he was sleeping and didn't even look alive."

"But he was. His life was being stored away. Do you know whether he recovered all his memory?"

"I don't know. He's hurt, very weak. He doesn't talk except to scream at the Queen. And we don't understand his language. Otherwise, he just suffers and laments. We know nothing about him. Not even if he can live..."

"Do you know if he seemed surprised by his surroundings when he woke up on Kah'B'La? To and Ta, who found him there, must have told you, surely!"

"Certainly. They told me that he shook his head, all full of anger. He pressed both hands against his forehead. He looked all around. Obviously, he recognized nothing. He scrutinized the sky. And he fell back on the ground. To and Ta noticed that his eyes were totally empty…"

"Do you want to help him?" The Old Man broke in. "Is that your desire?"

"Yes," Amo replied enthusiastically. "I want him to live!"

"Well, that's good. I'll teach you what to do. And you will manage it."

Amo learned many things that day. He felt less like he was learning them than remembering them. At every moment, when corroborating the words and gestures of the Old Man, something triumphant, deep in his heart, cried out, "That's true! Had I forgotten it?"

The Old Man first showed him how to gather the wild bees' honey without getting stung. He talked to the insects in an even voice with a great deal of politeness. He thanked them in advance for the precious substance they were going to give him. The buzzing swarms parted and he gently extracted the almost black honey that he dripped into a bark container.

"See, it's liquid sun. These bees are intermediaries between the world of Ooh'R and the earth. Their task is to harvest the Gift of Ooh'R on the plants and to put it in storage. It is the best food there is for an Angel who, mysteriously, is a little like Ooh'R and who, like the bees, is an intermediary."

Amo opened his eyes wide and dipped a finger into the honey, tasted it…

The Old Man familiarized him with certain herbs and a type of root whose flower resembled an orchid. Once cooked under ashes this root crumbled easily into a fine flour.

"You will mix it in the milk of Mou Touh, mix it with the honey. It will be the first drink you give to him. See that purple fruit in the bushes. They're good for him. He will accept them readily because it is light food. Angel, who is not like you, cannot eat what you think is good. It's all too heavy, too strong for him. Blood, meat, fat, they're all things that horrify him, that smell of death, that belong to the realm of the dead. You can keep him alive if you offer him honey, fruit and plants. But again you have to go about it the right way. Overall, he needs something different from you who feels pleasure at the mere sight of abundance. He is very subtle. It's the details, the intentions especially that count. Therefore, if you want him to accept the food that you must hurry to bring to him, take these flowers and tie them together. You will garnish the plate on which you put the food. You will wake him up gently, calling him by his name. Here, add a few feathers from my birds to your flowers. You will see. He will appreciate them. I'm sure he'll keep them. Get back before nightfall, Amo!"

The day was ending.

The tall redhead, carrying his harvest, took his leave unopposed. The birds were already falling asleep. The Old Man waved farewell.

A cool breeze blew over the lake. The fog slowly lowered to cover again and hide the domain. At the rocky entrance pass, Amo turned around. The peninsula was no longer visible. The fog enclosed the lake.

He started running. The will and the certainty of saving the stranger gave him wings!

He was still full of joy from the day, but when the usual shock of getting back inside the magnetic aura of Kobor struck his instinct, all that was left of the joy was a dull reflection, already fading away, almost lost.

The usual despondency draped him in a heavy shroud that restricted his movements and hobbled his will.

He suddenly thought of Abim whose silent power was expressed in Kobor's aura. Abim held them all! What could be done against this? She was inapproachable. Present in everything, yes, but untouchable... Lingering odors of the magical night resurfaced in his memory. He pushed them away, frightened... Oh, how long it had been since he had visited Méè-Nê!

But first of all, he had to save Angel.

CHAPTER XV

During Amo's absence, a strange lethargy weighed on Kobor. Neither the weather nor the ambiance inspired anyone to do anything. Most people spent all day sleeping. Waking up late, they fell back to sleep, sickened as soon as they gave a quick glance around: grayness, no other sound but the occasional splashes from the last batrachians in the puddles, shut in by the fog, beads of gray humidity on everything.

So, they pulled down their pudding caps and snuggling for warmth with their families or in couples, they closed their eyes again.

In a corner of their pit, the lethargic Ananou were tangled together.

Right above them, behind her stone doors through which the guards who never entered were snoring, Abim was waiting with great patience for the time of awakening, which she trusted was coming.

She meditated. A thread of red light between her eyelids was the only proof of life. Sometimes, however, with her hand, without moving her head, she brought a cluster of Dongdwo eggs to her lips and chewed them with haughty contempt.

She was thinking... She was seeing. A fleeting smile crossed her lips. She was waiting. Actively. Time meant almost nothing to her. It did not affect her. It only brought what she always desired. She just had to wait.

On the lookout for subtle sounds, for fluid forms... She perceived, on the horizon of her hearing, the Laugh, the clear Laugh! A geyser of white flames sprang up, untouchable... Soon, soon, He would be here, before her, TRULY. And Opak would be standing next to him.

Abim knew that the Beautiful Being was going to live! Yes, LIVE! She knew it... She had to touch nothing, do nothing, say nothing, not move, just wait. Things were headed in the right direction.

This morning Opak was tired from her night and was sleeping, too. The daytime did not wake her up. Nothing budged in the Chamber of Men.

The T'Lo were awake as always, without a sound, respecting their masters' rest. T'Lo Dê chose this moment to slip into the room with the Beautiful Being. This desire had been simmering in him for a long time.

After a short hesitation, the other T'Lo followed. But they stayed to watch from the doorway while T'Lo Dê tiptoed to the bed. Very little light filtered through the heavy drapes, but the eyes of the T'Lo were sensitive to the faintest rays. T'Lo Dê, therefore, saw perfectly well.

At the sleeper's bedside, he was enraptured in admiration. He seemed unable to pull himself away from the sight. He leaned over a little, eventually, one hand held out in a gesture that was never finished.

The other T'Lo, as if sharing his distress, huddle together, holding each other. They stuck out their pug-nosed faces, their eyes sparkled.

After a while, T'Lo Dê pulled back his hand, then squatted down, stayed there, straining his neck, his wide eyes riveted on the Beautiful Being. His emotions escalated. Soon he was panting, tears ran down his cheeks. He trembled and shivered.

Near the door, his brothers were suffering the same phenomenon.

A little light fell upon the bed. The sleeper opened his eyes and stared right at T'Lo Dê. Neither of them screamed or recoiled. And yet, it was a collision of two worlds! But these two worlds, so different, so extreme, both understood that they were confronting their two sufferings.

And at the same time they understood (by some miracle of sympathy) that their grief, their constraints, came from the extreme worlds that they each represented, the world of the T'Lo, the world of the Beautiful Being, in relation with the intervening world, the race of Kobor Tigan't to which neither of them felt allied. The T'Lo because they *could* not. The Beautiful Being because he *would* not.

When they had finished gazing deeply into each other, T'Lo Dê lowered his head as a sign of submission and started sliding away in order not to offend the stranger any longer. The other T'Lo were already withdrawing soundlessly into the Chamber of Men, going back to their usual places.

But the Beautiful Being sat up on his cushions and held out his hands with a little yelp. T'Lo Dê came back and put his head on the edge of the mattress.

The Beautiful Being whispered to him in his own language, which the T'Lo did not understand, but somehow all the intentions were passionately grasped by his sensitivity.

For his part, the stranger "heard" the T'Lo's thoughts as their mute tongue could never say a word, but whose huge eyes reflected so clearly their emotional fluctuations.

Thus, they proffered mutual compassion. The understanding between them was immediate, natural and profound. It bound them together stronger than a pact. They knew that neither of them would threaten the other's liberty.

T'Lo Dê made no overtures because he sensed that the Beautiful Being was not interested in eroticism. So, he straightaway discovered, by his kind of sensitive genius, pure admiration and unblemished affection.

The Beautiful Being, who noticed everything, wanted to reassure this heart thirsting for love and to compensate for the gaping solitude of the T'Lo with his treasures of tenderness.

He did not know exactly what the Giant Men used these creatures for, but he figured rightly that they were not free. Nevertheless, he was puzzled seeing his pretty jewelry. What kind of slavery was this, then?

Showing interest in someone had made him forget his wounds and weakness a little. But he got tired quickly. Lethargy took hold of him again. But he would not give in until after an understanding was reached with T'Lo Dê: no, he would not leave his bedside and he would watch over his sleep.

Which was done.

When Amo arrived quietly, carrying his plate of fruits and honey, he was surprised to be greeted by T'Lo Dê. For an instant, weird suspicions spun around in his mind. He had a bad feeling. It was not that he hated T'Lo Dê, but he feared his pernicious influence. He managed to put aside his thoughts. Clearly, he saw the sleeper was left alone, so pure, so weak! He had to wake him up now.

"Angel," he murmured.

Seeing Amo leaning over him, his face lit up. T'Lo Dê, taking great care not to touch him directly, adroitly got him sitting up on the cushions. And it was a wonder to see food finally accepted!

T'Lo Dê clapped his hands. Amo started laughing. And he repeated, "Angel, Angel!"

The Beautiful Being was delighted to hear himself being called by name and almost with joy in his voice asked a bunch of questions that Amo could only answer by giving his own name. "Amo, Amo!"

The Beautiful Being repeated it. Happiness washed over them all. Finally, something unwound. T'Lo Dê was also named directly by Amo and the Beautiful Being repeated it, thereby throwing the T'Lo into an ocean of gratitude.

Angel touched the flowers. Amo got him to understand that they were picked especially for him, just like the plants, honey and fruit. The patient nodded, slowly tasted everything with pleasure and gratitude. His cheeks turned pink. He was rubbing the feathers the old man had put with the food. Amo was not ready to explain where they came from. He could not talk about the Grand Old Man...

A cry: Opak was in the doorway, sleep-laden and worried about abandoning the stranger. The scene she was witnessing, therefore, looked unbelievable: the Beautiful Being was eating. T'Lo Dê was supporting the cushions and Amo had just guffawed out loud.

At all this she roared as a matter of form, furious that this achievement was not hers. But she was happy that it was happening. Immensely, enormously happy! So relieved that she did not know what to say—her prisoner was eating!

She looked warily at the kind of food, even tasted it, dipped a finger into the honey and was surprised that someone could swallow such things. She unfurled the garland of flowers. She twirled the feathers in her fingers, unable to decipher their use.

With a feeble but precise gesture, which allowed no reply, the Beautiful Being took them back. He was clearly disgruntled. T'Lo Dê caught the hint and his eyes darted between the Queen and the Beautiful Being, terribly surprised that he did not love her.

Amo told Opak, "The Beautiful Being is called Angel."

Her eyes grew large, "Ang'h?" she struggled to pronounce.

Amo corrected her. But Opak was curiously resistant and after a few useless attempts she persisted in saying "Ang'h".

She liked the name and could not stop repeating it. Every time, however, hearing his name distorted, the Beautiful Being grimaced.

To and Ta felt great joy when they heard about the improvement in the state of the Beautiful Being. The news somewhat eased their remorse for contributing to his ordeals. They went to see him, were welcomed with a charming smile, easily pronounced the name Angel and showed deep interest in the new food. They got in the habit of adorning themselves in flowers every time they came. They brought some as well.

Without saying anything they guessed that Amo had seen the Old Man. Amo looked at them and they smiled, joined by their secret. Amo remembered all the Old Man's advice concerning Angel. He regularly brought the desirable food and offered it himself, which seemed to have a favorable effect on the patient.

To gather the honey, he went back to the domain of the birds, but the Old Man, he was very sorry to see, was no longer there.

Amo, who was keeping these things in the secrecy of his heart, was saddened by this. He traveled farther into the region without any other encounter. The experience taught him that he could find the fruit, plants, roots and honey pretty much everywhere. He chose the flowers with more discernment than before.

And because Angel requested it, he started partaking of this new food with him. He also took on teaching him the language of Kobor. He named everything he brought him. He pointed to objects, named them and patiently corrected Angel's pronunciation. Angel had great fun. He proved curious about everything. His excellent memory helped him make quick progress.

A close friendship bound him to Amo. With him he shared laughter and whims that cast a shadow over Opak who was still always so scornful if not hateful of the Beautiful Being. All these new ways rattled the Queen. The idea of surrendering to them never crossed her mind and so she saw the time pass without anything bringing her closer to Angel. She took comfort, however, because he was getting better. The hope of seeing him on his feet soon made her tolerant. She waited and tried not to get too involved in what was developing there. But she was jealous of the obvious sympathy shown between Angel and Amo.

The latter always felt troubled around the Beautiful Being. In spite of himself, he could not forget the battle, that first moment when they clashed and grappled each other... Angel was soul-stirring like a woman of higher essence. Amo would have liked to confide in the Old Man.

T'Lo Dê, when not serving the Queen, spent most of his time with Angel. He felt as much love for him as he did for Amo and Opak. But one quality was very different. Angel made him feel good. Being around him exorcised the curse of his state of being a T'Lo. He was enchanted. He no longer ate. He floated in a state of simple bliss. The flexibility of his psyche put him in easy harmony with Angel whose rhythms he reflected like in a mirror.

Without ever getting tired, half curled up at his feet, he watched him, bathing in all that beauty. And he was never uncomfortable. A shadow, docile, almost beautiful sometimes because the Being in front of him was Beauty itself...

Angel's wounds healed. He gradually recovered his strength enough to get out of bed for short periods. Grown even leaner, he walked cautiously, leaning on Amo or on the T'Lo. He could not stand being supported by Opak, who was rather clumsy and whose contact always repulsed him, awoke the bitterness of their fight or the too recent tortures of forced feeding.

It has to be admitted, however, that the Queen made an effort. She, too, showed objects for the Beautiful Being to repeat the names. But by malice, he pretended not to understand, answered incorrectly, on purpose, to get revenge, to tire her out. He noticed, with a sneer, that she mostly pointed out things belonging to her, the Queen, that only bore witness to her splendor, to her power. He wanted no part of it. It was a dialogue of the deaf. They were equally stubborn. He in his refusal. She in her naïve selfishness.

To show him that she was the Woman, therefore the Power, she had her Men brought in, named them one by one and stripped them naked to display their strength and health. The Men, in their simple natures, were delighted with this game that flattered their value and their rank. Angel turned his back!

The males, whom the stranger intimidated and fascinated at the same time, did not understand anything about his attitude. Submissive to the appetites of their Queen, they were ready to welcome him among them, even as the leader next to Amo, as a bizarre favorite, a being whom they did not really know if it was male or female but who, for certain, attracted admiration and attachment.

Opak wanted to make the stranger understand above all that everything that was hers was his, too. That was why just like she had him try on her own finery (which he found ugly and heavy) and jewelry (which he threw off with indignant sighs), so she took his hand (spontaneously she claimed) and made him touch the handsomest of her Men.

Angel yanked back his hand in furious protest! The Man just stood there, baffled. The meaning of the stranger's reactions completely escaped him. All the more so when he tried to excuse himself and show that it was not the Man, he was upset with by smiling sadly at him from a distance. But the fact remained that he had slapped Opak's hand, which was holding the Man, screaming at her incomprehensibly in his native tongue.

A grave uneasiness loomed, therefore. The Queen wanted peace: she sent away her Men. For a time, while the Beautiful Being calmed down and handed some flowers to T'Lo Dê, who had learned to weave them into a necklace, and watched him with pleasure, she just stood there, stupidly and resentfully. Not knowing whether she should break down in tears or break out in anger. So, she stomped around, whimpering ridiculously, which the Beautiful Being completely ignored.

T'Lo Dê had, however, looked up worriedly from his work, but he saw that the Queen was not concerned with him. With her brow knit and eyes vacant, she was staring straight ahead. After regarding Angel's eyes and finding them paying polite attention to him alone, he reabsorbed himself in his work, happy to be observed, happy to be making the adornment that he knew would be preferred above any other.

He got the sudden idea to insert little feathers between the flowers. Was it really an idea? He only realized what he was doing when his fingers by themselves started putting the feathers on. Frightened by what he had done, which was not planned, not expected, he stopped and raised his anxious eyes. But Angel was already clapping in approval of the innovation. A rush of blood due to the emotion and to pleasure, colored T'Lo Dê's skin as he was overwhelmed with gratitude.

The work continued like this, pleasant and peaceful. Sometimes Angel chose the flowers or handed him the feathers. Both of them forgot about Opak... It was a nice day. The drapes were open and the stone tiles moved away from the window letting in more warmth than on previous days. A pinker light, too, because the sun was peeking through the fog a little bit more every day.

Lying on his cushions in the diffused light, Angel was reviving.

Still, he tried to pull together his missing memories. Before waking up on Kah'B'La, before his capture, where was he? A big, black hole. Unable to muster anything. His memories started from that moment... Before, there had been something else, another life, another Elsewhere, which were gripping him with nostalgia... Lightness and brightness. Grace. Happiness. Ease... He could conjure up nothing and form no image of it. Nothing for his thought to latch onto. Nothing but traces of sensations, palpitations. Nothing... He was there, stripped, exiled, a stranger in a heavy, thick, brutal world. A world that was not, could not be his world!

The first sign of a sob was rising in his chest. But the T'Lo's hand, attentive to every impulse, the weird reptilian hand, spread its delicate, mauve fingers and barely touched his foot. This meant: I'm here. Don't grieve. I love you.

That was what he figured T'Lo Dê was thinking. He smiled, knowing that the T'Lo was sadder than he was and he did not want to add anything in any way to his sorrow.

165

Behind them, Opak kept her head lowered, not moving. But she ended up raising her eyes at them without really seeing them. Suddenly, she seemed to snap out of it. Something flashed in her mind and she was seeing them next to each other, together, right there...

"Ang'h and T-Lo Dê," she muttered. T'Lo Dê, T'Lo Dê! But of course, how had she not thought of this before? Almost all the time, T'Lo Dê! Ang'h tolerated T'Lo Dê and she had not noticed it.

She repeated this carefully to herself, examining them closely, with an attentiveness that was unusual for her and that made her brow sweat. After a while, it seemed clear to her that this was the solution.

In her stubbornness and afraid of being found out finally, she waited a long time to see an erotic gesture exchanged between the T'Lo and the stranger. But nothing happened. Angel seemed to fall asleep while T'Lo Dê went on with his delicate task getting ever slower.

Opak stormed out of the room. The T'Lo looked up at the noise and Angel sighed out of his cushions.

The Queen, believing herself to be very clever, hid behind the door to spy on them through the crack.

The T'Lo's clairvoyance was fully aware of her action, but he was not overly surprised. It caused no reaction in him. He did not understand her ploy.

Contrary to what she imagined, Angel also knew that she was hiding behind the door. He sighed again and held his head in his hands. This constant surveillance was too much. What?! Was she always going to be spying on him, weighing him down with her blatant expectations? A prisoner, he was a prisoner being held within these stone walls! A prisoner in an unknown city, itself imprisoned by the fog! A prisoner of his own weakness and a prisoner of that black abyss that had engulfed all his memories!

He rolled his head from side to side. "Come, come, it must be possible to find out something about it. Just scraps, crumbs about That which had been His light, His splendor!" He stretched, tilting his face towards the light sifting through the windows. He appealed to the virtue of this light. It was there, on high, that the truth was found... Oh, would that a ray spring forth and light up his inner night!

With that gesture that was so curious, without realizing it, Angel wrapped his four fingers around his long, little fingers, as it to boost his power of concentration. But nothing came of it. He let his hands drop open with an expression of mortal despair.

T'Lo Dê had observed the whole pantomime without interfering, straining to understand its significance. He looked closely at the abnormally long pinkies. Then, all of a sudden, as an inner illumination lit up his pug-nosed face, he brought one of those fingers up to his ear. At the touch, Angel opened his eyes.

"Yes," he sighed, "O T'Lo Dê, your mute heart understands everything. There was a spirit in my fingers that commanded the heavens. That was before. Elsewhere. Through it I understood, I learned... Now, here, have I lost the power? Nothing comes. I'm too weak, I guess?"

Opak did not understand a word. She was tapping her foot. T'Lo Dê's gesture meant nothing. She left. Waiting. Waiting. Let the T'Lo do something...

Angel and Amo enjoyed each other's company. The patient really only livened up when his food supplier came. He arranged the meals to keep him at his side. Amo went along willingly, though still secretly troubled by Angel's voice and body and face.

He talked about what he had seen or discovered on his last expedition, describing the animals, nature, clouds. The Beautiful Being seemed eager for details, asked a lot of questions, thirsting for information as if he needed to refurnish his memory. He was struggling to find some traces of something somewhere that he might recognize.

When he learned that the birds had deserted Kobor the very day they had brought him here half-dead, it seemed like he might have found a little piece of what he was looking for.

He nodded. "Like so, like so!" he exclaimed softly, passionately, before asking whether, in the countryside, someplace, he had found the birds. Amo nodded. So as not to be heard by the Queen he whispered that all the birds apparently took refuge far away in a valley known to him alone, hidden at the foot of Kah'B'La. He has seen them more than once because that was where he got the first acceptable food for him.

Angel saw a sign in this. Also whispering, excitedly, he made Amo promise to bring him there when he had his strength back. This secret bound them together even stronger. They had something in common to share apart from the Queen.

Angel rejoiced. Amo wavered between the same feeling and another, more bitter, of separating himself even further from Opak. By force of circumstances, he was sharing less and less with the Queen. And what exactly had he shared? He wondered...

Of course, all was not finished between them. She often asked for him in her bed. She took her usual delight. But he no longer felt the bounty he had known. His power remained intact; the carnal delight erupted as always. But he was, in a way, separate from it. He saw in his mind, from a distance, the pleasure being experienced, he felt the stormy eruption, but it did not really affect him. And above all, it did not connect him to Opak anymore.

He wanted something else, stronger, but sweeter, too. Something of what radiated around Angel... He wanted, for example, between his eyes and hers for a look to be exchanged that was different from what she was giving him, this look just like (oh woe!) being satisfied after a hearty meal. He wanted her not to fall asleep right away but to talk about what was going on in her heart and head... But, beyond this appetite, beyond this rush to always be satisfied, beyond this massive conviction of being the Ooh'Rou of Kobor Tigan't, was there anything in her heart and head? When he talked to her at night, pulling her out of her sleep, she grumbled, barely answered or mixed everything up and called one of her T'Lo to help them arouse their tired flesh with ardent caresses. Oh, it was always the same thing!

However, she often talked about Angel. Even just to moan over his strangeness, weeping with desire, always butting up against the same problem: why wasn't he in her bed?

And since the answers never satisfied her because she did not listen to them, she suspected dark intrigues. Why did the stranger show so much obvious pleasure during Amo's visits when there seemed to be no erotic relationship between them. Amo tried to explain friendship, the confident joy in conversations or even the contentment of being together without saying anything. She did not understand, she did not accept any of it.

She became jealous of their closeness very quickly. The humiliation of not being fertilized by Ooh'R was ruining her. She felt shrunken. Her foundation was attacked. A Queen without hope of a child is a sign of coming calamity for the realm. And the Great Child, when would it come? When would Abim acknowledge it? Alas, was it truly not yet found among all her children? Was the Very Huge truly right to say that Ooh'R rejected Amo? And this, too, the Queen did not understand why. But eventually, she ended up not hating her favorite but rather fearing him, fearing the curse that he might be stricken with...

168

Amo seemed to be an enigma to her. What was he cooking up against her? And with Angel, what was this bond she could not fathom?

Running into the same obstacles threw her into a fury. She quarreled, then, with Amo. And since the angry man with eyes afire and nose flaring aroused her sudden desire, she mated with him, almost ferociously, wanting to exhaust him, to destroy him by yanking out his life, all his life! But she fell asleep without warning and he left her, his soul oppressed but his body intact, his huge store of power barely touched.

He left in the night and walked for a long time in the dark through the deserted streets of Kob Ooh'R.

When he got back, just before dawn, Opak was very often no longer in the Chamber of Men. Shouts and the sounds of breaking objects came from the room where Angel was lying.

Amo ran in. Often, he bumped into T'Lo Dê in the hallway, trembling and panicking. As soon as the door was pushed open, he was struck by an unexpected spectacle: the dismal dispute. Opak, naked, had tried to slip in next to Angel who was white with rage, ruffled like a bird, standing up despite his weakness and, strangest of all, despite her he looked dangerous. Mysterious waves emanated from him. He shouted belligerent words in his own language. The Queen got scared. What powers, then, did the Beautiful Being have at his disposal for them to feel strongly that he was gathering invisible presences around him?

In his first defensive outburst he had scratched and bit Opak. Under his angry assaults, she staggered, gazing in shock at his bleeding hands.

But Angel could not sustain the tension for long. After these fits, he became sick again, refused to eat, seemed to be at death's door.

They had to start everything from the beginning. Opak wailed in dismay, repentant, devastated.

It was Amo once again who nursed Angel back to life with his gentleness, his attentive care and his mere presence.

T'Lo Dê, who was brought to the limits of nervous tension by these crises (because all the motives were beyond him and he suffered through them like terrifying hurricanes) helped as best he could, unhappy that all these being whom he loved so much were tearing each other apart. He wanted only for them all to unite in the intimacy of sharing. Why did this intimacy not develop?

Why was the Queen not satisfied? It was enough just to be with Angel, to see him and listen. Nothing else was necessary.

Why was the Queen trying to act with him like with her Men? He, the T'Lo, knew very well how Angel, first of all, wanted his friends' heart...

CHAPTER XVI

Méè-Nê was worried about Amo, her spiritual son, the favorite of her Great Brain. She saw him less often than before since the night of terrors when Abim had used her secret arts.

Yes, since that night something had broken in the vital system of Kobor Tigan't. Wasn't this break the first signs of the decline? The B'Tah-Gou sensed it grievously.

The place where the whole edifice was cracking had been shown to her by her subtle senses. In the heart of the City, this blemish, this erosion... Nobody saw anything yet on the outside. And nobody wanted to see anything. As always!

Even so, there were portents: the persistent fog, the foul spring, the odd retirement of the Queen, the stranger so gentle, peaceful and beautiful, brought here by uncustomary violence, wounded and not healing, and then there was the desertion of all the birds and the exile of Ooh'R. Plus, Amo whose inexplicable disgrace shocked everyone so much that no one would utter a word about it. Oh, so many signs, so many alarms calling for vigilance, resistance, to wake up!

But no, the people, the entire race was escaping reality in sleep. Their sleep, this spinelessness that the B'Tah-Gou saw condensed in the aura of the City in thick fumes that helped maintain the fog... And the fog, the fog that drove so many to sleep, oh woe!

After these thoughts, Méè-Nê called for little Ata-Réè. She exited, in hushed tones, for her alone, the need for staying awake, for vigilance and lucidity, knowing she was being heard and understood. The Great Secret was shared between them. Thus, the Storyteller began to shape the Little Brain of the child so that very soon her Great Brain could unload everything into it.

Méè-Nê spoke and her voice had never been so beautiful:

The Death Stones are at the end of the path.
Do not sleep! Do not go!
Resist the nocturnal call that gathers the Storytellers!
Reject sleep! Uncover your brow!
Your eyes must stay open, O Kobor, my city, my race!
It is not by fleeing the fog
In the mists of sleep

That you will flee Kobor's enemy fog!
Remember Ooh'R, arouse in you the gold of his memory
Because the Death Stone is also in the heart of the city,
In the heart of the race, O Kobor!

Afterward, while the vibrations of her voice rippled on, soothing, during a long, mute contact, she transmitted to the child Ata-Réè the entire heritage of her own heritage.

The whole line of ancient B'Tah-Gous were speaking through her. And just like during a chant when the vocalized treasure stimulated the mysterious memory of Ata-Réè's vocal cords, so the powerful thought of the Storyteller emanated without a sound, planted itself in the virgin ground of a young thought.

With a pious and sad heart, but inspired with enthusiasm because she gauged the importance of this transmission, the child received everything with the fierce will to prolong the tradition. She also knew that this meant goodbye already from her B'Tah-Gou... and already, by osmosis, she started to look like Méè-Nê. For, her features changed. Graver. Heavier. Her big eyes sunk in.

She started to grow taller. She had not yet filled in. She was still so young. She had not yet reached the required age for transmission. But Méè-Nê, assessing the scope of everything she had bequeathed to her, figured it was the right time. She especially wanted to anticipate the fatal time of the great splintering of Kobor. Her Mind, then, had to be completely absorbed by the child's mind.

Above all, she knew how much she and all her peers had been threatened by Abim. On that evil night, they had all lost their power. Abim had started invading the stronghold of the B'Tah-Gous. None of them had been able to completely escape her hold. All, since then, had been affected. No longer perfectly whole, no longer perfectly pure but from now on mixed, merged. In a corner of their being, henceforth, there existed, implanted, parasitic, a threat, this graft that was foreign to their nature but strong enough to take hold sooner or later and develop by transforming little by little.

A time would come when the tree of the B'Tah-Gous would bear strange fruit. Poisoned pulp, pernicious, spiritual food... Yes, yes, Abim had started invading. At first just satisfied with making her mark where she would return some other night. Then she would go a little further in her invasion.

Of course, Méè-Nê, by magic willpower, had infiltrated this deposit left inside her by Abim. She knew, alas, that her defense would not hold out forever. She only managed to delay it, to contain the influence a little. The day would inevitably come when it would give way. She would infiltrate again. And again. And so on, fighting to the end…

It was impossible to prevent. They could only gain some time, a little time… And everything transmitted to a young brain that was purer, stronger, able to defend itself because already a little "different" in its evolved structures, different from the Old Brain of the B'Tah-Gous that was really just a faithful Archive.

Méè-Nê knew perfectly well that the mentality of Ata-Réè differed from hers. She was glad for it. A subtler, more flexible brain and especially more personalized. Yes, the child of this generation had a new gift. She was able to invent using the fertilized soil of traditions. Until now the Storytellers "repeated". They developed nothing. Ata-Réè would not be satisfied with this. She would create new forms of thought using her heritage. This faculty made her independent. She would be able to transform without deforming. Abim's influence would not affect her.

And when all the old B'Tah-Gous had been demonized, flipped from the light of Ooh'R to the blackness of an unknown star, when they would all be absorbed by Abim and become her playthings, extensions of herself, the preserved heritage would already have started a new gestation in the psychic brain of Ata-Réè so that she can transmit a still pure tradition sheltered by new habits that her own genius will know how to adopt.

On this day, Amo was alone at the foot of one of the Sleepers of the Sun, the R'Lil as the Giants called them. It was the tallest and shiniest of the black mountains. It exuded a permanence that, for the first time, made him dizzy.

Wasn't their majesty funereal? Wasn't this, truthfully, the tomb of the Ages?

He went to stare for a long time at a huge slab that had been polished at the base of this R'Lil. In it he found rubies encrusted, tokens of all the ancestral royalty. How far back in time it went! His head was spinning. He told himself that all the Ooh'Rous had come here at the start of their reign to enshrine their rubies. The first Ooh'Rous, unimaginable their shape or strength, then the whole cohort of descendants down to Opak. All of them had touched this wall in the prime of youth of glory!

Suddenly he wondered how long the rubies would remain embedded. He had an astonishing vision of this R'Lil completely covered with rubies, standing tall in the golden glory of a future sky! Then almost right away he realized that it was false, that he was lying to himself. Everything would soon be over. Yes, here as elsewhere, everything had to end. And it was already ending, he thought with a shiver.

He knew that there would be no more superhuman Queens, but what would there be for adoration, for the necessary ecstasy, what would there be?

With a feeling of disillusionment that was already giving him an answer, he put his finger on the last ruby. "Opak?" The name had no more meaning... Opak? It was a sound made with the mouth rather than a name.

For a moment a horrible feeling of loneliness threw him into a panic. Then, he felt mute inside, disengaged from what he had loved so much. Opak... His inner longing searched in another direction, where, mysteriously, there was nothing but emptiness, absence. And yet, Amo kept loving, feeling a strong but fleeting impression. He said "Love?", questioning the space in front of him, above him, the sky, not knowing what to do. Ooh'R, however, was washing over his body and making him feel good. There was concern being poured down on him by another Solitude whose call he was hearing. Ooh'R was saying, deep down in its glare, "Come to me, come to me!"

How to get there?

Amo swayed back and forth.

He was struggling. The image of the Queen appeared out of his inner fog, then it turned around, dissolved, never to return.

Had he wept sitting on this rock? He stood up feeling confused. He had to move.

With his mind elsewhere, he stepped back to get a better look at the range forming the main Sleeper and her sisters.

The sun was setting fast. The oblique light sharpened the reliefs on the landscape. He watched the shadows gradually lengthening, those of the Sleepers and the other, straight, pathetic, which was his own getting longer and longer...

All of a sudden, with a start, right at the tip of his shadow, he saw a man of his race standing there, whose shadow was added to his, extending in a way so that the shadow became duel and stretched farther out…

He felt reassured and excited.

The man was also watching the Sleepers, probably pondering ideas similar to his own.

As soon as he realized that Amo was looking at him, he came up to him. Amo waited for him, not moving from his spot, with a strange feeling of fatal joy. He remarked that the stranger's face refracted the sun marvelously, like polished metal, in which two molten droplets had been embedded—his eyes.

He was struck by how tall the stranger was. He would put him among the tallest men of Kobor, but he held himself differently. Not heavy or massive, not jarring the ground with his heel, he stood up straight, a little stiff as if making an effort to contain such great forces. Still, his gait was supple, his step long. Moreover, on closer inspection, the man was not slender, not very muscular. Nevertheless, the impression of willful energy defied this inspection.

Amo figured that he must have a great responsive power. His straight, black hair, thrown back, revealed a high forehead. Garments of hide, tight-fitting, all of one muted shade, along with his clean look, made him a somber vision of rigor, severity, but also of health and certainty. He walked a perfectly straight line toward him. Amo was thinking that there was no escaping and the stranger might have deadly intentions.

But the thought had barely crossed his mind when he saw up close the beautiful oval face, so bright, that contradicted any suspicion with a trusting smile. His yellow eyes were enchanting.

"I was also wondering how many rubies more? And I was sad because it seemed to me that the R'Lil will never, not ever, be covered."

So then, they both had been thinking the same thing. Amo put his hand on his shoulder, "Our thoughts travel the same path. We should walk together, side by side, don't you think?"

"Yes, Amo."

"You know my name?"

"Who doesn't know the Queen's Man in Kobor?"

The Queen's Man! At this expression, which he was used to nonetheless, Amo blushed not with confusion but because his heart had beat painfully. He was now so far from the Queen's Man! It was better to hide it like an ugly wound that you know will never heal because something will always inflame it. It is always in a spot already damaged that the future shocks will hit.

He pushed away his embarrassment and said, "And what's your name?"

"The name that other beings give me isn't important between us. See, it isn't true. With you I stick to the truth of life. I am, therefore, your Friend. Call me that, would you? Don't try to call me anything else. We have very particular and very specific connections between us. You feel it, don't you?"

"Yes, I feel it. Very well. What you say is fair and good. So, you are my Friend." Despite all this, curiosity got the better of him, "But I don't know where to place you. What city do you come from? I've never seen you. It seems to me that you should live in Kob'Ooh'R. You are noble through and through. What woman do you belong to?"

He saw that the other let the question pass with calm indifference. It fell to the side, trivial rubbish that did not concern him. He just smiled and looked deep into Amo's eyes more gently and more intensely at every question, but without showing any irritation, just a kind of amused patience.

In the end, Amo smiled, too, and stopped interrogating him. "You're my Friend. I feel it. I know it. You remain free. Since you don't feel like telling me anything, I won't drill you with my curiosity. I only questioned you because I'm afraid of losing you very soon. And I've barely found you. I want to be sure that I can find you again."

"I'm a man of your race and your Friend. I will travel a very long time with you. We need each other. However, there will come a time when I will no longer be of use to you. I will know before you do. By then you will have become greater and nobler. I will have given you everything…"

He did not finish even though Amo pressed him worriedly. The conversation turned to other matters.

Following this unexpected encounter, Amo lived for while in contentment. Between him and his new companion there was an odd friendship, very gentle and yet bitter; enriching but depriving; full of unexpected contrasts.

Amo realized this gradually. He acquired an expanded consciousness, a refined sensibility, new ideas, the need to choose what was more in tune with him. This freed him from the daily routine that men endure, choose, accept. Amo now wanted to sift through life's choices, reject what he did not like and finally do things for himself, dictated only by his own conscience.

But prior to these outcomes, there had been a long period when they were almost always together. Limited by certain obligations, they managed this by always running into each other by chance at a turn in the road or on a street corner. They had fun together like they were playing games, enjoying the favorable climate that destiny seemed to grant them. Seeing them, they were always laughing, telling each other, "I knew it!"

And the reply was always, "Me too!"

As brief as their meeting might be, it brightened Amo's heart and made his companion's eyes sparkle more.

Yes, they were very comfortable together. Together they enjoyed the benefits of being alive. Meeting, talking, answering, walking together in step or even saying nothing, side by side at night, it was plenitude, harmony and especially *peace*. A peace that blossomed only for them, remaining for everyone else the forbidden flower with its bud always closed, a promise for the future that never reaches its springtime.

The two of them were granted this blooming flower. And in this climate, they understood each other easily, in total harmony. It was a satisfaction that could console many a woe! Amo, at least, felt like this for himself, but for his friend, he never felt very sure of what this consolation did for him.

On the other hand, he noticed very quickly that the more he saw him, the more he discovered in himself, from so much expansion of thoughts, all the sad secrets, a whole past buried in his reticent heart.

His Friend was all the more precious to him. He always appreciated talking to him, always had a nice smile for him, plenty of brotherly warmth, in spite of the grief that he never allowed himself to confess.

He overflowed with projects. Constantly, he proposed some stroll for the next day in out-of-the-way places or meetings with people in Kobor, adventures in short… He talked about it and arranged all the details in advance. All kinds of speculations would lead him into exciting and unforeseen developments. Amo listened, was thrilled, but saw the conflict between the brilliant imagination, which was living through these projects in advance, and the sudden obscure look in the Friend's eyes as he apologized for not being fooled by his own words that contradicted the reality of the enthusiasm. For, he never followed through on any of these projects. It was necessary to learn how to resign yourself to the situation.

Amo thought he understood. Had they not lived out these projects entirely on the plane of dreams where they saw themselves acting together? What was the point of living through the same thing twice when they knew very well that reality tarnishes the dream color, dulls every sensation, limits every power?

These were the subtleties that Amo learned. He started playing along willingly, by natural inclination. He was not fooled. His Friend neither. They both knew it. They agreed to play together in this conjuring of images. The evocations were so intense that Amo was surprised to find his real memories mixed up with the images from his dream life. There were moments when he could not tell them apart. He felt like his own thoughts and those of his Friend came from the same, single source. After all, perhaps it was Amo who was unknowingly thinking all the things that his Friend was saying?

He came to believe it. He looked at his companion as an emanation of himself, another Amo, not yet completely revealed, whose unknown possibilities remained to be discovered. He thought he could know him, he thought he could control him. But it was not true. He promised to come but he came not. He did not promise anything and suddenly he was there. A reflection. The unexpected, blown in on the wind... The wind, the unexpected, would it take him away? At this thought alone Amo was seized with panic.

But he comforted himself by clinging ecstatically to all that this friendship was giving him, even and especially in its weirdness, which he was trying hard to understand.

Moreover, he credited his Friend with special virtues. Among others, being able to modify destiny, to minimize its blows when he was around. Amo did not know how this happened but since they had met, he suffered less, he could remove his problems into a kind of magical domain where they resolved themselves, where they took on a different meaning.

The fact of living through so many adventures and experiences by this dream dialogue freed him, exorcised his demons. He thought a lot less about Abim whose looming threat had poisoned his life up to now.

He also went through a period of weakening of his sexual appetites. He barely even noticed it, replaced as it was by a new craving of his spirit. The life of his psychic being superimposed itself on his actual material life. Here again, he was hardly surprised.

His Friend, for him, was a being of good omen. As long as he was there, nothing bad could come. There was truly a benevolence surrounding this person. Amo attributed this, instinctively, to the Grand Old Man. He had no idea why. However, it seemed to him that a secret, significant bond united them. A day would come, no doubt, when all this would be made clear...

The Friend never did anything bad. Even the unexpected and the absences were not really harmful. But maybe he never did anything? Little by little this proved to be true. And many other things came up that he had to get used to.

Amo realized that he did not know where his Friend lived or how. His social circle and his personal activities, except for their relationship, he knew nothing about and could not even imagine. Whenever he tried to question him about it, he ran into a peaceful silence, like on the first day, with a smile. At this moment, more than any other, he felt like he was looking at himself, facing his own reflection like when he leaned over the lake in the realm of birds.

Several times at the beginning of their relationship, the Friend went away without warning. The very first time, Amo was really caught off guard. He had left him the night before and figured he would see him the next day. Nothing of the sort. The day passed in perplexity, then in worry, but nothing came of it.

This lasted for several days. Calling out, searching, all in vain. A blank. The feeling that the missing person would never return. An utter absence during which Amo, who found no clue anywhere, suddenly realized that no one had ever seen him with his Friend. He asked cautious questions that made him believe that no one in Kobor knew the man that looked like him.

He remembered that by some recurring chance, every time they were together, they had never run into anyone else. Chance led them into particularly deserted places: Kob'Lâm in the evening, in those silent districts where the storerooms lie dormant or very early in the morning in the countryside to see Ooh'R break through the fog. Plus, neither of them had sought out the company of others.

This prolonged absence was needed for Amo to become aware. He remembered having twice been at a meeting point planned by his Friend, once with Eqin-Go who he unexpectedly ran into, and again with To— both times there was no one there. His Friend showed up very late, only after Eqin-Go had left. Amo had the feeling that he popped up behind him! He joked about it but to his great astonishment the Friend, instead of laughing as usual or apologizing, just looked at him with such grave gentleness that Amo, confusedly, had the fleeting impression of a reproach. He could almost hear him saying, "Look, don't you know that I can only be here with you alone?"

The second time, To had talked on and on. Nobody came. Amo had no choice but to bid farewell to To and go on his way, leaving his gloomy thoughts to guide his steps. The day was almost over. An arm slipped into his—the Friend! The streets were utterly deserted.

Amo also remembered having never told anybody, not Eqin-Go nor To, that he was waiting for a Friend. He had meant to tell someone, but he had never done it. When the time came, it slipped his mind. During the long days of this absence, thinking about all these things, Amo did not really feel alone or abandoned: around him, invisible, was the presence of the Friend! And because of this, he was a little ashamed of continuing to search for him.

When he came back, unchanged, smiling, as if nothing had happened, Amo told him, before even thinking of complaining, "I felt you near me."

"So you see," is all he replied.

But the grievance sprang out nonetheless and Amo's face turned tragic, "But you left! And I never know where you go or what you do! I thought you were dead!"

"No, no, you didn't believe that, not for a single moment."

And it was true, Amo had to agree. Already his companion's enveloping tenderness and calm was putting everything back in place.

He was saying, "What does all this matter? What does it matter what I do or don't do elsewhere since I have reality only with you! Sometimes, you can see me, other times you can't. But I am always here with you."

They went off together for a long walk in the deep valley without straying too far from the farthest walls of Kob'Lâm. They met nobody.

After this, Amo's life was attuned with the rhythm of these disappearances and returns, a kind of alternating between night and day, between sunlight and shadow.

"I look forward to your return like I look forward every night to seeing Ooh'R in the morning!"

CHAPTER XVII

Laboriously, after several attempts, Opak managed to get through the reasoning she had set out on. Her head hurt the whole time but she succeeded in piecing together her slow thoughts.

She was jealous of Amo: he was taking her place with Ang'h. She had to prevent him from coming so often.

And then there was T'Lo Dê. Ang'h liked him a lot. And she, the Queen, was glad for this fondness. So, she had to let T'Lo Dê be around Ang'h, not to disturb him. But would this be enough to soften up the Beautiful Being? Would her emanation alone be sufficient?

She decided to let other T'Lo come into Ang'h's room. She decided that Amo would go on a long hunting expedition. The excuse was easy find: the storerooms of Kob'Lâm were dangerously low because the fog had obstructed, if not prevented, their restocking. The Dongdwo eggs were also lacking.

She summoned Amo.

"There are no more Dongdwo eggs. The cellars of Kob'Lâm are almost empty. The fog is lighter now. The men have to get back to hunting and searching for eggs. You will take with you anyone you want, a lot of hunters. We must completely refill the storerooms. Ang'h's food can be gathered at the same time and men will take turns bringing it back to Kobor during the expedition."

Amo obeyed—she was the Queen! She was right: Kob'Lâm was dangerously depleted.

It was an important undertaking. The first big event wince the Spring Festival when everything started to go bad. Amo called on around 1,000 men who were fitted out for what promised to be a long expedition to judge by the deficiency of stocks they had to replace. Eqin-Go as well as To and Ta were to be his closest companions. The Friend had promised to join them. A meeting was set up for the morning of the departure at the Gate of Kob'Lâm.

Intrigued by the preparations, the Giants of Kobor Tigan't emerged from their lethargy, which looked more like sulking. Surprised to find themselves revived by nothing but the sight of all these men being busy, the thought that maybe everything was slowly getting back to normal.

Thus, a murmur ran through the five cities. The people came out of their houses, one after another, waking up and getting excited. It was still wet, beads of water covered the terraces and walkways, the stairways still looked like spillways, but they saw the sky, finally! Therefore, they all found that the weather was better than they had thought in the depths of their homes.

The meditation caps were pushed far back from their foreheads. They could see better this way. They breathed deeply. And their eyes, unused to the bright light that was creeping back, blinked comically. They blew their noses, snorted and coughed. The movements of the early onlookers, at first heavy and stiff, became livelier as their numbers grew. Then, the people outside started knocking on the doors of those still sleeping.

On the eve of the departure, the blacksmiths of Kob'Râm made a big show of uncovering the melting crucible. They removed the lid that was protecting it from the rain that had hitherto been feared.

Come now, come now, it would rain no more! The worst of the ordeal was over with!

They were cheered on for this. Soon, the forges were aflame and roaring lustily again. The hammering resumed, which was like the sound of life, the beating of the heart of Kobor Tigan't.

In Kob'Lâm, the families put back out the bushes of Kah'B'La that they had protected from mildew. It was touching to see that on some of these bushes there were flowers showing signs of opening.

In Kob'Vâm, the good families started gardening again, fixing the leafy garlands of the territories, cleaning the springs and streams of the parasitic moss and all the vegetal waste that had littered them.

The next day, the expedition gathered in the center of Kob'Lâm. The hunters with their weapons and their provisions for the trip came running in from all corners.

There was an outbreak of joy. People were milling about from top to bottom of Kobor Tigan't, all the way down from Kob'Ooh'R where on the orders of the Queen the votive garlands, all torn up by the last storms, had been replaced and were flapping favorably in the breeze.

It was a rosy morning. Opak herself was seen waving kindly out of her window. The men from her Chamber of Men clapped their hands merrily, making wishes for a good hunt. Everyone there answered in turn with shouts of gratitude, then, as if they were late, they all clambered down the stairs, down into the other cities towards Kob'Lâm mostly where they could watch the departure.

But Kob'Lâm could not hold everyone. They were already being crushed. All of Kobor Tigan't was leaning over the storied ramparts, shouting and waving their arms when the column of hunters moved off and started on their way, marching in good order past the bridge over the abyss at the gate of Kob'Lâm. Amo was at their head. His red hair glistened.

A kind of disappointment floated in the air, however, especially among those from Kob'Ooh'R because they had hoped to see, next to their Queen, the white figure of the Beautiful Being. They supposed that he was still too weak or maybe he did not like bustling crowds.

It was neither of these. Angel was brooding.

This departure of Amo, on the Queen's strict orders, had deeply upset him. Feeling his exclusive friendship strained, he had barely responded when Amo came to say farewell.

Opak had been secretly satisfied by this coldness.

Na-Nood, the moon of the Giants, shined like another kind of sun. They saw very clearly this evening with only a little fog hovering. Just enough to occasionally swell the huge, iridescent hangings that were slowly fraying up and down the trees of Kah'B'La.

The hunting expedition set up its base camp near the holy mountain in a pleasant, sheltered area, a valley where there was a nice spring whose natural pond was full of green fish that amused the men.

From their arrival at twilight, the 1,000 men were busy from one end of the valley to the other getting set up. The first round of armed lookouts took their position encircling the camp while the provisions were unpacked to which some easy game had just been added.

All the aromatic high grasses were cut and are now piled high in lines of soft beds on which they spread covers and skins so they can sleep under the protection of the cliff that hangs over the end of the valley, creating a semi-circle of hollowed out crevices.

Countless are the fires that burn around the encampment. They are all being fed regularly with branches and twigs that crackle and spit sparks.

Right now, the meal is over. It had lasted a long time. They are finishing it more slowly than they started, with smaller bites that they savor. The conversations, interrupted by their powerful hunger that had to be assuaged, are now starting up again with snatches of sluggish remarks that are never completed but left floating like the layers of fog overhead.

Above the camp, halfway up the valley walls, the fumes of grilled meat drift in the air. They pour their favorite fragrant fats on the embers—musk that gives a feeling of weighty comfort and also keeps the pesky insects away. The flames attract them. They swarm in, relentlessly, and burst in the heat with the same sound as plant pods that mix with the sharp crackling of the sparks.

Very far away they hear the Mouh-Tou bellowing their misty cry. They men joke around: "Listen, Na-Nood is wailing!" The traditional expression that equates the big, milk-giving animals to fair Na-Nood.

They also hear, when the wind blows from this side, the distinctive gurgling of the some Dongdwo who cannot sleep because the commotion of the hunters has warned them that tomorrow the egg collectors will be in their swamps.

To and Ta are lounging near Amo with Eqin-Go, his bosom Brother. The others are spread around at distances fitting their hierarchy and their relationships. Everyone is very tired. They had marched almost without stopping for three days after leaving Kobor Tigan't, making only short halts for snacks and naps. Now, here, they are set up for good and can finally relax.

From this base camp the different activities of the different groups will fan out tomorrow since it is conveniently located pretty much halfway between the Dongdwo swamps and the best hunting grounds.

All along the way before arriving, secondary camps had been set up to serve as relay points for the steady delivery of fresh food going to Angel. The closest to the main camp will bring together all the game that will need to be dried and smoked before sending it back through the same relay points to the storerooms in Kob'Lâm.

Amo, who is responsible for everything, mentally checks the details of his organization. Everything is in place. The men seem content, a little melancholic, maybe, as usual whenever they left Kobor Tigan't. Tomorrow they will be excited by the hunt and will think no more about it.

Na-Nood is shining brightly. She is a presence that Amo understands. He feels uneasy from her. She makes him think of his B'Tah-Gou, Méè-Nê, who has not visited in a long time.

Eqin-Go seems to catch this because he says softly, "O Brother, where has the time gone when we used to both go to visit our Storyteller so often. You are no longer free like in the past, not since that Night you know about. There have been so many things, so much grayness since then. We are barely living! I never see you anymore. You disappeared. Nobody knows where you go. When you're around, you stay deathly silent, which I'm afraid to break. Besides, you don't really see me. You pass by like a shadow, your eyes are elsewhere and it's like you're whispering to invisible beings."

Amo is surprised and sorry for Eqin-Go. He takes his hand. "Is it true, Brother, that I've become like that? I didn't notice."

Eqin-Go nods in affirmation while To also agrees, "Amo, we too, Ta and I, have felt the same things. How many times you passed by us without seeing us! We wished we could've talked to you because we understand the torment you're feeling, you the bravest of the Men."

Amo's eyes turn very gentle. He pats the hands of his three friends in turn, too emotional to speak. He would say too much. And so many things must not be said, which is choking him. But then again, despite their good intentions, he is not sure to be understood.

Emotion gets the better of Ta whose pretty, amber face tenses up. She cannot contain her remorse, "It's all my fault! I should never have told the Very Huge about seeing the Beautiful Being! All the woe started on that day when I was foolish enough to tell her. Oh, the Terrible, how well she knows how to pull out of me what I want to hide, which should've stayed hidden because we are certainly suffering now, all of us since that cursed day when we captured Angel. He is suffering, too. And it's our fault. Now my sister Opak is unrecognizable. She barely governs. And she rejects you, Amo, whom everybody loves!"

She cannot continue. She weeps, overwhelmed, and hugs To tightly.

Eqin-Go tries to sound more hopeful, "I don't know the Beautiful Being, only you've got close to him. But if I believe all the rumors that are running around everywhere from Kob'Ooh'R down to Kob'Lâm, in every house, everyone wants the Beautiful Being to get better. We're all expecting miracles from him that our Race needs. Even if his great Presence is sometimes terrifying and incomprehensible for us. They say that well before the coming of Angel, it knew of his existence, it saw the white birds, heard the laugh that is more than a laugh, so much so that Ooh'R takes pleasure in it. All of us think that the presence of the Beautiful Being is beneficial to us despite all the harmful signs we've seen. But since he started getting better, the fog has thinned and the light has come back in our hearts and on our terraces. The birds will return to

Kobor, you'll see, very soon. Then, our Queen and the Beautiful Being will go forward together."

He stops talking abruptly because everyone is looking at him. The men are standing around him in a circle.

Eqin-Go blushes, a little confused, "I think Méè-Nê came visiting me with her Great Brain. Surely, she was talking through my mouth."

Amo hugged his Brother. "Your words will come true, Eqin-Go! The Beautiful Being will love the Queen. Because he must. If it were otherwise, woe betide us! Come on, let's rest. The first watch needs to be relieved."

The men scatter with approving whispers. They will tell these things before sleeping to those who were too far to hear. But first they stretch out their arms: "O Amo, we love you! You are the best Man of the Race!"

E'Ho-Ha, who is a very handsome, very strong man, almost as big as Amo, comes forward and speaks with conviction. "May you be beloved by the Beautiful Being and stay with him on both sides of our Ooh'Rou for the greatest good of the Race, for our peace and your honor!"

For a while the whole camp buzzes quietly with all these words.

Amo hears it. He is lying back. Eqin-Go has put his head on against his shoulder. Amo suddenly tells him, "We will go see Méè-Nê when we get back from the Hunt." He says nothing more. Maybe he is already asleep?

No, he is silently going over his organization again. His eyes are darting back and forth. All goes well.

Against the cliff wall the hunting weapons glisten, lined up by the sacks that will be used tomorrow for collecting the Dongdwo eggs, led by To along with his best men. Ta readily got permission to follow him. She did not want to stay in the camp waiting.

Other men led by Eqin-Go will hunt the big game whose meat is considered the best for drying and smoking.

Amo, tomorrow, will go alone to the place he knows to gather honey and pick fruit and plants.

Everything that has just been said soothes his heart. Yes, he is loved by all despite the falling out of favor. He very much appreciates the fact that nobody mentioned the non-fertility of the Queen. Will the Great Child, therefore, never be born of him? No, it's not true what Abim said, that Ooh'R shuns him… Ooh'R has a secret plan. Soon Amo will know it…

And then something crosses his mind that he had not thought of since their arrival: soon, tomorrow, or later, but without a doubt, he will see his Friend. Because he was not at the meeting point at the gate of Kob'Lâm the morning of the departure. What does it matter! Amo knows that he will see him again… soon… very soon… He falls asleep without realizing after having checked one last time that the watchmen were surrounding the camp.

Eqin-Go is not sleeping. He sits up, smiles at seeing him finally asleep, pulls up the cover and lies back down, but keeps his eyes open.

The general hum of the camp dies down and the conversations fade away, gradually replaced by the breathing of sleeping men.

To and Ta walk off, arm in arm. They had prepared their bed farther away, apart, in a cave where they will be alone and where the kindling fire awaits them.

Eqin-Go would have like to talk about other things with his bosom Brother. A little more about Méè-Nê, for example, whom they had so neglected and who had just proven through inspiration that she was not forgetting them… And then to reveal something else that is more intimate and is tormenting him…

He slips off to sleep. At the end of the night, in his dream, there are the golden eyes of a T'Lo lit up… there is the graceful crawling to come to him… there is the very slow, very fluid pleasure that never really ends, that keeps going, that drugs…

Na-Nood is shining. The shadows of the watchmen are dark blue on the white ground. They stretch out, gigantic, determined. The guards protect the camp. The whistling, croaking and rustling that suddenly thunder from the depths of the woods, the stalking and pouncing, all this will be kept out by their vigilance. Nothing will break the circle that protects the repose of the men of Kobor Tigan't!

In the back of her house where only the rosy light of the embers is glowing, Méè-Nê is rocking back and forth. This evening, at length, she spoke of hope, the fog dissipating the next day, her fervor in the race. The men she was teaching, who had participated in her rhythmic speech by swaying like her, had all left.

She sighs. Ata-Réè glances at her. Alas! The place reserved for Amo in the middle in front of the others stayed empty again. And empty, too, next to it, the place for Eqin-Go.

"How fast things have gone since that terrible Night!"

But silence was needed. They will not break it. They listen. Are they not guards?

Amo was walking alone, rapidly, to the Domain of the birds. The night had gone very well. He had given orders for the day and knew they would be carried out. Therefore, he had left the base camp wisely organized. The day watchmen took their posts while the men inside the camp got busy with their tasks.

Early in the morning Eqin-Go had taken most of the hunters while E'Ho-Na went with the others in search of the milk of the timid Mouh-Tou, always hard to get close to.

To and Ta had left at the head of the egg-collecting party.

Amo was going at an even stride as if something were calling him. He still heard some of the hunters' shouts driving the game. The sound faded. All that was left was a very faint whispering. Or was it only the wind? Now Amo heard nothing at all. Everything was calm. In this part of the region, there seemed to be no animal life. He had noticed this the other times. He saw only big, glistening insects darting through the air, very high, very fast, drunk on the light.

His Friend popped up in front of him just when he entered the narrow gorge that led to the Domain of the birds. And he said, "I've been waiting here for several days. I left before you."

He was jittery with joyful impatience.

"You took so long getting here!"

Amo was speechless.

The other dragged him along, "Come quickly, I found out where all the birds are hiding."

In a daze Amo followed him without breathing a word. Was he really leading him to the secret little lake? Yes, there was no mistaking the path.

His Friend gloated, "They're all here! All the birds, Amo, all of them! And do you know how I discovered this miracle? Thanks to you! Yes, I dreamed about you. You came to get me and you brought me here. It was so clear, so real that I wanted to see for myself. I couldn't wait for the hunt to leave. It was too long for me to find out. So, I left. I ran the whole way. And I found them! All of them, just like in the dream, Amo! It's true, true, all the birds are here!"

Amo was watching him in his joy and found him beautiful. His Friend stopped, comprehending, and spoke gravely, "You knew it, didn't you? You knew where the birds were?"

"Yes," Amo said.

They spent a magical day together. Once again, as if it were needed, they reaffirmed their perfect harmony. They picked plants together, filled up the honey pots that Amo had brought. Then, they dove into the lake to relax. The Friend lay down under a tree on the shore to take a rest. They talked for a while in soft voices that dwindled away and finally stopped because the Friend was asleep.

Amo had no desire to sleep. The whirling hither and thither of the birds and their chattering made his head spin, not in a bad way but they put a kind of spur in his blood, a kind of yearning for something unknown... that was waiting for him, that was making a sign to him...

At first he took a few steps, worried about staying by his Friend's side, then, slowly, he wandered off.

Now he is walking, absorbed in his thoughts. The jabbering and the winging of the birds are intensified. He watches them. So many birds! Thousands of black eyes staring at him. All the ledges on the cliff are teeming with these light creatures. Clouds of feathers bursting in the air! A whirlwind.

And all the winged folk resting in every way, like a handful of white dust tossed up.

Mysterious orders seemed to be controlling their flights. There is a sudden calm. They are all perched, very high up on the edges of the rocks. And here is Amo, utterly astonished, starting to follow, docilely, this little ruby red bird fluttering in front of him, settling down three steps ahead, then soaring off a little farther, leading him on like this...

The little red ball bounces along and Amo lunges forward again and again. The bird is always out in front.

Amo climbs up a ramp that rises along the wall. The little bird of fire is leaping a little higher. It alights. It waits for him. Amo hurries up.

All of a sudden, he notices that he is overlooking the lake from very high up. How far away the peninsula is! Because of a bend in the ramp, it is now behind him. He had not realized it. And now there is a very dark, very deep gorge beneath him where plants and trees are tangled together.

How could he have climbed so high without feeling tired or surprised? He has a weird feeling of being accessible. He wants to be. He accepts it. He is happy to accept it.

The bird is quite close, watching him with keen attention. Is it going to fly off farther ahead? In that case, it will be impossible to follow it because the ramp stops right after a slab juts out of the cliff. The little bird shuffles behind the slab! Amo does the same. Here is where the ramp stops. And before him is a deep, dimly lit rift in the rock. The ruby red bird stands at the entrance along with a handful of other birds of all colors.

At the sight of Amo, they soar off, peeping joyfully, back through the rift. Do as they do, he tells himself, and he enters.

Right away, his sense of time abandons him. He loses the memory of what is behind him. And who is he? He no longer knows. But it is not important.

He walks like in a dream. Does he have a body? All his consciousness, his whole universe is focused on this concern to keep following the handful of precious birds that land and fly off incessantly, leading him onward, ever deeper, inviting him with their sparkling eyes.

After an indeterminable time, he realizes that he is following the Grand Old Man, haloed by birds. The air is glowing blue, which he had never seen anywhere but he is not flustered. He is content with it. It reminds him of both the intensity of the sky and the luminous depth of water…

He follows passively. Ahead of him, the tall figure with an outline fringed in light. A silent march. Solemn. Patient. The Old Man wields a tall staff. A cluster of birds grips the top of it, beating their wings, elated, quivering. Below, in the sand, at the bottom of the staff, a snake is slithering!

And then here: Amo is sitting, serenely, in a vast cave. Is it a cave? It is so blue! And there is no end to it… He looks… And here: before him stands his Friend, who is facing him and whose tall figure is hiding something… And then what happens? What mysterious phenomenon is pushing his Friend slowly closer to him? Amo gets up. And his Friend is right up against him. His outline is all blurry. And now they are one, a single creature because his Friend is absorbed inside him. Amo hears: "Finally, finally, here I am!" And he is full of joy. And solemn too. And the plenitude inhabits him. And he sees like he has never seen before.

He sees: there in the middle, with his back turned, the Old Man is working at a mysterious task, full of grace and power. From every finger come threads of light. They are shooting out!

The Old Man is holding these threads horizontally between two kinds of pillars that rise up from below and are lost sight of above... And the snake is spinning around on the ground. It spins and swirls. While up above, without stopping, the flights of the birds burst in the air and blend into whirlwinds!

Amo sees the threads multiplying. First at ground level—and the snake spins—then some above others, the threads rise, rise all the way to the roof—and the birds fly and soar—the threads are lost even higher, in the highest, just like the pillars, just like the birds... Amo guesses that they keep rising up. Nothing stops them. Isn't he, too, rising up? What are all these lights, all these colors bursting around him in this ascension? Could it be the birds around him whose movement is so strong, so decisive, that they are carrying him with them?

Up above, Amo is rich, happy, he is noble and at peace. He has glory. He is himself. Finally, finally himself. Healed... The Old Man is holding his hand...

And then, from on high, with all the threads raining gently, vertically down, he descends, Amo, with the others. And with the others, the fingers of the Old Man take hold of the shining thread that he has become... The fingers of the Old Man take the threads and stretch them out from top to bottom. And now the threads are all intertwining. And at every point where they meet, stars shoot out, bright and twinkling...

And here: Amo knows what all this means. All these threads have a name. He knows them just like the Old Man knows them. There are: Amo and nearby these two other threads so like each other, To and Ta. All of them intertwined, bound together. Opak. Angel. Abim. And the work of the Old Man goes on. And all together they are destined to form a fabric, a design on this fabric behind which Ooh'R, Na-Nood and the Other Shining Ones, unknown, go back and forth like watchmen, like attentive guardians who keep an eye on what the hands of the Old Man are weaving and if his threads, all his threads are obedient to the sage rhythms that govern them, the stars, and which they all obey!

Oh, how immense is the nocturnal space! Who is it, Amo, spread out, floating across this celestial vault? The threads of the Old Man connect all the stars. Na-Nood is there. Ooh'R goes up and back down. It is night, then day, then night again. The cold prevails and the night. The warmth comes after. Then the heat of the summer... He, Amo, at the heart of it all, a child now, whimpering. A royal man now, his voice calm: "Ooh'R!" Why such profound desperation? Because Ooh'R grows big, pours forth, bursts like at the orders of one who truly knows his Name!

From where is he returning? How much time has passed? What age? He knows that he is called Amo. He has already been in this cave where he is now. He has already been like this, standing still. He feels strong and calm. There is power in him. A being is keeping watch deep down inside him, which is both his Friend and himself.

In front of him, with his back turned, the Old Man is working on To, Ta, Opak, Angel, Abim and on him, Amo. They are coming toward one another, attracted, repulsed and bound together. Their coming together and breaking apart form signs and figures that the whole sky remembers and is touched.

They are all like the threads in the hands of the Old Man.

And here: One snaps... Angel? Another frays... Opak? That other one that was seen here, where has it gone? Where is To? This one is becoming white, refined... Ta? That one resists and stays bound, thick... Abim? Amo bursts! Where, o where, is he?

But all is calm. He is in a cave. The Old Man has just come back to him:

"My Son, my Son Amo, you re the first one to enter here. You will always be able to come back if you need help. I am always here. You see, I work. I fix the broken threads..."

The Old Man must have talked for a long time because the memory of his voice, the music of his inflections still cradle Amo on his way back, on the dark and narrow path where all the birds are chirping as they accompany him... Amo is exhausted. Like never before. It is if everything has been shattered inside him. And yet, it is a pleasant shattering.

And now the exit, the bright day, the ramp descending steeply, dazzling under his numb feet. Down below, the lake, the sun that bounces off its surface.

Amo goes down slowly. Everything is so punishing for his eyes. Ooh'R shines so strongly that he feels caught in a trap of light. He cannot think about anything. The lake is getting nearer, with its green peninsula, and under that tree over there, his Friend is sleeping.

Amo walks along the shore. He keeps his head lowered. Every footstep in the sand occupies his mind completely. He tramples the grass on the peninsula. He stumbles. How will he walk without the help of this ruby red bird hopping along to guide him?

Here the one sleeping under the tree. How calm he looks! Amo kneels down. He wants to say something, to express his flood of thoughts, of visions, of dreams unfurling inside him! He wants to say that he knows, that he has seen, that he has understood! But it is impossible. Not a sound comes out of his mouth. And sleep falls upon him. The world recedes. He wants to touch his Friend's shoulder. He has not got the strength. He slides down on the grass, relaxes, stretches out. The mass of memories retreats unto the horizon of his mind. Is he going to lose all this? He does not want to. He wants to remember, to remember…

Amo falls asleep, dark, empty and deserted. The little, ruby red bird who had nuzzled against his cheek flies off.

And he is startled awake. His Friend is leaning over him, shaking him. "Amo, wake up, wake up!"

He struggles to sit up. Fog and mist in his head.

"What a sleep you were having, Amo! So frightening and I couldn't wake you up. But now everything is fine. Listen, Amo, I had a dream. I was standing in a cave. I was standing in front of you. You were sitting down, looking at me with such extraordinary eyes that were calling me, luring me in. And I felt that I had to go to you. And yet, I was craving to turn around and see what was behind me. But I couldn't. And you couldn't see what was behind me either because I was blocking your view. And I couldn't turn around. Or even step aside to let you see. I could only come closer to you. And then, O Amo, all of a sudden, I was inside you, united with you, one with you. And there, through your eyes, with my consciousness, which was also yours, I saw everything that you saw. O Amo, the Old Man! In his hands were threads of light…"

He told the long tale. Amo listened attentively, facing his memories, some of which were already obscured in him so that he had the sad feeling of having lost pieces of his treasure.

By listening he understood that there were differences in perception between his Friend and himself. He had experienced marvels. His Friend only dreamed them. For him, there was no ramp, no ruby red bird and the crucial passages of the grand experience were missing.

But Amo looked up at the cliff searching for the ramp. He jumped to his feet. It was not there! There was no rift in the smooth, white wall that looked so tranquil.

Amo put his hands on his head. The more he wanted to sit back down, the more the details of the adventure escaped him. He ended up sighing without saying more about it.

"O my Friend, I, too, dreamed the same thing as you."

They headed back to the camp. The shadows were long and the night coming on.

Before entering the narrow gorge that led out of the Domain of the birds, Amo looked up with hope like a madman to prove the reality of what he had experienced. A small, red spot up above on the cliff? No, it was not a bird, they were all sleeping, nestled on the ledges. They were white, gray or beige. There were no birds the color of fire. There was just a red reflection of Ooh'R as he set.

When the darkness had come, his Friend, who was walking silently next to him, suddenly touched his hand, "I'll leave you here. You will find me again later. The first chance we get."

Amo wanted to hold him back but he was already gone.

CHAPTER XVIII

Abim stays in a kind of morose reverie where she barely feels the time passing.

She is floating. During the entire period of the rain and fog, she slept almost constantly, always half breathed out of herself. She barely woke up when some silent servants, responsible for her needs in the absence of Ta, came to replace her supply of Dongdwo eggs. She ate almost nothing else. She had no need in this particular state where her exteriorized spirit drifted with no awareness of time. A form of herself in thin shades, in pearly gray. A rest. Contemplation without object, still sometimes interrupted by lively images.

Thus, she very often found herself back in the solitude of the Grand Va-Hôh, to the West of the Ancestors. Sea and waves. Fire and geysers. Cracked earth. Creeping lava. She saw all these things, hovering like a cloud at an unspecified point in space. In her vision, Ooh'R never appeared. Not even Na-Nood—no, it was not night either! But the twilight of bygone days, of the Ancestors, with that star of dark light, the star forever extinguished except for her alone, Abim, to be able to revive sometimes, to recall in the depths of her extensive nostalgia. She was there, yes! She brushed the tall stones erected in a circle…

The commotion of the Hunters' departure, which aroused all of Kobor, had hardly bothered her: less than a wrinkle on her surface! What was the point of being disturbed? She knew that she had to let them go. She incited something by the capture of the Beautiful Being. Now, it had to run its course.

Abim, the Very Huge, is resting. She is saving herself, holding back. Because she knows: soon there will be great effort needed to redirect events in the desired direction. All her willpower will be necessary, all her force, all her powers too… So, with foresight, she is gathering, building her inner resources. Oh, it is because Abim is not depleted like the cellars of Kob'Lâm!

When the moment comes, right on time, she will get rid of Amo. In his place will be the Beautiful Being beside the Queen… In a short while, very short, the Beautiful Being will be on his feet. There is no stopping it. Things are rolling down an implacable slope…

All of a sudden, through the fluid of her astrality, she perceives a signal: an unusual event is buzzing somewhere in Kobor Tigan't. Oh, it is not an alert! Simply something that piques her curiosity. Her attention focuses... Where is it? She wanders, searches, perceives better, gets closer... There, in Kob'Lâm! There is a light leaking through a door in the blue house of Oda-Néè, the woman who keeps Eqin-Go, Amo's bosom Brother.

Oda-Néè appears. She is a pretty woman who interests Abim because even though she has few men—Eqin-Go is her favorite—she nevertheless possesses many T'Lo.

After a cautious glance outside, reassured by the calm, she goes back into her house and softly calls out to the shadow that is waiting there behind the door. A T'Lo steps out.

Abim recognizes him with rush of interest and approval. It is T'Lo Gâ. He is highly renowned. Almost as much as T'Lo Dê. He has a long history with human intimacy. Transmitted by inheritance to Oda-Néè who stands by him like a family coat of arms.

The other T'Lo, a little scared, huddle together at the door not daring to leave.

Abim understands the meaning of Oda-Néè's whispering as she puts her hand on the T'Lo's neck, pointing into the night, "Go to him, T'Lo Gâ, you who are our ardent link! Bring my love to him along with yours!"

The amusement expanded in Abim's consciousness like when a shiny pebble makes waters ripple—a never-before seen event, this T'Lo going off alone in the night!

For, it is true, he goes, with specific intent, a decided goal. First, he sniffs the air, keeping his hands in front of him, his mauve webbing spread out. Now he sets off and Oda-Néè closes the door. The lamp goes out. No more noise.

But there is this T'Lo going down the walkway that connects the highly perched house to a first terrace. He feels his way along the railing. He has found the stairs that lead to the big flats where he scrambles farther down, despite his nervousness, toward the red smoke of Kob'Râm at work.

Once there and even though he has seen no one, the sound of the forges, the throbbing of the bellows, the banging of the tools, all this active wakefulness so typical of the city frightens him. He runs, not knowing where, holding his head as if disoriented. He ends up crouching in a bushy garden in Kob'Vâm. Leaves are dripping on his spine. There is water in a basin. He leans over, dips his finger in. Then he is off again and does not stop. He crosses Kob'Lâm where everything is dark, where nothing moves. His big eyes shine in the blackness. Now he is crossing the bridge…

Abim still sees him as he slips down into the hollow valley, through the grasses. He knows where he is going…

Abim knows, too. What a curious event. The incident has entertained her. Now she turns away. No need to follow him. He will not get lost.

Abim gets back to the stillness of her indefinite contemplation. The T'Lo are part of her occult power. They incarnate the memory of the Ancestors. Wherever they are, she is, implicitly. This one will provide her, if need be, with a listening post where he is headed.

Abim rocks in her somewhat gloomy grayness.

In the hunters' camp, Eqin-Go cannot sleep. He tosses and turns on his bed. The dry leaves crackle under him. He is suffering from a racking sensation of emptiness. A corner of his being is deserted. It is a kind of hunger that he is familiar with. Nothing appeases it. Nothing but the object itself of his torment.

He cannot stand it. He gets up, without a sound, and crosses the camp. He climbs up to one of the cliff ledges where he finds a watchman named Ka'Ok. He touches his shoulder. "I can't sleep. Get some rest, I'll take your place."

Ka'Ok looks deep into his eyes. Something passes between them and the watchman mutters, "Me neither, I can't sleep… far from Kobor."

The last three words mask others. Eqin-Go stares at him. Do they both belong to the same Secret?

Ka'Ok speaks again, "Here, in the camp, a lot of us are like you, like me. It's hard to be away from them… who are suffering, too, being away from us."

The two men touch each other's hands. The watchman makes the expected gesture and takes off the big bracelet that protects his arm. The bracelet is hollowed out. Inside is a smaller, thinner ring: a T'Lo insignia.

Eqin-Go does the same, shows a similar bracelet. They are both complicit in the Secret.

Before leaving, yielding his place, Ka'Ok speaks again, "In Kobor, when we get back, the Secret Festival has to take place! We should have got all of us together. The evil spells should have been broken. Instead of that, we took a long time…"

He went off, respecting Eqin-Go's desire to be alone. And he stays alone. Time passes slowly. Na-Nood is enthralling. Eqin-Go ends up seeing nothing but the intense brightness of the light that absorbs his gaze… What is slipping through the grass? He grabs his weapon. A deep breathe, a lunge. He is about to strike but holds back just in time. T'Lo Gâ has just collapsed at his feet, exhausted by the frantic run that has brought him to his master.

With Ka'Ok's help, Eqin-Go will hide his T'Lo. The news will spread very secretly. Only those who wear the other, smaller bracelet hidden under their big bracelet (by which they recognize one another) will know about it.

But in the final days of the hunt, when the camp was almost deserted, the last forays having taken the hunters farther away, Amo chanced to enter a cave he had not noticed before, hidden as it was behind a curtain of leaves, and discovered all the traces of a ceremony of T'Lo worshippers.

"Almost the Secret Festival," he grumbled.

Annoyed, he stamped his foot and looked around in search of more telling details than the overall picture. How many of these T'Lo are there. Who brought them?

But quickly he had to face the facts: there was only one T'Lo here. He knew by the way the bed had been set up on the sand with the marks around it.

The furious desire to unmask the guilty parties surged up in him. He would have to search the camp, interrogate… Oh, who was hiding a T'Lo? This T'Lo who might have been in the cave just last night, maybe a whole group of conspirators came to render him homage… Oh, he could see them huddled together around the bed, keeping deathly silent, watching the insane mating: Man and T'Lo… An absolute mockery of the Fertilization Festival when the Queen is on the High Terrace! With horror, Amo repressed these memories, so recent but still fading away, getting lost in the distorting mists of all the sorrowful events that afflicted him recently.

He stared. Yes, there, all of them, in a circle, all night long, watching Man and T'Lo… The T'Lo, sometimes man and sometimes woman… A mystery of the double nature. A mystery known to the most distant Ancestors, the Huge, the Unthinkable… He shudders… All night long! Until the exhaustion beyond which, apparently, open the countless delights of the Other Pleasure, That-which-is-slow, That-which-never-stops…

Amo repressed the assault of other similar images that rushed into his memory. He knew only too well the infatuation Opak had for the T'Lo. Deep down, the Queen never forgave him for not ever having given in with her to the embraces of T'Lo Dê. Did he really hate T'Lo Dê? No, not really…

His anger subsided, replaced by a bitter clarity. He left the cave. What good was it to search the camp and turn everything upside down? It was only one T'Lo after all, not an enemy. He would only succeed in sowing trouble and disorder by tracking him down. Weren't the usage of the T'Lo permitted? It never gave rise to cruelty. Nothing bad, apparently, ever came of it… It was worse, perhaps? He did not really know… Weren't those who love the T'Lo likeable and peaceful? There was, however, this softening, this twilight of the being that took hold of them…

Amo sighed. Was it necessary to take action? His reproaches would not be understood. He would only arouse astonishment, grief and bitterness. Maybe also scorn? For, this refusal of the T'Lo, in the eyes of some, belonged to the type of people who took care of the stocks in Kob'Lâm, who were crude and blinded to the point of having lost the meaning of the ancestral ways.

Amo kept quiet.

But it was a very painful restraint. At the first opportunity, he opened up to his Friend when he showed up at a turn in the path. He told him about his find, explained things to him, tried to express all the disapproval he felt for practices, especially tried to understand himself and maybe after all was said, to find a way to justify his being different from those who were considered the noble successors of the Ancestors.

But to his great surprise, his Friend interrupted him with smile to tell him point blank, "Do you know that your bosom Brother Eqin-Go is also a worshipper of the T'Lo?"

Amo jumps, "What? Eqin-Go, my bosom Brother?"

He turns pale, is outraged and grabs his Friend's calm hand.

But it was obviously true. He had noticed for a long time, more so lately, certain signs in his Brother's behavior, that special gentleness, that tender lasciviousness he emanated. And then that detachment, the evasions. And the inexplicable absences. The image of the cave behind the curtain of leaves popped up in his mind: so, that was it, Eqin-Go with T'Lo Gâ, Oda-Néè's favorite!

After the first shock, he was eager to know more and asked, "You, Friend, how did you know?"

The Friend smiled frankly, "I know, that's all. And I know there's no doubt about it."

Outrage and bafflement arose in Amo, who was shifting from side to side. "But why, why exactly Eqin-Go? He never told me anything?"

"Maybe he tried but you didn't listen or understand."

Amo shook his head, "Oh, those T'Lo, I hate them!"

"Why, when you know nothing about it?" The Friend laughed and made Amo sit down so he could talk to him. "Don't get carried away like that, Amo! Listen instead. Before judging these things, you have to know them. Now, what do you really know about our origins, those of the T'Lo, of the Ananou? And the Greater-Than-Us, what do you of them?"

"Not much. I'm not a B'Tah-Gou. They know!"

"Maybe a little less than you think."

Amo was calming down, as always when his Friend talked to him. "Oh, you're probably right."

The Friend gazed at him, "The Great Secret, do you know it?"

"No. Obviously not. I only know that the worshippers of the T'Lo say they know it. They also say that it justifies their way of life. I don't know if they should be believed. Maybe it's a way of bragging... But you, my Friend, where'd you get the Secret from because I see from the look in your eyes that you know everything? I can't doubt it coming from you."

"I do, indeed, know the Great Secret. And I want you to know it because in this Secret lies all the past of the Ancestors and... mine. I am here to share everything with you. Listen!"

He leaned closer as they were wont to do during serious conversations. And during the whole conversation he held his hand.

"Here is the whole Secret. In bygone days, long before Kobor existed, long before our Ancestors, fleeing the cursed West, coming to set themselves up, the Greater-Than-Us were living on the High Plains."

"That I know."

"Yes, but you don't know who the Greater-Than-Us were. They came from the Land Beyond Kah'B'La."

"The dead land? The land of the Beautiful Being?"

"Angel is nothing like them. Angel is something else. But keep in mind that the dead land was once a living land, rich and fertile, marvelous, full of things and creatures that you can't even imagine. Now, there came a time when, for some unknown reason, the earth dried up and life withdrew. The Greater-Than-Us died off in droves. Some of them owed their life only to their flight into the High Plains. They had to live there, to survive. They were few in number but determined, powerful and strong-willed. For their race not to go extinct and because they couldn't multiply fast enough, they coupled with the very tame but very big lizards that peopled the High Plains. They gave birth to hybrid creatures, the first Ananou whom they raised to obey them and serve them. These Greater-Than-Us, therefore, got in the habit of practicing two kinds of mating. They kept coupling with each other, between families, which perpetuated the race and produced the Noble Caste. But they also procreated with their servants, which made a kind of people. Over the ages, the lizards went extinct. There remained only the Ananou, crossbreeds of man and lizard. They evolved like that. Oh, they were weird men the Greater-Than-Us! They certainly built cities stronger than Kobor, but you see, nothing remains of them."

The Friend paused for a moment.

"What kind of life did they have?" Amo asked.

The storyteller shook his head, "We have no details. It's too far from us. But still, the memory of the Tradition preserves the main events that were decisive in their destiny. See, they were bold men who feared nothing. They had no taboos like ours. But there came a time when, just by living, as the generations passed, their opinions, at first unanimous, diverged. Their solidarity weakened because no danger of extinction threatened them since they were well established on the High Plains. So, they split into two factions. One wanted to preserve the live of the Ancients. While continuing their human procreations, they were also happy with their Ananou, begetting servants with them, which was becoming a more essential part of their domestic life."

"Were those servants already basically T'Lo?" Amo asked.

"Almost. But the other faction didn't want to live like that. The people of this opinion wanted to mate with humans only. They figured that the Ananou, who were numerous enough, should mate between themselves only. These people called themselves the Pure. They thought that they alone were the true nobles. They called the others the Mongrels.

And for them this was very pejorative because they were extremely proud. What happened between the two factions? A fight, a war, followed by a compromise? To tell you the truth, we don't know. The Mongrels kept living on the High Plains while the Pure left for the West. And these two fragments of the Race had no more contact. They even forgot about each other over the Ages.

"The West? How did they survive?"

"That, too, Amo, has been lost. But we know this: the Pure had brought their Ananou with them and had no intimacy with them. But it happened that one day, one of their Queens, after losing her favorite spouse, fell in love with an Ananou. What can I say, it was a fatality of race! The old instincts resurface... Now, a strange event occurred that was unique in history and that was known only to those closest to the Queen: she conceived a child with this Ananou. She had a huge daughter who was a Great Queen. They say that these Queens preserved the secret tradition of a T'Lo Spouse. But they maintain that never again was a woman fertilized by a T'Lo. The Stones of Grand Va-Hôh were erected at this time to commemorate these things."

Amo was waiting for one more detail that he felt was coming. The Friend told him:

"Yes, they say that terrible Abim is descended from this Queen. That's why she tolerates the use of T'Lo. That's why she draws her strength from the Ananou. But, O Amo, others, whom you know not, also say that the terrible lineage stops at Abim and will not continue through Opak. The Very Huge would like her daughter Ta to take a T'Lo..."

Amo wanted to speak because he was shaken up, but the Friend imposed silence.

"Listen to what came next, it's almost the end of my story. In the ancient city before Kobor, the Greater-Than-us, the Mongrels who no longer knew anything about their families in the West, were afflicted with a sickness. The High Plains were covered with noxious fog... Now you see why, instinctively, we're so afraid of the fog... It lasted for ages. The Mongrels disappeared. Some died, others maybe left? We're not sure. The fact is that only the Ananou remained, thanks to their reptilian nature, surviving despite the humidity, sticking to the High Plains. Time, a very long time, passed. Then over in the West there was a great disaster. The Pure were decimated and were led by some latent atavism towards the High Plains, now free of the fog. They had saved only a very few of their Ananou, but they found the descendants of the other Ananou, those of the Mongrels. So, by necessity, they had to mate with them… And everything started up again! The same and totally different. This was Kobor, Amo!"

To and Ta eventually got tired of always leading the egg collectors. The atmosphere of the swamps oppressed them. The young woman had showed great courage and endurance, willingly taking part in the search for eggs, but it was obvious that she needed to breathe some fresh air, even just for a few hours.

Amo showed up. He had come to see them because he was visiting, one at a time, the different centers of activity for the hunt, from the mobile camps of the big game hunters who had to move often and always farther away so that they could no longer come back to the main camp every day, to the Mouh-Tou milkers who also moved constantly because the timid animals kept getting away from them.

Everything was going fine everywhere. Crops and game promised to be abundant. The relays were working well, bringing back fresh food to Kobor Tigan't on a regular basis. The meat was prepared in a special camp, the first stop quite close to the main camp so that the game would not go bad on the way. In that camp, they dried and smoked the meat over fires fed with aromatic herbs that burned all day and night.

The Dongdwo swamp was, perhaps, the least healthy of places. So, they worked in shifts, changing frequently so that no one got sluggish or sick from the stench.

Now, To and Ta, taking their work very seriously, had remained at their post without rest or relaxation. Amo was worried about them. He saw the young woman's complexion had gone bad and To's cheeks were sunken. He told them that it would behoove them to take a break since, all in all, given that all was well, it would be easy to find someone reliable to lead the collectors.

The young couple was overjoyed. They left at once because they really needed to. They would walk and camp in nature, free for a few days, before returning to the base camp, they said, adding that if they happened upon any roots or good berries for Angel to eat, they would be pleased to pick them and bring them back later.

Amo watched them leave, happy to see them prancing away with joy. And he had a sweet, tender feeling for their intimate happiness, their unique harmony. He loved them only the more, all the while thinking sadly that he too, like To, would like to be the only man of the Queen.

Thinking again about Opak turned his heart inside out. He looked around in the hope of meeting his Friend. But he was nowhere to be seen.

It was Amo's turn to leave the swamp. On the way, full of sad images that, seemingly, were piling up in him as if they were summoned, he brooded on his recent sorrows once again: Angel's coldness when he went to say goodbye? Why had he looked so frigid? Why those hard eyes, that scornful scowl that said (and he understood it) "You others of Kobor Tigan't will always disappoint me! A stranger I am and a stranger I will remain. I thought I had a friend here, but this friend is going on a hunt without even a thought of staying by my side!"

Yes, that was what Angel's coldness was saying at that moment. He had turned his back. How hard those goodbyes had been! He could still see the scene: Angel went to the far end of his room, sat down under the hanging fabrics that protected his bed and called over T'Lo Dê who had sensed what was happening and stayed there to swing his grief-stricken eyes from one to the other as if to say: "Don't do this, don't do this, please!" But come now, is it necessary to heed what seems to appear on the face of a T'Lo?

Amo braced himself against this emotion that he deemed unworthy because he was true that the T'Lo often destabilized him and affected him more than he let on... No, assuredly, he did not hate T'Lo Dê! He only regretted that this was a T'Lo, nothing but a T'Lo, and not a woman...

More than anything, he remembered the weird expression on Opak's face when Angel turned his back to him. She looked Amo straight in the eye, not like a Queen, not even like a woman, but really like an enemy who had triumphed. "You go and I'll keep him for myself!" That was the meaning of the grin that flared her nostrils and bared her teeth, exactly like when she was hungry and the longed-for meal arrived.

But come on, what could Amo do? It was the Queen. He still belonged to her. She had not really rejected him yet. Plus, weren't the cellars of Kob'Lâm dangerously depleted? The long hunt, therefore, was justified. And Opak was trusting him again since she had put him in charge of it...

During these bitter reflections that made him feel the full measure of his loneliness, To and Ta were floating in the purest bliss. They were thinking of nothing but themselves. But their affection for Amo had risen to new heights after the sign of friendship he had just shown them.

To and Ta sprinted or strolled according to their fancy. They slept in moss-covered caves where nothing came to bother them because there were no wild animals around and everything was quite timid, scampering off silently at the approach of men instead of attacking them.

They almost did not feel time passing. But one morning when they woke up late after a night of perfect harmony together, greater than they had ever felt before, they realized that their feet were guiding them back to Kah'B'La.

Laughing, they hurried to the ascent. It was a clear day without a trace of fog. The rising heat lulled them a little, added to the lethargy of their long night of love, which had really been longer than ever before.

With their thoughts wandering, they helped each other on the path rising like a green tunnel from all the plants and trees along the sides. And they remembered more and more excitedly and anxiously the first time when they went together to the top and looked together onto the other side.

Today it was exactly like that day.

But the fatigue got the better of them halfway up. They lay down to rest, in each other's arms, in the shade of a big rock that hung over their heads like an awning. When they opened their eyes because of the wings fluttering and the birds chirping, they really believed that they were dreaming. And they could not move because their minds were floating outside their bodies.

The Grand Old Man was sitting and leaning over them. It was just like the first time. "Beautiful children, don't forget to never separate. Don't let them ever separate you. For no reason. For no excuse. Because you are two halves of a one."

And he was already gone. Already there were no more colorful birds that were so delightful to see.

To and Ta got up, still groggy. But their strength was back. So, without a word to each other they ran straight to the top of the mountain as if they were once again about to discover the miracle of Angel.

It was something else they saw when they leaned over the flat rock of the summit that was like a platform and where relics of the fight between Opak and Angel were still visible. The rope used to haul the net was rotting in a corner and the white skeletons of dead birds were all scrambled in the most pitiful way.

Finding these vestiges, these mute witnesses, they again felt guilty, really to blame for Angel's capture. Especially Ta, who had still not forgiven herself for being so easily taken in by her Terrifying mother.

But what they saw on leaning over the Other Side took their breath away. On the rocky cradle where Angel had spotted them the first time, now there was a trickle of water welling up, strangely, and flowing in a straight line around which myriads of multicolored insects were teeming.

The trickle of water was so thin, so meager that, of course, it did not flow down all the way into the Dead Land. It evaporated well before, dissipated in the intense constancy of Ooh'R. But Ta, on seeing this, perceived strange things and she was suddenly in that visionary state that sometimes took hold of her. To, therefore, listened to her in fear because she was truly seeing through time and her words then became just like those of the B'Tah-Gou, irresistible and engraved in the memory and above all never to be doubted.

While listening he had to hold her tightly in his arms: the vision was so powerful that her body shook and if she had been alone, she would no doubt have rolled over the edge, borne away by these things that were being expressed through her before their time had come.

It started with a groan. Ta wrung her hands like a woman alone who has lost hope in everything. She did not seem to see To anymore. Her eyes were gazing upon terrible things beyond.

"O solitude! O what a desert of white solitude. I, Queen, what sadness must have brought me to these places. I have seen them arid and desolate. I have seen them when the sign of water was placed over them. Oh, that was the first sign of the start of the Terrible Things. And everything I have experienced has no name. Nothing for me but the name of Solitude. And here now I am leaning over what is no longer the Dead Land where I was young, happy and passionate, no longer the Land of the Return of Water from when I was still and even younger, happier and more passionate, no, no, now there is a cataract that has been roaring, rushing and crashing for so, so long! See, see, people of Kobor, it is a huge river that now rolls its raging waters through the Land on the Other Side... Listen to all these waters rumbling! How they sparkle! How they spread! Will all the Land become a region of water? Then... and then, oh, I have grown so thin, oh, I am all white and the women of Kobor, too, who tried to match my paleness... in Kob'Ooh'R there is now a Great Place where people go. They enter it. They stay there, silently, facing the beautiful, mute Witnesses erected there before them… O sad queen, poor Ta, here in this place of time, what have you found?"

Ta, struggling in the arms of To whom she obviously did not see anymore, showed signs of greater dread.

"See them, see them, what a crowd! All of them with her, all with Ta—yes, yes, she is the white woman—they are straining to see… Oh, how loud are the clamoring voices and what echoes they make! Yes, yes, they are saying it's true: the cataract has dried up. The Land sparkles like a crystal. All is dry. Dead again. Another kind of death. And look, look, there, down below, a miracle! He is there, it's him, the Vanished whom we have searched so long for. See him in the cradle of rock, become himself like a sparkling rock…"

Her eyes rolled up. She fell back into the arms of frantic To.

Before sinking into an uncanny blackout, her voice faltered, becoming almost inaudible. She was still muttering, however, more and more confusedly, more and more murkily. To tried desperately to understand. He caught a few snippets:

"See, O queen, sad queen, see in your extraordinary solitude, to the Great Enclosed Place of Memory they have brought you. Here next to other memories. It is him. They come to see him. He sparkles. Unchanged. Pure. The waters of the cataract have turned him into a sparkling stone…"

Her voice failed. Her eyelids draped her eyes. She was soaked in cold sweat and the color was drained from her cheeks. To felt like he had saved her just in time from the waters she was seeing. She had not drowned, no. She was breathing calmly, very relaxed, apparently in a deep sleep. To could not wake her up.

He wrapped her in their two blankets and ran feeling that if he ran fast enough, he could ward off the fatal destiny that the words of the prophetess seemed to foretell. He carried her back to the main camp by the shortest route.

But night overtook him. He got lost abruptly without understanding how it could happen. All of a sudden, as he was making sure that his precious bundle was well protected, he tripped. Without letting go of Ta, he rolled down into what seemed to be a deep, mossy ditch. He was only dazed, with no injuries.

But thick clouds masked Na-Nood, so much so that when recovered a little he barely saw anything at all around him.

Finally, after a moment, he realized that he had really fallen into a very narrow space, a kind of shaft covered with dry grass and moss, from the bottom of which he now saw, very high above him, the edge of the rock that had tripped him. Then his eyes adjusted to the dark and he made out the faintly lit mouth of a cave in the wall.

To felt exhausted, his legs were trembling but he was hesitating to take shelter in the cave and await the day when a beating of wings followed by a little chirping drew his attention.

He looked harder.

And it was a little bird, all excited and merry and round and red as a ruby whose glistening eyes seemed to be inviting him.

All of a sudden, seized by a feeling of safety and joy, he thought of the Grand Old Man. He was not mistaken because almost immediately his voice was heard, "Come in, Beautiful Children!"

He went in. And barely over the threshold, Ta warmed up, woke up and smiled at the same time as him on seeing the Old Man who was bidding them come to the back of the cave, bathed in a pale blue light.

Then To became aware that was sleeping there with Ta under the protection of the Grand Old Man who, once in a while, spoke to them. Their souls received the message.

...There were also long, ineffable stretches of rest and then, once again, To awoke a little.

So, unsurprisingly, he still saw, in a quivering halo, the Grand Old Man working, holding living threads in his hands. He knew that Ta was seeing this also. And they fell back into a warm and revivifying sleep.

Always, always the Old Man pursued his vast labor. The threads intertwined, from the bottom to the top of the world, and strange, telling designs were formed over which hovered assemblies of stars... strange designs that were called To, Ta, Abim, Opak, Angel, Amo...

"Beautiful Children," the Old Man said, "remember well to never separate! Never... Never..." The voice faded away.

The morning light woke them up completely. Had they dreamed? There was no trace of the Grand Old Man nor anything else.

The cave that had seemed huge before, now looked rather small. They left, mystified. Almost at once they found some natural steps, they could climb up to the rock they had fallen over.

And they went back to the camp.

CHAPTER XIX

During all this time that the hunt was going on, things were not going so well between Angel and Opak. Especially at the beginning.

In the first few days he was in a really nasty mood, to the point of losing his natural grace. Surly and sulking he looked exactly like a bird balled up on a branch in bad weather.

He clung to the bad feeling he had at Amo's departure. He also missed To and Ta. Therefore, for a while he barely said a word, shuffled around dolefully, and could only be around silent T'Lo Dê.

He pretended to ignore the Queen, adding this new resentment to the long list of others. But Opak, for once the diplomat, managed to show surprising discretion, given her intrusive nature.

She came, of course, several times a day, to take a look or to ask after the needs of the Beautiful Being. He, true to his pattern of conduct, did not answer and did not even stop whatever he was doing at the time. Moreover, he spent most of his time at the window staring at the sky as if something or someone would be coming to him from there. Or else, frustrated by this repeated wait, he took a break by appreciating the view, finally cleared of fog, that looked out over the steeply layered terraces of the four cities below Kob'Ooh'R.

If Opak brought food, he just flicked his hand behind his back without even turning his head: "Put it there…" And that was all. The Queen made a sour face but turned around making no other show of her bitterness, just a sign to T'Lo Dê who dutifully went over to Angel.

This tactic was hard for the Queen to keep up and most contrary to her impatient temperament. But she controlled herself, inspired in a way by the unusual intelligence that allowed her, for the first time, to see a thought process through to the end with a tactic worked out: sending Amo away and gradually taking his place with the Beautiful Being.

While waiting for his spite to simmer down, the Queen obviously had to keep up her strength for hope by eating a lot (the only really useful distraction!) and gathering her Men and T'Lo around her in the Chamber of Men. At these gatherings, she paradoxically started to miss Amo. He alone had the resources that could make her forget her worries. She knew he was still the most satisfying of her men, the only one whose mating always gave her the longest and most climactic pleasure. With him she had the thrilling feeling of seizing a masculine force for her own use. She came out of his embraces richer and more the Queen, having conquered the essential and particular vitality of this man through the muted craving of her femininity.

Her other Men did not give her the same feeling. They were there, handsome and tame, flattering the massive vanity of the Ooh'Rou, but they did not bring her anything special, no magic, no effusion of power to steal. It was good, healthy and pleasant to mate with them, to consume them, to feed on them. The erotic games they distracted her with were the just desserts of her status. But it was not enough. There was something else she wanted to take and assimilate. Something else that did not belong to her. That she might not really have the right to take? And for this very reason she wanted to take it.

She came to think that there was certainly some similar resource, intimate and secret, in the Beautiful Being that she had never tasted before. There was surely a superior Amo there whose magic she had to acquire to be the greatest, the most fulfilled of the Ooh'Rou of Kobor Tigan't, the one they would later say: "She gave birth to the most celebrated Great Child the Giants have ever known!"

However, time was pressing and little by little, almost imperceptibly, she was starting to use the services of the T'Lo more often than before.

Now, it happened that one night, after quarreling with her men who bored her, she sent them away to punish them, keeping only the T'Lo around her bed. So, this night, as they persisted in reigniting her passion, under the effect of the erotic drug they secreted around them, Opak reached that dangerous orgasm that they alone could give.

All night long, with their strange genius of fondling and stroking, they had systematically exhausted the usual climactic pleasures in her, thus bringing her to the limit of her responsive resources.

And Opak, contrary to her habit, after the pleasures, did not fall asleep. She stayed awake, so weary that she could not move. Everything around her was shaking and she was almost scared. But she could not stop it, already gone too far and too deep, she saw the T'Lo leaning over her, all the T'Lo whose soft hands and tongues and genitals went on without stopping, like in a weird ritual, appealing to her, dragging orgasms out of her that took longer and longer to finish as the resources of her nerve impulses steadily petered out.

And every time they were more intense, more grueling and then she collapsed, more broken but unable to sleep. The T'Lo, with no pleasure in it for them, intensified their efforts with infinite patience, with tireless attention, a will to win her over to them forever by their love for her while an odd, bewitching light glowed in their pug-nosed faces.

...An instant! Oh, it was just a brief glimmer, enough, however, for her to remember afterwards when it was too late, for an instant, yes, she felt that the Ooh'Rou ought to be on guard, that in the domain she was venturing, she would find nothing to grab, nothing to capture, nothing to bring back to show for her victories, but quite the opposite, she would break down there, slip away, always farther in, and never be able to stop going in there or getting lost... Yes, she knew that past a certain limit, there was great danger lurking and afterwards, nothing would ever be the same...

She was about to break out of the hold, to shake free of the intoxication when suddenly T'Lo Dê was there with the others above her. It had the unfortunate effect of reminding her of the nights with Amo when so often, to whip up his male ardor, she had called him over. At the sight of him, therefore, she gestured for him involuntarily.

T'Lo Dê, as master, joined the others. He was more accurate, more ardent, more discerning and more captivating as well.

When his long, stiff, reptilian member penetrated her, she felt her humanity shatter inside her, explode so that she could no longer recover it. But this too was but a brief glimmer. Already she was losing all awareness of it.

...So, from afar, from the depths of her annihilated mass that could no longer even speak: no, the Other Thing started welling up, a slow, piercing, reptilian sensation, endless and instead of making her erupt in pleasure and letting her drop off into stillness, it started infesting her, slow, slow, gnawing away relentlessly, without anything to stop it, loosening the fibers of her being that were unknown to her, razor-sharp, in a constant, almost disembodied stimulation, which swept her away helplessly into the heart of a gyrating movement at the bottom of which her incessant moans were spinning, spinning, spinning...

And it was from this night on that, truly, she started to decimate her vital sources, to abdicate her role as queen and as woman because there was no human presence to alleviate the bewitchment of the T'Lo.

The type of intelligence that had surfaced in her, instead of developing more, wavered, faded away a few times, then came back, depending on circumstances, until it was nothing but a smoldering ember in a blackened hearth.

But it was not instantaneous.

The next day, she awoke very late from a lethargy in which almost all the memories of the night had been diluted. The gravity of her act was totally unrecognized by her. She only felt muddled at the sight of the T'Lo. Her mind was floating in euphoric vapors and she desired to decorate them more lavishly than usual because she found them more beautiful than the night before.

She called for her shamefaced, repentant men to give them a lesson. "See, my T'Lo are better and more devoted than you. I'm so satisfied with them that I'm giving them all new jewelry. And I want them to wear it from now on as if every day was a holiday!"

And she did start giving them all bracelets, necklaces, all kinds of trinkets that she pulled out of her chests while the men lowered their heads.

T'Lo Dê was not there. He had quietly gone back to his duty at Angel's door, waiting for him to wake up and call for him to weave a garland of flowers or simply to say nothing and do nothing but be there to contemplate the sky where, maybe, the Beautiful Being would see the awaited sign.

Everyday life began again like before. It was like nothing had changed. And, in fact, the men suspected nothing. That special night was like many others for them when the queen got mad at them.

She was not mad, though, because she was keeping them with her afterwards. But she proved more insatiable and more demanding than ever. This flattered the men. She, on the other hand, just felt irritated because they were not really satisfying her. A part of her, far away, was yearning for something else. But what? No matter how much she tortured her brain, Opak could not imagine what it was she desired.

She tried to shrug it off. Oh, these men cannot live up to Amo!

Then she brought the T'Lo in when she lay with her favorites. For them it was like before, the usual habits. But for her it was different even though she knew not why.

Emotionless, unchanged, gentle, obedient, ready for anything, the T'Lo, whose golden eyes saw through walls and looked into the expanse of time to come, the T'Lo waited silently. They knew that there would follow similar nights that would become more and more frequent until she would, in the end, never stop.

They loved Opak so much!

The ennui of dreary days got the better of Angel's bad mood. He felt more and more annoyed, almost disgracefully so, seeing that the queen was paying less attention to him.

The better he got, the more the sun poured into his room and the more clearly he saw the daily lives of the inhabitants during his long meditations at the window, the more he started wanting to live, to play a different role than the patient and prisoner. He started wanting those big laughs, that vital energy that was coming to him, faintly to be sure, from the Chamber of Men. Was he jealous? When Opak came to visit he was suddenly awakened, present, charming. The Queen was greatly surprised. So much so that she was momentarily speechless. But since she was bringing something special that Amo had sent to Angel, she it held out to him.

The Beautiful Being shrieked with delight. They were two white birds in a kind of cage made of supple branches.

T'Lo Dê, shivering, withdrew immediately into a corner of the room while Opak and Angel, on seeing his distress, broke out laughing, which had the sudden effect of establishing the first truce between them.

T'Lo Dê, like all his kind, was scared of all animals. The opposite was also true since no animal ever dare come close to a T'Lo! Not that they were cruel—they were atavistically incapable of that—but there was the barrier of Horror.

It was so sudden for T'Lo Dê that he quietly broke down in tears. Angel was in a good mood and the Queen felt the resurgence of interest that her T'Lo had awoken in her. They both, therefore, were there to comfort him.

So well did they do it that he ended up not acclimating but at least resigning himself to the presence of the white birds whom Angel very quickly tamed, letting them fly around the room, which they did not try to leave.

This episode helped to bring Angel and the Queen a little closer together.

He had been dragged out of his inner gloom by Amo's gift, which reminded him of a precious friendship and not forgotten as he was wont to imagine.

Other presents came later from To and Ta.

Opak got herself in his good graces by bringing them to him.

Angel stopped brooding. After all, she was his only distraction! He was really bored with too much and since he was feeling better his curiosity was piqued by all sorts of things. He wanted them explained to him. He thought that it might help him recover part of his lost memory. He felt separated from his own memories only by a thin veil. Details shown through a little more every day. The sight of the white birds had been like a flash of joy to him and when he looked at them, he always felt an intense tremor inside, an exaltation that almost made him cry out... but he kept quiet, unsure.

Therefore, he engaged in conversations to master the language of Kobor. He spoke almost fluently by now. The Queen marveled at him. And he saw this. But when he tried to teach a few words of his own language to her, her eyes gaped in fear, almost in a panic, and she shut up right away, not wanting or not able to pronounce a single syllable of what Angel was repeating patiently. He was disappointed and also upset because he realized that his own language was slowly slipping away from him.

This forced him, then, to delve deeper into his new study. He dove in, getting told and explained all the habits of the Giants. Thus, he learned what the different annual Festivals were, what the fears and pleasures were in Kobor, what made them happy, what they desired and how, in fact, the Women and the Queen in particular governed everything.

He showed great interest and reacted alternately with surprise, ridicule or disbelief. Sometimes also utter disapproval or disdain for the practices that Opak pointed out as important.

The Queen, who got more tired by these intellectual debaucheries than other kinds of excess, still did her best to tell him everything. It was ripe for her, moreover, to leap at the opportunity to flaunt the magnificence of an Ooh'Rou, of Her who always "possesses the handsomest males of the realm whom she is free to capture and renew at the Spring Festivals."

At this Angel frowned, muttering under his breath that "he wouldn't like to be chosen like this."

Opak shot him such a sharp look that for the first time made him turn red, flustered by the fact that he had been captured himself! And under the Queen's glare a sudden anger welled up in him. But nothing serious resulted because Opak had the rare wisdom to stay quiet. Even though her mouth was already half open. See, the thought of the Very

Huge had flashed through her minds, in such a way that she was almost afraid. It seemed like her Mother was advising her to wait and say nothing because the secret trap was slowly closing in, as it should, on the Beautiful Being.

Therefore, she lowered her eyes. Angel was thankful for this discretion. With utmost surprise, it must be said!

So, a certain form of tolerance and intimacy gradually grew between them.

In order to leave Angel as seldom as possible, Opak arranged to have her meals with him, more and more frequently, even though he refused to share them. In truth, he hated these spectacles and so he always gave her dirty looks with an unforgiving eye that caught every last detail of her gluttonous behavior.

She ate with her typical, voracious haste that was always considered an inherent particularity of royalty. She seized her food like she did her pleasures. She snatched the meat from the platters with a rapacious hand. She sniffed the aromas, commented on the succulence of the dishes with her mouth full, giggling, cooing or grunting. Her strong, white teeth crushed and ground while keeping an eye on the rest, which she swallowed up as soon as she could. She clicked her tongue and laughed with such good humor that she was sure it was shared. And then she hollered out for more, always more!

Her favorites, whose simplicity during these spectacles was always a blessing, stood timidly in the doorway, their eyes sparkling, tender, in awe of such a vast power of consumption.

The T'Lo, too, stuck in their bald heads, looked on, but in a completely enigmatic way. Their golden pupils zeroed in on the Queen, contemplating her in a very different way from the men. They perceived a waiting period whose possibilities seemed to extend unto infinity. Yes, they were waiting for the Queen. They would wait as long as necessary. She would come back to them, one night... The Queen all alone... They alone knew these things... T'Lo Dê even more precisely... Opak was satisfied with eating and having the pleasure of seeing them all there.

Two or three times at these feastings splattered with sauce, blood and grease, Angel could stand it no longer! One day, exasperated, without having time to wonder what was happening, he saw himself kicking over the platters! Everyone watching shouted in outrage. Opak said not a word. She stood up, huffing a little, and wiped herself off absent-mindedly. It took a little time to understand the meaning of this outburst.

Then, she had the rest of the dishes brought in and she cleaned them off, deliberately, staring maliciously at her guest.

In the doorway, the men turned pale. The T'Lo withdrew swiftly, except for T'Lo Dê, wary and already distraught.

Angel, who would not back down, stood rooted to the spot, staring defiantly back at the Queen.

She did not hate him. He saw this. Quite the contrary. She was showing off because she had seen his eyes light up with anger, his cheeks turned red, he was breathing fast, his nostrils flaring. She felt it as an arousal, his blood pumping faster than usual and might this be nearly desire? She was hoping to fan the flames, the anger, the blood, to push him over the edge so that he might, for example, throw himself on her, grab her... He had never even touched her. Maybe if their two bodies grappled each other, the flame of anger would turn into a flame of desire spurting between them?

The men understood this perfectly well. They blushed, engulfed by the eroticism emanating from Opak.

And true, she was beautiful like this, in all the glory of her mighty life, of her rosy orange flesh giving off the musky scent from her innermost centers.

And Angel saw this. For the first time, something coming from her affected him. He clearly saw what it was. And yet, he was no longer fighting so hard against it. It found in him something akin to the start of an echo. He managed to let nothing show and surprised them with an outlandish reaction that nobody was expecting.

With a thin smile on his lips, he leaned over and while Opak, being full, pushed away the final remains, he heroically fished out, with his fingertips, a fat piece of meat that he held out, dripping and greasy for her to swallow.

How helpless she was! She ate what he was holding, her head spinning, without knowing if he was mocking or admiring her. Maybe it was both! For, yes, she was beautiful despite her excesses. Her men agreed with the general opinion and found her beautiful because of this, since she surpassed everyone in everything!

Angel, who was aware of this detail, did still not want to share in this kind of esteem? But she left him dreaming of it. So much strength in everything, so much absolutism, such total power to assimilate what she coveted. Oh, she was frightening! He stared hard at her... But no, she was not frightening. She was Life, unrelenting, Life, gigantic, Life, devouring and yet multiplying...

Afterwards, Angel broke nothing else. He pretended to sleep sometimes when she was eating, a new way of escaping the spectacle.

She had tears in her eyes because it was a most unworthy attitude! And her men shook their heads in disapproval. But come now, they could not get angry with the Beautiful Being! Was he not a stranger? Besides, he was so irresistible with his charm! His beauty aroused all desires!

So, while he pretended to sleep, he felt the ambiance change around him. They held their breaths. He knew that the Queen had stopped eating and like them was gazing at him. All eyes were on him, scrutinizing him, becoming quickly intolerable. He had to wake up!

More out of mischief than vengeance, he came up with something else. As soon as the Queen had finished her meal, he ate next, in his way, with a different kind of bravado.

Delicately, he chose a cooked root, dipped it in honey, opened a piece of fruit chosen for its shape and color after a long, admiring inspection, then he breathed in its aroma; he sipped without ever spilling as if the milk or water was liquid light or something exceptional, divine, kept for him alone, whose exquisite pleasures he alone could taste. Everyone gaped at what he did! He refined it more: he took his time, pondered between mouthfuls. His little birds came and pecked morsels from his lips.

He smiled, distantly, as if to himself and if anyone talked to him, he did not answer. His face was pink, his eyes a little misty.

Opak was not mistaken: it was pleasure! But what sort? Pleasure from these little things? How could he feel it? She did not understand. She really tried. It never gave her anything but sticky hands and unquenched hunger!

Waves of despair washed over her. She struggled not to shout out! He was escaping her! Anyway, he was still escaping her, like before. She was making no progress, accomplishing nothing and getting annoyed with suffering his charm.

Because despite herself she had to watch his slender fingers making those mysterious gestures, different from hers, deliberately or unpredictably choosing, squeezing, taking, mixing, slicing fruit or herbs, a drop of honey in a dollop of milk... Hands with those long pinkies... They touched the fruit like insects, like leaves, without a sound, without anything that clashed with the flow of the ceremony.

Opak thought this way of using food was abnormal. This slowness, these tiny quantities taken after all kinds of manipulation, it all seemed so perverse, disturbing, magical… He was torturing her! She loved him a little bit more.

These differences, inexplicable to her, in the way of living: so many obstacles between them. She felt it wholeheartedly. But it brought her no closer to understanding. She did not know what it meant to adapt oneself, for example. They always had to do like her. It was unthinkable for her to do like another, even if he were the dearest, most cherished in her heart. On the contrary, to the extent that the object of her sentiment or desire surpassed the others, she had to conquer it, bring it to her, absorb it, consume its virtues for her own benefit.

Therefore, she changed none of her habits.

Angel was stubborn, too, and stood his ground.

In this he was at fault because, being more evolved than her, it was up to him to compromise. Even just to get a little closer, to offer his hand and lead her slowly to other refinements. For, truthfully, Opak loved him. She loved him in her way, of course, but with all of herself and by the transformative power of love she was susceptible to evolution, to awakening.

But Angel did not love her. He was self-absorbed, in search of what he had lost: his powers over nature. Instead of finding new possibilities, certainly available on this ready soil that was Opak, he persisted in focusing on his former state without understanding that these things had to be surpassed and joined to others and, all in all, transplanted from his mysterious place of origin to this Land of Giants, which had reached a turning point in its cycle and had desperate need of being gently pulled out of its rut.

He had a mission as educator and he was thinking only of himself, of his own contentment.

He realized this once in a while. And this made him feel sad. So, with a kind of self-betrayal, he put aside the real problem, placated his scruples and acted as a teacher to T'Lo Dê whom he taught to make garlands, to choose fruit and flowers, to contemplate the sky and clouds.

And he got this surprising result: one day, shyly, T'Lo Dê started eating like him, honey, fruit, cooked roots, green plants. What utter amazement in the Chamber of Men at this news. Curiously, Opak, instead of being outraged, felt a secret admiration for her T'Lo, which she did not hesitate to show by elevating him over all the others. He got new jewelry and was proclaimed the First T'Lo, the one who would be inherited by the Great Child.

At this point, after all this time had passed, the hunters announced their imminent return.

The cellars and silos of Kob'Lâm were overflowing.

A secret panic took hold of Opak. She figured that things were moving too fast, that she had not made good use of the time. Amo, whom she had sent away, was coming back; his seat of friendship was still warm with Angel; he had not lost any ground. Quite the contrary! She fully realized this when the Beautiful Being had tears in his eyes as he petted his birds while thinking of the imminent return of his precious friend. Meanwhile, what had she accomplished? The right to stay in the same room as him!

She was scared. Everything was mixed up in her head, forcing her to think fast. How could she take advantage of these last few days? She had to slip into Angel's room at night. She had not tried again after her last unfortunate attempt.

She could only think of a fake temper tantrum to throw out her men one evening. But she had to wait, alone, for Angel's light to go out. And he was dreaming of the stars in front of his window. For a long time. She got bored. The T'Lo came over to her...

When she awoke from her heavy sleep, which she had fallen into after her debauchery, she was conscious of nothing but a slow spiral that spun eternally on itself, tearing off pieces of her... she was crumbling slowly, slowly, like an eroding mountain...

It was morning under a bright sun and all the cities were hustling and bustling. Laughter and shouting: "Welcome back! Welcome back!"

The hunters were coming in.

Opak was vaguely aware of it. She had to reconnect with things. She made an effort, tried to get up, but failed. So many problems to face while somewhere a lazy tenderness was calling her. She could hardly see. Everything around her seemed to be floating in a golden mist like in the eyes of the T'Lo, like the tenderness at the bottom of which there was... What was there? She did not know.

She thought of the hunters. Amo? Yes, Amo! She had desired him a lot lately. But today she was doing nothing, drugged... With him would be To and Ta... certainly, certainly... They were happy, those two! With

Angel it might have been like that... She had got nowhere with him. It was too late now. It was almost the same as before the hunters left.

Despite everything, she barely felt upset. And no contentment at all to see Amo again. Everything was so far away from her in this golden mist! She kept going reaching out for the murky tenderness that was signaling to her, that she could not reach and that she was already feeling the cruel loss...

She looked more beautiful to everyone, with a new halo, a radiance, something indefinable that made her languid and charming. Only the pale purple halos around her temples were a sign of her encroaching intoxication.

In the hubbub of the return and the joyful crowd pouring into her rooms, she forgot his night.

The hunters recounted their feats with freer, fuller gestures than the citizens. They were a little thin but darker, disheveled, too, and their clothes were a little shabby; many had repaired their harness with whatever they could find, vines and raw strips of hide yanked off some prey. They had the strong odor of earth and wood.

Amo's red hair had lightened in the sun. His eyes, too. He was laughing with To and Ta who were reacting to the cheerful welcome of the Beautiful Being.

Even though Opak was the focal point and all the gifts of honor were piled at her feet because everyone wanted to bring her the best catch or the most amazing discovery, she felt strangely alone, separated from the others. She wondered what was happening to her and found help only in the eyes of T'Lo Dê, so gentle, so gentle, never taken off her...

She got served a grand, general feast and for the first time Angel took part, eating in his fashion, of course, surrounded by everyone besieging him with curiosity and politeness without ever bothering him and whose constant admiration and kindness to listen to him and watch what he was doing were a moment of happiness for him.

Eqin-Go was sitting with Oda-Néê and Ka'Ok near the Queen. Suddenly, he noticed her temples. He was startled and discreetly warned his woman and friend. For a moment their gaze lingered, was fascinated, then turned gloomy. There was no doubt about it! And they glanced quickly at one another. They, too, bore the same sign. And they gloried in it. Opak was a great Ooh'Rou!

220

At the end of the night, Opak thought she had rediscovered satisfaction and joy with Amo. And he thought so too.

But it was but a flickering flame. In the morning, Opak was sleeping, thinking she had devoured her male's strength. Amo was awake, disappointed, not reunited, never reunited. She was still the Female, the Queen who took and never gave. Insatiable. A bottomless pit.

They were not coming together. Both of them, during this period of absence, had gone their separate ways, too separate. Now they were lost to each other, hopelessly. And this difference could only get worse.

Amo, after these sad reflections, quietly left the Chamber of Men to see the sun.

... Over the next few days his inner solitude is going to grow stronger.

What he had feared is happening, sooner than imagined: his dear Friend, whose presence purifies him, is nowhere to be found.

On the same day as the return, in the deserted hallway of Opak's rooms, while Amo was wandering alone, he appeared briefly at his side: "I will see you at your B'Tah-Gou's. I will go to Méè-Nê one evening very soon." And he was gone without Amo, in his astonishment, being able to say a word. Footsteps were heard, people were coming, talking loudly. They looked surprised to see Amo standing there petrified, alone in the middle of the hallway...

So, he went to Méè-Nê several nights in a row, but the Friend remained absent.

The B'Tah-Gou and Ata-Réè clearly see his woe. They both welcome him affectionately, as if he had left only the night before. They hold no grudge for being neglected. They know perfectly well what is happening and for the rest, for Amo's secret torment, they guess it and offer him kindness and compassion. The other men there, with Eqin-Go, support them.

But Amo finds that his B'Tah-Gou has changed. She is weaker and more distant, with her clouded gaze and gravelly voice.

He blames himself, chiding himself aloud for not having visited enough. But she quickly set him straight, "No, you are guilty of nothing with respect to me. It is something else afflicting me."

She looks ready to say what it is but then no, she strays, "It's time, see! It's the age, it's a great weariness..."

And she acts so tenderly that soon it is Amo who is opening up, who talks about his Friend disappearing. He expresses his despair. He also expresses how futile his searches are. And even though he does not explain clearly, Méè-Nê understands more than he does himself. And she tries, mustering her strength, to give him a glimpse of the enigma.

Those present try hard to follow what the Storyteller is going to say in order to respond appropriately when the story's rhythm demands it.

Here is Méè-Nê in the proper hieratic attitude:

A Friend came out of the edge of my shadow.
He walked towards me.
And it was as if I were meeting myself.
Have you seen Him who looks like me, my Friend?

The audience responds in sooth:

No, no we haven't seen him!

And Méè-Nê goes on:

He was walking by my side, faithful as a shadow.
But he was all light like the Sun-Ooh'R.
I called him my Brother, my Likeness, my Friend.
He instructed my heart, made it rich and beautiful.
Have you seen Him who looks like me, my Friend?

Response:

No, no, we haven't seen him!

Then:

This Friend went back into the edge of my shadow.
He went back to the place whence he came.
I am searching outside, searching everywhere.
I am asking everyone, shouting all around.
Have you seen Him who looks like me, my Friend?

Response:

No, no, we haven't seen him!

Then:

My Friend is in me, deep in my shadow. He was there before I saw him, shining like the Sun-Ooh'R.

He will venture outside no more, but I will enter him, at last. I will be alone no more. Even death will not cast me out. For, He who looks like me will be there, my Friend!

Done. They stay long in meditation. Amo lets his tears flow freely. Eqin-Go is both sad and glad that Méè-Nê, with her usual clairvoyance, has so well responded to the secret of his bosom Brother. Amo is brave. He will heal.

The B'Tah-Gou is tired from this great effort. She would like to say something more but her labored breathing does not permit her to speak. Everyone is worried. Amo most of all.

"What's wrong with our B'Tah-Gous?" Eqin-Go asks. "For a while a kind of spell has haunted them all. And now it's affecting our Méè-Nê."

The Storyteller makes a sign to Ata-Réè. The girl will explain instead of her. But everyone turns pale, their hearts pinched, because the young servants are not authorized to speak to men except when they become the inheritors of a B'Tah-Gou as death approaches their mistress.

Ata-Réè speaks to Amo. Her voice is clear, young. Resonant harmonics ring forth in it.

"Amo, our B'Tah-Gou wants to tell you that she has been sick since the night you know about, the Terrible Night."

He understands immediately. He remembers all the evils of that night when Abim took possession of the Storytellers' astral bodies. He remembers what he saw down there when he was dragged along with them. And the fight he put up. He remembers the circle of Ancestral Stones and the tallest one standing in the center. He knows very well what it represents. Horror shivers down his spine. And in spite of himself, he hears:

"If the Center Stone falls, there will be no more evil spells."

The men say nothing. They are entering forbidden territory here. They must speak indirectly. As little and as briefly as possible so as not to be heard by the one always prowling, always spying in Kobor.

Ata-Réè speaks boldly to verify Amo's ideas:

"At the heart of the Race there is the greatest danger. A Stone blocks the way. What is there is like what is here. It is danger and Death."

Amo suddenly sees himself pushing over the Center Stone. He hears the Great Va-Hôh rumbling all around him. It is so vivid that he believes he is there.

He knows what he will do.

He says nothing. His silence is already meant to protect his future act. He simply nods his head.

Méè-Nê's eyes stare deeply into his. She has understood. She says nothing either. Ata-Réè will say nothing. If they are needed, he will find their help.

CHAPTER XX

Amo is dragging. Despite his will and desire to understand and to admit what is happening, he has a feeling of numbness and dizziness facing the incomprehensible void of his existence.

The episode with his beloved Friend, even though very recent, now feels like a dream.

Amo looks at himself in the water, questions himself. His own face knows nothing either, shows no change. He is like before, like always. There are only traces left in his heart and head.

At one moment he jumps: "The flash that struck me during Angel's capture, had it broken my ties to the world?"

He runs through his memories, relives the fight with Angel... and suddenly he feels, very acutely, this distress grab hold of him when the body of the Beautiful Being was grappling his own... He wants to forget this. He has often pushed this image away. But it comes back whole, just as warm and vivid... He does not resist it this time. He contemplates it with impassioned astonishment. His heart beats faster. His heart of love so preoccupied with finding his likeness.

But what can this tender heart, this burning love attach itself to since the Queen is an abyss and his Friend no longer exists, can never again exist? The face of Angel takes shape before Amo. He is suddenly scared and pushes away, with great difficulty, the appeal of this sweet vision.

Then the despair of living like this hits him immediately and brutally. A current carries him away, he knows not where, towards fatal conclusions. He is utterly incapable of controlling the direction. He is going to crash, far away down there in some dark calamity. To fight back he has to attach his unsatisfied love onto a living subject. Oh, to be alone no more!

Amo is wandering. He is wandering on walks. They lead him nowhere; he gets lost. He is wandering in actions; countless things he starts and never finishes, eventually forgetting all about them. He is wandering in his mind. His sleep is a wandering.

Kobor Tigan't looks foreign to him. He feels like he has come back from a voyage that lasted almost a lifetime and during which he had lost his memory of familiar sites. But the hunting season had not been so long!

225

He has strange suspicions: "Have I died in the meantime?"

He feels young and old at the same time. He feels both worn out from searching in vain for his compatible love and brand new again for not having found it. He looks around and finds no contact with anything. Of course, he is not crazy since he recognizes the city, the people, the things, but all of it looks like reproductions of what existed before his encounter with his Friend.

They greet him everywhere, however. They show him respect and kindness as always.

"May the Gift of Ooh'R be lavished upon you, Amo!"

This is the most common salutation because in everyone's eyes he is still the Queen's Man. He answers in kind and thanks them, all the while telling himself how foreign all this feels to him.

Even the air he breathes in like a stranger in his chest!

Later, he feels guilty for wandering around like this, detached from everything. For, surely, they are calling for him elsewhere! Somewhere there exists what he is searching for!

A warm palpitation flows through the air around him then and he feels it. Where are they calling for him with an urgency to match his own? Who is calling?

Amo turns his face to Ooh'R. The mysterious call resonates down to the marrow of his bones. Where should he go? What should he do? Who should he love? Who, like him, has such great need of being loved?

Is it You, Ooh'R? Is it You?

Full of love and impotence, he watches the sunset and sunrise. At noon he lies down under the vertical sunbeams, letting them burn his skin and the void in his head turned red.

He searches no more. Does not want to search.

"Set on me, Ooh'R! Burn everything!"

He burns without moving and finds, strangely, in this blaze, compassion, attention, almost a presence... Then, again and again, the face of Angel rises as if coming from the solar heart itself. And little by little, Amo does not push it away, but he lets it join with the sun in the devotion he renders less and less bitterly.

Amo thinks that the Beautiful Being is alone, cut off from his kind, yanked out from his origins and even more than him, an exile.

Amo has to confess the tender compassion he has always felt. Between their two beings, since Kah'B'La, something has been connected. And in his bright eyes there glares the same question that he asked during their confrontation. Angel is always saying, "Why are you capturing me like this? Why are you hurting me?"

Amo slowly walking up to Kob Ooh'R. To and Ta turn up, skipping across the terraces to meet him with great joy painted on their faces.

They each grab an arm. "We've been looking for you, Amo, because a marvelous event has occurred. Angel has suddenly become like we saw him on Kah'B'La. He's regained all his powers. They're saying he remembers. He's making sounds like birds. They've never heard anything like it before in Kobor! Come quickly!"

They start running. But Ta keeps talking impulsively.

"It's like at Kah'B'La! We both knew it! From the moment his voice came out, the air in the room became vibrant, crackling. Do you remember how he gathered the lightning in the cloud? Well, you'd think Ooh'R had answered him by letting loose myriads of sparks... The whole sky started gleaming. Look, look, way up high, aren't those birds there? Are they coming back to Kobor? Is his voice calling them?"

Indeed, Amo can see tiny dots moving in the sky. It is so high up that he cannot tell for sure. It is already fading. But they can hear the tones of Angel's voice. And they can see him standing in the window of his room. He is looking up.

They rush into the palace. They run into people who, like them, are hurrying to the Queen's rooms. Without a word, bumping into one another, they enter. It is an indescribable spectacle in the room of the Beautiful Being.

Opak is there, in the middle, as if she had been caught off guard and frozen in place. She opens her huge eyes and looks almost scared. All her Men have entered, as if against their wills. The rapture and incomprehension form an odd mix in their eyes.

The T'Lo are lying in a pile, their necks strained toward Angel who, transformed and larger—or so it seems to Amo—pays no attention to anything but his resonating modulations. His hands are raised in the weird gesture of appeal that is particular to him. His long pinkies are clutched between his other fingers. And as if by this gesture he was channeling, guiding and controlling a secret, inner force, he *sings*, modulating a long melody whose high-pitched sounds interweave in coils.

They do not sing in Kobor Tigan't. They hardly understand what is about. How can anyone produce sounds like this? What does this language mean? The heart hears, the head listens!

Everyone submits to the charm. They feel the blessing, the caress. They want it to last, to never end. Moved, captivated, bewitched! All the developments of the melody are reflected in their faces.

And what is even more marvelous is that they can see way high in the sky a golden-headed white bird appears. Angel has seen it. He emits a shrill call. His melody cuts off. Why does Amo think he hears, "Take me!"

Up above, it spirals, seems ready to come down, but no, it shoots back up and disappears. Had they really seen it? Was it real?

"A bird like the ones on Kah'B'La," Ta mutters.

Angel has lowered his head. Then he looks at them like he is back to himself... Yes, these are strangers to him, these beings of Kobor Tigan't. Must he abandon all hope of escaping them? This only flashes through his head. He abruptly closes his eyes so that they cannot guess his thoughts.

Amo saw and understood. Therefore, he watches more carefully. Angel is facing them, separated by his undeniable mystery. It is a kind of mute confrontation between him and those of Kobor. It does not last. A disillusioned, proud expression slips over his face. Still, he smiles at Ta because she is holding her hands clutched to her heart. Then he spots Amo and gives him a big grin. When he speaks, it is to him he turns:

"Amo, I am going to find my birds again, Mine!" Is this a warning or a confession? Both, perhaps.

"Your strength is back. You are back to yourself," is all Amo says.

But thereby he acknowledges, already approves Angel's secret desires. They understand each other.

Opak does not get all this. Her head is buzzing. Angel, for her, is even more beautiful; more surprising, more inaccessible and more desirable. She sighs at him, "Ang'h is the most beautiful. Ang'h is the greatest. He is the jewel of Kobor Tigan't. The sky answers him when his voice carries over our heads. This is a wonderful, mysterious power. Ang'h, come now, bring back Ooh'R's goodwill and happiness for us!"

They are in awe. For, she rarely says so much.

Angel seems touched by her plea and very solemnly assures, "Soon, all the other birds, yours, those you miss, those that deserted your city, they will come back."

And seeing the joyful astonishment of all present, he looks like he is contemplating the future and adds, "Yes, yes, believe me, soon, very soon, I know, I see, the birds will be here."

228

Abim had Opak summoned.

She is talking to her with her usual intensity. She has her daughter right next to her but the latter struggles to understand what she is saying because the thread of thought breaks off constantly.

She listens, strains and certainly hears, but it is as if her mind keeps slipping away from one moment to the next. The words are a jumble. She stares hard at her Terrible Mother's lips, which move when she talks and stay still when, at the end of a phrase, a question is asked.

But what question? Opak did not hear anything!

Abim repeats it, seeing that something is happening and snubbing her. So, she is going to have repeat what she says and to do this, in order to keep her fierce gaze trained on her and to infuse her will, she leans over so close that her cold breath fans her face.

"I am telling you that the Beautiful Being will be your spouse... Repeat!"

Opak makes a supreme effort to obey. But even though she repeats it word for word, she does not understand: words devoid of sense. She becomes drowsy and her head nods. She cannot show this. She fights as hard as she can...

Abim goes on hammering away:

"You will put your belt around him, here before me and before the world after I talk with him. Amo will drop to second rank and serve him. In the presence of everyone, these things will be done by my will. Do you hear me, Opak? Because if we leave you like this, you will never do anything by yourself."

She leans closer again, back to the subject at hand.

"The Beautiful Being will be your spouse. You will assemble the cities. You will appear in full regalia. It has been a long time since they have seen you. It will be a gala. You will make a procession across Kob'Ooh'R with the Beautiful Being at your side. You will put Amo behind and then all the Males from your Chamber of Men. And the nobles of Kob'Ooh'R will follow you and everyone will come here with you to see what I will do."

She pauses to stare at her daughter, then in confidence, half threatening, half mocking, her face even closer now, "A piece of advice, my daughter, do not bring your T'Lo on this day, leave them in your rooms!"

Hearing this, Opak snapped out of it a little—she flinched.

Abim graced her with an ambiguous smile. And she pointed briefly to the pale purple marks she saw on her daughter's temples.

"Be careful where you go, Opak, because you do not share in the strong Race of the great Ooh'Rou of old! You cannot take the liberties that they did. You can only take some, like everyone now!"

Opak can only babble incomprehensible denials. This only makes the Very Huge shrug her shoulders before continuing.

"Get the ceremony announced and prepared! Tell them I want to see the stranger now when he is available!"

The fog suddenly lifted from Opak's head and it flashed through her mind: she has just understood. Her eyes squint and she asks, "Will the Beautiful Being be my spouse?"

Abim grins, like a sting, fierce, scornful, amused. "Yes now. I keep telling you. He will be your spouse by my will. The ceremony will take place in three days. From now on you will say nothing about my intentions or else—Repeat this back to me!"

Opak does as told. The Very Huge, who sees her struggle, furrows her brow. "You must be stronger than your T'Lo, Opak. Watch out! You must take strength from them, not give them yours..."

Since the Queen barely seems to understand, Abim gets angry for real, grabs her arm and starts shaking her furiously, "Are you sleeping or what, my daughter? Wake up! And answer me this: are you staying alone with your T'Lo?"

Opak shoots her a sharp look. She is scared and her mother is hurting her.

Abim realizes this and lets her go. "So, are you going to answer? Or should I shake you harder? Come now, talk! Your T'Lo?"

Opak wipes her forehead pathetically. "I... I don't know... no, it's not true... no, I don't stay with them..."

Then she breaks down in hysterical tears, struggling like a madwoman, frightened to death, to free herself from her mother's grasp. She screams, "I... I don't remember, I don't remember!"

Abim has turned purple with fury. She lets her go and pushed her away. She straightens up to her full height without deigning to look at her. "Enough! You will do what I tell you. And say nothing about what I want of the stranger. This must succeed. You must be a worthy Ooh'Rou. The Beautiful Being will be your spouse. You have to have the Great Child by him. I will recognize no other. If you fail, hear this: Ta will reign and you will be nothing!"

Opak hurries away.

In the meantime, Angel and Amo were getting along, the confidence between them thriving.

Angel sighed, "Amo, my head is like a vast garden devastated by a storm. What a mess! Ruins... and wonderful things, too, that you can't imagine, that I can't describe."

"What things? Try to tell me."

"I can't. I don't understand them because they're separate. I don't know how to find my way through them. A devastated garden! Nothing's left but a few parts of a road that really leads nowhere. I can walk a little way, but not long. They stop. They end in nothing."

Angel became agitated but he looked sad.

"If only you knew! In places there are still... oh, how can I say it? There is glory, light, flowers, all right. But it's all alive, intelligent, extraordinarily present and active. They're beings to delight the eyes and senses. What a poor gardener I am! Flowers, yes. But I don't know what they really are..."

"What do you think?"

"They're my memories. At night, faces gather around me. Beings whom I know appear to me."

"Do they look a little like us?"

"No, no, Amo. Not at all. They're not like you but very different. You're colorful, strong, big and powerful like your trees, like your stones. You make noise. You move the air when you move. They are white. I can almost see the light and other things through their bodies. Some are a little like water, clear and sparkling."

"But then they're fragile like children?"

Angel burst out in a sad laugh, "Oh Amo, they're stronger than you! You get tired, they never do. Their spirit is like a flame. They are obeyed by everything around them. They set everything around in order. When they command, their will springs forth like lightning."

"You did, too, Angel, when I saw you the first time. You haven't done it since. Are you too weak?"

"Yes, in a way. But really, since I've been among you, I've forgotten. All this thickness hampers me and hold me back."

Amo took his hand compassionately, "I know you'll find this power again. You've already rediscovered the power of your voice."

Angel shook his head doubtfully, but Amo's conviction still affected him. So much so that he ended up whispering, "Maybe, maybe…"
And he leaned over to confide, "These beings are my people, I'm sure of
it. I come from where they live, Amo."

"From over there, you mean. From the Other Side of Kah'B'La?"

"No, not really Kah'B'La. Much further. But in that direction, yes.
There's a passage, understand? A possibility to leave."

The redhead reflected. "I think I understand. You came from over
there. We found you here. Try to remember what was there before that
moment. Did you walk for a long time, for example?"

Angel wrung his fingers, "I don't remember anything. Before I was
Elsewhere, I was living Elsewhere, in plenitude, in ease and freedom,
with gestures of power and my voice of power, with beings of my kind…
Then, I was alone, with an empty head and a heavy body, with a feeling
of panic in my heart. I was lying in the hollow of stone. I needed nothing.
I could do nothing. Everything was in suspension around me."

"How long were you there?"

"How could I know? Sometimes I was like that. Sometimes I realized that I was running over the side of the mountain with birds around
me. It might've lasted a long while. Or only a moment…"

"Do the birds come from your land?"

"Yes. They're my sign, my mark. You here have your marks on
your jewelry. For us in the Elsewhere, it's the same, but the marks are
never on inert things. They are alive and we can use them. The beings
like me each have their own kind of bird according to their hierarchy.
And these birds, it's like they come straight out of us—they incarnate our
specific qualities."

Amo was listening and thinking that very often his own thoughts
and desires were turning around him, flying about like birds, albeit invisible and which he did not have the power to really control. He contemplated the Beautiful Being, touched by understanding so well his crisis.
"You want to leave us, don't you?"

"I know I have to stay," Angel lowered his head. "And yet, I yearn
for my freedom!"

"But where would you go? You don't know where it is what you're
looking for. Beyond Kah'B'La there is nothing, Angel! Nothing! No one
goes there, neither man nor animal. A desert. Empty. Nothing but stones
and death!"

"Yes, I know. You've explained it to me often. To and Ta have told me as well. Let's not think about it anymore."

Opak came in. They stopped talking.

Her face was mottled with the tears poured out during her meeting with the Very Huge and she seemed a little lost as she bumped into the door on the way in. She seemed to recover somewhat when she saw them. A disgruntled glance at Amo because he was too close to the Beautiful Being, but for the latter she blossomed in a sudden burst of energy.

"Ang'h, my Mother Abim, the Very Ancient who keeps silent and apart, wants to see you to honor you. It will be in front of everyone and in her room."

CHAPTER XXI

Abim goes to great trouble for the stranger. As per request, Ta came early, well before the ceremony, to help the Very Huge get herself ready. It has been a long time since she has done this once habitual service. But from the day Ta dared to rebel openly, Abim no longer asked for her, leaving her to her hard-earned freedom.

Today is something else.

Although Ta arrived on time, not a moment later than agreed, she found her waiting with cheerful impatience and a restrained smile that would soon amaze the others.

Right away, Abim gives orders. Politely. "My Daughter Ta, come close. I'm going to teach you something that might serve you well later since you will be the only one to know it, but which will serve me at the moment… Look, a few slabs on the floor there have indentations in which you can put your fingers."

"Yes indeed," Ta says, having never noticed this particularity before.

"Well, put your fingers in the closest one and pull. The stone will slide over."

Ta obeys. And the first stone slab slides into a slot and reveals a hidden compartment with a chest inside.

"Take it," Abim orders. "Bring it out and do the same with the other three slabs."

Four chests are lined up now. There are four more indented stones, but they are obviously not relevant since Abim ignores them.

"Daughter, open the first chest! You're going to take out some objects you have never imagined existed and whose significance you will not be able to grasp. I can only tell you that they are objects of power and they were useful to me in the past… yes, they were useful to me but not exactly as objects, more like servants… But that is of no concern of yours or anyone else in Kobor. I alone know. I alone have the right. First of all, you are going to fix my hair according to my exact instructions. Open the first box you see there in the first chest."

Ta does so and takes out some pins and three-pronged combs made of an unrecognizable metal, black and translucent and certainly very old.

234

Several times during the hairdressing, Abim makes her change the arrangement of the braids around her head until they form a kind of pointed tiara. The black combs and pins gleam on the dry whiteness of her hair.

"Open the second box!"

There are jars of the same ancient metal. Abim points to one. It contains a very strongly scented grease that goes straight to Ta's head. A powerful musk with a bitter, sinuous aftertaste, tinged with something peppery. An erotic wing spreads over a serpentine coldness. The young woman has never breathed in anything like it. She feels a little dizzy, tinged with dread.

Abim gets anointed all over. On contact with her skin the scent changes. The pepper fades away to thin layer and the musk tones down but spreads. The whole atmosphere of the room seems to transform. A new element has entered, suggesting the pomp, the reign, the power, the majesty.

In the midst of this scent Abim confirms her secret reign. On her orders Ta takes out from another chest some jewelry of extraordinary splendor since she intends to dress herself so that her clothes express the essential quality of her power: permanence.

Thus, she dons a heavy, reddish gold robe that drapes her without a crease like a big cone. Over this she puts on a kind of mantle made of shiny black hide whose origin Ta cannot guess—she has never seen the like and it seems almost metallic.

The mantle, open in a triangle over the robe, forms only two folds, one on the left and one on the right. The edges are incrusted with gold bars inserted between rubies and dull green stones.

Over everything lies a breastplate necklace held by thin chains. It intrigues the young woman who thinks she can make out the shape of a black snake coiled around a ruby red tree. But she cannot verify it because the Very Huge does not let her and forbids her from even asking.

When a black and gold ornament, like a big tree branch, has been put in her hair on the back of her head, Abim orders Ta to keep her distance. She has her light some scented wood in the cups placed around the room, then unroll the skins, hides and furs that were lying dormant in the other chest.

When everything is ready, Ta gazes at her mother and gets scared because in her garb she looks less like a Queen than a monumental pyramid with a Queen's head laden with ancient, perplexing influences.

Abim was a creature come from elsewhere; her race buried in the olden, unspeakable times of which she is undoubtedly the only living example left on earth.

For the first time, with all this regalia, she was openly confirming that she centralized the kingdom. Never had her formidable presence been more worthy of the epithet "Very Huge".

The stone doors swing open; the curtains are rolled up. The scented smoke rising straight up gathers together and is sucked outside. The arriving guests are hit with it and can see nothing at first. Then, the procession passes through the screen.

Opak in front turns pale at the sight of her mother. She was not expecting to find her in such adornment. The surprise freezes her to the spot. She knows not what to do or say.

Everyone else stops, too, by necessity. Those in the hallway did not understand while those at the door crammed together, jostling, on tiptoes, trying to see something.

The representatives of the noble families were standing around Opak as if on alert, not knowing whether they should be in awe or in fear.

Amo and To exchanged brief glances: they were on their guard because for them and for Ta also, whose silhouette they saw through the smoke, Abim being defined like this by her ornaments was nothing but a visible danger. More even: she was the Danger, the Opposition, the Obstacle, the Shadow decked out in borrowed light.

The Very Huge was calmly enjoying the effect. She stayed motionless for a long time, which held all the others just as motionless! No, nothing moved she made the decision.

But bursts of laughter, natural and carefree, broke out to deflate the gravity of the moment!

Abim shot down a look—the spell had been broken. It was the stranger. He was laughing! All eyes converged on him—huge astonishment—only to turn away almost immediately because birds were flying back and forth in front of the window.

What was happening? Abim, too, strained her neck. What birds! The sky was overshadowed by them!

The people present looked at one another stupefied, without daring to show it in this place. But, in the hallway those not yet inside shoved so hard that the crowd poured through the door, jeopardizing the orderly ranks of those already in the room.

The stranger's delight was not hampered by any self-control. He pointed to the sky and laughed, as if to say, "I told you so!"

And this first cascade of laughter was followed by another, heartier and louder, on seeing the tumbling, stumbling people.

He had been pushed right in front of Abim and there, still laughing, he pointed to the sky full of birds. The rest of the people had held back and so he was alone. But this did not bother him. On the contrary, his amusement only grew when he eyed the Very Huge from top to bottom and saw that she did not understand anything at all about the source of his joy.

Was he mocking or just stupid? Was he being provocative or completely unaware? Or was this his way of exposing her useless tricks?

She did not know how to tell. She was much too shocked! Confusion and fury were spinning around her. More laughter erupted, abruptly cut off. On all sides, they were muttering incoherently, over here with worry and over there with joy at seeing the birds come back.

However, for the more observant few it was obvious that two posers were confronting each other, the one dark, the other light. They were waiting for a kind of thundering storm to erupt from the conflict.

The laugh went on, with variations. Abim's silence continued as well. But the laugh was already sweeping away the fears—it was so truly robust and merry! And then, outside, the birds were soaring through their dizzying dance, squawking and chirping, cooing and whistling.

All of a sudden Abim's face took on an expression that made Opak, fearing for the Beautiful Being's life, throw herself between them. He stopped laughing, became very calm. Ta was already next to To and with Amo out front all the nobles closed in around them. Abim remained like stone.

Then the stranger looked her straight in the face, fully aware of everything she represented. A gentle, superior, insolent, friendly look. And when she had clearly received this dart, he laughed again without looking away. It was no longer because of the birds but as if to offer her this enigmatic laugh, as if to conquer her by it.

It was too much; she was on the verge of being disgraced.

Then she saw the only way out: she, too, laughed, mightily, massively, shaking her whole frame, jangling her pendants, to show that she understood, that she approved the laugh with a similar one and that everyone ought to be laughing too!

And so it was. Her huge hilarity, in awe of itself, poured out.

Stupid Opak let herself get swept away. Flipping directly from fear to relief, she brayed, sniveled, hiccupped and turned purple with her mouth agape.

The stranger gave her a cold look. He let the fit run its course without taking part in it. It was not worth it anymore. Serious now, he looked around for To and Ta who were lost in the crowd, not laughing. He saw in their eyes their desire to flee. He seemed moved by this: sympathy, a wave of tenderness lit up his face, then brusquely turned indifferent until he gave to Amo alone a look of friendship, understanding and shared secrets. They smiled at each other. Opak caught this and her face clouded over.

Likewise, the general laughter had just died down because Abim had finally stopped.

The multitude of birds was still shrieking the same call anxious for an answer.

Then Angel issued a vocalized sound and opened his arms. The birds came rushing into the room and flying around him. They all had little green herbs in their beaks and they dropped them on him. The expression on his face was indescribable. It was like he was hearing news of his family. He picked up one of the herbs and waved sweetly farewell. The birds left, tamely, and continued their ceaseless circling high in the sky but this time without a sound.

The Very Huge finally spoke up. Her eyes were half-closed. She did not move. Her hands rested on her mantle. She spoke only to Angel, just as if they were alone. At first, she seemed to exhale the words from the depths of a deep reverie, which had the desired effect of attracting all the attention. Necks strained, breaths were held.

"Stranger, say they? For whom could you be a stranger amidst people who are destined for you? You are not a stranger for old Abim because when I see you I say, 'It is you, surely!' Just like when I see these people I say 'they are yours who will receive your mark!'"

There were ohs and ahs, muffled, but Abim went on undisturbed.

"I have been waiting for you for my people. I have been living only for this. I was hoping, hoping! Thus, I was not dying… I had seen you in my deepest thoughts when I was sad about the sadness of my race and I would float outside myself to venture down the invisible slopes. And I flowed like water in the night. I was blind and I had no feelings, nothing but my sadness. But I heard your laughter every time. I heard it! I went to it without seeing anything and I found you. Yes, I found you! But without really seeing you, just dazzled by the luminous force that came out of you, just intoxicated by the magic of the words with which you enchanted the air. There was always the storm around you. Its barbs stung me. It was like I was in the middle of a furious swarm. And a tempest of white wings threatened to carry me away, to dissolve me. For, nothing could get through your guard… I was broken when I came back and disappointed at brining nothing back. I could not give a name to what I had seen. But I knew unquestionably that I had encountered the Force that was missing from our cores."

She paused a moment before stating plainly, sure of the effect:

"I am your oldest admirer, me, the Very Huge. And at last, today, I can name with your name what I have known for so long."

She paused again, looked directly at her guest and in a slightly more resonant voice, though at the same volume:

"Ang'h, if, like my daughter Opak, my throat deforms your name, my heart, whispering it softly, does not mangle the strange marvel. Listen: my mouth insists on saying Ang'h while my heart knows your real name… But who knows my heart! The homage that my heart intones becomes an insult to your harmony when it passes my lips. Alas, you see, it is like that with everything for us. Giants from a rough epoch, we remain rough, even though the times have softened. Peace reigns but we are still troubled beings. We live sedentary lives on our terraces amidst our fountains, but the nomadism of our hunted ancestors is in our blood, a wandering soul whose thirst is never quenched."

She sighed.

"Ang'h, you have invisible wings, lights escort you. We are heavy stones. Our feet alone keep us upright. We are desiccated trees imprisoned down below by the matrix of our roots. We are suffocating, our blood is heavy, our heads in a fog… Time has left us behind. It marches onward, far ahead of us, we cannot catch up, we stay here, abandoned, suddenly, in a renewed nature, turned into the Ancients, the Old Giants! Fruits of last season that have shriveled on the branch without releasing their seeds. That's what we are!"

Everyone present was emotionally hammered. It was true. All of this was true!

"We are behind," Abim went on. "You, Ang'h, you are ahead. Time runs through your life like joyful blood and the stars are reflected in your blood. The sun beats down on your heart. Are you not like the Son of Ooh'R? When you regard the sky, nothing is hidden from you, the secrets of the Above shine in your spirit like sunrays in clear water. But not us! Ooh'R, whom se celebrate, does not shine through our thickness! You get your powers from where the lights coalesce up on high. Ours, which I hold, are old powers, old serpents with sick skin, which come from the deep, dark earth down below. We can do very little with them, nothing but destroy to defend ourselves... You, your presence fertilizes the flower whose fruit will ripen in the sun later. All your gestures germinate. All your steps offer promises to the earth. O Stranger, we still have among us the Creatures of the Error and we do not hate them, whereas you already have the birds of truth. Every morning your knowledge revives. Every evening we grow dim, our flame is always lower, we forget the past without gaining anything in exchange. What we lose the night before, we do not find it again the next day. You awaken more every morning. We fall deeper into sleep every night!"

Abim sounded desperate.

"O Ang'h! Death is at the gates of Kobor Tigan't and you, only you have life. Only you are life! Agree to share it with us! Revive us! Instruct us! Make us change! You are a young sun; we are just the remains of a very old earth. Winter and darkness—that is who we are!"

Everyone was panting. The Very Huge let her head drop as a sign of desolation, just long enough to get a good feeling for the intensity. Then she finished with a prayer movement:

"Let the springtime of your reign come upon the Giants!"

A long, approving rumble rises from the crowd.

Opak, who had not grasped all the subtleties of the speech, was reassured because the Very Huge had the prudence not to bring up, as she had feared, the subject of her union with Ang'h. If he had heard this straightaway, he might have run off. But now, having lost his taunting attitude, he seemed deeply affected by the Very Ancient's words. He was clearly waiting for the murmurs to die down before responding.

Opak sighed softly in admiration of him because, obviously, he had understood everything that was said. He was incomparable! Love gripped her. She almost cried but she held it back just in time.

Ta was sunk in an abyss of confusion. Did she suddenly have to revise all her judgments of her Mother? Had the Very Huge really spoken from her heart and revealed a hidden sensitivity? The young woman had been moved many times. Seeing the face that was slowly withdrawing from the light of a dying wish, Ta was ready to admit Abim's sincerity.

But she saw, sneaking under the eyelids, in her direction, an ironic look: the Very Huge was using her as a witness to her prowess! She even underscored the complicity in her eyes with a frown and a tiny jerk of her finger like flicking away a kernel. Then, in total control of herself, she was back to her hieratic, vaguely sorrowful attitude.

Ta was struck with horror! What was the Very Huge plotting now? What monstrous thing had she set in motion today that probably would not come to fruition for a long time? Something hidden, something invisible, but inevitable! Whatever Abim wanted always happened, so slowly that it was never seen until it was too late—the thing dropping on you in the middle of the night or jumping out in front of you in full daylight! She shot To a look of despair. She felt like he was answering her, "We'll leave. We'll leave before."

Amo was absorbed from the start in contemplating Abim. His face showed no emotion except the fierce desire to force out whatever was lying in wait there in the depths of the old woman.

When the approving whispers had dwindled away, Angel's voice rose up, clear, melodious, different from anything that could be heard in Kobor Tigan't. He still stumbled a little over the pronunciation of the language, which made him sound unusually suave.

"Old Queen, your wisdom is great. You see straight and far. Your words have convinced me. You have spoken so tenderly about your race that I see it better now. I find it beautiful. And I want to satisfy your wish. I will stay among you, therefore, to teach you to live differently. When my magic is exhausted for your benefit, only then will I leave for my true life."

Abim bowed her head in a sign of consent, which needed no words of support.

Once again, an approving rumble ran through the room as shouts of joy and various wishes sprinkled over the background noise.

Opak was breathing heavily, anxiously. The moment was coming. Now she wanted to warn Angel, to tell him herself first, maybe to ask him if he would accept. But it was too late. Everything was going so fast now, too fast for her to pull herself out of her habitual slowness.

And now: Abim was giving her the sign. She had to step forward. But Amo was in the place she was supposed to be. Opak joined him. She said nothing to him either.

Angel was watching them without understanding. He must have thought that it was a customary ritual.

But Ta had the sudden revelation of what was going to happen and her heart wrenched. To also saw what she saw.

Amo and the Queen were face-to-face, chest-to-chest, right between the stretched out arms of the Very Huge. Slowly, without taking off her necklace, Opak put it around the neck of her favorite. Amo immediately realized what this meant and turned pale. Nevertheless, he followed suit and put his own necklace around the Queen's neck. Then Abim's hands came crashing down and broke the two necklaces, which fell to the ground.

The people were astonished beyond measure, a muffled exclamation followed this gesture. While Amo backed away, Opak briskly joined Angel and threw her belt around his hips.

The voice of the Very Huge boomed, "Here is the Queen's Man! Give us the Great Child, Ang'h! Put your sign on it and I will recognize it!"

The walls rang out with the cheers of the people. The news had already spread like wildfire outside where more cheering thundered forth. The scene had played out.

Angel was stunned, looking one by one at the players on the stage: Amo, Abim, Opak, To and Ta who were trembling. The truth, the unbelievable truth was dawning on him: Amo had been denied and he had been forcibly united to the Queen!

His paleness turned white. His eyes fired an icy glare at Opak. She could not tolerate those eyes that reminded her of the worst moments of Angel's fury at her blunders.

"I wanted to ask you first," she stammered.

He did not hear her. He said nothing, did nothing, just stood there in silence, looking around him, more a stranger than ever, while disdain, sadness and disgust flashed over his face.

Without budging, he received the broken necklace from Amo, offered as a sign of servitude. "Consider me your brother. I will serve you."

He simply said, "I'll need you."

But this sadness had broken his already weakened resistance. The sound, the heat and the emotion hit him hard—he wobbled slightly. A strong shoulder supported him: Amo.

Everyone present went into the big, bright rooms that opened onto the terraces overlooking the land. Abim had arranged presents and food for all. Angel leaned on Amo. Opak was about to follow them, but on orders from the Very Huge she had to stay behind for a private talk. Ta threw off her jewelry and ran out without a word.

Opak was waiting, ill at ease.

Abim beckoned her closer. The Ancestor suddenly looked very tired and very old without the splendor of her ornaments. Her bulging fat was covered with wrinkles. The bright orange of her skin shined a little less than before. Gently, she rubbed her forehead where the diadem had left marks. A moment of silence when her daughter dared not say a word, then she let her hands fall as usual and after a deep sigh, she spoke, almost whispered.

Opak had to lean close in. And she trembled because she could not avoid feeling the discontent and menace that rumbled under every word.

"I talked a lot just now… to make my reputation deceptive! I am tired of all these words. They are still flying around in this room on big, echoing wings. I am no longer at peace with myself. They weaken the strength of my hidden spirit. I yearn for silence. I want to get back to my potent vigil. Too many words blind my inner eyes. So, I am asking you to listen to what I am going to tell you because I will not repeat it, my Daughter! And if you misunderstand, as usual, rest assured that it will cost you dearly. Queen of Kobor Tigan't, you are dragging us down to defeat. Your face has the color of Nood on a night in a bad winter. You have red fumes around your head—so much stupid anger!—and the few thoughts you are capable of are worthless."

Opak's silence must have frustrated her because she was clutching her daughter's hand and starting to shake it as she growled:

"Opak, you will die tomorrow of your love if you don't dominate it tonight! You will die unsatisfied, vanquished! And the people will hurry to wipe out your humiliating memory. You will die, Opak, understand? Stop consuming yourself with unhealthy sweating! Mate with Ang'h, you can do it, you must do it, he is yours, he belongs to you! But understand that I am holding him for you in the web of my will like all things and all people in Kobor! And what do you do when my magic offers you this prey? You weep! Foaming rage, stomping anger, shouting and bellowing, these are not royal strengths. They are weaknesses, the worst! They are of no use for you. OF NO USE, Opak!"

She hammered this out without loosening her grip.

"Your love itself is of no use to this undertaking. Without love you would already have succeeded. What has it brought you, this upside-down love where a male laughs at you without letting you mate with him as is the custom? You have not taken one step closer to Angel since his capture. Nice capture, right, when you don't even hunt. Because you are running in circles, my Daughter, while he has secret wings!"

Opak manages to squeeze out, "Why isn't he with me like all my Men?"

Her depression was so visible that the Very Huge looked more mildly at her, understanding that her daughter, barely able to see or reflect on what she saw, had not adapted her behavior to the stranger's personality. She tried to explain it to her.

"Why? Because you do not show him a reflection of himself. You should be his water mirror, pleasing to his beauty. You look like your Men and they look like you. That is why it is so comfortable with them. But to him, what are you? A wall. He sees nothing of himself in you. You blind him. You suffocate him. How can escape into the heat of love when you appear only as the one holding him here. You are his locked prison. It is what is not you that delights him. This being is different from us, always trying to see in the eyes of those looking at him how he himself is reflected in them. And he instinctively goes towards the one who shows him his best image. He loves when they do like him."

Opak understood this, partly, but she it seemed so hard to overcome that she started to cry silently.

The Very Huge switched to irony, hoping to make her react.

"My Daughter, you are not capable of enlightening yourself. For you to see the light, to reflect it back, you need to take desperate measures! Listen to my advice. And consider them more as orders! First of all, do nothing, do not lurk around, do not try to take him by surprise or by violence if you desire him. Watch him carefully. And then, be like him!"

"How?"

"Simple: just do as he does, copy his manners and the way he does things. Even if you don't understand them. I know you well enough to know that you will not understand anything. And I'll warn you again: be his reflection. Do you have light colored clothes? Make yours the same as his. He wears no jewelry? Leave yours in the chests or give them to your Men, to your T'Lo. He drinks no blood and eats no meat? Do the same. Sacrifice yourself... or hide when you eat—should be easy enough. But make sure to ask him politely for HIS food. And eat like him. Then, when he's softened up because you will have surprised him and he will be vulnerable, make him feel that he is superior to you. Cry a lot, yes, you can do that! It will relieve in the meantime… Cry without talking and lie at his feet. You can't conquer him with our ways. Look on him as if he were Ooh'R in person. And make him see this. Tell him that you need him, that your head needs him. He will be moved! He will give you his food and his knowledge. He loves to do these things. You will imitate his gestures, his voice. You will move your lips when he talks as if his words were animating them."

Opak looked up. Something was opening up in her understanding. Yes, yes, she could do exactly what her Mother told her!

"Don't be the first to touch. Wait! If he touches you, don't respond, don't touch back. Wait! Tremble a little. And make him see it. If he comes to you at night, if you hear him coming, don't run to him. Wait! Cry a little. Tremble a little. Don't ever act with him like with the males of Kobor. Ask him for help. Help, you understand? He loves to help. He loves to teach. He loves to give comfort."

Abim saw in her daughter's face that she understood. She urged her almost tenderly. "Go, my stupid daughter, join him!"

Opak got up but her mother held her back in order to make sure.

"Tonight, when you eat with him, when you ask him for his food, say: I need you. I know nothing. Teach me. Make me like you."

She had Opak repeat this back.

"You will remember?"

The Queen repeated it again. Yes, she would remember.

"Good," the Ancestor said. "One last thing. Tonight, he will take you to task for tricking him and capturing him. Promise him his freedom."

She did not understand.

"Idiot!" Abim fumed. "I'm not telling you to let him go. He couldn't anyway. You'll just say it softly. 'Oh, what does poor Opak matter if she hasn't been enlightened by you. I'll give your freedom and I'll go die from it but that doesn't matter…' Understand, Opak? It looks like you're scared. Believe in the Very Huge. I know this: when he gets his freedom, he won't use it. Never, understand! Because his spirit will feel involved. And especially because I will hold him here in Kobor with all my willpower. You understand what I'm saying? Yes? Finally. Now, go, obey, succeed and don't ask me anything else."

Opak was already at the door. Abim muttered one last thing.

"But if you fail in this project, then Ta will reign in your place."

It was as if the Queen was nailed to the spot. She raised her imploring hands to her Mother who granted her this relief:

"I will name the Great Child whom you will have with the Beautiful Being."

The curtains closed behind her and Abim was alone, withdrawn into silence. She continued weaving around Angel the invisible net that would keep him prisoner forever. But she was not forgetting about Amo either...

And Amo was not forgetting about the Very Huge.

Seeing her had revived his certainty of the occult danger that she represented. He knew that she was entirely enemy. He also figured that she was trying to stretch the snare of her influence all the way to Angel. She would draw from him, through easily manipulated Opak, a greater power.

He did not believe her pretty words. He did not believe her concern to truly help the Race. No. This woman wanted to keep ruling secretly. She wanted to feed her store of occult forces. She would consume Angel, dissolve his energies...

Amo was glad to think of the Beautiful Being staying in Kobor. He knew that his precious gifts would be bestowed on all just by his presence. But this was not enough for his heart: he wanted him happy, free to use his strengths, free to spread them around as he wanted and not under the influence of an invisible leech who would suck them out of him until he ran dry.

The words of Méè-Nê echoed in his memory and he thought that, yes, it was true, soon, he, Amo, would be alone at Grand Va-Hôh... and he would topple the High Central Stone!

Amo's face had darkened and Angel, leaning on his arm, seemed to be following his thoughts, even though secret. Until he finally leaned over and whispered in his ear, "Amo, don't think that I'm replacing you at the side of the Queen. I was ambushed. Neither you nor To nor Ta are guilty of anything in this situation. Your Ancestor is the main cause, the only real cause. Opak has no personal willpower, except to live on consuming air, food and love. I know this as well as you, Amo. Come, it is said that together we will put a strange end to things."

Amo was too emotional to respond, so he squeezed his hand.

But people were crowding around them. Angel signaled that he wanted to return to the palace.

CHAPTER XXII

After bringing Angel back, Amo did not have the heart to celebrate, so he slipped away from the crowd, escaped the women who were already menacing him, knowing he was free, by smiling at their belts to honor him.

He went down city by city towards Kah'B'La, at first in a hurry, then more slowly as his ruminations deepened.

He remembered bitterly that during the whole speech, not once did Abim's eyes look directly at him. And yet, several times—he was sure of it—she had scrutinized him, studied him, without getting caught because she was so clever at concealing. She kept her eyelids lowered, but she saw very well through those thin slits in the shadow of her eye sockets.

He started to recite certain phrases from her speech, recalling the intonations. In all this it was also like a sneaky look, the spying of a dangerous intelligence, traps laid bare. The worried whispers of the young noblewomen seeing him for the first time had amused him. But now, after reflection, he thought they might be right.

He sighed, ill at ease. That heavy, hot hand—a stone of the sun—that grip, without any real human contact, weighing on his shoulder and pushing him back according to the breakup ritual, oh, he could still feel it! It was still there, weighing on him, still pushing him back, to the potential limits of life, farther back, back! It was making him dizzy. He feared he might fall backwards at any moment. He struggled. But he felt, at times, like the ground and all it supported, walls, houses, railings, fountains, terraces, the High Plains themselves, were retreating from him, slipping away, far behind him, where everything dissolves... A metal thread had been stuck in the base of his neck.

Afterwards, these dizzy spells came and went at irregular intervals, sometimes strong, sometimes weak, but nevermore did Amo feel fully balanced. This added to his despair and most certainly forced the decision he made to strike down the impious power of the Very Huge.

Night fell. Greenish strips unfurled over the red haze of the sunset. Amo was wandering through the low city. He met no one. The shadows darkened quickly under the high walls. He heard water trickling pretty much everywhere under the stones. Sometimes his feet got wet in a real stream flowing out of the narrow space between two buildings. Then he was walking on dry stones and the vast silence of the storehouses surround him, the reserves stuffed with provisions. He had to feel his way along the walls to keep going.

At a corner, the brightness of the moon fell upon him. He looked up: a rift had been cut out of the wall. The light filtered through it. It was like a lure. He found the steps that the watchmen used and climbed up. He sat in their deserted place on the top of the rampart, feeling the enigmatic breath of the void on his face and chest.

The night of the world spread out before him. On his right was Kah'B'La, surrounded by lighter purple, marking out the land. In front, at the deepest point, by a kind of darker sheen than the rest of the night, he imagined the three R'Lils. On his left, the air bore the fetid stench of the Dongdwo swamps. The thought he could hear the sighs of the Moon's Widows—the ill-intentioned Aâz. This was not a good sign. The wind carried other noises as well, but so faint that he did not recognize them. He was afraid it was the voices of the Great Va-Hôh."

The sounds got louder and suddenly became familiar to him: animal growls, loud slapping, two or three muted leaps, the weird cry of a big bird—yes, 'They' too had come back, the ones that cleaned the heaped up waste in the chasm under the bridge—somewhere, a rotten branch snapped off, causing frightened howls from the animals nesting above and below it, then there was silence, immobility.

For a long time, the clouds drifted by. And the wind shifted. And the streams all around trickled, flowed, endlessly, hopelessly…

Amo suddenly hated this place, this time, this destiny. Hated so deeply that he jumped up like a child overcome with fear. What was he doing here? The wind blew, the water flowed and the clouds…

He wept long and hard, lying on the rock.

Then he stopped crying. He was thinking of the unfathomable and disappointing Queen, of his vanished friend, of Angel who also desired escape. And still he was picturing someone, a familiar figure, coming to him somewhere through the grass and calling softly to him at the foot of the ramparts: "Come, come, everything's ready, I'll take you."

And they left in the night, the two of them—the Queen, the Friend or Angel? Who was with him? He did not know—both of them left. With their united wills they destroyed the unwelcome fate of loneliness… the thin, warm arm on his… the confidential whispers on his cheek… the eyes of mystery of a very lively creature borrowed a softer glow from the moon… Sad and gay, eyes that comforted… And all night long, the walk they took, tirelessly, on strange paths... Whither? No matter! They were already elsewhere, released! The air was already full of unknown scents! In another sky, right in front of them, the promised dawn was already rising!

Tears flowed down his face again. He was alone. The thick, dark night enveloped him. The clouds were passing by and the wind and water—his life!

Angel's face popped up in his mind again. Was it not superimposed with that of the Friend? His tears dried up. His heart was touched. He was suffused with gentleness. Was he rediscovering promises?

With a heavy step, brooding, he changed place to go sit more comfortably in a hollowed-out part of the wall garnished with moss. Without realizing it, he fell asleep.

Night fell. Laughter and cries crept up from down below in the flickering fires.

With his back turned, Angel was silently watching the sky through the window. He was alone. The males had gone back to the Chamber of Men and the T'Lo were making no sound.

Opak quickly tore off all her jewelry when she got back and changed her ceremonial garments for a soft, ivory colored shift. Expecting almost immediate results from these preparations, she stood for a moment behind Angel, waiting. She was breathing heavily, but nothing happened. He did not budge, lost deep in thought. He looked formidable to her, so she did not dare speak or touch him. And yet, they were there together! Shamefaced, incompetent, once again, she could do nothing but squat on her bed and wait there in the dark, trying to ignore him.

Time passed. The watchmen with their torches were walking tranquilly at the edges of the vast terraces. The people everywhere were rejoicing. To and Ta had left so exuberantly! Amo was not there either. People were gathered merrily around fires in all the cities. Food was being grilled and the love chambers in the houses were already alive with pulsing bodies.

Opak felt doubly frustrated: she was very hungry and her desperate need for love made her unhappy. Steadily she sank into a stupor. Did she sleep? The thought of Abim flashed through her mind so clearly that it was like her mother were actually there, insulting her ruthlessly. She jumped. It was very dark. The festive fires were almost all gone out. On the terraces the guards were on their stationary shift.

Angel had not moved from his place. He was just leaning on the windowsill. Once again, she got scared. She could not see him breathing! Was he dead on his feet? Everything was spinning in her head. She got up, knocking over a metal vase that made a loud crash. Angel did not even flinch.

It was too much for her. Opak let out a hoarse cry and threw herself at him. She touched his warm, firm shoulder.

Disturbed, he swung around but at the same time, kind of nonchalantly, he looked completely unconcerned. He walked slowly to light the fire in the big brazier. Then he looked at her like a thing. And she got even more scared when he started to pace the room mechanically. She gazed upon him. She could not even call out his name. Oh, it was too hard! She wanted to go hide among her T'Lo, to forget, to give up. But the invisible presence of her mother was torturing her, threatening her. If she did not succeed "then Ta will reign! Ta will reign! You will be nothing!"

Angel gently toed the hides and cushions, sometimes turning them over to examine them, lost in thought. He mumbled strange things like "No, it's not possible, none of this is possible."

A halo of sadness encircled him. He slouched.

Then he kicked the furs and snarled, "I hate these things!" Opak felt the blow and trembled. He still did not see her. He smiled suddenly and spoke as if to himself in a loud voice.

"They're light and shiny! Strength comes out of their words. So, the birds, the clouds, the lights are all arranged according to their desires!"

A bitter laugh shook through him until it ended in a sob.

"It's not possible," he repeated.

All of a sudden, he was standing in front of Opak before she knew it. And he shook her.

"Tell me why I'm here! Tell me! Why? You must know. You wouldn't be sticking around like this. Answer! Why here? And why am I deprived of my powers, cut off from my ties, separated from my glory?"

Opak understood nothing. Only one idea was mulling through her mind: she had changed her clothes like her mother had ordered and he paid no attention, nothing had happened. He was just shouting these incomprehensible things.

Angel furrowed his brow and grabbed her wrist.

"You lied to me, Opak! You trapped me! You bound me to this realm to keep me prisoner forever within your walls, upon your bed!"

He was choked up with rage.

"But can I ally myself to you, me, me, whose nature you can't even imagine? What are you to me? You're nothing. You're not even a kind of T'Lo. I have no connection to you or to this city or your race or even your dark and narrow world! You are like mud on my ankles. You are bogging me down, me a free being, a radiance that nothing had ever constrained!"

A perilous fury was blazing in his eyes. A mysterious energy was radiating around him. The air sizzled and stung. The fire was leaping around in the brazier under some invisible impetus.

Spurred on by terror, the lesson jumped out of the Queen's mouth as if Abim were whispering to her. It was probably the case because Opak was too scared to think by herself in such circumstances. Angel was shaking her, his hand gripping her like a bird's claw as he lashed his prey with hard words. And she, under attack, wanted to scream. But instead she heard herself reciting her lesson and even elaborating a little.

"Excuse me! Oh, please excuse me! I don't know what to do. I wanted you here always. You're too beautiful, Ang'h, much too much! I'm dying. I don't know what to do. I never know what to do. Excuse me! You can leave tomorrow. Yes, I'll let you. Tomorrow, yes. I'll die after. It doesn't matter. I'll die. You're too beautiful, Ang'h, much too much!"

She broke off. The sudden outburst left her head empty. So, she cried. This, at least, really came from her. Angel was stunned, calmed down, still holding her. He was clearly baffled by her speech.

"Opak, you've treated me treacherously from the start. It's bad! I am bound now. How can you free me? And where, really, would I go?"

She looked at him. "Excuse me! Tomorrow you can go. Excuse me! I'll let you go. Tomorrow..."

She started in again on her litany in the same words, unable to find anything else to say. He smiled at her awkwardness. He kept holding her, scrutinizing her curiously, but already less suspiciously, with little bitterness. He thought that maybe he had misunderstood her fervor. So much nonsense confessed outright was disarming.

"You're very stupid, Opak."

She nodded, yes, she was very stupid.

"Poor Opak," he went on, "and yet you're very beautiful, but you exist only to act like an animal. And how clumsy, what a crude creature you are! Oh, it's so hard for you to say what you think and feel. You can barely even express your suffering. No, you're not bad, are you?"

She shook her head, no, she was not.

"Excuse me! You can leave. Yes, tomorrow," she panted again.

He stopped her talking.

"Very well. I'll do it, tomorrow. I'll leave in the morning. They'll think the birds carried me off, right?"

She shuddered to hear this. What was he saying? He was going to leave? Her mother had told her that she would not understand anything. No, indeed, she understood nothing anymore! He had accepted and was leaving tomorrow! It was an unbearable prospect! She could not control her nerves, suddenly trembling like a leaf. Her eyes gone wild, biting her lip because if she opened her mouth she would start screaming, "Stay! No, I don't want you to leave, ever!" And she must not scream, Abim had warned her: "Succeed! Or else Ta will reign!"

Then she remembered something else she had to do and she dropped to the floor at Angel's feet.

He bent over, compassionately, "But are you really so upset?"

Oh, she remembered everything now. Abim was supporting her. Everything her mother had said was happening. It was like a miracle of her magic.

Angle was rubbing her shoulder a little, brushing aside her hair, looking at her face. She was trembling, was scared… and she showed it. But this was not the lesson, it was true! Angel was bent over her, Opak thought she was losing her mind—he was so close!

But he just helped her up, put her on the furs. He brought her some food and said, "Eat and pull yourself together."

She was about to accept when the terrible shape of the Very Huge sprang up in her mind. Oh, she was forgetting again.

Right away she refused the treats and pointed a shaking hand towards the food prepared for Angel. "Give me yours. I need you, I know nothing, teach me, make me like you."

She shut up again and hung her head in shame. How much she wanted that meat! But she had to stick to the plan. She realized that if she strayed, the slightest mistake could be fatal. She saw the fruit he was holding out to her. She ate it slowly, managed to finish it off under Angel's watchful gaze.

"Come on," he said, "calm down. I'll stay for a while to teach you. I won't leave right away."

And he helped her with the rest of the meal. He ate, too. She did her best to imitate him, too preoccupied with it to think. He did not talk either, but he kept explaining things in detail. She was afraid that he was seeing through the ploy. He seemed to be thinking.

He was serious, a little severe. But several times, he picked up what she had dropped and smiled at her indulgently. This reassured her a little.

However, his gaze made her dizzy. Her desire for him was growing beyond measure. Her head was abuzz.

Nothing of what she ate pleased her but she was sorry it was over because she did not feel full and she would have to keep up this charade.

Then Angel was sleeping in the cushions like someone who had simply gone to bed as usual. Opak stayed awake, troubled, gnawed by desire and tormented by an empty stomach. What, finally, had she accomplished? That he stay for a while! But "awhile" was not "forever"… She mulled this over without finding a solution. So, he was going to leave anyway? Yes, he would leave anyway. In a little while! Everything was falling apart.

She crawled, inch by inch, over the furs towards the sleeper. She kissed him, drunk, breathing in the scent of his flesh. When she touched him, he started and instantly reacted by shoving her away.

She fell back without complaining. Her clothes had fallen open. Angel was completely awake. And there on the floor she suddenly looked so weak, so totally helpless, covered in tears, her hair untied in a halo, which put him in the throes of confusion.

She looked back at him. It was a gentle, warm, intimate look that humbly called to him. The flash of revealed skin glowed with a weird poignancy. Opak had transformed. Who was she? This grand image of woman was silently saying, "See, I am the temple of your lost glory!" And her arms and breasts and belly and legs, were they not suddenly the fraternal valleys of a land of comfort and promise? "In me lies your lost glory".

And Angel paled, bent over this revealed phenomenon of the Ooh'R, the trap of the Ooh'R…

Meanwhile, Amo, sleeping on the deserted ramparts of Kob'Lâm, dreamt of his Friend. Angel's face did not appear in this dream. Amo had even forgotten it. He no longer thought about it, no more than Opak. And it was a sweet forgetting, a rest.

This dream brought back pieces of the past into the present. And yet, this episode did not exist in his memories. Curiously, he knew it but he tried to change what had been into what should have been.

It was a troubling dream that he felt that he was guiding by thought, by desire. Basically, he had found, without being amazed, the power to influence events. By thus mending the causes of his grief, he gave himself some compensation. He believed he was living through it for the simple reason that he did not know he was asleep.

First, he had walked through the grayness of Kob'Lâm without looking or hoping for anything. A steady, rhythmic stroll that he performed with care because it was freeing him and taking him closer to possibilities… And then he stopped, surprised, content: how had he not seen this before, this lodging? It was at the darkest place of the low city, the very last house before the rows of storerooms and warehouses. All silent, dark and this house before which—he remember now—he had passed 100 times without seeing it and without an inkling of its existence. This time he recognized it! He went in…

Behind the stone, double doors, the outside universe had no access. It was something completely different. There was a big inner courtyard, emptier than it should have been. Maybe because of the blinding light shining down? Amo felt good. Abim's impact had not followed him nor anything else. Nothing. He was free. A great relief. Safety. An isolation had been preserved here that escaped the usual constraints. It was located beyond the laws. Yes, it "escaped", truly. A piece of another world…

An old man sitting down stood up, came over, serenely, to greet him. "It's been so long since I've seen you! Your Friend will be glad. Come in. Look."

Amo entered the house.

Oh, HE was here in the soft light. The Friend was here, he had not left the city. He had always been here!

Sitting on the ground, nude, very beautiful, very pure, less like a human being than some exquisite object of unknown use. But he was alive! He welcomed the newcomer with his eyes unchanged, half cheerful, half sad. And the old harmonic affinity was re-established.

There were a lot of people around him—parents, friends, women. His entourage that Amo did not know. But they made no sound, they were not a bother, had no opinions or independent movements. They were around the Friend like his own, personalized, scattered, diverse but still obedient thoughts.

Amo sat among them. He also felt like one of his Friend's thoughts. But he was happy. He was the closest, he, Amo, was the most intimate thought.

His Friend smiled at him. Warmly, he took his hand and kept hold of it. Time passed, tranquilly. Everything was in its place in the world.

Amo found everything happening here strange, but he did not worry himself. It was just that the actions of these people remained a mystery. It looked like they were doing nothing known, that everything they did was hermetic. It could make no sense of it. Their goings and comings, their way of walking, crisscrossing one another, their gestures and words, so much never seen before, so many enigmas. Their docility in always keeping his Friend at the center of their movements without ever touching or speaking to him or even acknowledging him. But it did not matter! He was among them, safe. And he, the closest one, with his hand held, he was happy.

After a while, Amo realized that a man was squatting some distance away, working on some earth in his hands. He was kneading it, turning it, giving it form, all the while casting keen but peaceful glances at the face of his Friend. With indescribable amazement Amo noticed that a face was gradually being assumed by the earth. Vaguely at first, just a hint, then it appeared more and more clearly between the skillful hands.

What magic! Amo watched unafraid. He saw nothing bad, quite the contrary. But he wondered, unable to fathom, what was the goal?

The man answered him, as if he had read his mind, by showing the finished face. "Much longer than the man, much longer than the man."

Everyone around smiled. His Friend squeezed his hand more tightly, smiling also. "Much longer than the man," he whispered like a promise.

Without fully understanding, Amo's soul was comforted.

More time passed without any new developments. Nothing changed around them. The Friend did nothing but hold his hand. Everything Amo had suffered was abolished in him. He was healing, happy, released from himself thanks to the power of this faithful hand…

The scene blurred. In a confused transition between waking and sleeping, Amo saw nothing but the miraculous face of the modeled earth that alone remained perfectly distinct. He still felt the pressure of his Friend's hand and his sharp voice engraving in his mind "Much longer than the man will last faces like this. The man dies or disappears, but this earth, shaped in his image, you will keep!"

Everything went up in smoke. Swirling vortices in the middle of which Amo was tossed and turned. At every jolt a face of modeled earth leapt out of the smoke in front of him. Thus he saw, in turn, the face the Friend, of the Old Man, of Angel and of To. Amo's hands were frantically kneading the earth… He woke up with a start.

"Much longer than the man!"

It was his own voice. He rubbed his eyes with a trembling hand. He was rich, powerful, rejuvenated, he, too, was going to capture in the earth the features of those he loved and they would never fade away!

"Much longer than the man, I will make them last much longer than the man!"

He jumped to his feet. Cold was crawling all around him. It was till dark. Dawn was wavering on the horizon. A strong wind was shaking the trees, the tall grass at the foot of the wall. It made a noise like a marching herd.

The feeling of the friendly hand holding his own persisted. He looked at his hand. The feeling faded away and was replaced with that of moistened earth, smooth, fresh, supple. In a burst of joy he started running. He would tell Angel about this; he would make his face and To's and his Friend's and the Old Man's!

His way led him straight to the place where the dream had put his Friend's lodging. Seeing it, he was startled and stopped. Then he entered after hesitating briefly.

A black, gaping courtyard. And at the very back, blacker still, there was just a vast, abandoned cellar, dreary and moldy, open to the winds. Unidentified objects were lying around in the dust.

He backed away quickly, comparing his inner treasure to this decrepitude and fearing lest the latter effect the former.

But no, no, he was happy. Faces were going to emerge from his hands! His hands were full of faces!

CHAPTER XXIII

A sudden flourish of being bloomed in Amo.

"Longer than the man!"

Amo kept repeating this to himself. And in these sounds the entire range of his emotions was expressed. The more he said it, the more certain and the more intoxicated he became. He was powerful and different. He, Amo, was daring to start an unsung deed! He could and had to do it. So, he would leave after him a trace, a witness: faces, presences, full of a magical life that time would never wear away.

He felt sustained by the obligation to accomplish this work. Now he had extra life. He felt like his Friend was really living inside him and at any moment he could see and talk to him. Moreover, he could hear his voice, his advice permanently in the middle of his chest.

Not for a moment did he fear failing. He could not but succeed! Angel, who had heard his secret, understood him, talked for a long time and encouraged him in his project. He was moved. He remembered that in his own land "Yes, certainly, there were great, eternal faces decorating the façades of buildings and the inside walls of the houses." He also remembered that before certain of these faces "they went silently to kneel down."

Amo's eyes widened. He did not really understand what this last detail meant because it seemed beyond his scope, which was to "make" these faces. For a brief moment, however, the thought flashed through his mind that maybe later in Kobor Tigan't people would go silently to see his Faces?

But this seemed so far away, so problematic that he immediately forgot about it, just happy to be starting his work.

His project took form. He searched around a little before finding earth that was good for modeling. His first tries crumbled to pieces. He was obviously a little annoyed, but then he recalled that in his dream the earth had looked slick and smooth.

It was To who brought him a kind of clay that he recognized right away as the earth of his dream and that was suitable in all respects.

So began a frantic period in which the normal world literally disappeared from his senses. He started living inside his dream.

He had withdrawn into a big room in the palace. To be left alone he posted a guard before the door, one of the Queen's males who was devoted to him and whose bewilderment at Amo's activities soon became unfathomable! For, it must be admitted, Amo had completely changed. Neither his personality nor his behavior was recognizable. His face, so expressive before, reflecting all his feelings, was frozen in inflexible concentration. His eyes saw nothing but the ball of clay between his hands.

He worked tirelessly, with a somber passion and haste that left him no rest. Take the earth, moisten it, fashion it, whisper to it like it obeyed or understood and sometimes also keep repeating the name of the one whose face would gradually appear as the features took shape…

Amo slept little, working even in the glow of the fire. He kneaded the earth until it became warm, alive. His eyes stayed half-closed to remember better.

The miracle started slowly. It could not be rushed or muddled; the shapes appearing were timid. He felt a spirit animating his fingers and the secret images of his heart were starting to bestow themselves… The shapes formed into faces. Or rather One face, started over and over again because he was never satisfied, despite the many exemplars that were now lying around him—the face of the Friend.

He refused visitors and his dumbfounded guard obeyed his orders, letting only Angel, To and Ta enter.

Opak came one day following Angel but at the sight of what was happening she screamed and ran away, never to return to the room.

Soon all of Kobor was buzzing with this strangeness. To and Ta could not take a step without people pressing them with questions. Some more curious folk snuck into the palace and when they could not get close to the guarded room, they found ways to shimmy out to the main window. What they saw was enough to make them more astounded than ever. They had no time to dwell on it, however, because Amo saw them and shouted furious orders so that the guard rushed in and chased them away.

But their story made the rounds of the cities! People invited them home to hear. They were even summoned by Méè-Nê who nodded gravely as she took Ata-Réè once again as a witness to this new sign of the times.

Personally, Amo knew that he had little time to finish his project. The series of initial faces, those of the Friend, at first rough, then more detailed, gave him the desire to do exactly like in the dream, meaning to have a in front of him a calm friend whose features he could then try to capture.

To, Ta and Angel patiently participated in this endeavor. It was a turning point. It was harder, but more thrilling too! He undid and redid, never satisfied and frustrating his models who thought his creations were so precise!

Then he caught the essence of To's face. Ta was watching the development with a kind of vague anxiety. Seeing the copy of her lover taking shape in front of her made her tremble. Instinctively, to protect it from any threat, she wanted to take the face to her own rooms, but Amo curtly refused.

"Until further notice the great faces have to stay together in this room." Standing his ground, he added, "When I am no longer around, you can do what you want because they will last longer than the man."

Ta's face soon joined her beloved among the others.

The room was full of vibrant presences. It could not be denied that a secret vitalization was permeating these faces.

To and Ta found themselves walking silently or whispering. They told this to Amo who said nothing but remembered Angel's opinions and for a second time he thought that later in Kobor people would come quietly to honor the Great Faces.

He succeeded particularly well with Angel's, expressing it wholly in a long, refined mask with two oversized eyes.

Finally, after several days spent alone, he piously produced the face of the Grand Old Man. He created in plenitude with the feeling of saying farewell to all around him. He was becoming detached. He had almost no time left before the deadline he clearly saw approaching: the tall Stone against which he alone had to fight.

He started hearing rumblings from the Grand Va-Hôh. He asked his faithful guard if he heard them too and by his negative answer, he understood that the sounds existed only for him in foreknowledge of imminent events.

He figured that it was time for him to see Méè-Nê.

The presence of the Grand Old Man mysteriously joined his Friend's in his heart…

While Amo was thus heading consciously toward his destiny, it was the same for Angel in the palace.

There was no lasting arrangement between the Queen and the Beautiful Being. Paradoxically, they were both too different and too alike because, in fact, their two natures were divergent: the one descending, crude and unchanging, the other ascending, refined and volatile. On the other hand, they both converged in the same stubbornness, each as unwilling as the other to make concessions.

So, a few days passed in mutually frustrated efforts to sustain this challenging life together before the situation deteriorated quickly. They could not manage to strengthen their common accords but found countless points of disagreement. And soon they saw each other as before, each of them back to where they began but with a grudge!

And the climate turned bitter. Moreover, curiously, it seemed that everything was racing around them. All of Kobor was living faster than usual. In a kind of frenzy they were trying to catch up on the good time that had gone missing since the Spring Festival.

They saw To and Ta like when they first met, running through the countryside, passionate, exhilarated and dancing. They came and went in a flash. Amo was in his new creative fever. Everyone was talking about this miracle. The B'Tah-Gous said that the dawn of a new era was heralded by all these signs.

Over all this loomed Abim's mediation, more vigilant than ever. And maybe it was, in the end, because of this that they were so impatient to be happy?

Angel and Opak were far from it!

The Beautiful Being, defiant and disdainful, trying all possible ways to point out, to remind her that he was the Stranger come from Elsewhere to whom she had done violence. He made no more pacts and no more compromises. Again he closed himself off, more and more often, in outraged silence. He systematically multiplied his pouting, his refusals, his denials, which threw the Queen into states bordering on madness. Thus satisfied, when she was yelling and crying, he contemplated the sky, letting her understand that he was getting ready for his coming freedom.

Opak prowled around, anxious and voracious, suspicious and unsatisfied. She resumed her despotism, keeping a close watch on all his comings and goings.

But hadn't he just said, "I'll stay for a while"? Opak, who was obsessed with this, thought she would keep him here at any cost and it would be only right for her to take precautions.

Feeling hemmed in, he got much worse, losing his appetite, on the point of falling ill again, then he hardened up. And their secret war was thus declared.

Opak answered with a disastrous multitude of dishonesty, blunders and demands, besieging his lordly frigidness with her oppressive desires.

The Men of the Queen quickly realized what was happening and prudently kept silent, apart. They were so very sad and shamefaced that they dared not whisper a word of it outside, which was why the disharmony was not known to the people right away.

The T'Lo, informed in their way, were waiting for the right time to approach. Their Opak, already so subtlety invested, would inevitably fall under their power for good when her desires remained unfulfilled for too long... since they knew how to comfort her, to enrapture her, to get her drunk on fluids and rhythms, in the endless paradise of pleasures!

Other incidents helped to ruin the situation.

Opak was stupidly caught eating a big meal of meat in secret. Angel exploded in bitter laughter and in retaliation forbid the Queen to share his meals of fruit and herbs.

Opak got scared: now she had failed in what her Mother had ordered her to do! To make up for the adverse effect she straightaway tried her sorrowful speech of the first night, begging for help, but she could not remember the words she had used. She was pitiful and stuttering. Angel laughed in her face, baring his teeth like he was going to bite her:

"Liar!"

Then he turned away and started chanting those words that she did not understand and that frightened her because, in answer to him, the sky started shimmering and sparkling. Was he going to fly away and disappear?

In a hoarse voice she called for the guards who came in and stood on either side of Angel, ready to hold him back. He kept singing with growing tension, invoking help from above as he gripped his long, little fingers. High in the sky an indigo whirlwind took shape, dotted with white spots and twinkling gold.

A shrill cry: "Carry me away!"

But everything faded. Defeated, Angel dropped his arms and stayed quiet. No, he did not have his full strength.

The guards were at a loss. They looked at the Queen. The other men appeared in the doorway as usual to hear the song. They looked at the T'Lo who were also there, coming up quietly, one after another, their enigmatic eyes darting from Angel to the Queen, envisioning mysterious outcomes.

Sometimes, at the end of such scenes, Angel wept silently in frustration. Then everyone present, in different ways, felt painfully troubled and powerless in the face of this tragedy that was beyond their ken.

Only T'Lo Dê looked undisturbed and unchanged in the midst of all this. He was doing his duty as usual. Obeying Angel, he stayed at his feet, delicate and considerate. He had learned to make all kinds of things with dried herbs and flowers. Thus every day he created the adornments that Angel liked to wear.

Obeying Opak, he joined her when she was with her Men seeking compensations of love that would get her revenge on Angel.

And in his own heart, in his non-revealable inner self, he loved and admired Angel, Opak, Amo and he did not understand why they could not find a common point to come together and attain, with him, the permanent ecstasy of the T'Lo…

He day waned. A few hours earlier, Amo had finished the face of the Old Man and put it with the others along the walls. Afterward he daydreamed while contemplating them: To, Ta, the many copies of the Friend, Angel, the Old Man… His eyes never tired of looking at them all, scrutinizing, comparing.

From their side, the Faces watched him, too. He felt it. Strangely, he thought that these Faces had, in their way, also made him, Amo, such as he had become at present. He felt that he, too, would no longer be subject to change. He would last longer than the man…

He was holding a ball of clay in his hand. It was dry. He had no more desire to work. It was not worth the trouble. His creative fire was rapidly dissolving. His heat, his frenzy were leaving him, exhausted, deserted, but at peace. What good was it to hurry! Had he not fulfilled his duty today? He waited patiently for the next step, certain that it would not take long.

And indeed, Angel burst in while Amo knew, at that very moment, that this was the next step. He sent away the guard whose footsteps dwindled down the hallway. Then he looked at Angel calmly without saying a word. He was ready to do and hear anything.

Angel stepped forward, "I caught Opak alone with the T'Lo."

He was livid, his mouth contorted. Amo kept looking at him. He was his brother, his friend.

"What do you want of me?"

Silence. Then Angel licked his dry lips, bent over closer and whispered ardently, insistently, "I can't take it anymore, Amo, I can't stay it any longer! Help me! I'm not from here, I'm not one of you, I want to leave, it's too much!"

"I'll help you," Amo said flatly.

But Angel did not seem convinced. He begged, "My people are waiting for me, you understand. I've seen their signs. They came. For days now my prophetic birds have been flying around over Kobor. They're waiting for me on high!"

"Tell me what you want and I'll do it," Amo agreed.

"I have to get back to the place where you found me. That's where I came from. That's where I'll leave from, I'm sure. You'll bring me back, won't you? You can help me escape!"

"It's fine, you'll escape."

Angel was feverish, "Listen, if you talk to my guards, tell them you're taking responsible of me, you know they love you and will obey you. So, we can leave without an escort... If you don't help me, I'm going to die, Amo!"

Amo stood up, smiling, "Tomorrow evening, I'll take you without Opak suspecting a thing. I'll tell the guards that you're coming with me to visit my B'Tah-Gou. I'll go with you to Kah'B'La for your people to take you back. And I won't come back to Kobor. I'll go on to the Great Va-Hôh to topple the stone that represents the Very Huge."

The night before their planned escape, Opak felt her old soft spot for her former favorite. A whim. She had laughed a lot at the meal, using Angel's grim, stern face as an excuse.

Lately, she was acting bizarrely, now dejected, now excited, babbling nonsense for hours, then abruptly silent, as if she had been slapped on the neck. Then she would sit with empty eyes, drooling a little, while her hands fidgeted on their own, always making the same movements. After a while she would look like she was in pain and jump to her feet. She would curse everyone, scream, send away her men and shut herself in with her T'Lo.

But this night, it was different. She seemed clearly out of her mind, in a fog, barely conscious of what she was doing. The purplish spots on her temples had grown much larger. But Opak was watching Amo as if seeing him for the first time. With her customary spontaneity, she jolted out of her lethargy, pointed all her men to the door and threw out all her T'Lo along with them in order to stay alone with him.

She proved herself passionate, greedy, unchanged: the Devourer, once again disappointing for him.

But his soul was not with her. He realized what he had suspected for a long time: he had lost his taste for her.

When she agreed to rest, he went off to lie down on another bed far from her. But his peace had been shaken. He was not satisfied. Despite Opak's passion, or because of it, he felt burned inside again, unappeased, this desire to join in love with another him, luminous, welcoming, complementary, who would instantly shatter his loneliness.

He no longer felt the Old Man inside him nor the presence of his Friend. Tomorrow, he was going to leave everything behind and a great need for love moaned in his heart. Not knowing where to turn, he found his old, intimate devotion and murmured, "Ooh'R, Ooh'R!" almost without being aware of it.

Fever started running through his blood. He tossed and turned, softly, soundlessly, drifting while lightning flashes cleaved the darkness.

Then the heat stopped flowing, remained still, and enveloped him...

Was this a dream? In this universe of sensations engulfing him the stripped body of Angel, as soft as a woman, started to thicken under the intensified touch of his fingers. And it was agreeable, all golden, mysterious, like the reflection of himself that Amo was searching for in the Queen or in the sun...

And a balanced swaying, perfect, a consolation of harmonizing, primordial movement joined two principles that were floating in front of him, at first suggested, then drawn near, then fused into a spurting golden geyser!

The gasp of pleasure carried Amo beyond everything.

... And then... something exploded in his consciousness. And ice ran through him with the horrible feeling of the irreversible.

... He propped up on an elbow and he saw, under him, T'Lo Dê whose dilated eyes expressed total fervor and the most complete communion!

Amo thought he was mad. He broke out in desperate, uncontrollable laughter whose convulsions ravaged him even more.

How could he have been taken by surprise like this? A T'Lo, a T'Lo! It was just a T'Lo, nothing but a T'Lo!

Amo opens the door... Angel has come in at the same time. Total silence. A watch fire was burning in the room: Méè-Nê and Ata-Réè are alone, side-by-side, and appear to be waiting.

At the sight of them the women raise their eyes without a trace of surprise. The men have stopped, the door closed behind them. They have the unmistakable look of those setting out on a long trip never to return.

The two women are not mistaken. Have they not sensed this so many times already?

A poignant sentiment unites the four of them in this confrontation. Each incarnates his own destiny openly in the eyes of the others. Here is Méè-Nê, resigned in her almost completed extinction; here is Ata-Réè in her youthful ardor who has to endure the New Age heroically; here is Angel who is going to disappear as mysteriously as he had appeared; here, finally, is Amo heading off to one of those victories that you win through sacrifice...

"He's leaving. I'm going to topple the stone," he says simply to Méè-Nê.

She nods her head. She knows. But she stays silent. Maybe it is already impossible for her to talk?

Ata-Réè is half risen at the sight of Angel. She has stopped, however, because the contemplation of the Beautiful Being demands all her senses. He, too, is not moving. He stares back at her. Where does their intimacy come from? They do not know. They are meeting too late. But they cannot stop believing that there is a reason for this encounter where one is entirely clear to the other. They also cannot stop the swarm of passionate messages between them.

Then Angel makes up his mind. He holds out his hand toward the girl. "Listen, I want to leave you something before I leave. I can't give it to anyone else—I couldn't have imagined!—but you can receive it. It's for you that I came. Listen!"

For a long time he sings, chants, intones.

Ata-Réè listens, communes, receives. Something opens up in her consciousness. She understands. Better: she hears! She knows where he gets this harmony because high up, far away, above everything, there is a radiant center endlessly emanating this language that is music and that one can imitate when one has access to it.

She is transfigured, in ecstasy.

Soon, without realizing that Angel has gradually gone quiet and is watching her in tears, she starts singing herself with her clumsy throat, she signs, imitating the sequence of sounds that are accessible from now on.

Méè-Nê tells herself that all is well. She will soon be able to pass away. She has transmitted everything to her heir and now here is a new gift to enlarge her inheritance. Yes, the transmission is assured. She will stand firm against the New Age of which Amo is the willing architect by leaving for the Great Va-Hôh.

The old B'Tah-Gou shudders. How terrible it will be when the center stone down there is assailed by the hero and starts to fall!

CHAPTER XXIV

The next day, Opak woke up in the afternoon. Every day was later than the last and it took her longer every time to resign herself to being awake. Get up? To go where? To break the enchantment of her slow eroticism? The outside world bored her.

She could not remember what she had done the night before. She yawned. She was there among her cushions, with her T'Lo... But now she was hungry, she had to eat. It was a pleasure well worth the trouble!

She became aware of an unusual hum buzzing through the palace. People were astir, running around. It must have been later than she thought. That was why she was so hungry.

She called out.

They must have been watching out for her to wake up because her Men and guards immediately came bustling into the room.

"Oh Queen, we've looked everywhere and been calling out for them!"

Who were they calling? She did not understand. And yet, she was already sweating nervously, unable to utter a sound.

All her Men were struggling with desperate outcries.

"They haven't answered. We can't find them. Nowhere. Nothing. Nobody. Neither Angel nor Amo... Oh Queen! They're gone!"

It took a moment for the words to reach her brain. When she realized what had hit her, when she truly understood that the Beautiful Being and Amo had disappeared, Opak jumped up and turned instantly into the Ooh'Rou she had been when Angel was captured.

She orders and organizes, her wildly toned willpower galvanizing everyone and forbidding any backtalk.

She has them search all of Kobor. To no avail. Not a trace. No one has seen anything, knows anything. But this helps spread the news like wildfire. Everyone starts looking but shadowed with dejection: what new calamity was afoot? The two most beautiful jewels of Kobor Tigan't have gone missing: Angel the transcendent stranger who had won over all their hearts, and Amo the peerless, the handsome Man of the Queen!

Neither Méè-Nê nor Ata Réè says anything. Everything happening is in accordance with destiny and beyond momentary appearances. When the sorrow and grief that begot these two irreversible events is over, the salvation of the people of the Old Giants will return.

Opak has the entire region searched. She is thinking only of Angel. Was he captured by the Aâz? Did he fall into the Dongdwo swamp? A flash of inspiration: maybe he went back to Kah'B'La?

She puts herself at the head of her best men. Her attitude galvanizes them, makes them forget for a moment the mounting pessimism from their fruitless searches.

The Queen wants to believe, wants to hope—it is not possible that they not find Angel! The Men are also thinking of Amo. Their affection searches for him at the same time as the Beautiful Being. But the Queen has forgotten Amo. They realize this and feel a superstitious fear as if it were jeopardizing any chance of finding him.

Opak speeds toward Kah'B'La. Never has she looked so beautiful. Would this be her final blaze?

She is not decked out in jewelry but in armor. She is ready to fight any dark enemy to snatch Angel from their grasp. She wants to know nothing else. He is held prisoner somewhere, by someone, beyond Kah'B'La.

She marches quickly, with giant strides. Her haggard face is more pathetic. They feel her strained to the limit. She is thinking and acting faster than she ever has. Her forehead is beaded with the sweat of concentration. Her hands are burning. She is going without breaks. She does not even catch her breath or drink or eat. She will not stop.

At once that are on the holy mountain.

A rare havoc awaits them. The air is saturated with mist. When they lean over the Other Side, they see a huge waterfall in a rainbow aura, bellowing its downpour all the length of Kah'B'La. The Dry Land is now a lake, flooded as far as the eye can see!

Rocks are hurtling through the water, entire walls breaking off. The whole place is being challenged by sovereign nature, which is heading toward a different order of things.

How are they going to look for Angel in such a place?

They are all terror-stricken. Ta has fallen into the arms of To. She is hiding her face. She does not want to see the waterfall, the first materialization of the relentless images glimpsed in the hunting season. To is there holding her. No, no, the white solitude is not, cannot be true!

Opak has nothing to say. No screams, no nothing. And it is more frightening. She is motionless on the platform. Does she even understand what is happening? Seeing her, one could doubt it.

Then she swivels around to face the path. With her fists squeezing her head she lets out an inhuman howl. "He'll never come back! Never! Never!" And she collapses.

She regains consciousness only when they are back in Kobor. Ta is holding her hand. When she sees her, she shoves her away and calls out for her T'Lo, shutting herself away with them until their erotic drug takes over her brain and senses and abolishes her pain.

Later she will refuse to leave or show herself. She gets food brought to her and eats lavishly after which she breaks down sobbing, screaming, waving her arms around and banging her head against the wall. They cannot reason with her. She looks to be suffering physically, not just a broken heart. All her flesh is plainly in torment. They have to lock her in with her T'Lo to calm her otherwise she bites and claws anyone getting near her.

Alone in the semi-darkness of her sealed room, surrounded by calm, golden eyes that distilled so much gentleness at her, she cries softly, not quite a wail that they listen to with horror in the hallways. She lays listless util the T'Lo approach her and their lavish caresses transport her elsewhere.

The news of her sickness spreads through all five cities. Faces grow dark and stern. A sick Ooh'Rou is not a good omen since she necessarily must personify health and unassailable life, being, in sum, the strong Earth, spouse of the fertile Sun.

Sullen crowds climbed up from Kob'Vâm and Kob'Lâm. People from the old families of Kob'Ooh'R openly pouted. The blacksmiths of Kob'Râm were in a fuss because they claimed that the metal had never been more uncooperative and since spring all the weapons forged were wretched.

Gossip and squabbles were rife. More in Kob'Lâm than anywhere else. And all the nasty rumors infesting Kobor Tigan't from top to bottom came, for the most part, from the Low City.

They were soon speaking out loud everywhere about the fact that the Great Child had never appeared among Opak's offspring. They pointed out spitefully that she had not been fertilized during the Spring Festival. They recalled all the disasters since then. They kept bringing up the season of rain and fog. And especially, without fail, they grieved deeply over the sad fate of Angel. Everyone figured they had been guilty of violence to the stranger by capturing him and obviously because of this he had leapt to his death.

Opak was a bad Ooh'Rou.

The news spread fast that she never left her T'Lo.

In Kob'Lâm where, as a rule, they frowned upon the tradition of the T'Lo, they shouted out bitterly that they had seen it coming!

Her confused men wandered the streets. Some of them openly visited the prostitutes in the Low City. The people invited others home and shared their sorrow in order to get information.

It was a disaster.

Furthermore, they wept for Amo. He personified excellence and an unjustly sacrificed life. They remembered his face and all his virtues. They started to devote a veritable cult of remembrance to him.

Ata-Réè was visited often after the definite enfeeblement of Méè-Nê, essentially making her the heir. They kept asking her for the verses the B'Tah-Gou had dedicated to Amo.

As always in such circumstances, the Old Giants thought of the hidden presence of the Very Huge. Would it not make the looming woes come crashing down on them if they spoke of her? They eyed one another knowingly, fully aware who was the subject of this grimace. They were breathing bad air.

The general tension increased over the days when they saw no improvement. On the contrary, they saw the cursed situation getting worse.

Instinctively, they turned to Ta.

The loss of Angel and Amo along with the defection of her sister had made her suffer an abrupt maturity. Her face was taut, pale. However, she had a determined look they had never seen before. She was suddenly interested in all the affairs of the kingdom and proved herself active and competent. When she appeared, the people were reassured.

They followed her. They talked to her and since she answered everything with wisdom they started going up to Kob'Ooh'R in the mornings to see her as early as possible and hear the news, which was, unfortunately, always the same: Opak sick, the missing unfound.

But Ta always added very convincingly that the dark time could not last and something was bound to change. They just had to wait. She did not hide the fact that it might be long.

They listened faithfully. They believed her. Did not this princess, so sure of herself, know everything? The Ooh'Rou hardly used to say a word. And they always regretted it.

So, the people replied devoutly, "Ah, you're here! Thanks to you, we'll wait!"

Ta was surprised to find herself interested in them, all of them and everything, which she knew better than she imagined. She also discovered that she was taking care of them, that her mind was always busy now finding solutions to the various problems that came up.

At night she woke up To to discuss things with him. Both of them felt a strong desire to help the people. They needed to reassure everyone, to give them back their hopes. They started going through the cities, talking calmly about the future of the race, of the good times coming back. The people believed them wholeheartedly.

They morning in Kob'Lâm a woman shouted, "Oh, if only you were our Ooh'Rou!"

There was a long silence. Ta shuddered and hugged her lover—the vision of the white solitude had just struck her again.

To whispered in her ear, "What are you afraid of? Aren't we *already* together? Why would you be a lonely Ooh'Rou?"

In her lair, even though she had full knowledge of all the news as always, Abim has judged it better not to summon Ta. She wants to rest longer in meditation in order to see more clearly the double event that both appeased her old hatred and enraged her with her frustrated hopes. For, in the end: Amo has left, never to return—she is sure of it!—which is one result. She got what she wanted. But alas, for what purpose since the Queen has foolishly lost Angel!

Abim is startled awake. Black night. Who is hitting her? Pushing her? She pushes back but her body is leaning to one side. On the other side, she clearly feels the thrust against her.

She feels bad.

Underneath her, far below, in the refuge of her hidden casing, her fluidic root is cracking and suffering.

Who is attacking her?

Warning! Her life is in danger.

Abruptly she opens her clairvoyance. Her furious inquisition instantly sweeps the dark depths of the night. It is here that her search is focused. First, she hears. Yes, it is the quiet rumbling of the Great Va-

Hôh. Then she smells. Yes, it is pungency of sulfur and the bitterness of worms, it is the piercing saltiness of the shore... The Great Va-Hôh, her stronghold! Who dares this? What madman?

She sees! Now she sees!

On the wan floor of the ocean, in the circle of grand, ancestral stones, Amo is trying with all his might to topple the biggest, the center stone—herself, Abim!

"Amo is alive!" The hatred of the Very Huge explodes.

And down there, as if he sensed the little time he had left, Amo attacks the base of the stone that he cannot work loose. He hammers away at it with a club. Sparks fly all around. And in the stone a crack opens.

Abim is alarmed, beside her herself, feeling all the blows. If he succeeds, all is lost! Her secret sap will pour out and Abim, uprooted, will die. A monstrous rage makes the Very Ancient blaze. As fast as she can she gathers her destructive powers to confront the aggressor. Her breathing is loud and heavy.

In the night the body of the Very Huge is already glowing red hot.

She draws in, unrestrained, fiercely, all available living astralities in the core of which she must infuse the demolishing Klimm, the anti-life force that destroys all cohesion.

The metallic force is already eager. "Klimm, klimm, klimm!" Down below, all the Ananou scurry into a corner of their pit and writhe in place. Then they lie limp on the ground as if completely drained. Are they going to die so suddenly and so totally ravished? No matter! Quickly, quickly, Abim needs all her forces, all together.

With the viscous astrality of the Ananou, Abim arouses that kind of dragon who is her vehicle and which she slips into after leaving her body. On the plane of this other existence the whirling, clicking Klimm replaces the blood that stagnates in the stagnant life of the abandoned body. In the darkness of the silent room, it is like a mountain of cooling stone.

Outside, a storm rages. It is as if all the blackness of the sky is unleashed on the five cities.

In Kob'Lâm, all the B'Tah-Gous who are sleeping have been drawn from themselves. All the bodies are lying frozen. All of them have been whisked away.

Except Ata-Réè who started chanting, in a high-pitched voice, like she had heard Angel do. And because of this, because of the vibration that protects her, she stays there, separate, spared, in front of the abandoned body of Méè-Nê.

Ata-Réè leans over her B'Tah-Gou and steadfastly continues her conjurer song. Will Méè-Nê come back? Ata-Réè already knows that she is essentially becoming the last B'Tah-Gou, the sole heir.

Throughout the five cities, all the inhabitants have woken up in a fright. Hastily, they shut themselves in, close all doors and windows, huddle together in their main rooms. The candles they light barely pierce the thick shadows. They fumble to burn scents. Isn't it the great Va-Hôh they can hear?

Pandemonium everywhere. Mad tempests. The earth is toppling, it seems... Then comes the shrill whistling. The clouds explode. And the flood hits them.

Oda-Néè and Eqin-Go peek through the slit of their shutters, see that all the leaves are glowing. The rain, too, is like a greenish light. They do not want to see any more. It is all the Great Va-Hôh, surely!

In Kob'Ooh'R, Opak, whose grief was keeping her despondent, comes screaming out of her lethargy: "Ang'h!" And she wants to run to help him, thinking he was being attacked.

The uproar of the elements is driving her crazy. Her men are struggling to hold her back, weeping to see her reduced to this. She fights, pushes them away. All the T'Lo are trembling in the clutches of an indescribable state.

Ta has come running in with To. They help hold Opak who is foaming at the mouth and whose voice breaks off at the peak of her howling. They lay her down on the pillows she had torn to open. She jumps up and escapes!

They catch her outside, passed out, lashed by the rain. The tornado has rolled her to the foot of the staircase. Her rescuers have to hook each other's arms to defy the storm.

The wreck of the Ooh'Rou is carried like a sacred relic they had found profaned. All the heavy stone casements are closed over the windows in her rooms to protect her. They can keep watch as they dry her off and warm her up. She just lies there with no other movement but her lips endlessly muttering incomprehensible words.

T'Lo Dê, who bears the traces of sorrow caused by the double disappearance, snaps out of his apathy to lay his head on her vacant hand. Opak calms down. Seems to be sleeping.

Ta feels older all of a sudden. She is no longer the same. Her clairvoyant eyes dilate. She squeezes To, who is observing her, he, too, heartbroken. She need not say anything. He knows she is thinking of the terrible vision of the hunting season when they leaned over the other side of Kah'B'La and saw the trickle of water.

"Oh, To!" she whispers. "Tell me that none of what I've seen is possible. Tell me that I'm deluded. It's a mistake, isn't it? A fever?"

"Yes," he nodded firmly, "yes, my only one, you thought you saw, but it's not true. We don't want it. We don't want these things. So, they won't happen."

He is lying to help her, to comfort her. Maybe to exorcise her, too? But grievously he knows that Ta is not deluded and that these are the harsh designs of the future.

The young woman is not fooled. He is lying heroically because he loves her. So, she pretends to believe him so that, besides the foreboding, he will not be tortured seeing her full of dread. She smiles bravely at him, laying her head on his shoulder where she usually falls asleep. He shields her with a tight embrace. Nothing can happen... She wants to sleep.

Half of Opak's men are sleeping. The other half are on guard duty. They change shifts regularly, smoothly, careful to protect the Queen and her sister.

To nods off. Ta cannot. Her eyes open. She meets the gaze of T'Lo Dê. What message is he sending her? She knows that the T'Lo are strong seers, T'Lo Dê in particular. Why does she feel that he, too, has seen the same things as her about the future? She does not know. But the longer she stares into those golden eyes, the stronger the impression turns into a certainty. Poor, poor T'Lo Dê, he knows and can say nothing. But isn't she, too, condemned to silence? She cannot, must not say anything about what she knows.

Will Opak recover from this new attack? Since the disappearance of Angel and Amo she has been but a shadow of herself. She stays shut in. She sleeps almost all the time. When she wakes up, she cries like a madwoman for her T'Lo to come as quickly as possible. That is her only way of calming down.

Her excesses have very noticeably put their stigmata on her face.

Saddened while watching her, Ta cannot help noticing this. The purple halo has spread over her temples, which are now hollow. Her eyes are sunken in dark circles. Her mouth is limp.

Suddenly, Ta understands with truly frightening clarity that the Queen is lost for the realm, that she will never, never reign as a great Ooh'Rou.

The future foreseen on Kah'B'La is much closer than the young woman wants to admit. She is trying to fend off everything rushing forth and assailing her with new, searing details.

And now what does hear in counterpoint to these images, the ravaging Klimm passing over the very heart of the maelstrom! Abruptly, the sound wanes and rolls out toward the cursed West.

The Very Huge! Towards what occult crime? It was not a natural upheaval, this sudden storm, but rather the cavalcade of Abim! What is going to happen? Ta remembers the noises that spread everywhere on the last Terrible Night. A few B'Tah-Gou died soon after. And they whispered that the Very Huge had sucked the life out of them. The first misfortunes befell Kobor Tigan't then.

Ta is stricken with horror. A nameless, vast horror and disgust and also revolt against the control of this Terrible Mother who ruins, yes, is ruining the land and the race!

She is not sure if the events are reality or a new vision. In the darkened room where a glowing mist rises, she sees a door open onto an unbearable clarity and the new Ooh'Rou of Kobor Tigan't, all dressed in white, thin and pale, enters slowly—it is herself, it is Ta!

The young woman shrieks, which wipes away the vision. All the sleepers awake. She is shaking and crying. She refuses to explain.

T'Lo Dê stares at the wall where the door had opened.

The rumbling storm grows dim as it rushes to the west…

That night, Amo had just arrived at the great Va-Hôh in sight of the Circle of Stones. It was his final stage.

Although haggard from the wearisome journey made without pause from Kah'B'La where Angel had left him to meet his own destiny, he did not think for a moment of resting. Furthermore, the permanent danger of the place would not allow it: the trembling earth, the flowing lava, the spurting geysers… Besides, Amo knew that he had very little time to achieve the final act of his life. And he had entered the Circle of Tall Stones to confront the tallest, the one in the center.

… He had already been laboring like a maniacal lumberjack when Abim's counterattack came whirling around him. Despite the uproar of the Great Va-Hôh, he felt it coming…

Fast! He had to succeed! He braced himself frantically against the Stone to topple it. Too late already! A funnel seemed to be dug out under his feet. And from there, from beneath, from the dark hollows, came the irreparable!

It was like a soft paw on his ankle, which was drained of blood immediately. His leg was already dissolving into rotting flesh. It was no longer a part of him.

It was all too late! Desperately he let loose a blubbery cry, "I didn't finish! I didn't finish!"

He had, in fact, only managed to lean the Great Stone over a little. Wounded but not vanquished, it would fall later...

Under attack, Amo collapsed in the middle of the abomination. The black force besieged him right away. A thousand feelers: "Klimm, klimm, klimm!" that cut and tore. A thousand mouths that sucked and swallowed. The Ogress! A mountain of devouring!

What was animating this force, he identified: rumbling of words, muffled syllables of an unknown language, beating of a monstrous heart, inexhaustible breath and there in the center of it all, that throbbing plexus: Abim whose foul magic was murdering him like she had always wanted to do!

"I have come!" she said starkly.

He heard her.

It was done then. He felt corrupted, dissolved, turning into a putrid grave. Sucked out on all sides, his life, his inner life was melting, rotting, literally spewing out.

But what the Great Enemy wanted to destroy was the human soul, which was still intact. And he knew it and he took refuge entirely in this soul.

Last to be attacked, the blood in his heart boiled. There was a final burst of full silence: DEATH!

... and in the inexpressible afterward that followed, all the waste starts descending with him, with his soul where he stays sheltered, into the terminal abyss... No, it mustn't be!

Ascending power swells the soul and in a vertical surge, Amo begins to separate from what was no longer him and was pouring down below. He partially succeeds.

... Even though still attached by a long cord to the decomposed mass, he rises up toward the heat, the sympathy of the Sun that he feels like a blind man... Ooh'R, Ooh'R!... he knew the name of this Divinity... Ooh'R... pleading aspiration, total faith: do not let me fall into abomination!... an echo of himself had always been received up above, an echo that had allowed him to love... Ooh'R, your refraction of love, this echo—almost an answer—that I loved, loved so much!... Ooh'R so sought after, so yearned for... Amo knew all this. He saw nothing, heard nothing. He just knew that this was what he had to do: rise up, tear away from the attraction that was struggling to drag him down. He knew that this was his salvation: Ooh'R, the Heart, the Love...

Afterimages were floating in him as if come from another age: Opak, beloved, her pretty face; the Friend, mysterious, beloved, too short-lived; Angel, peerless, beloved; all met, all lost, all inaccessible... But all so much loved!

The memories are wiped out... A greater effort. Everything is torn, ripped out. More suffering... But, oh, the Sun, the Sun is here, nothing but the Sun, instead of his consciousness! The Grand Old Man appears, here in the center, in his golden cave.

He stretches out his arms, "Come to me, Son!"

The last bond snaps. The final rupture. The unnamable separates forever from him to drain down, down. Elsewhere.

Amo, free, explodes into a myriad of golden particles, alive, that swarm together in an infinite expansion throughout the Creation...

Abim has not triumphed.

Everything she sent out comes flowing back to her chaotically. But it dissolves, disperses in the storm. Most of it will be lost, irrecoverably lost.

The general uproar quiets down.

Abim is back in her body. It is ice-cold, inert, as always on her return. She will not be able to warm it up again. She is caught in it like a trap. Locked inside a minerality that no longer obeys her impulses and that dies not move.

She is breathing, however. But she suffers a shooting pain. Her fluidic roots feel chopped, split. Her secret sap, her force, is trickling out there. Abim cannot even open her eyes. Just breath. That is all.

She is paralyzed.

She had not conquered Amo. He wounded her. She will not heal. In her room where the daylight filters in, her gray mass is motionless, leaning to one side. She cannot straighten up.

Because down there on the Great Va-Hôh, in the circle of stones, the tall central stone is also leaning, its base crippled by Amo's last-ditch efforts.

CHAPTER XXV

The Very Huge had Ta summoned. The young woman hastens to the room, worked up with speculations and foreboding. On the way, she reflects on how strange it was that the storm suddenly calmed down two days ago. In fact, during that dreadful night, the lull was taken a little lightly as the end of the storm whereas it was just moving west.

But after some dead time when they were already starting to step outside, it came rushing back from the west like a tidal wave. The howling and the unleashed force reached the heights of excess. It felt like everything was going to topple over, that the sky had ruptured, that the earth had gaped open and that it was the end of Kobor Tigan't.

And yet it was only a final spasm. As soon as the tornado reached Kob'Ooh'R, it abruptly subsided and was as if it had never been!

Ta looks around: people are cleaning up the debris and mending the churned-up gardens. But except for this, nothing was ruined, nothing destroyed. All the houses and heavy stone slabs had stoutly resisted.

The blacksmiths had relit their fires. They had once again replaced the votive streamers on the golden sphere of Kob'Ooh'R. The palace servants are currently distributing the food as usual throughout the five cities.

The young woman looks up: the sky is pure! The birds are gliding gently, alighting here and there to nibble at or smooth down their feathers. They drink from the puddles.

But there are other things, wicked things that cast a shadow over the scene and that keep people from even dreaming of any hope again. First of all, some B'Tah-Gou died the day after the storm. All of them were plagued by a mysterious illness, a lethargy. This morning more died and they know that others will take their leave in the night.

What can be done? They do not complain. They pass away without suffering like at the end of a long and lazy exhaustion. Like they were resigning.

Their devotees are disoriented. The young servants not yet confirmed in the spiritual inheritance are panicking in their grief. Their wailing and lamenting is heard all over Kob'Lâm. Ta wonders what will become of these girls later.

Only at the home of Méè-Nê is everything calm. The old Storyteller is still alive. But she is not moving or talking. Her eyes are almost always closed. When they do open, it is to look at Ata-Réè who sits very peacefully at her side. Now the girl has the full transmission. The whole inheritance is in her. The Great Brain belongs to her. She has become a true B'Tah-Gou. She knows it. But as agreed with her mistress, she is keeping the secret in her heart. The time has not yet come to reveal anything. She also knows that there will be none left but her in Kobor Tigan't. She will be the only one, the sole B'Tah-Gou.

She thinks of Angel. Their souls had embraced so strongly on the day of their only meeting! She has no sorrow. She listens to the eternal songs in the enigmatic Height where her consciousness can abide henceforth. She sings in harmony with what she hears faintly… Her voice has already softened…

Méè-Nê is lulled. From time to time she smiles. All is well, is it not? The future shimmers in large fragments in her pacified mind. She sees, she knows that a grand New Time is opening. Amo, her dear son, is he not continuing his effort? Wherever he is, is he not slowly putting an end to the Death Stone? It is leaning, this Stone, a little more, a little more, day after day! And then in a specific place, at the start of this New Time, Méè-Nê knows: the Stone will fall! And so will the occult reign of the Very Huge.

Ata-Réè shares these visions and because of this she also thinks of Ta, gravely, respectfully, compassionately, since what is awaiting the young woman is full of dolorous grandeur.

Ta is about to enter her mother's room when news is brought to her from To and Eqin-Go together. They have just learned that a frightened mob is running around Kob'Vâm bawling out that the green water in the sacred pond is far lower than before.

The two men went to see. It is true: inside the pool a dry film marks the old level. And the liquid is tarnished.

"The B'Tah-Gous are evaporating in the same way," Eqin-Go remarks. His eyes are red. The loss of Amo has hit him hard and the imminent demise of Méè-Nê is only adding to his depression.

When the Storyteller is gone, Eqin-Go will have nothing left but the T'Lo. Ta sees this. And she is surprised to once again be thinking: "What can I do for him?"

But there is something else more confidential: many Ananou have died in the pit.

Rumors are already spreading. Ta immediately gives orders for the bodies of the Ananou to be taken away at night, with no witnesses, and that guards keep away the curious from the Pit in order to count the survivors. These measures should stop the news from spreading too quickly.

For a moment she is astonished at having ordered so speedily. She feels that the burden of the kingdom has fallen into her hands and that her being has gone into action to assume responsibility. But she has no time to wonder at this. The two men are already hastening to carry out her orders. But in the hallway leading to Abim's residence, one of her personal guards has just shown up. He holds out his arms to stop the two men.

"What's wrong?" Ta says. "Speak!"

"I heard the Very Huge through the door where I keep watch. 'Go and tell To to stay and wait for me to talk to my daughter'."

Eqin-Go runs out alone with the orders for the Ananou Pit.

As the young woman walks down the long hallway where the guard pulls aside the curtains and opens the stone doors, she wonders in what condition she will find her mother since the green pool is vanishing and the Ananou are dying along with the B'Tah-Gou... And did Amo leave with Angel? Will she find out later when she is standing silently among the Great Faces, in her white veils and her white solitude? Ta stifles a cry—what is coming over her?

But she goes in to see Abim.

The room is dark. There is a scent of perfume hovering, the same that was used for Angel's reception. Abim is sitting strangely—leaning over. The little light filtering through a half-closed window makes the stiff, lopsided body even more tragic.

Nothing makes a noise. Nothing moves. There is only the body, huge, monstrous, that looks like it is held in mid-fall by some miracle.

It is such a bizarre sight that Ta feels afraid of it. Is it going to topple over?

She holds her hands in front of her and advances. But a few words, more breathed than spoken, stop her.

"Don't touch me, whatever you do!"

She stands there frozen to the spot. The body slumped before her has lost all color and probably all its heat. It looks made of gritty, cold lava. Not to speak of the gray, stony face with its two narrow slits that used to be eyes but where there is nothing now. And the mouth that is but a dark slash out of which the awful breathing voice exhales its message from beyond the grave...

"Listen... Come closer... Right there, next to me... Yes, my magic is dead. My Stone of Honor is almost uprooted... Listen... Pay attention... Soon I will speak no more and you will have to obey by remembering... because, you know, I will always be watching over... without speaking, without moving and probably without being... But I will watch over..."

Ta rebuffs, "I obey only what I think is good."

"Bah! I know that," the Very Huge grumbles. "No matter! I want to transmit everything to you. You will have much more than Opak. She has never been a good Ooh'Rou. It was not the Kingdom..."

Ta wanted to protest but:

"Drop it, then. You know as well as I that your sister is an idiot. Let her be with her T'Lo!"

"Who told you about the T'Lo?" the young woman stammered.

An odd laugh rose in Abim's throat. "My wisdom told me. My intelligence told me. The wind told me... Opak does not even have the possibility to open the Other Eye. You have it. And you have a lot of other things that I used to take for whims but that are really your willpower... Now your will wants to help the race. This, too, I know, my daughter... Plus, you guess things in advance. Plus, you know how to find what is needed. I haven't forgotten that it was you who found Ang'h... Me, I only heard him living and laughing in space. I knew he existed, but I never knew how to find him... Oh, I should have gotten rid of Opak right away to help you!"

"But I don't want to reign!"

"Ah ha? But of course you do. *Since you are reigning already and you know it and everybody else knows it*... Except you don't dare admit it and therefore the people don't dare admit it... Except you are not going to be an Ooh'Rou like the others... that's finished, that lineage! You will not be an Opak... and for that you will have to solve the problem of the Great Child in a different way. Because you won't have it. I know. You are something different. So, deal with your succession later... You will know what will work. I have no worries. That is your business, no longer mine..."

Ta speaks up clearly to ask a very specific question, "Would you have recognized the Great Child if it was from Angel?"

With all the energy left in her she croaks, "Certainly! Only him. No other. Amo's kids are nothing, nothing. And you would do well to destroy them if you don't want them to enfeeble the race."

She waits for an answer that is not coming, so she mutters, "Fine, fine. It is my advice. You do as you think fit. It is no longer my business…"

She starts to pant. Her voice is much weaker. Ta has the feeling that her body is listing more and more to the side.

After a moment, the Very Ancient starts talking again, but snatches of barely audible speech. Ta has to get even closer.

"The chests… under the floor… for you!"

"I don't want them!"

"Yes… of course you do, you will see… later… you will need them… certain ones… you will remember… there will be problems… the race in danger… remember what I tell you… the race… attacked… You alone… no one will know but you… the chests here… Bah! I'm not worried. You're strong… and sharp when need be… Oh, how you used to stand up to me! You combed and were furious… the rabid girl…"

She gets a second wind and is heard better.

"Ooh'Rou Ta, you have only one weakness—To. He is a male who resembles Amo."

Ta screams and it is a Queen's command: "Be quiet!"

Quite unexpectedly the Very Huge stops talking. Like a big, pathetic child. Her gaze filters through, enigmatic and troubled. Ta is wary. What is this inscrutable old woman cooking up? But then her face takes on a senile pout. A feeble spasm shakes her. She tips over a little more. She bobs her neck and moans weakly two or three times. It looks like she is afraid to ask something. Fake? Perhaps… Or an actual need?

Stiffly, uncertainly, but still disturbed seeing her in this state Ta asks, "What's wrong, my Mother?"

The Very Huge twists a long lock of her white hair. Her fingers are trembling. The lock slips out of them and clearly, she cannot get hold of it again. Her hands refuse to obey her. She is looking very intently at this and then realizes that her daughter is also watching.

Now she is drooling. She is awful and pitiful.

Ta shudders as she dries the face that is becoming more paralyzed every minute. Doing this, she cannot help feeling moved by pity.

Abim senses this change and tries to take advantage of it. She must make a huge effort to break through the ponderous barrier that is gagging her mouth. "Oh Queen, true Queen, true Daughter… you see… what has become of me? Weak, weak… I will not hold out much longer… so, listen, my daughter, I want…"

"What is it, my Mother?"

"I want… I desire… one final joy... a little whim… you know about whims, my Daughter… remember? Not a big thing… what I used to ask of you… when you combed my hair…"

The old woman is babbling, beating around the bush.

Ta is irritated, "What, Mother, what is it? What do you want? Tell me!"

"The eggs, my Daughter… fresh Dongdwo eggs… one last whim… tomorrow I won't be able to eat them again… tomorrow I will be closed, shut off, dead, Ta, imagine!"

"Eggs, my Mother, I can get you some from Kob'Lâm from the cold storage."

"No, oh no, no, fresh eggs, fresh, nothing else will do, just this once, this one last time… Tell To…"

The young woman stiffens up.

Abim is crying. It is a frightening spectacle, indecent. The sobs are jiggling her mass.

"Pity, my Daughter, my Queen, fresh eggs, just a few… I'm dying, don't you see! Tell To to go… now… it's not far… no need for a lot… He is here, he can do it… To with the little sack… just two or three eggs… He'll be back in no time…"

"It's too late. Tomorrow he can go and I'll go with him."

"No, don't abandon me! Tomorrow I won't be able to eat… Don't leave! Stay with me! Have mercy… Tell To now…"

… And so, at that moment, To left.

He did not want to obey when Ta told him. He thought it was a ploy of the Very Huge. Ta was upset. She brought him in so he could see for himself what bad condition she was in. And indeed, even more than before, she was trembling, drooling and crying.

But To persisted in arguing otherwise, "A ploy, it's a ploy!" he grumbled.

And he even dared to laugh when he pointed out to Ta the bright, vigilant glimmer peeking out from under the half-closed eyelids of the Very Huge.

But the glimmer immediately disappeared. Ta had seen nothing. Then, inexplicably, for the first time, she got angry at To, accusing him of being callous. They almost quarreled.

"Come with me then," he said.

But Ta stayed with Abim saying that she had to do her duty.

And To had to leave alone.

He had looked at her for a long time from the doorway with utter dread before deciding.

"What are you waiting for?" Ta yelled. "Go on!"

When the door closed, she felt an untold sorrow, an aching in her heart, a mad desire to run after him, to catch her love…

But the Very Huge was groaning and trembling. "Don't leave me, child!"

The Calamitous Valley stagnates in its perpetual fog. Does there really exist another world than this one? Can a world made of sun, movement, life and heat really exist?

Here one does not know. One never knows. Here time stops still. Here nothing is becoming…

Where is the exit of this existence?

To is startled. What is happening to him? What is this fatigue that has so insidiously crept over him, so entirely possessed him now so that he does not even want to move.

Why had he come here? He does not know.

How long has he been standing here? He feels unable to make the slightest guess. Besides, he is not really interested… is not really worried.

Through the gray stagnation of the heavy, steamy air, however, he feels like the milky light of day is slowly waning. Is it dangerous? How to know?

But yes, danger surrounds him! He sees them, the Aâz, all around him, those vindictive plants, enemies of man, swollen with their bizarre, psychic existence.

Yes, yes, he has dawdled. He can feel them casting their invisible nets. But since he knows it, why isn't he running off? Why is it that every instant is adding more and more control over him! It is because he does not want to leave. No… First, he has to solve a problem. But it is so hard! He keeps asking himself the same question: why is he here? He does not know. What should he do now? He does not know this either. Leave, perhaps? He is not sure, cannot put two thoughts together.

Nothing is connecting in his head. Nor in his body. An immense apathy has loosened his vital bonds. Desire, passion, thought, memory, projects, nothing is left. Even his name he cannot remember!

Without realizing it, believing he was still, he finds himself wandering. The spongy ground squishes under his heels. He hears it with odd curiosity. A step. Another step. And the little gurgling answers, talks back… The foot sets down… like a question… Is it far? Should he keep going? And the semi-swamp answers quietly, yielding softly: "Farther, farther… on and on."

And this goes on. To walks aimlessly.

Little by little he is in the thickest part of the vegetation. Something is calling him that he cannot resist.

The Aâz are beckoning him gently, limply, waving their fleshy leaves. He lets them touch him. The thick, white stems graze him. How cold they are! A cold passed straight on to him.

Countless small hands are laid upon him. The whole multitude recognizes him. He hears it, the news that is spreading through the bushy recesses: "It's him, it's him! Oh, how long we've waited! Come to us!"

The Widows of the Moon are calling him!

The young man goes. He cannot remember his name. He will not leave again. He knows not whether he loves a woman. He will not leave again… And yet, yes, a tiny thought, which is his whole life, fights back deep down inside his mental dissolution—there is a woman like him somewhere beyond the clutches of the Aâz, a woman whom he loves, whom he loves…

He repeats, "I love you; I love you." But he still ventures into the deepest of the pernicious plants.

… How long has he been sitting in this place? He feels very weak. The Aâz are covering almost all of him. The soft ground sinks under his weight. The pale moss scatters little bubbles and throbs quietly, quietly. What is it saying? He keeps trying to understand the language. He is also surprised to hear the sap flowing through the stems of the Aâz. The plants stick to his skin with weird intimacy. He is covered by their big leaves. He is quickly growing colder and colder.

At first, he had tried, flapping like a scared child, to peel off the vegetal vampires, but he only managed to tear off bits of them. The milky sap with its pungent odor seeped out of the mutilated parts. He breathed it in and fell asleep in the ever-growing cold...

In the distance, in the Dongdwo swamp, a hissing sound rises up, almost like the one given off during funerals. To starts. He listens avidly. Everything comes rushing back: the Dongdwo, the eggs, Kobor Tigan't! Where is the sack he brought?

He stirs. He thinks of Ta. What trap has he fallen into? "Ta, I love you, I love you, save me, save me!" his soul cries out.

But he, To, the hunter, is he mute?

"Ta, save me, I give up, I'm caught!"

He shouts in vain. He hears his cry echoing. He hears it as if lagging behind. Is it really his?

But still, it wakes him up. He wants to fight. He has to fight! Is he standing up or does he just think he is? He clutches at the stems. They stretch, break, drool lots of sap. The odor intensifies. He yanks out a clump of plants whose roots pull up from the soil along with big clods of moss. In the holes left there, water sparkles and fascinates him... How heavy the Aâz are! He struggles. At least, he believes he does. He screams again, "Ta, save me, I love you!"

This time he does not hear himself. But, she, she, always, she has heard his calls! She will hear, yes, yes, she will come...

He has fallen from on high. From the heights of his life. From the peak of a mountain. Is it Kah'B'La?... Ta is not coming. Ta does not hear.

He lies in the thickest of the growth. He grows cold. He grows weary. The secreted toxins are swiftly spreading through his body. He dreams. He does not know that he has fallen for good and is lying down, covered by the Aâz on the soft ground that is slowly sinking, in which his body is slowly sinking, toward the deep, greedy roots...

It is almost night. Again he hears the Dongdwo whimpering. It really is the funeral wail!

Then To sees the vast shadow of the Very Huge who has come to inquire of the fine work done by the Aâz. He screams in revolt. The final embers of his life flare up.

"Ta, help, come, I love you, I love you!"

He wants to escape. So, it was all a trap, a horrible trap set by the Very Huge!

He sees! He knows! It all explodes into fragments of revelation in his shredded consciousness: Ta promised to a solitary reign, all dressed in white! She had seen it, she knew and he, too, knew. It is fulfilled by the sacrifice of their couple... They must never leave each other, under no circumstances... The face of the Old Man flashes by, passes over and disappears... The suffocation and the paralysis swallow the surges of lucidity To has between long, ever-deeper spheres of shadow.

"Ta, help, come, I love you, I love you!"

The beloved's face fills the whole horizon of his consciousness. Why isn't she coming to him?

So, he runs to her, endlessly, he does not stop running to her... The distance remains unchanged... The distance is eternal... He runs to her, eternally...

In the center room the monotone, inarticulate babbling of Abim gradually puts Ta to sleep, who is tired from staying awake like this.

"Don't leave me," the Very Huge groans at regular intervals with a weird, little girl's voice.

Ta slips off into a half-sleep in which her thoughts run amok. What is her duty? Is it really to stay here next to HER who has become so monstrous? Who has always been so monstrous? The monotone moaning prevents her from thinking about it.

Abim repeats the same tedious things. "The chests... yes, yes, you will need them... There will come a time when the force from below will be necessary to you... for the people... Oh, there will be great danger, a great crack, perils, outside and within Kobor, sickness... Then, I'm telling you, you will come here for the chests under the floor... and you will summon the force from below. It will obey only you... not in the same way as me, but still, it will absolutely obey you. But you must put the ornaments on your body... the metal plates... the black bracelets that you saw... and the breastplate... Also the diadem... you must rub your body with the scented grease because otherwise you couldn't stand it... you are not as strong as Us, the Ancient Ooh'Rous, much less strong... and the jewelry will protect you... The Force from below will recognize you. You will be able to command it, to bring it out, to send it out, all around, as you want... and then bring it back once the work is done... Tell me you understand! Tell me you accept! Tell me you will do it!"

Over and over again Ta nodded. Almost automatically at the end.

Oh, this waiting is so long, with this anguish looming over there in the distance! She wants to think of To, but she is constantly prevented by her Mother who is talking, talking and her fading voice is so insistent that Ta has to keep getting closer, listening harder.

"Repeat what I said," The Very Huge mumbles.

Ta obeys. But she forgets some details. Abim catches this, repeats the words, explains, reiterates the chests and jewelry and starts over again, demanding a repetition when she is done.

An inescapable nightmare!

Who is crying over there in the distance? Where is To? Impossible to escape. The distorted voice brings her back, binds her in the same circle.

"… then you will put on the breastplate… Not before anointing your body with the grease… and you will put on the diadem. When you have the bracelets on, you will light the bowls in the four corners and you will sprinkle the powders on the coals…"

"Yes, yes, yes…" Ta utters.

"Don't leave me! Tomorrow I will talk more, O my Daughter… I have so much to tell you! You must receive it all! You will reign… a great reign! Oh, a very great reign! Different. Completely different from all the others… come now, you will be Queen Ta, the White Ooh'Rou, the Unique…"

Why does this phrase go straight to her heart?

What is suddenly exploding?

What is tearing apart?

What is sinking?

She pushes away her mother's hand. She straightens up, pale, horrified. Her entire being, in a single bound, flies to the place where she has heard the call for so many hours.

"To!"

She screams. Her cry cuts off. For, she sees the wide-open eyes of the Very Huge staring at her, ruthlessly.

"Ooh'Rou Ta, you will love nothing but your people!" The huge body is leaning over, lopsided. Drool trickles out and abruptly dries up in the corners of her paralyzed mouth. Her eyelids droop. She will not recover.

Abim is still muttering. It is barely audible.

"I… didn't… need… Dongdwo eggs... my daughter… not at all…"

The Very Huge will never move again. She just keeps breathing from the depth of her minerality that begins…

CHAPTER XXVI

This morning, very early, while everyone is still asleep, Ta climbs up alone to the sphere of Kob'Ooh'R. She goes to sit there where it is possible to contemplate the great panorama of the terraced Cities of Kobor Tigan't. Thus, she will meditate. It has been a long time since she has been able to do this.

She is expecting a visit. Someone is supposed to come to her this morning. Her foresight, her clairvoyance, grown stronger through grief and sorrow, told her so. She also knows that if this meeting takes place, it will herald a new time for her Race.

Around her, the air is all bleached by autumn. A sweet scent blows: overripe fruit, yellowed leaves, the soil digesting the early debris.

Ta climbs slowly, step by step. She is wearing a white robe. She has grown thin and pale. She is not aware of it. She has not looked at herself since the day To was found dead.

She thought at the time that it would be unbearable, that she would explode in agony… Some time passed. Days. Maybe months. She does not know anymore. Half of her being disappeared with To. The other half, thenceforth cut off, had to confront so many things that the passing time meant nothing to her. She lived through her mind, through insight, through endless vigils. Without believing it was possible, she survived. But day and night became one and the same for her, during which she developed the urgent solutions for all the problems of the realm.

All the people, with a great surge of trust, flocked to her. She could not let them down.

She had, therefore, curbed the initial panic that gripped everyone after the successive disappearances of Angel, Amo and then To, and after Opak's defection and also the dense mystery surrounding the Very Huge.

Ta talked to the people. Her voice reassured everyone. They found her beautiful and radiant despite her obvious sorrow. They admired her. They had needed to admire a noble for a long time. Their devotions, therefore, went en masse to her. And everything she said or ordered was received enthusiastically. They believed. They obeyed. They relied on her.

Now they know that the door to the Room in the Center is closed forever. The guards have been removed and posted farther away in the outer corridors. Nobody will ever enter there. Except, if she decides to, the new Ooh'Rou can push open the stone door...

But Ta tells herself that she will never go. The Very Huge has no need of anyone.

As for Opak, she seems to have completely lost the little mind that she never really had. She does nothing, never leaves, leads a vegetable life, totally devoted to the satisfaction of her appetites, only with her T'Lo who act on her like a drug. They never leave her. She lets herself be coddled and cuddled by them constantly. She eats and sleeps. The caresses or hunger might wake her up a little. She is very fat, very heavy.

Rumors have spread. Is she expecting a child? In that case, would it finally be named the Great Child?

They think that only Ta knows the truth. But she keeps silent and looks so severe when she hears such things that no one ever dares to ask.

The rumors continued against her will. She has forbidden any talk about Opak. The very name is no longer pronounced. And they obey. Does she desire so ardently to supplant her sister that she can thus order her total obliteration? Some believe so. But they are not shocked. For, everyone knows that Ta takes good care of Opak, personally ensuring the quality of her food and comfort. They think, therefore, that she is firm, able and good.

One day she gathered all her sister's children. She looked at them in bewilderment for a long time. She admitted that they were all good-looking, healthy, bright-eyed and nary a one showed the signs of sloth like Opak. But which one was the Great Child? Ta could not tell. The Very Huge had not revealed to her the nature of the mysterious Sign. Maybe there was no Sign? Maybe it was all just another of Abim's many tricks to keep her monopoly on determination and choice. In order to always be in command secretly. Then the reign of the Ooh'Rou would be a second-hand authority...

But now the door of the Room is closed.

Ta was reigning in a way that for many was new and surprising, but from which they expected great things.

She set aside the identification of the Great Child, but she figured that it was best not to keep raising these children apart from the others because they were developing less quickly. On becoming adults, they would obviously make up the royal noble caste but with this isolated upbringing it would be destined to the indolence of pleasures. And the worship of the T'Lo was never more thriving than among this nobility.

Ta made the decision to personally supervise the education of these children. Here as elsewhere, everything had to change.

But who would help her in this huge task? If To were alive, he would be at her side... With this thought she chokes back a sob. She has come to the sphere of Kob'Ooh'R. She sits down to wait.

Her thoughts turn to herself. She judges herself harshly, cannot forgive the guilty frivolousness she had shown. The fickle, dizzy Princess, they used to call her not very long ago... No, she had not loved To enough. She believed she loved him but in a way, she betrayed him and sent him to his death. This is now and forever the doleful ground of her being. Ta had indeed become the white Ooh'Rou...

She understands now, in the light of her mourning, how even in her love she acted carelessly. She could have, she should have prevented To from going to his death. She was never supposed to separate from him... The Grand Old Man, on that radiant morning on Kah'B'La, right before discovering Angel, had warned them: "Beautiful children, never separate!"

Alas, how selfish she was, too! She should never have become so indifferent to Kobor Tigan't and her Race! Everything is mostly her fault, she tells herself. Because when she noticed the nascent tragedy, she should have acted. Since she knew well in advance that her sister Opak was incapable of ruling. Opak was not a Queen. Due to this, Abim had long ago usurped the power she had no right to.

Ta knew it now. To govern a land, it takes more than just calling yourself the Ooh'Rou Opak. It is not enough to appear before the people in all your regalia or to possess the greatest number of strong males. On the contrary, you must integrate the Race in yourself, as deeply as possible, have its needs be your only care and be open to inspirations that the Race will benefit from. It is necessary to imagine everything in advance, to pioneer the necessary evolution in time, to be the Queen evolved before the others. To pioneer, that is everything! To experience before the others at your own risk. To taste the new and strange fruit to know before the others if it is good or harmful for all.

Ta now knows exactly what must be done. She admits that she has always known... Alas, remorse is a bitter thing...

She cannot escape her own judgment. It is hard.

On this radiant, autumn morning, she confesses to herself without leaving anything out. Yes, she should have taken the power before the tragedies. If, then, she had asked Abim, she would have agreed. And then she would have reigned better even than now! She would have reigned with To! To, whose memory weeps far away in the fog with that long, misty call: "Come to me, come to me!" Why does she have to hear this day and night... He dies eternally... She cannot reach him down there... She could not have reached him in time...

So, she cries. Then her thoughts turn again to tackle the great problem. There is Opak, fat and heavy, who will soon have to be cared for in secret; there is T'Lo Dê, so strangely timid lately, always scurrying to the darkest corner when he sees Ta and who covers his belly now like a woman; there are the Queen's children, how to raise them?...

Her thought slips and opens up... here now Amo's Great Faces appear in her mind... oh, how they seem to be living a higher life... they are superimposed in an iridescent fog, in the waterfall on Kah'B'La... behind the sheet of water, that layered, crystalline form... what silence! It is not water flowing, it is the fumes of the incense in the vast room where the Great Faces are gathered... the people enter solemnly... a form like crystal glistens in the back, in the center... Ta is there in a cold peace... she feels a small child's hand squeeze hers hard... Who is it? She turns toward the girl who for so many years has been at her side...

The vision fades away. Ta shivers. It is daytime. The sun is shining.

Someone is coming up to her, terrace by terrace. A woman. The same who was next to her in her vision: Ata-Réè, the one who will soon be the next, the only B'Tah-Gou.

Ta stands up straight. Ata-Réè is running now. Here she is right in front of her.

"White Ooh'Rou, tonight my vision is open to the rays of the future. And I was next to you."

Ta smiles for the first time in a long time.

"Look, Ooh'R is accepting us!"

And it was undoubtedly true because the great autumn sun was shining so brightly before them that for a moment, they felt covered in the hot cloak of life itself. Then, the golden, glorious blessing spreads over the five Cities.

So, the people wake up and come out on all the terraces, surprised by the unusual morning splendor. They are filled with joy. All together they turn towards the white figure up above, over everything, near the sphere of Kob'Ooh'R.

A long ovation fans out.

Ta takes the hand of Ata-Réè, "B'Tah-Gou, this is the turning point of the Ages!"

"Yes, White Ooh'Rou, it is yours, this New Day of the Giants of Kobor Tigan't!"

To be continued in
THE REIGN OF TA
When Giants walked the Earth – 2

OTHER CLASSIC FRENCH FANTASY
FROM BLACK COAT PRESS

Marie Catherine d'Aulnoy. *Tales of the Fays* (2 vols.)
Honoré de Balzac. *The Last Fay*
Theodore de Banville. *Magical Tales*
Mme Barbot de Villeneuve. *The Naiads * Beauty and the Beast*
S. Henry Berthoud. *The Angel Asrael*
Aloysius Bertrand. *Gaspard de la Nuit*
Jean Carrère. *The End of Atlantis*
Charlotte-Rose Caumont de La Force. *The Land of Delights*
Comte de Caylus. *The Impossible Enchantment*
Jacques Collin de Plancy. *Voyage to the Center of the Earth*
Comtesse D.L. *The Tyranny of the Fays Abolished*
Comte Duclaux de L'Estoille. *The Miller of Carnac*
Comte Duclaux de L'Estoille. *The Song of the Skylark*
Comte Duclaux de L'Estoille. *Argentine*
Marie-Antoinette Fagnan. *The Enchanter's Mirror*
Paul Féval. *Anne of the Isles*
Charles de Fieux, Chevalier de Mouhy. *Lamekis*
Judith Gautier. *Isoline and the Serpent-Flower*
Nathalie Henneberg. *The Green Gods*
Eugène Hennebert. *The Enchanted City*
Gustave Kahn. *The Tale of Gold and Silence*
Françoise Le Marchand. *Florine and Boca*
Marie-Jeanne L'Héritier de Villandon. *The Robe of Sincerity*
André Lichtenberger. *The Centaurs*
André Lichtenberger. *The Children of the Crab*
Monsieur de Listonai. *The Philosophical Voyager*
Jean-Marc & Randy Lofficier. *Edgar Allan Poe on Mars*
Jean-Marc & Randy Lofficier. *The French Fantasy Treasury* (anthology) (3 vols.)
Charles Lomon & P.-B. Gheusi. *The Last Days of Atlantis*
Marie-Madeleine de Lubert. *Princess Camion*
Charles Malato. *Lost!*

Maurice Magre. *The Marvelous Story of Claire d'Amour*
Maurice Magre. *The Call of the Beast*
Maurice Magre. *Priscilla of Alexandria*
Maurice Magre. *The Angel of Lust*
Maurice Magre. *The Poison of Goa*
Maurice Magre. *Lucifer*
Maurice Magre. *The Blood of Toulouse*
Maurice Magre. *The Albigensian Treasure*
Maurice Magre. *Jean de Fodoas*
Maurice Magre. *Melusine*
Camille Mauclair. *The Virgin Orient*
Catulle Mendes. *The Little Fays in the Air*
Henriette-Julie de Murat. *The Palace of Vengeance*
Gérard de Nerval. *The Prince of Fools*
Charles Nodier. *Trilby* * *The Crumb Fairy*
Edgar Quinet. *The Enchanter Merlin*
Henri de Régnier. *A Surfeit of Mirrors*
Restif de la Bretonne. *The Story of the Great Prince Oribeau*
Restif de la Bretonne. *The Four Beauties and the Four Beasts*
Marie-Anne de Roumier-Robert. *The Voyages of Lord Seaton to the Seven Planets*
Louis-Claude de Saint-Martin. *The Crocodile*
Edouard Schuré. *The Angel and the Sphinx*
Nicolas Segur. Penelope's Secret
Brian Stableford. *The Queen of the Fays* (anthology)
Brian Stableford. *Funestine* (anthology)
Brian Stableford. *The Origin of the Fays* (anthology)
Brian Stableford. *Fays of the Seas* (anthology)
Brian Stableford. *Tales of Enchantment and Disenchantment* (anthology + non-fiction)
Kurt Steiner. *Ortog*
Simon Tyssot de Patot. *The Strange Voyages of Jacques Massé and Pierre de Mésange*

www.ingramcontent.com/pod-product-compliance
Lightning Source LLC
Chambersburg PA
CBHW060431030726
47495CB00003B/834